Cynicism Management
A Rock & Roll Fable

Bori Praper

River Boat Books

Printed in the United States of America.
Published by River Boat Books. St. Paul, MN.
First printing January 26, 2021.

ISBN: 978-1-7332565-5-1

Cover artwork adapted from a poster for the punk rock band
The Altar Boys announcing their appearance at House of Blues
Anaheim on September 2018 with the new wave pop band
Crumbacher opening.

Cynicism Management was first published by the author as an
eBook in 2013 and a 2nd edition was published in 2015.

Other books by the author:
Pendulum Pet (2016)

"*Cynicism Management* reads like a satirical novel about Slovenia written from a foreign point of view, but Bori Praper is a Slovene, born and raised. So it comes as no surprise that after finishing the novel, he moved from Slovenia to Berlin. And then from Berlin to Tenerife, because he likes to keep it thorough. He also likes to keep away from any pitchfork-and-torch-wielding mobs, unhappy with their portrayal in the book."

Boštjan Gorenc - Pižama, Slovenian writer, translator, podcaster, and stand-up comedian

"In *Cynicism Management*, the foreground illuminates the background no less than vice versa. All the while, as Bori Praper introduces us to his dishevelled cast of dislocated characters and embroils them in a bizarre international conspiracy, he peppers the narrative with barbs, equal parts piss-take and grievance, at the stupidities and annoyances of the life in the post-Real-Socialism Slovenia. While *Cynicism Management* does comment, however, it never pontificates. It's not a 'statement' book by any stretch. Instead, Praper uses the plentiful parody to fuel up his Yugo 55, then takes the reader on a weird, meandering ride with plenty of beer stops and no suspension to speak of."

Dušan Rebolj, Slovenian translator and film critic

A Few Words About The River Boat Books Edition

The *Cynicism Management* scheme was hatched more than ten years ago, towards the end of 2008. Disillusioned by our previous musical endeavours, we (my wife Monika and I, I have to admit) devised a "literary musical" experiment, initially just for fun: the idea was to write a novel featuring a fictional band called *Cynicism Management* and record music to go with it.

The band soon attained a life of its own: a few fellow musicians joined us and we performed at quite a few concerts between 2010 and 2012, despite our initial reluctance to launch yet another live group. Our first album, poetically titled *Tit* (a small bird of the Paridae family), was released in 2011, well before the novel. The last live incarnation of the band was disbanded in 2012, when my wife and I decided to leave our native Slovenia and move to Berlin, Germany. Nevertheless, we kept working on the musical part of the project, though mercifully without the exasperating complexities of struggling to maintain a live band in the morbid quagmire that passes for today's music and concert scene.

In July 2013, the first edition of this novel was published by a UK e-book publisher that vanished a couple of years later. Frustrated by the lack of control over my work, I decided to dive in, tackle the self-publishing process, and re-release an updated e-book before focusing on the launch of my next novel.

Pendulum Pet, the second novel in what was gradually turning into a loose series of sorts, was released in 2016. What ties the books together is the actual music by the (now once again studio-based) band *Cynicism Management*, referenced in the novels, while the stories are – in spite of certain characters appearing in both novels – self-contained and can easily be read independently.

In 2017, while I was still writing my third (and at this time still unfinished) novel titled *Dog Days* and composing the music to go with it, Monika and I decided to raise anchor once again and move to the Canary Islands, the remotest part of the European Union that we could think of and much more pleasant than the ever more expensive and increasingly gentrified Berlin with all its hustle, bustle, and six-month winters featuring eternal darkness, constant drizzles, bone-chilling Siberian winds, and hence an overabundance of doom and gloom. The move resulted in my two-year hiatus from writing and music, as I focused on other things (mainly flat renovations, chilli pepper cultivation, and nature). In 2019, this sabbatical has recently been interrupted by my unwavering friend Rick Harsch, who has kindly invited me to contribute to his experimental "communal" novel *The Assassination of Olof Palme*, which is still in the works.

Shortly after that, when I had already started writing again, I was utterly honoured that the publisher River Boat Books saw fit to include my debut novel *Cynicism Management: A Rock & Roll Fable* in its list of upcoming releases. Due to this remarkable development, I decided to radically renovate the songs from Cynicism Management's original 2011 debut album "Tit" in time for publication – simply to do them justice, as the original songs had been produced well over a decade ago in much less than ideal circumstances. Next year, on the "official" tenth anniversary of the aforementioned debut, the new versions will be released as a standalone album. Until then, these tracks will be available on my website and SoundCloud page – head to http://boripraper.eu/portfolio/cynicism-management for a free download and streaming of the entire original soundtrack; or to https://soundcloud.com/cynicism-management for the band's most recent (as well as older) tunes.

If you happen to like this yarn, feel free to head to my official site at http://boripraper.eu/ to find out more about my projects, hear the music, and possibly sign up for my mailing list. I look forward to seeing you there soon, but – first and foremost – I hope you'll enjoy the story.

– Tenerife, August 2020

Acknowledgements

First of all, I'd like to thank my wife Monika Fritz, whose contributions to the development and plot of this novel as well as her uncanny and uncompromising ability to get me to edit out around fifty pages of superfluous rambling have been instrumental to the project.

Big thanks to Rick Harsch for his unwavering support and input. Hats off to my cherished "beta testers": Jure Rudolf, Igor Unuk, Sunčan Stone, Sašo Mermal and Aljoša Mislej, as well as to Larry Riley for proofreading – your insight has been invaluable. I would also like to thank everyone at the real Rock 'n' Roll Tavern in Malečnik, Slovenia, as well as all my truly wonderful friends, bandmates, fellow musicians, acquaintances, and other peculiar individuals – you have been an endless source of inspiration throughout the years. Finally, I would like to thank Matej Peklar – my best pal in primary school (in another millennium, in a now deceased country) – for his witty original e-book cover design and fantastic illustrations for the album *Tit* and the upcoming release *Tit Augmented* by *Cynicism Management* (the band).

Needless to say, all characters appearing in this novel are fictitious, and any resemblance to real persons I may have met – living or dead, but all certainly getting there eventually – is purely coincidental.

Speaking of the dead, however: I would also like to take this opportunity to bid farewell to Pero and Stana, the two hilarious eccentrics that the characters Ray Kosmick and Willit Lonch, respectively, have been loosely inspired by. You've both left much too early, but I keep you in my thoughts whenever Ray or Willit speak. Rest easy, my friends.

About the Music

The following novel contains references to songs, recorded specifically as a soundtrack for the story. However, the music is in no way necessary for following the plot, so you will miss nothing if you cannot or will not listen to it. Besides, it is always possible that you might like the writing but hate the soundtrack... or vice versa. The novel as a purely literary work is my top priority, and therefore I by no means wish to force my musical escapades on you.

As the original music for the novel is now more than ten years old and my technical capabilities as well as expertise in music production have improved quite a bit during the last decade, I will have – in honour of the tangible, paper River Boat Books edition of the novel – already released the so-called "augmented" versions of the relevant tracks (not remixes, but thoroughly reworked versions of songs).

All of the "rejuvenated" songs will be published about a year from now, on the 10th anniversary of the original *Tit*, as a new music album called *Tit Augmented*. However, the new versions are already available on my website and SoundCloud page, so if the idea of songs enhancing the story's atmosphere appeals to you and you'd like to be among the first to hear them, head to http://boripraper.eu/portfolio/cynicism-management, where it is possible to stream and/or download the entire soundtrack free of charge; or to https://soundcloud.com/cynicism-management for the band's most recent (as well as older) tunes. You will find a link to each song in the text of the novel where that song is first mentioned. You can also refer to the comprehensive **List of Soundtrack Songs and Relevant Links**.

In addition, River Boat Books is partnering with VizVibe to bring you a Special Edition of *Cynicism Management: A Rock & Roll Fable* that will allow you to experience four of these sound tracks through the magic of augmented reality. To participate in this feature, you need to download the Augmented Reality (AR) app on your phone for free. Go to https://www.vizvibe.com/arLaunchpad/ for more details.

DOWNLOAD THE FREE APP

Scan the Rock & Roll Icons found throughout this book for exclusive access to AR enhanced content.

Whenever you come across one of the Rock & Roll themed icons in the book, simply use your phone to scan the image and your phone will come alive with digital extras to enhance your enjoyment of the novel. You will find these symbols on the following pages: Rock & Roll themed icons are found on the following pages: 92 (Touring My Backyard), 242 (Iniquity), 469 (TV Turns On You) and 521 (Another Place Another Time).

Each Icon is only part of the trigger. The complete trigger is a rectangle approximately 2.25 inches in height and 4.75 inches in length. The icon should be in the center of the rectangle. Also, please rotate your phone or viewing device to a "landscape" position for optimal viewing. Some devices may not properly display the AR content. AR functionality is dependent on the year, make, manufacturer, processor, storage, speed and/or operating system of the device.

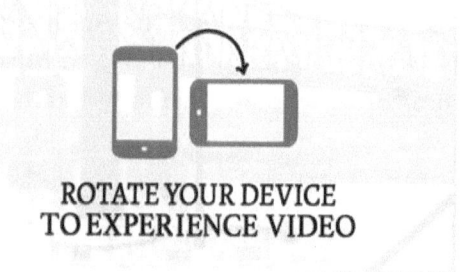

**ROTATE YOUR DEVICE
TO EXPERIENCE VIDEO**

Music Credits
   CYNICISM MANAGEMENT:
   Monika Fritz: vocals
   Jan Urbanc: guitar
   Borut Praper: drums, keyboards, programming, bass, guitar
   Aljaž Tulimirović: guitar and bass on Iniquity; guitar on Herbal Haze; guitar, e-bow guitar and kazoo on The End of the Vilewood Road
   Stojan Kralj: guitar on Herbal Haze
   Jure Praper: lead guitar on *Four-Circle Penile*

Substitute

All tracks written and arranged by Borut Praper, except *Iniquity* co-written by Aljaž Tulimirović

All lyrics by Borut Praper ©

Recorded, produced and mixed by Borut Praper

Vocals co-arranged by Monika Fritz

Mastering of the original 2011 Tit by 808mastering.com

Mastering of the upcoming reworked Tit Augmented by Andrej HrvatinRecorded in Studio S.U.R., Izola *(http://sur.si/)*

Additional material recorded by Stojan Kralj in Juice Plant Studio

RAY KOSMICK AND HIS PORN GROOVE CREW:

Jure Praper: lead guitar

Borut Praper: drums, keyboards, programming, bass, e-bow guitar, additional guitar

All tracks written and arranged by Borut Praper

Produced, mixed and mastered by Borut Praper

Recorded in Studio S.U.R., Izola *(http://sur.si/)*

Lead guitar recorded by Jure Praper

AUTHOR'S SELECTED DISCOGRAPHY

2015 - *CYNICISM MANAGEMENT: Pendulum Pet*

2013 - *CYNICISM MANAGEMENT: Shadow Chasers* (EP)

2011 - *CYNICISM MANAGEMENT: Tit*

2016 - *RAY KOSMICK: Short and to the Point* (EP)

2014 - *RAY KOSMICK: Aperçus*

2014 - *RAY KOSMICK AND HIS PORN GROOVE CREW: Something for Nothing*

2010 - *RAY KOSMICK AND HIS PORN GROOVE CREW: Bat Left the Belfry* (EP)

For the author's complete discography, head to author's music production site at *http://sur.si/*.

For selected free downloads, head to author's blog / home page at *http://boripraper.eu/*.

Books by Bori Praper
  Cynicism Management (2013; 2nd edition 2015; River Boat Books Edition 2020)
  Pendulum Pet (2016)

Cynicism Management
A Rock & Roll Fable

For Monika,
who suggested I write
instead of just making it up.

Table of Contents

1. Prologue:
Finnegan's Blog Entry No. 1

I've been told I can't be a "proper musician" if I don't start "blogging" about my dubious musical career (and other fascinating exploits). I must admit I don't completely understand the concept – people are seldom interested in what I have to say. They keep ignoring me even when I address them personally, staring them in the eye and screaming my guts out on stage, so why would anyone want to read about it online? But – what do I know, right? After all, I see people posting earth-shattering news and photos like *"Pooch mooning the camera," "My wee little treasure mastering the art of burping without throwing up" and "My spellbinding breakfast"* all the time, to the liking of an amazing number of their friends. So I guess it's just my own perception that's a tad skewed – which is a concept I'm already used to.

Well, if people want to be constantly reminded of the torment that is everyone else's daily routine, who's to say they won't be interested in all the impossibly intriguing plots unwinding before my very eyes and the countless momentous occurrences I keep witnessing as a musician. I may be hesitant to contribute even more junk to the vast collection of questionable online ramblings, but since my life is so fantastic, that could never happen, could it? I'm confident that people all around the world would probably be ecstatic to study these deliberations of mine.

I'm joking, of course, I'm sure nobody gives a shit about what I think or do. However, I've always been a man of intricate schemes and improbable plans, so perhaps spelling these out for all to see could just be another one of my twisted plots. Hence this blog – and maybe that'll make me a "proper musician" now.

So here's my cunning idea: I'm leaving. Yep, moving

someplace else. Before all four listeners of mine over here start to implore me not to do it because the Kirkwall progressive rock scene will surely perish without me, let me explain. Amalia, my old co-conspirator, called yesterday. She went on and on about this little former communist country she and her half-brother Randy had found somewhere near Italy about a year after she'd left the Orkney Islands. She said she'd discovered her ancestors hailed from that place, so she'd wanted to see it. And when she finally got there, she liked it – allegedly it spoke to her somehow, though she wasn't able to confirm the ancestral bit.

At times, I don't know why I listen to her. Much of what she's up to or says is bollocks, anyway. But she's a good conversationalist, an excellent drinking buddy, and a fine lay when she feels horny, which is usually the case when she's drinking.

So Amalia prattled on about this little backwater place where she'd finally ended up during this walkabout of hers, I thought it was Slovania or something like that... I know it wasn't Slovakia, I remember that because she said the locals made quite a fuss about foreigners getting the damn name right. Nevertheless, everyone kept confusing this wondrous little country of Amalia's with Slovakia, and the natives were insulted by that, so I remember it was definitely not Slovakia. Of course, I looked it up when we hung up, it was *Slovenia*. Po-*tey*-to, po-*tah*-to.

Anyway, Amalia kept on saying how cool this country was and so on. She'd even got her brother Randy to join her there, although he seemed to prefer the Netherlands. About half a year ago, at the beginning of the second semester at the local university, she'd landed a job as a guest lecturer, teaching English language and literature there. How she, an English lit dropout, had managed to do that, I'll never know. She said it was on account of her being a native speaker, and at the interview she'd claimed she still studied but had just taken a wee break, and they were all over her like frogs in heat. They'd said it was important that the students got to talk to native speakers. So for a while Amalia had pretended to be a teacher and she said it was great. Now she just shot her mouth off and made her students write essays, that was it. Not a great salary, but good enough, and she and Randy had even found a cosy and reason-ably-priced apartment. Apparently most Slovanian landlords preferred drunken foreigners who pretended to be teachers to drunken Slovanian students who didn't pretend to be anyone else.

While Amalia was blessed with her own room, Randy had to put up with this Portuguese nymphomaniac roommate who was supposedly planning to leave soon. Randy was looking forward to that, even though, as he explained bitterly, he'd been smitten with her when he'd first met her in some bar about a year before. He said he'd felt drawn to her like a mosquito to a bug zapper, and that's how his desire had in fact been extin-guished: the painfully alluring, delectable young temptress had first agreed to move in with him and Amalia, and Randy had been sure that as her roommate he'd have plenty of opportu-nities to expose her to his irresistible charms and ultimately butter her biscuit, of course. But, shockingly, it turned out that the girl was extremely liberal with everyone and everything – and her generosity was alarmingly *loud*. Which would have been fine, Randy hastened to explain, if she had ever been generous to him as well. However – oh! the torment of Tantalus – she didn't mind having it off while he was in the room, as long as he wasn't the one she was having it off *with*. Randy found that very hard to take. Moreover, he even suspected she might actually not like him very much, because she frequently gave him the evil eye. Perhaps, he admitted, it was because he snored, or maybe it was just that she and her wide array of playmates and playthings preferred to play alone. Be that as it may, poor Randy couldn't wait to get rid of her, although I must admit I loved her already.

Anyway, Amalia had come up with the idea to have me move in instead of the Portuguese lass. She said I could do some proofreading jobs or something for a bit of cash, or maybe even what Randy did, so as to "contribute to the household". Apparently Randy simply talked to people for money when he wasn't playing his bass. He called his services *oral communica-*

tions with a native English speaker. I'm wondering how *oral* he gets with his female "students".

Amalia also claimed that this time we would most probably make it as musicians. She explained this was a great opportunity because the local population of Slovania had a funny attitude to foreigners, especially foreign musicians. Supposedly you could (no sweat) even arrange for appearances on their national television, in particular if you were a really pale black alternative musician named Finnegan Frotz from the Orkneys and a red-headed singer of suspicious, supposedly Scottish-Slovanian origin, named Amalia Winegirl Paulin... Because the aboriginal population of Slovania thought that foreign musicians, especially if they were from the UK or USA, were somehow by definition far superior to any local yokels. It also helped a lot if you persuaded a couple of random Slovanian musicians to join your band, no matter how bad they were. Which wasn't hard, precisely because Slovanians were so often impressed with foreign musicians even if nobody had ever heard of them or their masterpieces.

The most important thing was, though, that you were *definitely* going places in Slovania if you knew the right people and hung out with them a lot. Which was no problem, because Slovanians loved to hang out with foreign artists, especially if they were somewhat exotic. And, of course, the loose lass she'd always been, Amalia partied with the right people all the time.

Anyway, since my nebulous career seems to be at a little bit of a standstill here in Kirkwall (as well as in all of Scotland, for that matter) and I haven't been able to muster the strength and determination to move to Edinburgh, Glasgow or London just yet (maybe even because I fear I'll have a hard time finding another singer and boon companion like Amalia), I might just give this crazy idea a shot. We'll see what happens...

2. Amalia

Amalia Winegirl Paulin's eyelids unglued and creaked open while her mind juggled double visions, bringing her staggering attention to the inside of her mouth, which tasted as if a syphilitic rat with a chronic case of diarrhoea and perhaps gangrene had crawled in there and died. Keeping cautiously still in order to avoid having to cope with gravity in such a blurry state of mind, she tried to grasp some idea of her whereabouts.

Amalia became aware of her face resting on her arm, which had long ago fallen asleep and now lay there dead, limp and utterly disillusioned. She must have been motionless in this position for a while, because she felt saliva drying on her cheek – probably she had been drooling in her sleep again. So she tried to focus her eyesight on the surface that her insubordinate arm was stuck to, and the feeble attempt made her even more disoriented. She concentrated and became aware that the vile surface in question smelled suspiciously reminiscent of a certain table with a very poor sense of personal hygiene. Stale stickiness and stench of beer spills, the lovable odour of cigarette butts extinguished long ago, decades of nicotine sediment on the walls... The familiar whiff of urine crept in from the corridor, through the slightly open door, and tap-danced on the tip of her nose – urine that had gone rank ages ago and was now referring to the nearby toilets and the floor around them as its retirement home. It suddenly dawned on her where she was. The realisation was like a ray of light piercing the oily darkness of oblivion.

"Hey!" she croaked inadvertently and coughed like a poster girl for pulmonary disaster, lurching for her last breath. "Boris! Goddamn it..."

Amalia gave the vile table a puny push and managed

to lift her head, which felt exactly like she imagined a 26-inch bass drum would feel if some mischievous prankster stuck a bunch of especially disagreeable tomcats inside and started beating on the double bass pedal. She blinked at the floor and felt a wave of relief roll over her annoyingly persistent nausea when she confirmed she must have done nothing worse than taken a Superman nap, as some Slovenians liked to refer to the phenomenon (her right arm, hand in a fist, outstretched, her right cheek using her left arm as a cushion) on her favourite table in her favourite of the most carefully selected seedy dives – Beeba and Boris's Rock 'n' Roll Tavern. So a quick pint was at her fingertips, and her condition was nothing one (or three) of those couldn't fix.

"Boris!" she managed to utter loudly without choking on her breath. "Beeba?! Where the hell is everyone..." she grumbled and looked around.

"Good morning, sis!" a voice chanted. Randy was sitting at the bar, smoking a joint.

"Oh. Randy, what's up. Where did you come from? Where's Boris?" Amalia blurted out apprehensively.

"Running some errands, stocking up, I think. It's the weekend, and it looks like you may have emptied a barrel or two tonight. Boris's cellar is not inexhaustible, you know, even if it looks that way sometimes," Randy stated the obvious.

"And Beeba?"

"Somewhere around here, probably in the kitchen or in the garden. Boris said you fell asleep on the table at around three in the morning, and they just let you take a nap. When I came to get you half an hour ago, at around half past seven, you were still snoring. How are you feeling?"

"Not too good. Tough night. Could you pour me a beer? I'm sure they won't mind."

"Sure, sis. Beer makes you strong, even if it's not Guinness," Randy laughed and abandoned his joint to smoulder in the ashtray, reached over the bar, grabbed a random dirty glass, rinsed it under the tap and filled it with draught lager. He refrained from attempting to adorn the

feeble foam with any four-leaved clovers or similar superfluous ornaments.

Randy stood up from behind the bar, handed the
salvation pint to Amalia, and resumed his position on the
barstool, relighting his pungent reefer. In the Free Territory
of Boris Birman's, the anti-smoking and anti-weed legislation
was conveniently not enforced while the place was officially
closed.

"Hey, thanks," Amalia said, grabbing the glass greedily
and gulping down half of it in one go. "I feel better already,"
she said.

"You know it's Saturday, right?"

"Aye, sure, the weekend. I wouldn't be here otherwise,
and so tired, too, would I?" Even before she managed to
complete the sentence, she started doubting herself, narrowing
her eyelids and focusing on her own treacherous subconscious
fabrications. "Besides, it hasn't even been a month since my
birthday, I'm still grieving," she added sheepishly.

"I don't care if you get drunk or not, sis, it's just that
Finn is coming today, remember?"

"Damn... Well, aye... Sure I do!" she said unconvinc-
ingly, as the ways of the world were still a bit blurry to her.
She finished the pint, checked the time on her mobile phone,
and instructed Randy:

"OK, hand me another and then we're off."

3. Finnegan's Blog Entry No. 2

I have this thing about airport toilets – I resent the cameras I imagine spying on my haemorrhoids in there, so I always try to resist my bodily urges at airports.

Don't get me wrong: I'm no paranoid conspiracy theorist. I despise the crap out of those. However, I really wouldn't be surprised if these arseholes that I sometimes feel are watching us all had cameras installed in the toilets. Behind the suspended ceilings with all those little nooks, crannies, rifts and fissures – countless spots for spy cameras. All kinds of ill-natured voyeurs, taking advantage of the world after 9-11, could be watching from up there. Hell, I've heard of cameras in clothing store cubicles installed for fear of theft, so how implausible are airport toilet cameras for fear of terrorism? Really, I'm not some foaming delusional lunatic or an Orwell fanatic, but, shite, if they spy on people everywhere you can think of, which I'm positive they do, why wouldn't that include airport toilets? You know, the place where people are usually off their guard. As we all know, even in *The Godfather* they hid pistols in toilet cubicles, and I'm the Pope's favourite altar boy if airport security hasn't thought of that. Security guards surely find anyone who possibly comes by with the idea of taking an innocent little dump suspicious, and would like nothing better than to barge in on their privacy and possibly accuse them of ulterior motives.

Unfortunately one can only resist one's bodily urges at airports for so long. Especially when waiting to board the damn plane frequently takes longer than the flight itself. So, after I'd finally had no choice but to heed nature's call, I made a show out of using inordinate amounts of toilet paper and mooning the ceiling for good measure before pulling up my drawers and letting down my kilt. Just to spite them all.

That amazing adventure was about the only interesting

thing that happened to me on my flight to Slovania. Despite my legendary rock star status – yeah, right – I had to resort to flying economy class with an ordinary Slovanian airline, so there was no free liquor or airplane food, of course; and while I normally love staring out the window, I, naturally, ended up sitting right on top of the damn wings. On the other hand, the flight only took about two hours – turns out Slovania is much closer to London than I might have thought; the stewardesses successfully kept up the appearance of being perky, upbeat and agreeable; and my trust in the pilots and their ability to land the plane successfully was well placed.

So I'd have no complaints (for a change) – if only planes were off limits to children under the age of 10. But, since infantile sonic terrorists are allowed to board (instead of being packed in with the luggage and larger pets, preferably properly sedated), I always end up listening to slobbering tots tirelessly protesting the awkwardness of air pressure changes. As a rule, while the brats keep drilling into everyone's brains with their shrill screams, the parents beam at them benevolently, wearing that *everyone-look-at-my-cute-little-treasure* expression instead of making their kids shut up already. Parents these days seem so eager to see their children as miracles that they let them get away with murder instead of just giving them a good old-fashioned whooping. I hereby thank the universe for the short duration of the flight, otherwise I might have considered slapping around both the parents and their puny progeny myself in order to demonstrate a thing or two about constructive upbringing and healthy discipline.

While trying hard to ignore the excruciating screaming of some snot-nosed little twerps a couple of rows away, I found a Slovanian magazine of some sort. It was translated into a lovely variety of British English, but all it contained was a careful selection of exceptionally boring and downright cheesy articles. At least I could enjoy the pretty pictures.

Anyway, there was also a short item about a famous Slovanian band that caught my eye. I don't know if I remember what they were called exactly, it was something like *Shaft Rock*.

And these *Shaft Rock* guys were really proud to announce they were going on the road in — listen to this — the ONLY touring bus in the whole country!

I found that so fascinating that even before I saw the place for the first time I'd decided to write something about it: a little ditty called *Touring My Backyard*.

4. Coven of Bitches

Deep underneath the surface, lost in the tunnels extending under the airport control tower like an underground maze burrowed by workaholic coke-abusing moles, Coven of Bitches pored over the video feed from the toilets.

In a time when political correctness seemed to spill out of the United States like a fetid cloud of appallingly bad taste, the female security guards working in their menacing high-tech chamber within the subterranean complex took it upon themselves to live a little and practice a bit of political *incorrectness*. Hence their idea to call themselves *Coven of Bitches*. How ironic it was, then, that their group was actually a result of that same feigned oversensitivity towards the delicate feelings of fellow human beings. When the authorities decided it would be a good idea to install spy cameras in the public toilets without, of course, informing the public of that, they were not in the least concerned that somebody might find out about their cunning little scheme and reveal it to everyone. Should that be the case they could always resort to the fabled argument that in order to improve everyone's security, the people's very assholes should be subject to unannounced official investigation at any time. However, the authorities were nevertheless concerned with gender issues and equal opportunity. Therefore female security guards observed the female toilets as well as male toilets on alternating weeks, and so did the male guards, in order to avoid arguments that heterosexual security guards were discriminated against. See, if gay guards could peer at passengers of their own gender, then surely the straight ones could have a jolly good time gazing upon the buttocks of the opposite sex too! It still remains a mystery why, until the day of Finnegan's departure from London Stansted, the airport authorities had not yet considered simply putting female *and* male security guards together in a single room, in front of rows and columns of monitors displaying both male *and* female toilets. But let's leave that to their Streamlining Department.

Anyway, that week the merry band of well-trained security wenches watched the men's faces and behinds. Indeed, by no means could any pimples on anyone's posterior go unobserved: every orifice had to be supervised and accounted for in case somebody tried to stuff something up their outlet. To this end, tiny self-cleaning cameras (equipped with minuscule lens wipers) had been – apart from every-where else – also installed *inside* the toilet bowls, of all places.

"Damnation, this is certainly going to hurt," one of the Bitches remarked as she watched an obese gentleman enter the toilet. "He's looking around very carefully and impatiently, looks as if he's in a terrible hurry... He's pressing his hand against his gut and checking if anyone else is in the stalls... I suspect he's got a big one to unload," she mused.

"You think he might have eaten at the airport?" Another One snickered.

"Deactivate the lens wipers if it looks like he's about to dump a really sticky one on the camera," Arch Bitch ordered. "I don't want last week's fiasco repeating itself."

"Absolutely," The Watcher agreed. "Getting the wipers fixed is a real pain in the ass. We'll wait out the worst of the fallout, use water jets immediately after, and then turn the wipers back on. The chap's private parts might get sprayed a bit, but I'm sure he won't suspect anything. He'll just think the toilet's equipped with some kind of an automatic flushing system or something."

"I must stress that this is not in accordance with the official protocol," remarked Grim Bitch. "Our superiors may find this procedure inappropriate. We could miss something while we aren't watching."

"I concur, but if sticky excrement hits the lens – no pun intended – we won't see anything anyway. Those poor little wipers will just struggle in vain. Then we'll have to use water jets anyway, but the wipers might still burn out before they get unstuck. I'll explain our actions to the superiors if need be," Arch Bitch concluded. "Make it so, Bitches, proceed with emergency safety measures if it looks like a viscous explosion."

The Watcher nodded: "Aye aye, ma'am."

"That disaster last week... I still think it was burritos and beer," Another One remarked absent-mindedly, seemingly to no one in particular.

"And I still bet it was Indian curry with a hearty side dish of Serbian bean soup," a Bitch of Serbian ancestry responded promptly.

"Let's avoid dragging ethnicity into this. We may be Bitches, but we're not bigots," Arch Bitch lectured.

"Well I'll be, how about that! Behold a really pale African-Scottish man enter after the fat guy!" The Watcher interrupted the digestion debate.

"I told you, no references to ethnicity! Not even in what we currently deem as a politically correct manner! Better safe than sorry. Who knows what any of the words coming out of our mouths today might mean tomorrow. It's all on tape, and you know the bosses are watching. And stop calling people fat already – are you nuts... I mean, uniquely mentally endowed?! By the way, how can you tell that the toilet visitor over there is... Well, an inhabitant of Scotland?"

"He's wearing a kilt."

"Oh, I see..."

"I bet he's actually just a tourist who got far too excited in a Scottish souvenir shop," Serbian Bitch offered.

"Look at the fat... I mean, gravitationally-challenged person, he got startled a bit there!"

The voluminous man turned around to check out the newcomer, looking surprised as he spotted the pale black Scotsman. He also appeared rather guilty already in advance. Then he retreated – as swiftly as he could squeeze himself inside and shut the narrow door – into an empty cubicle. The pale black kilt-wearing man, having observed the telltale urgency and purposefulness, entered a stall as far from the rotund gentleman as possible. Unfortunately, it was not a very spacious restroom.

"Look at them! What a display of unlikely outfits, gestures, peculiar appearances and distressed facial expressions there!" The Watcher clapped enthusiastically.

Serbian Bitch laughed. "This is so awesome, when you get into it a bit... I bet we could win cash awards at Funniest Home Videos with these tapes. Or maybe we could base a new reality show on this. *'The Toilet Chronicles'*, we could call it."

"Oh, sure. What loads of fun that would be!" Grim Bitch grumbled. "Who'd want to watch such crap – no pun intended."

"I beg to differ! See if I don't do something about it. When I strike gold with this material, don't you come a-knocking."

"Note that your aggrandisement of scatological humour is progressing towards the utterly vexatious," the slightly eccentric Bitch known as Accumulator of Unwonted Locutions remarked after a short pause.

"Whatever you say," Serbian Bitch sighed, rolling her eyes and shrugging at the others.

"Here it goes, yellow alert..." Arch Bitch turned towards The Watcher – the camera systems operator – and urged her: "Be careful, now, and do shut down the self-cleaning systems in case of emergency."

The Bitches fell silent and tensed. They did not have to wait long.

"Boom! There he goes! Perfectly liquid, so we can all relax now. Well, this guy is definitely not carrying anything solid in there," The Watcher sighed with relief.

"Stand down," said Arch Bitch, and added: "Condition green."

"Whoa, wait a minute, check that out!" The Watcher pointed at another monitor.

All six Bitches turned and stared motionlessly at the monitor displaying a pale black posterior and associated paraphernalia. Quiet murmurs, sighs, suppressed sounds of surprise and stifled syllables of splendour filled the control room for a few long seconds.

"Wow, that's nice!" Another One finally admitted.

"And daedal!" Accumulator of Unwonted Locutions added.

5. Finnegan's Blog Entry No. 3

Light beer. A collocation that rolls around your mouth effortlessly, much like *light mayonnaise* or *Bacon Light™* – lighter and healthier. You know immediately that the product the suspiciously coined trademark defines is supposedly better for you than your average *Dark Ale, Pudgy Cola or Profuse Pig Shanks*. The whole universe of marketing seems to be getting quite obese on lightness these days: because what harm is any *light* product going to do. Even light coffinettes don't sound as terminal as massive burial vaults.

So there I was, twirling my thumbs in the alcohol-free low-cost airline plane, thinking along the lines of: "Well, if I stop by the bar before actually getting out of this airport, I could probably squeeze in around three light beers before my conscience ever noticed I'd even had one. Sure, I've promised myself I'd never ever again start drinking before noon (or 11 am whenever I return to the British Isles from here and enter another time zone), but since I'm only considering downing a light beer, that's alright. And since it's only light beer, I might as well consume three of those while I'm at it. That's because three cans of light beer roughly translate into a moderately generous pint of Guinness. This little transgression probably won't in fact be completed before noon, thus constituting no sin at all… And, admittedly, in case I may be willing to sin a little, which should be no dilemma at all for a rock star, I may as well drink around four or five light beers and still remain within the limits of what seems appropriate for a relatively benign high noon wrongdoing under the guise of being an artist."

However, my meditation was interrupted by a fasten-your-seatbelts sign, and a stewardess informed everyone indifferently that we should close our trays because "we are about to land at the *Letališče Jožeta Pučnika* airport".

"What?!" you ask. "At the *what-the-hell* airport?"

Well, these Slovanians must be quite an intriguing nation, to name their only airport worth mentioning (as I found out later) something that no sensible sentient soul in and around the Milky Way could possibly hope to remember, pronounce, or, god forbid, spell correctly. Except for Slovanians, perhaps, but even that I am not completely sure of. I don't want to go into details, but believe me when I say that those funny little marks above the ss, cs and zs are not good news at all as far as pronunciation is concerned! They denote sounds that must surely have been invented by a colony of particularly malevolent airborne viruses with the intention of introducing them to this nation deliberately and thus spread more easily: because there is definitely much spitting involved. The name of the only significant Slovanian airport sounds as if a bunch of shrieking cicadas gangbanged a cockatrice. (I wonder if the flu in fact spreads more easily here than it does in, say, France, for example? That might be worth looking into if one wanted to win the Ig Nobel Prize.)

Phonetic deliberations aside, I was looking forward to getting off the plane and checking out this place. We had landed in the middle of trees and corn, on a runway the size of an aircraft carrier deck, right next to an airport terminal about as large as my neighbour's barn. It was almost like landing in someone's backyard. The plane came to a halt... Then a bus came to retrieve us and hauled us the whole nine yards to the tiny terminal like a load of sardines. Literally – I do not exaggerate: before the bus even switched into second gear, it had already come to a halt. I mean, of all the ludicrous things...

Later, after considerable deliberation, I attributed this display of utter folly to that undying wish of all nations: to be large, mighty, grand and consequential, potent and unyielding, dauntless, heroic, bold and brave and brawny and brash – in short, to be Klingon. You know: if all you have is a radio antenna, pretend it's the Eiffel Tower. Or maybe it was all a ruse to throw all those nasty terrorists who might want to bomb this highly important strategic goal off guard.

Why anyone would want to target this place was beyond

me, though: the airport was like a mortuary. It had such an all-pervading funereal atmosphere that everyone kept whispering. It was almost as bad as the Kirkwall public library.

Ten minutes later, while I was once again brooding about the ways of light beer and simultaneously praying to the mysterious forces of the universe to get my luggage back unshattered and unscattered, Amalia rolled up to the airport with her brother Randy. When I had finally picked up my luggage and gone out to meet them, she seemed a little cranky. I suspected that was the result of all these "naughty evenings" she said she'd been having lately. Whatever the case may have been, she readily lit up at the prospect of celebrating my arrival with innumerable undiluted Slovanian wines, which she promised were indeed worth indulging in.

Finally I was able to make my much coveted light beer transgression a reality, as Amalia and Randy were both all too willing to have a bit of a break at the bar before doing anything else.

Half an hour later, while ordering my third light beer, I was already pondering Amalia's succulent curves. Five minutes later I thought of her secret crevasses and tight ravines, and my mouth watered. After another gulp or two she was reminiscent of the second coming of Aurora Haze, the manifestation of Loree Ferrari, the moistening of Candi Sunrise. I may have not mentioned it so explicitly yet, but Amalia could definitely be exceedingly voluptuous if she wanted to. So I started worrying about the prospect of spending months upon months living with her, trying to resist the temptation of jumping her like a horny cicada gangbanger mistaking her for a cockatrice. She must have read my mind, as she was usually able to, so we hugged while I wished I wore pants instead of my kilt – it would have been easier to conceal my excitement into a trouser leg.

Though slightly embarrassed, I was already convinced my stay in Slovania would turn out to be a great source of inspiration.

6. Randy Jiggler,
Paloma Mala & Desidéria

Mercifully bestowing a welcoming hug on the apparently libidinous Finnegan, Amalia asked softly and, as far as Finnegan was concerned, rather sensuously: "What have you been up to?"

"Oh, you know, same old bollocks," the distracted Scotsman blurted out, his mouth overtaking his lubricious mind. He suddenly started worrying about the beery quality of his breath.

"Anything worth mentioning happened to you since I've been away?"

"Nope... Can't think of anything meaningful. Kirkwall is the same as it's always been. The local drunks still couldn't care less about my artistic achievements, and neither do the other two townspeople. The trip here was also quite uneventful... Oh, with the possible exception of the airport toilet. I felt really weird in there. I could swear I was being watched. Of course, I didn't take my absurd hunches very seriously, must have been an acid flashback originating in the late nineties," Finnegan smiled.

He, Amalia and Randy slowly squeezed themselves into Randy's rusty excuse for a car... *A Yugo 55*. Randy said he'd bought it because it was hilarious and dirt cheap. Cheapness was Randy's middle name, all right. As far as humorousness goes: Finnegan usually didn't find cars hilarious, but this piece of junk was indeed a tad on the funny side. And it was imaginable that with a bit of herbal inspiration it *could*, perhaps, actually become hysterical, so he could see what Randy was talking about.

Randy Jiggler was Amalia's kid half-brother, almost five years younger than Amalia and three years younger than

Finnegan, so he'd always been under their protection. He'd
never found much pleasure in shaving, so he usually looked
like an Al-Qaeda lieutenant. His black hair, though he kept
it as short as possible all over his skull, grew in abundance
wherever else it possibly could, and that only contributed
to the jihad impression. Randy had found much pleasure in
playing bass guitar, though, even as he'd been struggling to
graduate from primary school, which he'd eventually accomplished without flying colours.

However, bass guitar must have motivated Randy,
because he'd had no trouble finishing high school. He claimed
it was just because he'd been listening to all these tall tales
about high-school bands, so he'd actually had fun there while
trying to form one. Perhaps he'd also fit in better because in
the second year he'd finally discovered pot and chicks on pot.
By the end of the third year he'd figured out most of the tracks
by *Primus's* Les Claypool, and since then things had been
looking up.

However, in spite of his obvious talents, Randy had
wrapped up his education without ending up a member of
a major label band (endless improvisations with Finnegan
and Amalia didn't count as a particularly striking success).
That had been a few years before Amalia decided to put
her English literature studies on hold for a while, so Randy
resolved to accompany his sister on her quest for heightened
self-awareness: he figured he would just play bass, smoke
ganja, and hopefully stumble upon a group of people
indulging in meaningful musical endeavours someday.

The gang dumped Finnegan's luggage into the miniature
trunk of the ludicrous old Yugo, and Randy pulled away from
the airport. Finnegan meditated on how their infamously
anonymous jam session group had managed to find itself in a
faraway former communist land, and steeled himself for what
he expected to be a long drive to the centre of the Slovenian
capital. Amalia, who'd obviously had a rough night, took a
quick nap while Randy explained to their kilt-wearing friend
how Slovenian girls were easily impressed with Scottish

teachers of oral communication packing contraband from Morocco.

"Man," Randy explained, "You should see how easily impressed most local girls are with Scottish teachers of oral communication! Especially if they are introduced to a little contraband from Morocco, if you get my drift. You wouldn't believe how often they can't help grabbing me shamelessly by the…"

As much as Finnegan would have loved to listen to Randy's elaborations, he focused on trying to survive in the back seat of the little *Yugo*, gazing upon its sickening amber dashboard and moth-eaten upholstery, reeking of ganja, gasoline, cigarettes, wine cellars, ancient beer stains and ineffective, annoying, even reeking, car perfumes. However, before Finnegan could even wrap up a single sensible paragraph of his exasperated complaint to the car perfume manufacturer, they arrived at their destination.

"Huh?" Finnegan gasped.

"We're here," Amalia told him, her eyelids creaking open.

"…and those naughty identical twins actually begged me to wear my wee kilt so they could check out what was under there," Randy chuckled randily.

Contrary to Finnegan's expectations and in mockery of his neurotic mental preparations and breathing exercises, they arrived at the centre of the vast Slovenian metropolis called something not many people could possibly spell without looking it up (*Ljubljana*, for crying out loud) in little more than half an hour, and not one iota of New York was in sight. If Finnegan wasn't such a bitter bastard, he might have even found the place moderately charming for a couple of minutes, perhaps, before succumbing to the unavoidable impression that he was back in Kirkwall with its population of 9000 weirdoes.

The merry band promptly picked up Finnegan's bag, backpack (with his precious portable four-octave keyboard sticking out) and laptop, and lugged it all up to the apartment where Amalia and Randy roomed with a girl they constantly referred to as the Portuguese nymphomaniac (who obviously had not moved away yet). As Finnegan set foot through the door, he was suddenly jumped by a smelly ball of fur bent on licking his face. The fur ball also whined and wagged its tail as enthusiastically and affectionately as if Finnegan was its long-lost pal, if not a steak Florentine.

"What the…" Finnegan started as he tried to push the slobbering abomination away, "Down, you mutt! Relax, will you! Jesus…"

"She's not a mutt. She is a purebred Irish Soft-Coated Wheaten Terrier. Don't you insult her, she's just happy to see you," Amalia chided.

"Happy to see me, right. She doesn't even know me. And she smells as if she's just been through your garbage, which she must have washed down with the water from your toilet brush bowl."

"Yuck, Finn, don't be disgusting. She's just having a bit of a dental hygiene problem, that's all. Apart from that she's a darling. Right, Mala? Yes you are, yes you are…"

"Mahler? As in Austrian composer? Why would you give her a boy name?"

"Her full name is Paloma Mala. That's Naughty Dove in Spanish, you retard."

"What's she doing here? Did you hire her to keep the burglars out by means of olfactory warfare and needless displays of mindless canine affection?"

"Shut up, Finn. She's my darling, my best pal…" Amalia kneeled and let the dog lick her nose, chanting: "Yes you are, yes you are…"

"Perfect, congratulations. You never cease to amaze me."

Amalia ruffled the dog's wheaten coat and let her nibble on her ear.

"And thus she gradually drifted into bestiality. And with an *Irish* pooch, at that," Finnegan grumbled.

Amalia punched him in the shoulder and told him to get his stupid Scottish arse inside already. First she took him to the place where his dishwashing expertise was desperately needed (the *kitchen*, a word Amalia always spit out with utter disgust). So Finnegan first declined to wash any dishes, then fumed at all the intricate cobwebs revealed by what had once upon a time been airborne droplets of cooking oil, and finally deliberately left the toilet unscrubbed, leaving that privilege to someone else.

The pale black Scottish artist unpacked, checked in his toothbrush, and inspected what were for the time being his clean socks. He saw to it that his underwear stash was accounted for, and then looked around the smallish room he would share with the reputed Portuguese nymphomaniac until she finally packed her belongings and left. In the meantime Randy would sleep on the couch in the living room.

The entrance door opened and Desidéria, the Portuguese nymphet, walked in, chirping: *"Hei!"*

So Finnegan finally met and thoroughly checked out the unusually sexy (perhaps also due to his preconceptions, of course) Portuguese roommate of Randy's, who seemed to go forth and prosper without any skills in any languages other than Portuguese. Granted, though – if Randy and Amalia weren't making it all up, of course – she was adept at many other uses of her tongue.

Desidéria was a voluptuous olive-skinned lassie in her early twenties, her curves coiling like the face of a cumulus cloud, shifting and swaying with the intention of making even the most conservative of swans renounce monogamy. Finnegan wondered, his mouth watering, what it took to sprinkle dew on that particular flower. He must have felt frolicsome due to the lightness of those light beers, so he promptly tried to grope her posterior. Alas, her response was quite unexpected and Finnegan simply failed to understand why these nympho-maniacs – the quite disturbed needy women he could definitely help out, if only temporarily, or at least give it a shot – always appeared in someone *else's* stories, but, when he was in the picture, they tended to resent him for trying to alleviate their terrible condition. After the humourless

voluptuary taught Finnegan a lesson in adult and responsible behaviour by means of a quick slap and a well-practiced
contemptuous though still enticing expression on her face,
Amalia declared: "Now you're ready to meet your band."

7. Largo "Fidel" Cabaleri, revolutionary drummer

Largo "Fidel" Cabaleri was an Italian from Trieste who had emigrated to Slovenia because of the Berlusconi horror show a couple of years before Amalia and her brother Randy found the charming little place.

In Trieste, Largo went to primary and secondary school with a lot of Slovenian kids, many of whom he called good friends. Unlike many other Italians, of course, who called them Slavic scum – that was just the way things were in Trieste with regard to the Slovenian minority. But Largo Cabaleri boasted the nickname "Fidel" for a reason: he was raised in an openly anti-fascist and pro-socialist family, and he often preferred to hang out with Slavs instead of his fellow Italians, with whom he never quite knew where they stood. So Largo had already known a little Slovenian (he was especially adept at ordering small beers and burek) before he ever thought of moving to the tiny country where the language was spoken.

When Mr Berlusconi's evil media empire started gaining momentum, Fidel began to write articles for various obscure liberal publications and organise frequent political gatherings involving him and his friends meeting in bars where they hatched various revolutionary ideas, got drunk and gorged themselves on burek and hamburgers. Sometimes they would attend concerts in nameless underground clubs, where they would simply get drunk because they could not hear each other speak and disseminate revolutionary leaflets by throwing them on the floor in the dark. Largo also played drums in a revolutionary underground band, so occasionally he and his band would even get on stage and yell various revolutionary slogans at the crowds of normally not more than ten or twenty drunken and stoned revolutionaries, who could not discern any words anyway because of the terrible sound system.

After Largo "Fidel" Cabaleri had studied philosophy at the University of Trieste for four years but failed to pass any exams due to his many pressing revolutionary responsibilities, his father became a bit unreasonable and found Largo a job at his friend's construction company. Largo went to work a couple of times just to make his quite wealthy though annoying father happy but found the routine completely unworthy of a political activist such as himself. This, together with the fact that he had somehow been unable to undermine Berlusconi's menacing media empire, was enough for Largo. He called one of his Slovenian friends in Ljubljana, who had recently opened a language school there, and arranged for a job as a teacher of the Italian language, which he was actually quite good at.

Largo hoped Slovenians would be a bit more open to aspiring socialists such as himself. They were a former communist country, after all. But, alas, the emphasis was on former and some of the more indoctrinated liberal capitalist loudmouths of Slovenia soon informed him that:

"*Everyone is in charge of their own destiny!*" ("And while they're busy being in charge of it, they don't notice their only destiny is to work their asses off for next to nothing so that Capital may prosper!", Largo would bellow, his fists raised up high in the air);

"*The poor should thank the rich, for it is the rich who create new jobs!*" (although Largo has always thought that it was the rich who got what they had by abusing as many of the poor as possible);

"*This is the land of equal opportunity and everyone can succeed if they work hard!*" ("Sure thing, the uneducated daughter of an impoverished seamstress stands on equal ground with the spoiled self-absorbed son of a filthy rich white-collar criminal who hasn't worked a day in his life, as long as she works hard!" Largo would yell feverishly);

"*If you are poor it is your own fault because you are lazy!*"

("The oldest trick in the book, except for the *'you're paid less today so that our Company may grow and you can be paid far more tomorrow'* gimmick," Largo would scoff in mockery);

"Workers mean expenses; expenses should be streamlined!" ("Instead of *'my workers make it possible for me to get obscenely wealthy while I don't actually do any work myself, so I should cherish them like the purse I stuff their money in to the best of my abilities'*, right?" Largo would ridicule).

"It is the workers who need capitalists, not the other way around!" (At that point Largo would only sigh and perhaps order another small beer dejectedly).

One day an accomplished hard-line free-market zealot even told Largo that *"Workers themselves are to blame if they're losing their jobs as the production is being relocated to China – because it is they who are the first and foremost consumers of cheap Chinese products!"*

"Now that is cynicism if I've ever heard a perfect example," Largo muttered to himself while trying to decide whether to laugh or cry at the implications of the aforementioned statement. Of course, why the thought of investing in Italian-made *Armani* designer suits instead of buying that cheap Chinese crap had never crossed the mind of the working class was beyond anyone's imagination (if any clothes were still made in Italy at all – Largo suspected the good people of Singapore sewed on the *"Made in Italy"* labels in the name of outsourcing anyway).

Such finely-polished pearls of free-market capitalist wisdom (or truckloads of putrid, bottom-dwelling, gutter-infesting bullshit, depending on one's point of view) were imported directly from the USA and applied in the new capitalist Slovenia in the most obtuse and brutal manner in a period of no more than 15 years or so.

"In only 15 years, Slovenians have managed to establish a dog-eat-dog mentality where everyone looks out only for their own ass," Largo mused.

"In only 15 years, most people have become convinced that any achievement (as well as failure) is yours only and that you exist individually, outside society," Largo chided.

"In only 15 years, Slovenians have dismantled what was once an exemplary state-financed health care system where everyone without exception had access to the same kind of medical care and almost succeeded in turning it into the ultimate and far superior *we won't scrape you off the pavement if you don't pay us to* utopia promoted by the United States," Largo lamented.

Only bits and pieces of the old socialist system remained here and there, and these were promptly done away with and privatised in the name of anti-communism as soon as they appeared on the radars of the former communists, now born-again capitalists. What had once been a one-party system was now a multi-partisan sham in which all the parties were the same and equally corrupt, and where "liberal" meant "free to pinch money from your pockets in broad daylight without ending up in jail for it".

"Ah, much better," Largo sighed at the thought.

Largo sometimes saw himself as a contemporary *Don Quixote*, struggling against the brutal oppression of the free-market ideology, against capitalism at its worst, against the unending tyranny of globalisation at its most ruthless... The only difference being that Largo owned an *Armani* coat and rode underwear with *Calvin Klein* skidmarks instead of Rocinante the old nag.

However, Largo Cabaleri had not given this much thought at first. His enthusiasm hadn't begun to wane until he was charged a small fortune for his tiny little apartment in the centre of Ljubljana. He sighed after he was informed that he would pay considerable taxes on his wage at the language school, and more taxes on any of his own work he would dare to be paid for as a musician, writer or journalist. When they told him that electricity and water were not something that everyone could afford anymore, but instead became goods marketed for as much profit as possible, he rolled his eyes and felt really disappointed. He bit his lip as he found out he was also supposed to pay for his own health insurance. When finally he realised that food was bloody expensive, he decided he needed more cash. Were it not for the fact that beer was far cheaper in Ljubljana than in Trieste, that teaching Italian was far preferable to digging ditches, and that Berlusconi, wearing more makeup than the whores of Napoli, still stalked the TV screens, Largo would even consider retreating back to Italy.

Instead he complained about these horrible capitalist horrors to his father, who, by that time, had already turned Largo's old room into a painting studio. His father was so happy to be rid of his aspiring political activist that he agreed to help him out with a considerable sum of cash every month. He even threw in a still life depicting a goose feather in a little bottle of ink and an old typewriter he had recently painted. Largo "Fidel" yawned and sighed at the painting, but hung it above his desk in his Ljubljana apartment nonetheless, just in case his father ever visited.

For the next couple of weeks Fidel taught Italian during the day, while in the evenings he would wear his revolutionary *Armani* coat, don his revolutionary beret, and comb through the local bars in search of co-conspirators. He particularly liked a seedy little pub, the so-called Rock 'n' Roll Tavern, on the outskirts of the city. There, an aging hippy named Boris Birman and his plump hippy wife Beeba very successfully kept the number of guests down by refusing to serve anyone they found in the least irritating. Boris and Beeba merely strived for serenity and had long ago resolved to keep their stress levels down.

Boris spoke English very well, as did Largo (which was rather surprising for an Italian): Boris had played drums in an international lounge jazz band on an English-speaking luxury ocean liner for a few years, and Largo liked to study his revolutionary literature in English. So they talked a lot and soon established that they were both drummers as well as revolutionaries (although Birman's revolution ended when all his hippy friends became white-collar criminals or went into politics, which boils down to the same thing).

Largo and Boris became good friends, so Largo had the

honour of becoming one of the few customers Boris as well as Beeba served without a frown. He also became one of the few people who could bring his friends to the Tavern without Boris and Beeba eyeing them too suspiciously.

Largo met Amalia in a library, of all places: he was searching for some literature on teaching Italian, while she was searching for some literature on teaching English. That and the fact that they both spoke to the librarian in English was quite entertaining, bordering on pretty cool when later, over beer, they discovered they were both passionate musicians. Compatibility like that could only result in Largo soon introducing Amalia and her brother Randy to Boris, Beeba, and their irresistible hospitality industry, so that is how Amalia found her place in the new world.

8. Kip Ducker,
heavy metal guitarist

"Think inside the box", Kip's aging mother said for the thousandth time in Alice Springs, Australia, one morning in 2007, to her quiet but theoretically rebellious boy pushing forty. Kip's age-old reputation as the heaviest guitarist in Alice Springs had, to that day, failed to result in any financial remuneration worth mentioning, and the last blowjob he had received (a couple of years earlier) was not bestowed on him by a succulent sixteen-year-old groupie after a monumental concert, but by a foul-smelling punk-rock grandma after a bottle of appalling whiskey.

For more than two decades, Kip had tried to do something meaningful with his life – like becoming a global superstar guitar player. However, by no means had he wanted to move from Alice Springs to somewhere more receptive to heavy metal artists, because he felt just fine where he was. He knew everybody there. He had charted every street in Alice decades ago and was always able to turn every corner with absolute confidence, because he knew nothing would ever pop up suddenly from behind any of them as nothing ever changed. He bought needless things in stores that had been there forever, and got terribly nostalgic if even an inch of their shelf space was ever rearranged in any way. He drank beer in bars that he had frequented since the tender age of thirteen, so he was on the first name basis with all the waitresses. He even knew the precise parameters of many of their private parts, too, so he was always able to fall back on some of them when others told him it was over and that he was a goddamn loser.

Furthermore, Kip's mother cooked and shopped for groceries and washed his underwear, while his father, a wealthy man who died when Kip was twelve, had put a decent sum in a trust fund for his son. So Kip was reasonably well off without ever getting a real job.

Kip thought of serious labour on a daily basis as tiresome and meaningless, anyway, so perhaps it was best he had never experienced it, for it could be a bit of a disappointment for him. It might even leave noticeable scars on his sensitive artistic soul. However, in order to keep his mum happy, Kip worked as a part-time stuffed animal repairman in his uncle's antique shop, and he was good at it, too.

Kip Ducker had long ago decided it was a very good idea to focus fanatically on his own well-being by avoiding stress at all costs (he had heard that stress was the first and foremost reason for cancer, mental problems, hair loss and general disagreeableness). Hence stressful jobs were out of the question. Actually, any regular jobs were out of the question, because they tended to become extremely tedious very quickly, and tediousness equalled stress in his books. Kip also kept himself in shape quite passionately, methodically expanded his guitar and amplifier collection, and practiced his guitar technique occasionally (but only when he felt like it – obligation was even more stressful than tediousness). Since he was quite talented, had heaps of time on his hands between his stuffed toy repair projects, and because he soon owned a collection of the most enviable equipment imaginable due to the advantages provided by his trust fund, Kip became one of the best and heaviest-sounding metal guitarists in the Northern Territory at quite an early age. He refused to acknowledge, though, that this local fame of his could have something to do with the fact that heavy metal guitarists were few and far between in what could almost be referred to as "the middle of the godforsaken desert" by certain people far more bitter and sarcastic than himself.

For years, Kip had also refrained from figuring out that perhaps his reluctance to leave Alice Springs and put his amazing skills to a test somewhere else had something to do, perhaps, with the aforementioned fact: that being the heaviest guitar player was far simpler in a town with a population of

30,000 souls than in Sydney or New York, for example. So years slipped by him unnoticed while he enjoyed stressless bliss in an optimum quiet little dreamworld of his own design.

However, the going got tough once, unbeknownst to him at first, his heavy metal hair started departing the back of his head after he hit thirty, despite all the stresslessness. He gradually came to resemble that prototypical over-the-hill rocker that every town seemed to contain at least one example of. He did not immediately realise why, but suddenly he started hanging out with increasingly older and decreasingly attractive women, until finally it hit him hard: he who had once enjoyed a far-reaching reputation as an awesome guitarist and relentless womaniser was now only known to a very restricted group of people, consisting mostly of himself and a couple of his equally forgotten friends. Besides, heavy metal was out; didgeridoo accompanied by electronic beats was in.

Kip finally started thinking – occasionally, during moments of weakness at first but ever more persistently as time passed – about where he would end up in fifteen years and what he would do then: would he be the local greasy-haired and bald-spotted metalhead known to a very limited number of a select few acquaintances for his exploits in the olden days, or would he ultimately achieve something?

After half a decade of careful deliberation, Kip finally decided he did not like his mother's idea of thinking inside the box at all. He resolved it was time for him to leave his mum, even if his father had died all those years ago and Kip had ever since believed she needed someone in her life. Eventually he even dared to consider – however horrific such thoughts might have been – that perhaps she needed someone else, not her 36-year-old sonny boy. Kip, to his own dismay and to the dread of his mother, decided that conceivably he might even be capable of loading his own laundry into the washing machine, wash the dishes like the select few who possessed the arcane knowledge of dishwashing, shop for groceries, and even go so far as to fetch beer from the fridge by himself.

In light of his sudden enlightenment, Kip packed his best guitar, stuffed his least worn T-shirts, socks, drawers and pants in his backpack, and finally moved out, leaving Alice Springs together with his family and his uncle's vintage teddy bear collection behind. He refrained from saying much. A man of few words: that was the way he had liked to lead his life for as long as he could remember, since all he had ever felt the need to say he expressed with his guitar (plus distortion and a brutally thunderous amp).

Kip told his mother he was moving to Sydney, and at first he thought that was what he would do. But then, once he realised how many guitarists, perhaps even better than him, populated the Australian metropolis, he felt slightly uncomfortable. By that time, he had fortunately already met a certain theatre critic who had just spent about a year in a funny little European country and loved it there. This theatre guy was terribly enthusiastic about that remote and mysterious place, and it was all he could talk about every time he got drunk. After a few late-night drinking sessions with the guy, Kip became convinced that the country in question had to have *something* about it that made it so alluring. Once he looked it up and saw how small it was, he simply knew it was an incredibly convenient place to make some noise.

And so it came to pass that Kip Ducker moved to Slovenia, a country so far far away and so small his half blind mother would never find it on the map, which was a big plus... A land so tiny they would hear his guitar rig on the other side of it whenever he decided to fire up all his equipment he would later have sent over from Alice Springs. He finally found his raison d'être, sensed his most precious desires, got in touch with his innermost core, and suddenly saw clearly what he wished for in his heart of hearts: to shake the fillings out of the teeth of the population of a whole state by strumming a single mighty earthshaking power chord.

A couple of months later, however, when he attended a peculiar theatre performance (written, directed, produced, designed, performed and soundtracked by a bizarre male stripper who was also his own makeup artist), Kip Ducker was more perplexed by the developments taking place on the back of his head than by what transpired onstage. Some time ago, he had finally noticed this unfortunate phenomenon that nobody had brought to his attention and blamed it ever since for his decreasing eminence in the sexy heavy metal girl circles. So, while the stripper twanged and tapped something by some classical composer on his guitar and shook his naked booty, Kip was busy worrying that his expanding bald spot was getting far too shiny, that everyone sitting behind him was well-aware of that, especially because some of the lights happened to be aimed at it, and that too many of his once voluminous heavy metal curls were packing up and departing for fields far more fertile than his unbecomingly barren scalp.

After the performance, Kip even felt compelled to slip to the toilets and abuse the mirrors there to check whether any grey hairs had in the meantime decided to pay his thinning mane a visit – a brief visit, that is, before finally falling out with the rest of them, obviously. But instead of dwelling on it too long, he decided he would rather head to the nearby pub for a beer and try to come to terms with his terrible fate. There he chanced upon Amalia and the stripper he had just watched perform, but who was, to Kip's profound relief, wearing clothes now. Amalia and the exotic dance artist started a conversation with Kip simply because they had heard him ordering his beers in English. None of them held his bald spot against him, so Kip soon warmed up to them. In fact, they made him feel so comfortably mellow that he soon let them charm him into becoming their heavy metal guitarist, although he still refrained from saying too much: Kip Ducker was simply a quiet guy (except for his heavy metal guitar).

9. Bogomyr Yadvig,
fusion guitarist

About a year earlier, Bogomyr Yadvig, a bitter vampire with occasional suicidal tendencies and an inclination towards compulsive bitterness and melancholy, decided to take off from Vinnitsa, Ukraine, and fly to Vinica, Slovenia. His inability to gain any recognition for his twofold art in Ukraine had depressed him terribly: his dream was to become an accomplished exotic dancer/guitarist. Admittedly, that was a slightly peculiar goal at first glance, but his act was in fact flawless and fascinating, though nobody seemed to care. Bogomyr complained about this injustice to every one of his friends and acquaintances to the point where they actually encouraged him to emigrate.

In the aftermath of his nearest and dearest practically begging to be rid of him, which stung like a rabid bee and only fuelled his gnawing suspicion that nobody exactly yearned for him to stick around, Bogomyr fired up his computer and kept staring at Google Maps for weeks upon weeks, studying, examining, weighing his options.

In his opinion, Britain was too expensive, rainy, and conservative. He had already spent a few years in London in his mid-twenties, trying to make it there but failing miserably (as well as investing – although he was broke all the time – far too much money in umbrellas he then kept forgetting all over the place). He had mastered the language, at least, so that presented other options. That said, Australia was too far away, and he despised the United States, for he'd deluded himself into thinking he was a bastard by-product of millennium-old Romanian aristocracy, whereas Americans kept forcing their way of life upon him and depicted his kind idiotically in books and movies. Bogomyr took himself very seriously, so when what he saw as a heap of cheesy third-rate vampire

54

pop culture junk suddenly became peculiarly popular again towards the end of the aughts, he felt personally insulted.

Belarus, Romania, Moldova, Kazakhstan, Uzbekistan and Turkmenistan were familiar as Bogomyr had already performed there, though, alas, once again without much acclaim – thus he knew moving to these places wouldn't contribute anything useful to his much coveted career as a versatile artist. Bogomyr also considered Austria and Germany, but was dismayed at the thought of lederhosen, sauerkraut and white sausage. He scoped out Scandinavia, but, surprisingly, the very concept of a months-long night depressed him so much that he even regarded impaling himself on a beanpole as a more convenient way out.

Bogomyr also looked at Italy, but was appalled at macaroni and Berlusconi. He did not speak Spanish; he couldn't care less for breakfast in Székesfehérvár, Hungary; he would never enjoy studying the Greek alphabet; and the ways of Turkey and The Middle East were of no interest to him.

Thus Bogomyr Yadvig started zeroing in on what had once upon a time been Yugoslavia, for one thing because he knew he could become reasonably adept at a kindred Slavic language relatively quickly – at least that is until he ultimately got sick and tired of his exotic dances and vintage guitar and moved to a remote island somewhere, to the dismay of the local population. Suddenly, by pure coincidence, he spotted the little village of Vinica on the border between what were now Slovenia and Croatia. Despite the fact that he didn't believe in any deities, regardless of his thoughts about his own peculiar origins, and that he abhorred horoscopes as well as the entire range of various New Age beliefs, Bogomyr took this as a kind of sign... Or at least an incentive to get a move on. People more reasonable than he would have probably found this idea dubious at best, as ultimately it might have been smarter to give London a second chance, for example, despite the pesky climate. Bogomyr, however, was adamant.

And why did Bogomyr Yadvig not choose to move to Stockholm or Oslo, even Trondheim, and delight in endless

winter dusk and the allegedly loose and lecherous disposition
of Scandinavian girls?

Alas, even Bogomyr himself could not explain why.
He would probably suggest, though, that he had never liked
cold days ending in freezing nights... That he had never
wanted to be awake for months on end... And that stretches
of long-lasting freezing darkness would only make him even
more despondent than usual. He had always envisioned
himself living in a place where sunrises took place at the same
time every day of the year, a place of rhythmic regularity
where he would never get confused after pursuing his
bohemian pursuits too intensely, a place where the nights
remained as sultry as the juices of his women (at least until
he sucked them dry and they became empty husks of utter
despair). He would prefer The Equator. So Bogomyr was
intrinsically southbound.

However, before moving to Jamaica, Bogomyr had
to put his pride aside for a while. Also because he was
hopelessly broke. So he had to move carefully and gradually.
As a thoroughly unremarkable vampire he was unable to fly
all that well, especially during daylight, but he also sucked
at it during the night. So he travelled very slowly, resting
in Khmelnitsky, Kutkivtsi and Vil'khivtsi, as well as taking
a break and grabbing a bite in Zbruch, Velyki Chornokintsi
and Mali Chornokintsi, before deciding it might be a good
idea to use the last of his savings and just board a plane. So
he struggled to the nearest airport without any adventures
worthy of our attention, and finally reached the *Brnik* Airport,
Slovenia, via Frankfurt.

"What?!" he asked a dozy and resigned-looking
stewardess. "We're landing at the *what-the-hell* airport? How
can I ever hope to remember that and pronounce it correctly?
Especially with these fangs of mine?"

(He had got stressed out about this problem a couple
of months before Slovenia's greatest airport was kindly and
thoughtfully renamed the *Letališče Jožeta Pučnika Ljubljana*.)

The stewardess looked at him wearily and said

firmly: *"Dol mi visi,"* after which she turned on her heel and proceeded to her seat. Back then Bogomyr couldn't understand her yet, but her intonation certainly seemed to imply that she couldn't care less about the outlandish problems of the pesky Ukrainian.

After the plane landed, Bogomyr became slightly peckish but not exactly starved enough to start looking for a suitable girl to suck dry. Sometimes, during his more optimistic periods, he could go for months without seeking out a fresh victim. So Bogomyr simply ordered a hamburger. When his dish was served, he grabbed the eating utensil he had received with it – it said *handmade toothpick* on the wrapper. It startled the bejesus out of him.

"By the night, what's this all about?! I could actually use this to off myself,' the miserable vampire thought and wondered why in the name of everything he held dear would someone need or want a toothpick so obviously *handmade* that even a walrus would have trouble putting it to good use. "Must be some kind of a cultural difference thing," he muttered under his breath.

However, the thought of cultural differences and handi-crafts led him to consider the possibility that the Slovenian hamlet of Vinica with its population of 210 souls might provide him with a pretty boring diet, which might in turn cause him to seek out one of these handmade toothpicks and impale himself on it willingly. After all, what were the chances of an exotic dancer/guitarist ever successfully staging a late-night contemporary performing art experiment in a village whose only claim to fame was a plain little room where a legendary Slovenian poet had despaired and withered away a hundred years ago?

After careful consideration, while nibbling on his hamburger and fries, Bogomyr Yadvig changed his mind and decided it would probably be a better idea to head to Ljubljana, the Slovenian metropolis with a slightly superior selection of art venues and tasty women.

For about a year thereafter, Mr Yadvig tried to survive

from putting on bizarre acts at the local theatres, which were sadly mostly frequented only by a bunch of heavy drinkers bent on putting on similarly bizarre acts of their own. That, of course, meant that monetary rewards were few and far between, but they at least allowed Yadvig to despair in a century-old room resembling the dilapidated chamber of the fabled poet from Vinica.

One day a juicy drunken songstress named Amalia Winegirl Paulin dropped by the theatre where Bogomyr Yadvig performed by himself in his newest production – a remake of Swan Lake, involving him dancing butt naked exotic dances while performing Pyotr Tchaikovsky's greatest hits on his vintage *Gibson Les Paul* guitar. The distortion involved made such a remarkable impression on the not-so-virginal but still stunning Amalia that she invited him to join her imaginary band, which did not yet have a name at that time and for which no songs had yet been written. But she explained that in Slovenia the average female singer did not need much more than a pair of tits to become a national superstar, and any piece of music involving anything more elaborate than a 1/1 beat and playback accordions was actually an obstacle on the path to fame. So they would most likely become instant superstars the very second they finally decided to graciously present their unrivalled creative geniuses to the local population, which could undoubtedly hardly wait for such giants of everything artistic to take pity on them and enrich their previously boring little lives with unparalleled and monumental musical compositions. Bogomyr saw this as an opportunity to become a superstar himself, because who knows what might happen in this country if one was capable of playing an instrument live reasonably well while exotically dancing butt naked. Admittedly, Bogomyr had no tits to flash at the audience, but apart from that his dance moves were positively breathtaking.

So it came to pass that Amalia and Bogomyr Yadvig joined forces and started hatching a devious master plan that involved a couple of other characters: an unusually pale black Scotsman named Finnegan whose posterior has already been exposed as well as the other band members and unyielding support crew Bogomyr would soon get acquainted with... Not to mention the nascent band's tracks, of course: elaborate musical masterpieces which, unbeknownst to them, no audience in its right mind would ever want to listen to let alone invest any money in.

10. Boris Birman, sound engineer, producer, and barkeep

Some things you just can't believe in sober. Therefore gulping down truckloads of beer was Boris Birman's job while he recorded *The Bottles*, trying desperately to grasp all the nuances of what he was supposed to do in order to make the band marketable and yet not too horrible.

Beer supply was not one of Boris's problems, because he lived in a big house inherited by his wife: a tavern that she mostly tried to stay away from in order to avoid the boring and unpleasant customers. So sometimes Boris was forced to tend the bar himself no matter how annoying the customers whom neither he nor his wife had a particular urge to serve. But when Boris was not busy avoiding the patrons, he was involved in music production as a self-proclaimed but quite successful producer and sound engineer. Unfortunately, he was only well-known among his usual customers – desperate penniless musicians.

Once upon a time, Boris had been quite an accomplished drummer, and he still saw himself as a drummer. But one day he got involved in a fiasco with another one of his bands. Convinced that they would soon explode into an unprecedented success and make it big time, the band members, including Boris, hatched a cunning plan pertaining to a rather dubious investment: they organised a huge concert nobody actually bought tickets for. It all fell apart, of course, and Boris became so disillusioned he stopped plying the drumsticks. So, to fill the void that appeared in his drummer's soul after he had sold most of his drum kits as well as his best snare drum in order to repay the debt incurred by his latest entrepreneurial undertaking, he started turning knobs and soldering cables, so as to earn some money as a sound engineer. At least his wife's house was large enough, so Boris had more than enough room for a studio.

At first his new pursuit was entertaining, quite a relief after dragging his elaborate drum kit and a heap of other musical equipment to concert venues every other day. But his new vocation soon turned into yet another tedious job: in the mornings Boris was continuously forced to wrestle down the aftertaste of all the beer he'd had to drink the day before in order to put up with the bands he'd been forced to record. As a seasoned rocker he knew this was not a very healthy lifestyle in the long run, so he decided to ride his bicycle to work every single day to keep himself in shape. Alas, there was a problem with that: his workplace was located in his very house. It consisted of a large room where he kept a collection of instruments, a treasure trove of electronic gadgets, countless miles of wiring and cables, a couple of impressive vintage synthesisers that he absolutely adored but didn't know how to use, an assortment of computers, some items of unknown origin and a heap of nameless junk, as well as pieces of paper covered in peculiar outlines of what still needed to be done. Sometimes, during the night, he'd fill entire pages with scribbles and mysterious handwriting he'd fail to identify or decode in the light of the following day.

Anyway, since Boris Birman wanted to become more health-conscious, he made a habit out of rising promptly as soon as his neighbour's rooster cock-a-doodle-dooed. He'd swiftly fetch his bicycle from the cellar, ride it around his house a couple of times, and then pretend he had arrived at work. Then, as soon as he concluded whatever he was working on at his workplace every forenoon, he'd pretend to ride the bike back home, where in the afternoons he would dabble in something else.

However, every summer the situation would become intolerable: his neighbour's rooster would start arising at about 4 a.m., and far too many stupid kids in heat started rutting all night long outside his open windows like there was no tomorrow. The stuffy heat always made Boris's vision swim

like a stewing dolphin, so he'd gradually lose any leftover
enthusiasm for his bicycle. Soon the whole idea of going to
work by exiting and entering the same door every day looked
quite idiotic. Boris would start gritting his teeth, which made
his fillings ache and, in turn, gave him a lingering headache.
When he entered that stage, Beeba started giving her husband
a wide berth because at times like these he was too much of
a pain in the behind. In order to make her happy by getting
out of her way, Boris would always proceed to pitch a tent in
their backyard, away from the street where all the sexually
and chemically excited kids loitered, in order to at least sleep
where he didn't work. This way the whole bicycle trip would
not seem so bloody pointless – he could at least start at his
tent and ride around the neighbourhood for a while before
arriving at his front door, thus persuading himself to keep
up his athletic endeavours despite the damn heat and the
pointlessness of it all. Besides, the tent and the barbecue he'd
always erect nearby almost felt like a vacation spot.

This year the entire routine had once again worked
for him for a while. However, a couple of weeks before
Finnegan's arrival, as the production of *The Bottles* gradually
became more and more of a nuisance, suddenly little pointy
rocks started prairie dogging from the ground, poking Boris
in the hips during the small hours of the morning when he
yearned for sleep the most. Thus he laid laminates beneath his
tent, drilled holes through the laminated square in order to
be able to drive the wedges into the ground, and slept a little
better for a few days – until Niki Lipps, the Tit of *The Bottles*,
started demanding of him that he tune her vocals a little
better, improve the quality of her voice as well as her interpretation by turning a few knobs, and include more accordions
into the arrangements. Boris Birman almost snapped and told
The Bottles to sod off, but the money was good and he needed
it. So instead of throwing them out of his studio and tavern
or jumping through the window himself he told *The Bottles* he
needed a weiss beer.

When Amalia Winegirl, Randy Jiggler, Kip Ducker,

Bogomyr Yadvig and Largo "Fidel" Cabaleri entered the tavern a few hours later, *The Bottles* had gone and Boris was in the middle of tending the bar as an excuse for not having to mix that accursed band. Even *this* was better than pondering the vile *Bottles*. He already knew Largo, Amalia and Randy: they were among the few guests he could stand. Now that he laid his haunted gaze on Kip and Bogomyr for the first time, Boris saw something in their eyes (probably a certain mysterious glow of unknown origin) that convinced him not to call his wife and make her serve the new punters, thus avoiding serving them himself, which was his usual habit. Instead he poured them spritzers, a glass of red Merlot wine, handed them beers and sat down with them in order to clear his mind of Niki Lipps, her irrational demands and unparalleled intrusiveness. If at least she was as young and juicy and alluring as she thought she was...

Four hours later, quite enthusiastic because of all the beverages served and imbibed, Boris Birman agreed to become the sound engineer and producer of the band which his unusually amusing guests were planning to form with another friend of Amalia's who was about to arrive from Scotland soon. They would surely soon explode into an unprecedented success and make it big time! Though probably they'd have to work on some tracks and practice a little first.

11. Coven of Bitches

The Omnipile transnational corporation was one of those gargantuan conglomerates that made reasonable people grind their teeth in annoyance, while the majority of average consumers never even realised they were constantly being force-fed Omnipile junk. Omnipile made everything from shoelaces to spare space shuttle parts, and once they entered a certain market everything else could pack up and leave for greener pastures, none of which would soon remain.

When they decided to become the global leader in dairy products, Omnipile patented negative-calorie cream, weight-loss butter, miraculous anti-cholesterol milkshakes and health-boosting yogurt – the same shit in nineteen artificial flavours and colourful packages – and pushed out all the local dairy products in every country they invaded. Only certain sorts of French cheeses survived for the simple reason that the Omnipile scientists had not yet been able to figure out their all-pervading gym-sock effluvium and reproduce it as an artificial aroma.

After Omnipile had thought of pushing chewing gum and candy, their marketing wizards came up with an especially villainous shenanigan: more than thirty different brands of chewing gum and candy were designed, and 'new' flavours and lines and kinds and brands and packs and designs, sugary and sugarless, fruity and chocolaty, sour, sweet and a bit on the bitter side, kept coming out constantly. Their Marketing Departments even looked into prosciutto, bacon and beef Tartare flavoured chewing gum, as well as tofu gum for vegetarians, but they were not sure the market was ready for such a revolution. (Instead, Omnipile bought some potato chips plants, opting to test these new concoctions on a more familiar concept first before proceeding to mushroom-flavoured popsicles.) But they refrained from stating *"made by Omnipile"* clearly anywhere on the packaging (except for extremely fine print nobody could read without an electron microscope) and used the names of their countless subsidiaries instead. So when most chewing gum and candy plants not already owned or subsequently taken over by Omnipile went out of business, nobody except for the former workers really noticed. Omnipile had managed to ensure a covert candy monopoly for itself.

When Omnipile also started buying out fast food chains and making panty liners and tampons, detergents and washing powder, baseball caps, universal remotes and beer, this corporation's path to global domination was paved. After Omnipile purchased a bunch of fabled English Premier League clubs, the game was no longer played with the ordinary football – the trademark O of Omnipile was thereafter used instead.

Soon this exponentially expanding mastodon also went into the construction business, bought some weapons production plants, landed a deal with the U.S. Army and started first demolishing and then rebuilding countries in the Middle East, while simultaneously stocking them with ready-made bomb shelters, overpriced patented drugs, outdated GMOs, last-year's models of panty liners, tooth-brushes and parasols, as well as trading bottled tap water and rotten fruit that the French farmers had chucked out for their oil reserves. In the very unlikely and highly tragic event that peace should prevail on the planet for a week or two, Omnipile would soon cook up a little war or two of their own. That often involved staging a coup somewhere; sucking a country dry and then, when it wanted to liberate itself, accusing it of being a rogue undemocratic terrorist training ground; covertly selling some delusional dictator in a funny outfit loads of weaponised anthrax and then accusing him of possessing weapons of mass destruction; or at least bankrupting a country, privatising its water supply, turning off the water when the starving peasants could no longer afford it, waiting for them to burn something down during the unavoidable unrests, and then selling them fire extinguishers and fireproof insulation which would prevent their children from being incinerated in the future. Whether all of these schemes were in fact completely real or not depended on which conspiracy theorist you asked, but it was a fact that Omnipile's more important undertakings always involved operatives called the Omnipile Intelligence Agency Agents. These shady characters had made for themselves a reputation more ominous than that of the CIA in the olden days when CIA agents had not yet all worked for Omnipile – because many of the current OIA Agents had been employed by the CIA before the OIA offered them a better salary.

Whether outright malevolent or merely pragmatic and greedy without being burdened by useless concepts such as conscience, responsibility, ethics or morality, the Omnipile corporation was, without a doubt, abhorrent in the opinion of anyone in their right mind. Seeing David Beckham chase a smiling trademark O all over the football pitch could easily be interpreted as the ultimate victory of abysmally bad taste, further worsened only by Omnipile's horrendous marketing campaigns and especially their TV commercials. Why the people in the 'creative' departments of the most influential corporation in the world didn't get shot for producing the impossibly sickening jingles they used in their ads so as to peddle their wares was completely incomprehensible, but judging from their annual business reports, somebody in that conglomerate was doing something right. Maybe they had simply figured out that sickening jingles worked best on the simple-minded and unsuspecting population, while profits would dwindle the very second an ounce of sensibility prevailed in any way. However you chose to look at it, Omnipile's unstoppable expansion resembled the bubonic plague, and the well-known saying constantly repeated by ill-natured misfits – that Omnipile was a case of omnipresent piles on the sphincter of humanity – suited this sinister transnational abomination very well indeed.

Needless to say, the Bitches were perturbed when they were suddenly summoned for a meeting with an OIA Agent after work on Saturday. What could that possibly be about?

The six Bitches shuffled towards the meeting room hesitantly, glancing at each other quietly, their faces sullen and grey, and their postures reminiscent of reclusive paranoid creative bookkeepers facing an audit by the Tax Administration.

Serbian Bitch theorised: "I bet Omnipile bought the airport and we're about to be scrutinised by their Streamlining Department."

"We'd probably hear something if that was the case. They've probably sold new surveillance equipment to the British government and are about to bore us to tears with another one of those PowerPoint presentations of theirs," Another One cursed under her breath.

"We'll see soon enough," The Watcher sighed as they hesitated outside the meeting room.

"This is going to suck," Grim Bitch murmured.

Arch Bitch shrugged and gestured at them to get their behinds through the door.

Apart from the funky ties that these otherwise humourless people wore in order to alleviate the tension somewhat, the Omnipile Intelligence Agency Agents were your cliché men in black. This one was no different.

"Let's not waste any time on pointless niceties," the man cut to the chase, fired up the projector and began his *PowerPoint* presentation. The Bitches sat down, as enthusiastic about the whole affair as the founding members of the Fundamentalist Vegan Association at a butchers' convention.

"You are most likely aware that the Omnipile conglomerate likes to take things into its own hands, solve its own problems, steer its own destiny, so to speak," the Agent began, stroking his red-polka-dot-on-a-yellow-background tie confidently. "Even in our darkest hour we remain in charge of our own affairs. By all means we can all agree that the Corporation is more than capable of handling any and all crises it might face. That's generally a widely accepted fact, so all the governments we may be dealing with give us a lot of latitude when it comes to ensuring that our mutual businesses run smoothly. You're probably aware that we also maintain our own Security Forces with the mandate of investigating any matters we may be concerned with and protecting the interests of the Corporation as well as those of our business partners. In fact, in recent years the Omnipile Security Service has already become the standard by which all others are measured. I only emphasise this in case you don't thoroughly understand why the matter I'll soon brief you on is being taken care of internally, not by MI6, for example."

"I've heard MI6 agents are trained at Omnipile facilities and use Omnipile-made weapons, anyway," Another One whispered in Serbian Bitch's ear.

The OIA Agent paused and glared at them as if at unruly children. The Bitches stiffened and tried to show he had their undivided attention, just like undisciplined students might moments before pulling off an especially mischievous prank. The Bitches, however, did not feel especially playful at the moment – frankly, they were intimidated, even though they probably wouldn't have admitted it. Despite their clownish taste in ties and pathetically self-important demeanour, these Omnipile people certainly meant trouble.

"The information I'm about to share with you is on a strict need-to-know basis. And until very recently you didn't need to know. However, by witnessing a certain subject... well, frankly, take a dump about eight hours ago... you inadvertently got involved in a very important investigation."

The OIA Agent made a dramatic pause and let this ominous piece of information sink in as he fumbled with his laptop and finally displayed the fantastically charismatic visage of Finnegan Frotz.

"This is that subject."

The Coven of Bitches looked at the photo, and The Watcher immediately recognised the face. Perhaps her talent for observation was the reason why she was in her line of work and why she was called The Watcher, as well. "Oh!" she exclaimed. "The toilet show we witnessed in the morning, remember? You know, the guy in a kilt with a very elaborate..."

"Daedal!" the slightly eccentric Accumulator of Unwonted Locutions interjected, "...tattoo on his butt?" The Watcher finished.

"Of course, the Toilet Chronicles," said the Serbian Bitch and almost dared to snicker, remembering her new idea for a reality show.

"Quiet, girls!" Arch Bitch said, "Yes, of course we remember him. An unusually pale black Scottish guy, right?"

The Omnipile Representative said nothing. Instead, he clicked "next" and the projector displayed a map of the Middle East.

"Three weeks ago Ferdinand Fenton, president and chief executive officer of Omnipile, travelled to Yoman, a small new developing democracy in need of peacekeeping, rebuilding and advanced marketing in the Middle East, to carry out an inspection of certain facilities there. Contrary to the Omnipile Security Service recommendations and preliminary field assessments carried out by the Omnipile Intelligence Agency, Mr Fenton insisted that his wife and children accompany him."

The next photo showed the faces of two kids – a nerdy-looking boy of about fourteen and a cute girl in her late teens with an elaborate purple hairdo and pierced nose, obviously rebelling against her parents in the trendiest manner possible.

"Fergus and Fabiola Fenton. On the very first day of Mr Fenton's inspection in Al Awil, the capital of Yoman, Mrs Fenton and the children remained in their hotel, guarded by their personal bodyguards, while the majority of the Security Forces accompanied Mr Fenton, of course. In what must surely have been a very well-orchestrated and cunning terrorist act, the guards and Mrs Fenton were incapacitated, and Fergus and Fabiola Fenton were abducted. For now it's in the best interest of the investigation that we do not divulge any

other details about the situation or elaborate on the possible
motives of the kidnappers. What you need to know for now
is that about two weeks after this tragic event, Mr Fenton's
son Fergus was recovered. The kidnappers, or terrorists,
exchanged him for a, quite honestly, bizarrely modest amount
of US dollars and a few tons of *OmniBug* insecticide. However,
despite a thorough and careful examination by our most
capable experts we have been unable to recover much useful
information from Fergus. Even though the boy doesn't show
any visible signs of abuse or torture, he's virtually catatonic.
The only piece of information he could provide was the
number "6-4-7-3-8", which he kept repeating whenever we
tried to pressure him into telling us anything. Apart from that
he said nothing. Unfortunately, since he is the son of our CEO,
we currently can't resort to more... well... creative interro-
gating techniques.

"However, the boy did have a letter from his sister
Fabiola in his pocket and a video of her writing it on his
phone. Obviously the kidnappers wanted us to know that they
have Fabiola and that she's alive and well... For now, anyway.

"Needless to say, Mr Fenton would do anything to get
his daughter back unharmed... Preferably before these heinous
evildoers make any other demands. It is probably quite
unnecessary to underline that the reputations of the Omnipile
Security Service and Intelligence Agency have suffered a
terrible blow, and such an insult must be met with immediate,
decisive and forceful reprisals. Therefore we have immediately
launched an investigation to see who to aim our missiles at
and how to get Mr Fenton's daughter back before launching
them. Naturally, we have also been monitoring all incoming
and outgoing airplane traffic very carefully. And this morning
the following footage raised a red flag..."

The Agent clicked "next" on the laptop and an oversized
photo of Finnegan's pale black Scottish fanny filled the huge
screen on the wall of the meeting room.

"This is the backside of one Finnegan Frotz from the
Orkney Islands, who flew from London Stansted to Ljubljana,

Slovenia, on the 9:30 a.m. flight today. You were able to discover this extremely meaningful tattoo of Finnegan's thanks to our own ingenious Covert Posterior Surveillance System, which your government has had enough sense to adopt and install in all airport toilets as well as many other select locations in the United Kingdom. Let's go over this again..."

The Agent approached the huge behind that filled the screen. It was adorned with a beautiful, colourful, and clearly high-quality tattoo. An elaborate pentagram artfully framed Finnegan's sphincter. Two of its points were turned towards Finnegan's back and one point was aimed at his scrotum. The pentagram was encircled in a double circle, inside which a single number in Gothic script appeared where each of the pentagram's points touched it. An amazing rendering of a goat's head filled the inside of the pentagram, and Finnegan's sphincter represented the "third eye" in the middle of the goat's forehead. The whole masterpiece was tattooed in such a cunning manner that it made a perfect pentagram in a perfect circle only when Finnegan sat on the toilet and the third eye saw the light. And the numbers inside the circle were, of course, 6, 4, 7, 3 and 8.

"So, you see why this is so important? We don't know yet how Satanism, these numbers and Mr Frotz, currently the main subject of this investigation, are connected. We also don't know what all of this has to do with the kidnapping in Al Awil. But we're afraid these numbers are related to a profoundly malevolent terrorist plot of some sort, and we suspect the press may soon start muddying up the waters – two days ago a couple of paparazzi made a video of Fergus shouting '6! 4! 7! 3! 8!' through the window of the Fentons' mansion. The media aired it immediately, as you may have noticed if you watch sensationalist TV shows, and people immediately started coming up with all kinds of outlandish theories. This only made a mess of things and could hinder our investigation. And now that you've seen this written so elaborately on our suspect's buttocks, we thought it best to get a hold of you before you started talking, pouring more oil on the fire. That's one of the main reasons why we chose you for this mission: since you're involved already, it's better that you know what you're dealing with and work *with* us instead of representing a serious problem we can't quite control without adopting certain dire measures.

"The second reason is that you're already on our payroll, even though you probably don't know it, since the airport security matters are handled by one of our subsidiaries that we do not advertise as ours for... well... what we might call political reasons.

"Thirdly, as far as we could gather in such a short time, Mr Finnegan Frotz is some kind of a musician... So instead of sending the OIA after him, we believe it's more appropriate to use inconspicuous undercover agents, preferably youngish women whom he wouldn't suspect of being undercover agents so readily, who could even pretend to be his fans if need be, if you get my drift, women already well-trained in security matters, and by our instructors, too, although they might not have been aware of it. Youngish women who could use a pay raise and who owe us, because they already know too much, and because they also know they could be *nullified*, should they be unwilling to undertake the mission and carry it out appropriately. Your plane is leaving tomorrow morning, so you better start packing. What do you say?"

The Bitches looked each other.

"*Youngish... I'll show him youngish, the bastard,*" Serbian Bitch thought but maintained an air of indifference.

"*Wow, does this guy like the sound of his voice,*" thought Another One.

Arch Bitch said, however: "I feel like I'm already becoming a huge fan of Mr Finnegan's tunes."

12. Finnegan's Blog Entry No. 4

In the evening, after she was done laughing at my exasperation at the slap from the Portuguese trollop, Amalia organised a ride to Boris Birman's, with the suspiciously giddy Randy Jiggler at the wheel. Randy had a theory that the Slovanian police were supposedly not very well versed in looking into the bloodshot eyes of herb worshippers and thus preventing them from driving, and herbal haze failed to register on the alcohol scale. Alcohol was otherwise, according to Randy and his lush of a sister, the Slovanian drug of choice: the good people of Slovania regularly indulged in it in order to alleviate the pressures of driving and everyday life in general. Social life here was supposedly quite impossible without some heavy drinking, which was fine with me. Randy claimed that pot was also everywhere, and the Slovanian nation even boasted its own reggae band or two. I chuckled at that a bit.

So Randy rolled a spliff and puffed on it while driving, cool as a cucumber, on our way to Boris and Beeba's Rock 'n' Roll Tavern. To make matters worse, he put on a record by that Slovanian reggae band he'd just mentioned. Allegedly it was well-known, though I suspected all the fame was of a distinctly local nature. Believe me when I say that listening to those lads play Slovanian reggae – the singer pretending to have a Jamaican accent in what was already an incomprehensible Slavic language – was rather painful, so I couldn't stop myself from sighing loudly. I rolled my eyes and restrained myself from becoming too sarcastic, because this was almost as out of place as gangsta rap by middle-class white Presbyterian secondary-school students from downtown Dundee. Finally I decided to stare through the window blankly, while Randy enjoyed his reefer and the tunes with Jamaican-Slovanian lyrics he didn't understand a word of (and neither did any Slovanians, for that matter, with the potential but not definite exception of the singer).

The city of Ljubljana was actually quite likeable. It had a kind of a laid-back, relaxed atmosphere, despite the large number of people driving like maniacs. Quite pleasant to look at, with lots of classic architecture and few buildings more than four or five storeys high. Visitors from Kirkwall, Orkney Islands, didn't have many reasons to feel particularly out of place here, really. It was far less intimidating than London, for example, let alone some of the US metropolises I'd had the chance to visit. Amalia said that people here would almost always gladly go for a beer and just hang out with you, as if they had all the time in the world. Which they probably did, because it didn't look like too many things were going on around here.

On our way to Boris's, the police pulled over Randy's car because he'd abused the lane reserved for taxis and buses in order to avoid a minor traffic jam. Randy cursed under his breath while Amalia muttered something about him driving like a moron. Obviously she hurt his stereotypical male pride in his driving abilities, because just before getting rid of his joint, rolling down his window and greeting the copper with a silly smile and beady eyes, Randy proclaimed that he had no idea what she was going on about: all of them drove like morons, he was just trying to fit in. You know, when in Rome...

Seeing Randy put out his joint in the ashtray without blinking a glassy eye marked a moment of considerable angst for the more paranoid among us. Especially those of us still new to this place and conditioned to believe that former communist countries boasted especially malevolent police forces, trained in the dark and dismal times of totalitarianism and probably well-versed in inducing pain without leaving any traces that you could nowadays use in a potential lawsuit against them.

While the reasonably friendly and seemingly gullible Slovanian policeman tried to make sense of Randy's Scottish driver's license, Randy casually turned to Amalia, who rode shotgun. Reluctant to reach for it himself (the move might have been just a tad too obvious), he nodded at the pack of cigarettes he'd forgotten on the dashboard in front of Amalia. Muttering in plain old English, he asked her to clandestinely conceal the offending item, brimming over with fragrant greenish vegetation, into the glove compartment. Meanwhile, in the background Frank Zappa came on instead of those pesky Slovanian ragga-muffins and started elaborating on the *utility muffin research kitchen of the muffin man*.

The policeman, who stood within earshot of Randy and obviously, contrary to Randy's expectations, understood English well enough to comprehend what Randy was talking about, just smirked, handed the driving license back to Randy, sighed at the tower of ganja smoke rising through the half-open window of Randy's *Yugo*, rolled his eyes and made a scalding remark which went something along the lines of: "I should write to you a ticket and take your grass and give you blood test and take away your driving license. You're happy I don't have no time for strange tourist. But soon we get our little portable THC test, and it will be less nice for you then. You go now, I have enough other work today. And don't drive on bus lane no more, you understand?" To my profound relief the copper just reprimanded Randy and shooed us away.

As we pulled away, leaving the cops engulfed in a cloud of weed aroma and Yugo exhaust, I voiced my suspicions that even Slavic cops understood what we were saying pretty well nowadays. The downside of only speaking English, I suppose – one more reason why we should all have learned Gaelic better.

Amalia just giggled, pulled a small flask from her purse, and offered me a swig of cognac. I didn't mind: it certainly hit the spot.

We drove on for another ten minutes or so. It was surprising how quickly and abruptly we seemed to end up in the middle of nowhere, and the *Duelling Banjos* theme from *Deliverence* popped up in my mind. One minute we passed what Amalia said was the city's outer bypass, still driving through the commercial district... While a few seconds later I realised we were already in the countryside. I could still see the outskirts of the city through the rear windshield while we were already being hailed by the familiar whiff of cow dung and sight of cornfields. I looked around and noticed in the distance what looked like a big black and white portrait of Jimi Hendrix on a crumbling concrete wall. Indeed, we were about to arrive at the fabled Rock 'n' Roll Tavern, located far away from everything, though merely twenty minutes by car from the city centre. The location was perfect, because the place was also a small concert venue, and this way no tiresome neighbours with acutely sensitive hearing were bothered by countless aimless drunken excuses for jam sessions that supposedly took place regularly here, and which only the musicians onstage could possibly stomach. Any listeners not virtually unconscious were better off somewhere else, preferably behind the bar in the other room (sheltered by a couple of soundproof doors and a hallway separating the bar from the stage). In case of severe substance abuse on the part of the musicians involved in impromptu musical escapades, Beeba even stocked ear plugs, which she sold at quite a profit (sometimes the demand for them was incredible).

As we climbed out of the little car, my mind turned towards the upcoming meeting apprehensively. I sincerely hoped that the band members would not turn out to be a bunch of lunatics and drive me insane before we'd even had the chance of rehearsing a single track. I'd had far too many bad experiences in the past. I was already used to Randy's puffing and Amalia's guzzling, and I was hardly known for constant sobriety and clear-mindedness myself. However, I hoped this would not once again turn into one of those bands that only got drunk and stoned, never doing anything meaningful but talking, plotting and scheming, driving each other crazy without ever getting any tangible work done.

13. Cynicism Management

The merry band – Amalia Winegirl, Finnegan Frotz, Kip Ducker, Bogomyr Yadvig, Largo Cabaleri and Randy Jiggler – gathered at the Rock 'n' Roll Tavern. Boris and Beeba had already been alerted of the upcoming Cynicism Management conference by Amalia, so by the time all of the band members finally arrived, they were psychologically prepared: Boris had already downed three or four beers, while Beeba, who had a little bit of a cold, had somewhat increased her cold medicine dosage (tea and schnapps).

Beeba had prepared a huge platter of cold cuts and a heap of her locally-famous fried specialty. Randy, a vegetarian, grimaced and shuddered in dismay, figuring he'd just eat some fries.

"Here, special for eating," Beeba informed the band in a cute Slavic accent and beamed a smile at the guests as she put the food in front of them.

"Oh, this is awesome," Largo crooned, rubbing his hands together. "Beeba is famous for this – Viennese-style bull testicles, French fries and Tartare sauce."

Finnegan peered at the dish dubiously, almost forgetting for a second that his national dish was haggis, which was certainly not any less funky than bull testicles. Bogomyr sipped his Merlot indifferently, while Kip Ducker dug in without wasting a word.

Boris Birman arrived from the wine cellar and walked up to the table carrying an oversize jug of his best white wine, which was usually a sign of a very good mood.

"Bon appétit, everyone," he murmured and put the wine on the table indifferently. Even though he obviously did not mind the merry guests for a change, he had to conceal his joy somewhat for the sake of his reputation. But, nevertheless, he even went so far as to introduce himself to Finnegan: "Hello. I think we don't know each other yet. I'm Boris. Cheers!" Boris raised his glass.

"Nice to meet you," said Finnegan, taking the opportunity to pour himself a glass of wine. "Cheers!"

Finnegan soon learned that Slovenians had a habit of drinking to each other's health all the time, probably because everyone's health was constantly at stake due to all the drinking. Actually, cheers in Slovenian is *"na zdravje"*, which literally means *"to health"*. But these are not your ordinary toasts, oh, no. They also involve some culture-specific practices.

During a proper toast everyone in the group has to look everyone else in the eye, one by one, say *na zdravje* (in less formal company, *cheers* or *hey* or *yo* or *aye* or something that sounds like *chin* is also OK), and finally clink the glasses together. Then you have to proceed to the next person and repeat the process, preferably in a methodical clockwise or anticlockwise direction in order not to leave anyone out, because that's quite rude. In the case of men and beer steins, clinking in fact means smashing the beers together, preferably spilling some over each other in an energetic display of male bonding. If beer bottles are involved (real men in Slovenia often drink beer from bottles and frown upon glasses), the situation can get even more complicated. For purposes unknown, some men – after roaring *na zdravje* in a manly voice as rugged as possible and smashing beer bottles together with everyone – push their fingers into their bottles and then pluck them out with an audible pop (repeating the process persistently should the previous pop fail to be resolute and intrepid enough). For some unfathomable reason certain beer bottle abusers then even proceed to slam the bottom of their bottles on the table... and why this is, nobody really knows. Perhaps this particularly manly gesture is supposed to confirm everything said during the toast.

This process of everyone exchanging drunken wobbly stares and bumping their drinking equipment with everyone else at the table can soon become a tad tiresome. Perhaps all of this Slavic bonding, albeit somewhat gay, could even be considered a good way to remember new drinking buddies – were it not for the fact that all these toasts often result in blackouts, so you never really remember anyone, anyway... And were it not for the unfortunate circumstance that the routine goes on all the time, to the point of absolute tediousness, regardless of how well you know the people you drink with.

After a number of toasts, a few stifled burps and some clandestine winds (after all, the band members were not all that familiar with each other yet), Boris put another oversized jug and another litre of Merlot for Bogomyr on the table. The Ukranian exotic dancer – a droplet of blood-red wine trickling from the corner of his mouth – took the initiative and sighed painfully (which was undoubtedly a conscious and obvious hint at his tortured artistic soul): "Let's talk about this project a bit, I'd like to clear up a couple of things. First of all, I won't be involved in anything too cheesy, because I get upset if the artistic context is too shallow... Even depressed if the tracks are boring. I'll just speak my mind now, so that we don't have to talk about it later, when it might already be too late. I want my artistic freedom so that I can contribute certain ideas to the tracks and improve the arrangements when I feel they're too simple. I need to develop an appropriate feeling for the lyrics, melodies, harmonies, musical phrases and rhythm, otherwise I cannot invest myself properly in the composition. If I'm not involved enough, I may feel that I'm not taking part in anything meaningful. This may lead to my getting bored and distracted during live performances, or even unhappy with what I hear. The artistic as well as expressive value of this project has to be considerable in order not to end up on the same level with the rest of commonplace, banal, naive, prosaic, pathetic, casual, derivative, repetitive, transitory, vulgar, meaningless, unimaginative, ordinary ready-made little pieces of crap that people actually like listening to. I for one refuse to be a part of anything that mundane, ever."

"Wow... You've thought about this little speech of yours a lot, perhaps even opened a thesaurus, maybe? 'Cause I see you've learned all the synonyms for 'lousy' by heart." Amalia put in and rolled her eyes.

Finnegan thought: *"Fucking hell... Here we go, and we aren't even done with the bull testicles yet. I'll either kill this guy or end up best friends with him."* Instead of saying that out loud, he stated calmly: "Aye, I completely agree with you. Perhaps this would be a good time for everyone to express any preliminary thoughts and doubts before we actually get down to business. I know Amalia and Randy very well, we've worked together a lot, but I'd love to hear from you guys," Finnegan said calmly and even managed to smile convincingly at Kip and Largo.

Startled, Largo looked up from a fried potato, cleared his throat and declared: "Ahem... Well... I just have to know what the plans about the rehearsals are. You see, sometimes I can get terribly busy, even over the weekends. Especially over the weekends. And during the week, too, my teaching job is very demanding. Apart from that I also have loads of important materials to write and distribute... I still work as a journalist for a Trieste newspaper, and I often have meetings, which can be time-consuming. I'm just saying so now because I don't want to promise I'll have all the time in the world for this project, and then break my promise later. What I'm trying to say is, I'll certainly do my best, but I don't want to waste too much time on too many rehearsals. I mean, somebody has got to be in charge of this project. Of course, I'm willing to participate in the creative process a bit... But ideally I'd just like to contribute here and there, when I find the time, and yet feel I have contributed a lot, if you know what I'm trying to say," Largo smiled innocently, dipped a bull testicle in the Tartare sauce and stuffed it in his mouth.

Finnegan started: "Of course, I'm also not planning to waste more time on rehearsals than necessary. Besides, I already have some ideas, outlines..."

Bogomyr interrupted him firmly: "We're not going to

sound professional if we don't rehearse!" He glared at Largo and said: "How will you get into the groove with everyone if we don't jam together? How else do you think you'll get into the feel?"

Largo poked at the leftover fries with his fork and shrugged: "Don't you worry about my groove, man, I'll manage. I've always been able to cope just fine, thank you very much. But I'm not into jam sessions much, because they're boring and unconstructive, and I have loads of more important things to do."

Randy remarked: "Well, I like jam sessions. You know, just start playing something random and see where it takes you."

"Me too, sometimes... And sometimes not, depends on the people I play with," Kip mumbled around a bite of testicle.

"See where it takes you, he said," Largo smirked. "Sure, it takes you through a six-pack of beer and three hours of tiresome improvisation nobody wants to listen to."

"Excuse me if I like to have a bit of fun," Randy sighed.

From behind the bar, Beeba put in: "Sometimes is jam session nice." She glanced shrewdly at a large box of ear plugs, placed in a strategic spot behind the bar, bearing a bold inscription "EUR 10 A PAIR".

"Jam sessions are the stuff great compositions are made of!" Bogomyr thundered. "How else will you get to know everyone else in the band, understand how they play and develop a feeling for what they're about? How will you come up with new unexpected things and contribute to the creation of new ideas..."

"That's what I'm saying!" Largo said quite passionately. "I'm not all that crazy about contributing. I have my own projects for that. I just want to work on this project profes-sionally. I'd like to see someone else in charge of it so as to waste as little time as possible. If you want to torture people endlessly with your favourite guitar licks, wait until Ray and Willit get here. Then you guys, including Boris and Herb Boy over there, can jam until your eyeballs roll out of their sockets, but please leave those of us who have something better to do alone," Largo barked.

Randy raised his finger: "Speaking of the herb!"

He pulled his ganja smoking implements out of his pocket and started fashioning a joint methodically, obviously enjoying the whole ritual immensely.

"Amateurs! I can already see you're a bunch of amateurs!" Bogomyr complained.

Boris sighed audibly, slipped behind the bar and rummaged in the fridge, searching for one of his beloved weiss beers he liked to seek comfort in when the patrons got annoying.

"OK, OK, calm down, everyone, let's try to be practical here." Finnegan was a bit flustered already, and his blushing cheeks indicated an obvious disinclination to take on the role of the voice of reason. "Look. Occasional jam sessions are fine with me, no matter how pointless they might seem to any of you, but I'm not going to force anyone to take part in them. That's not the way I want to work here and..."

"You mean we're not going to improvise and work on tracks together?!" Bogomyr was getting increasingly irritated.

"Of course we'll work together, but I'm not going to force anyone to do anything they don't want to... To each his own. Look, let's get constructive here, alright? So, Largo... I get it, you don't like jam sessions and you don't want to have too many rehearsals. Still, we'll have to practice. So how often do you think you could manage to do that?"

"I can't have rehearsals all the time. Once every two weeks, maybe, I could probably find the time for that."

"Once every two weeks! That's nothing, we'll never play halfway decently at that rate," Bogomyr fumed.

"Well, some of us have work to do, other projects to develop!" Largo yelled.

"Amateur! I always have to put up with lazy-ass amateurs!"

"Oh, damn it, quit it already," Finnegan intervened, raising his voice. "Come on, guys! Jesus..."

Beeba stopped doing her nails, glanced at the box of ear plugs and considered offering some to Tinka and Stanko, an elderly married couple of drunken regulars, brooding over their spritzers quietly at a gloomy table in a remote corner of the room where they tried to enjoy their drinks in peace almost every evening. She decided not to. She let the old derelicts run a tab, anyway, so what was the point.

"Well, I might make it once per week, perhaps, if it's really so damn unavoidable," Largo muttered, his face already tired and eyes sunken at the very thought of it.

After a short pause, Finnegan said, already visibly impatient: "Fine, once a week will do, we'll find a way to make it work. So, to avoid additional confusion, since you keep bringing up all the work you have to do and all your other projects and so on, which I totally understand, to be sure... When would be a good time for you? Amalia told me she'd already arranged for us to rehearse here, if Boris will be kind enough to put up with our bullshit..."

Finnegan glanced at Boris, and Boris nodded, gulping down some of his special beer, thinking that at least he'd earn some cash from these passionate musos. So many of the other customers he was willing to tolerate were as destitute as the stooping shadows of Tinka and Stanko in the corner across the room.

"Amalia also says it won't be a problem for us to meet in the evenings, when everybody has the time," Finnegan added.

"Oh, no," Largo shook his head, "I usually have meetings in the evening. I'd rather practice in the early afternoon."

"Impossible! I can't have rehearsals during the day!" Bogomyr was suddenly worried. "I... I don't function during the day, not a chance. I'm an after-sunset kind of a guy!"

"No way, I have my political pursuits to pursue during the night..."

Now Amalia finally lost her temper: "Yeah, you usually pursue them here! You're here most of the nights, discussing stupid ideas with Ray and Willit!"

"But I work on a variety of projects with them!" Largo protested loudly.

"Yeah, you work on an extensive collection of idiotic plans and sandwiches," Randy across the table chortled like a mischievous child. "Anyone want to go outside for a puff?"

"How do you intend to play gigs in the evening then?" Amalia frowned.

"Well, that's different, I usually try to, you know, take advantage of my concert activities in order to further my other goals."

"Fuck your other goals!" Bogomyr barked.

"Oh, that's really nice and mature of you. At concerts I often meet many people I can mobilise for urgent matters of global importance you don't seem to either understand or care about."

Now it was Kip's turn to look concerned: "So you mean we're going to have a lot of gigs? Because I don't like to play live much anymore, I'm getting kind of old for that..." Kip Ducker scratched his bald spot absent-mindedly, suddenly putting a profoundly worried and even sad expression on his face. "I also don't like travelling very far to play. And I especially hate playing in dirty old squats for a couple of Largo's drunken pals."

"I can't believe what I'm hearing. The drummer won't rehearse, the guitarist won't play live... Amateurs! I knew you were just another bunch of amateurs! Fuck this!" Bogomyr yelled, grabbed his bottle of Merlot, poured another glass, splashing the deep red wine all over the tablecloth, and slammed it on the table in front of him angrily, not drinking to anyone's health at the moment. Beeba across the bar pretended not to see anything, but an image of miraculous sweet-smelling stain-eliminating washing powders popped up in her mind nevertheless, together with an excruciatingly annoying jingle from a certain obnoxious detergent commercial.

Finnegan's patience came to an end. He bellowed: "Fucking hell... I knew it! What a fucking idiot, I knew I

should have just stayed in Kirkwall. What the fuck was I
thinking, coming all the way here just to meet more people
impossible to work with, as if I didn't know enough of those
back home. I'm sick of this. I've spent years upon years trying
to put together a functional meaningful band, trying to come
up with cool material that actually meant something, and
even play the shit live – for nothing! I've worked on this
shit for eighteen years, give or take, never earned anything,
never wanted or expected much, anyway... Just to get some
gigs, have fun and play something I like playing. Shit! First I
wasted a decade on good bands that fell apart, every one of
them, because we weren't able to record anything meaningful.
Then I worked for years on lame ass fake-art projects nobody
gave a flying fuck about... And now that we have all these
computers and stolen software, now that I finally believe I've
come up with a couple of good ideas, now that we're finally
able to record any piece of crap we could ever possibly think
of... Now we have all turned into a bunch of whiners. Once
upon a time we used to be remorseless drunks and heedless
dreamers, but then suddenly everyone's got dogs, kids, wives,
in-laws, parrots, kefir mushrooms, fruit trees, tombstones,
lawns, mortgages, even jobs... I'm too old, we're all too
fucking old for this, it's over, we're stuck, held hostage by our
miserable lives, our fucking everyday horrors. Fuck this, I'll
never manage to do anything cool, for fuck's sake, and nobody
cares anymore anyway. We're done. Dead. What a fucking
drag. I don't know what I'm going to do, I'll just move to
the seaside and breed sheep. Oh, for crying out loud, I could
have raised them in fucking Scotland, if the weather wasn't so
goddamn obnoxious. I can't stand the constant drizzle, and the
sea is never warm enough to comfortably drown yourself in.
Fuck it all, I'm through! I'm through, you hear me?!" Finnegan
slammed his fists on the table, and his voice shook a bit as
he concluded his tirade: "I'm through with fucking wine,
too! Amalia, get me two beers and a quadruple single-malt
Scotch!"

Finnegan's voice dwindled away to nothing.

"I'm afraid we only have bourbon," Boris shrugged, feeling a bit sorry for the miserable Scotsman.

Finnegan slapped his forehead and covered his eyes in profound disappointment.

The room wrapped itself in a heavy cloak of gloom and doom and silence, and everyone in it suddenly felt an urge to scrutinise the spiders that lurked in the corners, pretending not to hear the strange people and acting as if they had to tend to their webs. In the far corner, Tinka cleared her throat softly. The clock on the wall ticked in time to the noise of Stanko scratching his scruffy nicotine-stained moustache and spritzer-scented beard. The refrigerator stuttered, trying to negotiate a peace treaty or at least a temporary cease-fire with the battalion of warm beer bottles Boris had put in there earlier. The candles Beeba had adorned the tables with in order to emphasise the outdated hippy atmosphere flickered noisily, enjoying their flames' reflections in the framed and glassed poster of *Jim Morrison*. In the candlelight, other vintage posters – *Bob Dylan*, *Jefferson Airplane* and *Pink Floyd* – looked down smugly on certain peculiar characters, obviously local legends who went by the name *Lačni Franz*, peering from the gloomy darkness of the opposite wall.

Boris Birman's cigarette enjoyed the serene moment, smouldering in the ashtray by itself, while its owner took advantage of the situation and disappeared to the toilet like a ghost, without saying a word.

Behind the bar a beer stein begged to be washed clean and put away for the night, feeling a bit sticky. The Merlot that remained in Bogomyr's bottle begged to be imbibed. Silverfish peeked out of their hiding places apprehensively, surprised at the sudden silence that came over the place, wondering if this meant it was already time to throw a party. Due to all the yelling they'd just witnessed at such a late hour, they hoped for many unwashed glasses and lots of leftover food, so they were getting somewhat impatient. The spiders in the corners stopped pretending to weave, shook their heads at the silverfish, warning them that the huge creatures with legs far too few and far between were still out there (they hoped to devour the silverfish themselves, not see them trampled on uselessly). They prayed that the tension they could feel in the air would not rip apart their delicate masterpieces.

Before he slipped outside for a smoke, Randy decided it was time to put an end to the awkward silence. He nibbled on a salad leaf and said: "Well, as far as I'm concerned, it's all fine with me, as long as it rocks."

14. Interlude:
Touring My Backyard

Later that night, when instead of bickering the band members started slapping each other on the back, hugging and saying things like "sorry, I didn't mean it, you know I get a bit emotional sometimes", "mate, this is going to be great, I can feel it", "whee, let's have another one" and, ultimately "I love you, man, I really do", the otherwise quiet Kip opened up and expressed some concern about the hair disappearing from his head and reappearing miraculously all over his back. On hearing this, Finnegan suddenly found the inspiration to wrap up the lyrics he had started thinking about on the plane while reading about the *Shaft Rock* band and their upcoming tour of two Slovenian municipalities by means of the only touring bus in the country. He slammed his fist on the table, finished his beer, ordered another round for everyone and stated resolutely: "That's it! *My hair receding down my spine...* Thanks, Kip, you've just written the bridge of the first track we'll work on!"

"What's it about, anything socially conscious?" Largo inquired.

"Absolutely," Finnegan explained eagerly. "It's about this Slovenian band of over-the-hill wrecks who try to pass themselves off as rock stars. They arrange for what they call an international tour, which in fact consists of a few concerts in a couple of towns twenty kilometres apart. But they go on this tour in the only touring bus in the country, and get all the newspapers they possibly can to publish a PR blurb about it. Of course, the music they play is pure and undiluted crap, and they know it, but the audience is deaf anyway, so who cares. So, as you can see, of course it's socially conscious. It's also a true story."

"Sounds good to me," said Largo.

Finnegan went on. Obviously he intended to bore everyone to tears, which was rather typical of Finnegan when he'd had too much to drink: "Obviously the music has to support the lyrics, so it'll have to be somewhat derivative of classic 1980s hard rock tracks, only humorous, you see. The tune should definitely get a bit of that *Shaft Rock* feeling across. You know, for example, we could start with classic hard rock perm-curl crap, like the Hammond organ, joined by an overdriven guitar... But maybe we could do the track in a 7/8 time, to make it just a tad weird, so it's obvious we're kidding. And the bridge, you know, the lyrics Kip has just reminded me of, that should be really biblical, true hard rock... Even harder. And we should definitely not let the track get too cheesy. It must be an evident, though not too blatantly obvious, attempt of introducing some humour in music, if you know what I mean."

Finnegan didn't wait to hear if anybody knew what he meant, he just took a short breath and rambled on: "What I mean is, we should make Mr Frank Zappa proud. The lyrics are indeed a bit similar to his *Bobby Brown* in some manner, anyway..."

Largo interrupted Finnegan's monologue, shaking his head and looking worried: "Oh, no, not the Hammond organ, I really hate that sound. And I'm not a really huge fan of Frank Zappa, either. Nor do I find any of those 1980s hard rock tunes very entertaining."

Finnegan took in a deep breath, let it out, breathed in again and tried to explain: "That's not the point, we're not *really* making a 1980s hard rock tune. Our purpose is to *make fun* of those tunes. And we'll especially try to ridicule all those outdated bands who should have stopped wearing torn jeans ages ago because their bald spots don't really go well with such juvenile outfits."

Randy puffed on his joint and laughed, his gaze darting towards Kip Ducker, who frowned at Finnegan a bit sternly, scratched his bald spot, glanced at his faded jeans, but chose to say nothing. Obviously the Australian guitarist understood that Finnegan was just arguing the idea behind a jocular track whose foundations were obviously supported by everyone in the band but the revolutionary Italian.

"Yeah, sure, fine, I know what you're saying," Largo claimed but wouldn't actually let it go that easily: "But, look, even if it's just a joke, this track will still contain Hammond organs and it *will* sound like a 1980s hard rock track. So whatever you say it's supposed to mean, it'll still be an annoying hard rock song with horrific Hammond organs, won't it?" Largo shrugged.

Poor Finnegan finally stopped shooting his mouth off and started blinking into emptiness. He covered his eyes with both hands and leaned forward on the table. His parade was being rained on by Largo's irrefutable logic, so he suddenly got terribly tired. He stammered: "Well... Yes... I suppose so... But for the obvious sarcasm. I wouldn't say annoying and horrific, though. Ah, whatever, I guess our musical humour isn't very compatible."

Due to thorough disillusionment, Finnegan was about to crumble and perhaps, in view of his poor blood to alcohol ratio, even take a Superman nap, as some of the more experienced Slovenians referred to the fine art of falling asleep on the table.

However, Amalia, used to Finnegan's occasional peculiarities and well-aware of his impending demise, felt sorry for her old pal and took over. She finally decided it was about time to introduce some healthy dictatorship into this band in place of what was already turning out to be a very useless and dreary democracy.

"That's enough, boys," she said and motioned at Beeba who promptly started pouring her another spritzer. Beeba had just been thinking about throwing everyone out – it was getting very late and they were becoming rather inarticulate – but she changed her mind seeing that Amalia had taken over. Beeba liked to see a well-aimed female kick in the men's behinds, so she served some more drinks and looked forward to the show.

However, it was soon over. Amalia slammed her fist

on the table and wrapped it up resolutely: "Enough of this. Finnegan has an idea for our first track and we should go along with it. I'm not discussing it anymore. If somebody can't tell sarcasm from naivety, that's his problem."

Amalia turned to Largo: "I don't care if you don't get it or like it, that's not why you're here. You're here to play drums."

She unpinned her rigorous gaze from the poor Italian activist and barked: "Does anybody have anything to add?" Amalia could be rather stern when she wanted to.

Largo shook his head, shrugged, and sought refuge in his small beer.

"Thought so," Amalia said.

Finnegan, suddenly looking quite pleased, pulled out the notebook he always carried with him and scribbled something in it. Largo rolled his eyes, gradually coming to terms with it all, and the rest of the band was glad to see that their bonding might actually result in a finished product one day. Finnegan wrapped up the lyrics and handed his notebook to the band.

When Kip Ducker read the fabulous lines proposed by the re-inspired Finnegan Frotz, he immediately saw himself in the verses involving the receding hairlines. He could genuinely relate to that and identify with the issue profoundly. After this pivotal point in time, Kip became even more convinced that his decision to give in to Amalia Winegirl's charms and join the band was the right thing to do. Maybe he could even put up with an occasional live appearance.

Here is what Finnegan's notebook said:

TOURING MY BACKYARD
[https://soundcloud.com/cynicism-management/
touring-my-backyard-augmented]

When I was just a boy I yearned to rock n' roll
But I didn't realise I was living in a hole
Then I grew a tiny bit, my vision kind of cleared
I popped a beer, caressed my cage and never really feared

Now I'm the coolest guy around, the only god with such a sound
I sell my twopence sermons every day
My nails are black my eyes are lined my pants are tight oh I'm so fine
I gloat in dismal dismay and decay

I rented the only touring bus in this godforsaken place
And published in every goddamn paper I was touring my own space

Oh wow yippee my gosh and gee
I'm tourin' my backyard
Rolling over my own mower
Bellyfolds o' lard
Mounted mirrors on the walls
My backyard's looking big
I'm bouncing reeling falling over
My excessive concert rig

In the mornings my head hurts, my double visions spin
But I know well that I'm the One so I embrace my sins
My proud dadland needs me to flash her stardom smiles
Distract the nation with pretence, wallow in shit piles

From the mountains to the sea
I sing my three-chord symphony
Nameless crowds beneath my feet
Look up at this astounding deed
My hair receding down my spine
But I still make these corpses mine
Dancing deaf to shit I spout
I dread what I have figured out

15. Fabiola

Fabiola roused as the two guards outside her room started performing *fajr*, the dawn prayer. For the first couple of days she'd hated these austere-looking men and their detestable habit of making strange noises in the morning. The doors in this dusty building were nothing that you would possibly see included in catalogues containing examples of supreme craftsmanship in the field of the fine art of sound-proofing. So these days Fabiola usually stirred wide awake at the crack of dawn, at the beginning of *fajr*. That was when the guards who otherwise loomed outside her door quietly like snails on dewy leaves of grass suddenly started shuffling their feet, grumbling and making sounds that could even be interpreted as grunts of annoyance... Similar to the sounds of annoyance she made when she was getting ready to fulfil her daily duty: 60 ab crunches, 20 press-ups, 30 squats and 20 toe raises. That was the least she could do, because hamstring pulls, inner thigh pulls and all those super-secret celebri-ty-endorsed butt exercises were currently on hiatus due to kidnapping, imprisonment, hostage situation, threats of throats cut, and lack of proper fitness equipment.

Well, "throats cut" might have been a bit of an exagger-ation. The guards never threatened her too seriously, even if occasionally they'd tell her to keep her dirty little infidel mouth shut, especially when at first she bitched at them for praying noisily in the morning and nagged their ears off with blasphemous ideas of sleeping until noon. The thought that they might have been less than thrilled to mope around outside her room during all hours of the night and follow her around all day never crossed her mind at first. So she kept pestering them, which did not preclude their ignoring her and concentrating on their spiritual affairs, backgammon, foul-smelling hand-rolled cigarettes and tea.

Despite this almost annoying silent treatment that the guards gave them, Fabiola and her brother were kept under careful watch at all times. They were forbidden from leaving the dusty old Arab mansion, but apart from that they could do whatever they wanted. Not that there was actually anything much *to do* within these otherwise pleasantly spacious and cool sandstone walls but bicker among themselves. Fergus was his usual self: a major annoyance. It was impossible to tell whether he was worried about their current situation at all. He was only interested in his damn computer games and all-important virtual characters. Every morning – the very second he opened his peepers and put on his nerdy glasses – Fergus would start whining and complaining, mostly about how his World of Warcraft guild now went to all the raids without him, how he'd be punished by his guildmistress for not letting her know he'd be gone, and how he would never get his hands on his coveted two-handed Infernal Sword of Massive Wart Infestation and Unusually Persistent Haemorrhoid Flaring +6. Another couple of days of this incessant torture and Fabiola herself would beg the mujahideen to shoot her brother or hang him or stone him to death or impale him on a stick or cut his little pecker off or otherwise dismember him and/or enjoy whatever other customs they liked to practice in this sun-scorched sand-stuffed slum. Fortunately, by some miraculous turn of events, she was soon rid of the obnoxious little twerp.

As it happened, apart from boring her to tears with his lamentations, Fergus also persistently complained to Habib, a young Arab who seemed to be in charge of them. Well, at least Habib was the only one to talk to them. (The thought that maybe some people on this planet did not speak English eluded Fabiola as successfully as Fergus's level 79 rogue in one of his computer games might elude an unsuspecting senile half-blind and three-quarters-deaf orc peon.) So on the third day Habib, perhaps even feeling sorry for Fabiola at the sight of her miserable visage, caved in and told Fergus: "Fine, my friend... Well... Almost my friend, if you not talk all the time. We also have computer. I take you to computer, so you play and your sister have some peace, yes?" he winked at Fabiola.

When Fergus was gone, Fabiola was finally able to gather her thoughts in peace. A computer? Perhaps, if her brother was careful and cunning enough, he could even get a word out? Tell everyone on Facebook where they were? Send them GPS coordinates or a Google Maps placemark? Summon all those mighty mages, clerics, hunters, paladins, warlocks, warriors, thieves, druids and other such helpful characters in his various guilds and call them to their aid? "No," she finally told herself after she gave it a bit of thought, *"there is no way even the Arabs could be that stupid."*

It turned out that stupidity had nothing to do with it, even though she was right about one thing, of course – Fergus could not get online and send an e-mail or instant message to their father. After the little brat returned, he rambled about the state of these Arabs' computers, their lame ugly excuses for games, having to use a screwdriver in order to get the damn pieces of software to work at all, obnoxious sound, horrific graphics, and so on and so forth. So Fabiola guessed the computers might have been a tad old. She wouldn't be surprised if they didn't even have fibre optics here.

Nevertheless, the next morning Fergus seemed marginally less tiresome than usual, though he still kept complaining about the backwardness of the local electronics. In the evening following that day he came back from the computer room almost calm and thoughtful, which Fabiola had otherwise only witnessed when her brother immersed himself into one of his online adventures. When she asked him what was up with him, he only said: "Studying a bit of programming. Good night, sis." And he fell asleep. Obviously Fergus had found something to do that interested him, and she was all too happy to leave it at that.

Last Sunday – two weeks after they'd been taken from the hotel and about a week after Fergus's sudden interest in computer programming, during which he'd become increasingly pensive and, thankfully, somewhat less difficult – Habib came to see Fabiola in the morning and told her: "Miss, boss decide it is time to let one of you go. The boy more naughty than you, so the boy go. OK? You please write letter to your father, telling you are good, yes? Then we discuss things with your father."

Fabiola suddenly felt as light as a feather on the Moon, despite the fact that she was still technically a prisoner – even though she'd obviously have to remain in the dusty mansion while her brother would be allowed to leave. She may not have let it show much, but for the first couple of days after she and Fergus had been taken from the hotel, she was a little worried about the whole affair. One might even go so far as to state she was somewhat afraid. But Habib was always polite and reassuring and whenever she cursed at him and told him to go screw himself, he would respond calmly with advice like: "Speak more nice, Miss, it is not nice for nice girl to speak ugly". She definitely had no reason to suspect Habib of anything particularly malevolent at that point. Her brother might have been a pain in the butt, but she still loved him. *"Well, put up with him, at least,"* she'd roll her eyes at such a cheesy thought. So she wrote the letter and let Habib shoot a video of her doing it. She let her father know that she was all right and that she too would be released if Omnipile cooperated with her captors.

Fabiola was surprised to see how calm and indifferent Fergus appeared to be about his imminent release. He was probably too shocked to rejoice in the fact that he would finally be able to go home, back to his annoying games. So she hugged him and told him to say hi to mom and dad and that everything would be OK.

Ever since they rid her of her obnoxious little brother, Fabiola had almost appreciated being able to watch the stunningly beautiful sunrise over Al Awil. Now that she was able to enjoy it in peace (well, apart from those religious noises outside her door which she had learned to ignore), she found it all strangely romantic and exotic... It was almost a relief not having to listen to her mother's incessant diatribes about pedicures and facials and the nerve-wracking carelessness of the household help. The fact that Fabiola started feeling flushed and queasy whenever she saw Habib, the unusually handsome mujahid, might also have had something to do with it. She'd thought all terrorists wore long goat-milk stained beards, but Habib looked nothing like a terrorist. He was thoroughly clean-shaven and sweet-scented, and there was nothing terribly "foreign" about him – Fabiola could definitely mistake him for a Londoner, were they in London. They were currently located in Al Awil, Yoman, though, which perhaps made Habib even more enticing.

Fabiola rose from her bed, stretched as gracefully and tastefully and delicately as only seventeen-year-olds can, and leaned towards the barred window of her room on the second floor of the mansion. As she rested her eyes on the fragrant Al Awil dawn, she let her mind dwell on the sudden onset of sensual pulpiness, soft moist rose petals, quivering fragrances and slippery soliloquies. She stroked her silky nightgown fleetingly and let the wind that washed over her tentatively from the receding chill outside caress her face and ruffle her hair softly.

16. Finnegan and the Smug Waiter

Finnegan was the first member of the newly established household to wake up on Sunday morning. His ability to sleep until noon had dwindled severely as he got older, or more "seasoned", as he liked to put it. Especially when he was a bit "tired" after the previous night's exploits did he often feel an urge to get up before everyone else, maybe because he wanted to show everyone how amazingly well he could hold his liquor.

Amalia and Randy didn't seem to be particularly concerned with how anyone held their liquor or what their new Scottish roommate had for breakfast, though. Feeling no urge to leap to their feet, make him coffee and ask him how he was feeling that particular morning, they just slept in insensitively and let him take care of himself. Even Paloma Mala the Deathbreath Rock 'n' Roll Bitch was nowhere to be seen. That was perfectly fine by Finnegan – he hated it if the dog followed him around, trying to lick the back of his bare legs. He was also perfectly happy that no one hastened to inquire whether he was OK and if he needed or wanted anything. That would only make him wonder if the people so concerned with his well-being harboured ulterior motives. Besides, he, Amalia and Randy were going to stay here together until further notice, so it was best that he got to know the place without relying on anyone too much.

Finnegan got out of bed and snuck out of the room in order not to wake the Portuguese trollop. Not that he cared about her feelings much, after she had slapped him in such a temperamental manner the day before. As if she didn't like his advances, the temptress! So he really didn't feel like spending the morning in a futile attempt to communicate with her in any way.

Finnegan's decision to turn on the TV (in spite of Randy snoring on the couch) and watch the Slovenian channels quietly while he had some breakfast turned out to be the first step on the path towards making that Sunday great. He almost let his fried eggs get cold while he stared at the screen showing a bunch of retards in absurd outfits yodelling and polkaing their asses off. "*By the gods, this is so bizarre,*" Finnegan thought, "*How adorable, I'll love it here!*" Little did he know how wrong he was about polkas being hilarious over the long haul.

After he was done chuckling clandestinely and feasting his eyes on the cleavages of the Slovenian songstresses of Alpine dancing tunes, Finnegan took it upon himself to tidy up the kitchen so as to feel useful (not one of Amalia's favourite activities, he knew; and obviously neither Randy nor Desidéria the Portuguese nymphomaniac ever concerned themselves with that much, either). Then, feeling charitable, Finnegan started cleaning up Randy's late-night and early-morning mess of half-full beer cans, weed crumbs and torn cigarette remains from the coffee table in their smallish living room (this was most probably a slightly neurotic way of subconsciously acknowledging that he himself should clean up his act). As Finnegan started wiping off the vile stickiness such coffee tables had been known to succumb to after prolonged periods of their owners' unrestrained giddiness, Randy moved his little finger ever so slightly and ever so slowly, opening one eye with an almost audible creak, coughed and uttered the following words ever so feebly: "Hey, mate... Wh... What's up?"

"Hey! You awake? Sorry to bother you, I couldn't sleep..." Finnegan whispered.

All Randy let out was a weary moan.

"Can't sleep, I'm going out for a bit," Finnegan explained apologetically.

Randy obviously decided to let Finnegan off the hook. He said: "Oh. Good. Why are you cleaning up then... Just go already..." Randy yawned, closed his eyes peacefully, and resumed his snoring.

Finnegan rolled his eyes and tiptoed away from Randy's

makeshift lair, but then Randy unexpectedly shot up in his bed and pierced Finnegan with an unfocused stare, uttering: "Finn!"

"Aye?!" the startled Finnegan turned around.

"Finn, man... A word of caution. Ask where the slippers are."

"Uh... What?!"

"Listen to me...," Randy abruptly struggled to rise from the dilapidated couch he'd sunk into, leaning on his elbows as desperately as if this was the last chance to fulfil some incredibly important deathbed purpose. As he endeavoured to hold on to the last thread of his willpower, Randy coughed again and whispered conspiratorially: "They're weird, you know... I know you think I'm exaggerating... But listen! Listen to me carefully, mate. If Slovenians invite you into their home... If you have to step over anybody's threshold... You take off your shoes and ask where the slippers are. It'll make your life much easier and spare you a very awkward situation..."

At the sight of Finnegan's vacant gaze Randy whined: "Oh, why do I bother, do as you like...!" and crashed back down on the couch, exhausted.

Finnegan frowned and looked at what seemed to be Randy's corpse for a split second. Then he shrugged, attributing the whole affair to the incomprehensible wonders of mind-altering substances, and left.

A fine day greeted him outside. It was late summer and it looked like it was going to be hot. Finnegan looked left and right, trying to get some impression of the foreign city in order to perhaps describe it in his blog later... And promptly decided to check out the nearest pub. There he could gather his thoughts far more effectively. It was a pleasantly warm morning, especially for someone who'd just arrived from the Orkneys, so Finnegan sat outside at one of the elegant wooden tables lining the street in front of the pub.

"Oi," said the waiter.

"Oi," said Finnegan.

The waiter looked at Finnegan funny and switched into what had to be his patented *look-everyone-we-have-a-tourist-here* mode. Finnegan couldn't understand how the hell the waiter could tell Finnegan was a foreigner on the basis of a single-syllable word that obviously meant "greetings" in both languages. Except if perhaps "oi" in Slovenian meant something completely different... Like "go to hell and your father is the Pope's favourite altar boy" and now they've insulted each other rather awkwardly. Probably the waiter did not mean "a type of music associated with skinheads". The fact that there weren't any other pale black men wearing a kilt and sporting a queer accent around escaped Finnegan, however. Of course, it had not escaped the waiter.

The waiter, probably tired of waiting for Finnegan to wrap up his internal monologue, asked politely, in smooth Received Pronunciation English: "What can I do for you, sir?"

Finnegan looked at the waiter, worrying about how he was also able to pick up on the country of Finnegan's origin so miraculously. Well, maybe Finnegan should have made a mental note underlining that not all waiters were idiots. And maybe Finnegan should have also made a mental note in bold, explaining that in countries as small as Slovenia almost everybody whom nobody knew was immediately greeted in English, especially strange men in kilts. Only then were any further attempts to uncover details about anyone's origins made. And, frankly, probably Finnegan should finally stop wearing the damn kilt – that particular prank of his was rapidly getting old.

"Decaf, please" said Finnegan – it was morning, after all.

"Sorry?" the waiter asked.

"A cup of decaf coffee," Finnegan elaborated.

"Sorry, we don't have that here," the waiter smiled, shrugging innocently. "This is a pub, not a yuppie café. Even in the mornings, sorry."

"A pint of beer, then," Finnegan said firmly. Yes, he knew he'd promised himself never again to start drinking before noon, but this was a special occasion. Besides, he allowed himself to do whatever he pleased when he was on vacation, and this could almost be seen as vacation for now. At least for as long as he wasn't doing any meaningful work.

"Sorry, we don't have pints," the waiter smirked smugly, "but we do serve beer in metric quantities."

Obviously the waiter knew English very well. Obviously he knew what he was talking about. Obviously he was also an asshole, and Finnegan was visibly annoyed by the man's self-important smirk.

"Uhm..." managed the previously relaxed, now slightly steaming Finnegan.

"Large beer or small beer?" the waiter offered.

"Large!" Finnegan was quick, resolute, and impatient, whatever quantity a large beer actually entailed.

He received a half-litre stein that he welcomed gladly, although he regretted that the "large" adjective wasn't even larger. This wasn't even a pint. As he gulped down a third of it, he relaxed at the thought that there was more where this had come from.

Finnegan soon started to enjoy the pleasant morning breeze and the relative laziness characteristic of Sunday mornings in Ljubljana's Old Town. It definitely felt like vacation.

A moment later – and what a pleasant moment it was – Finnegan heard a familiar tune coming from the pub. No, it was not bagpipe music that startled him, and it was not a pop song that he recognised: it was *Jakarta* by *Tribal Tech*, one of his favourite tracks of all time... At least as far as melodic, not very aggressive fusion tracks in 4/4 time were concerned. Finnegan was a bit of an odd-time aficionado, so most of his favourite tracks involved at least a couple of peculiar rhythmic twists and turns, and he also appreciated thunderous power chords. None of those elements appeared in this tune, though. This track was simply... beautiful. That's an adjective not many *serious* musicians would use, for *serious* musicians associated beauty with cheesiness. So, yes, one could even go so far as to say this tune was cheesy, were it not an absolute pearl performed by one of the greatest jazz/fusion bands of all time. And with a totally unforgettable and incredibly atypical, slightly "ethnicky" arrangement to go with it, too. Finnegan's complete immersion in this forenoon beerside lullaby was abruptly interrupted by surprised curiosity: how come he was hearing this from a regular pub on a Sunday morning?

As the open door was just behind his back, Finnegan turned around and peered inside, trying to make out what the waiter was doing through the heavy shadows. He half expected to see the guy reaching for the knobs of the pub's hi-fi system, in a hurry to replace the weird annoying music with another piece of pop shit with absolutely nothing to say apart from how some ho shook her booty in order to drive some nigga crazy. But to Finnegan's surprise the waiter nodded in time with *Jakarta*, obviously enjoying it, while he cleaned the bar. The waiter felt Finnegan's gaze on him, so he glanced at the Scotsman, who gave him the thumbs up. The waiter smiled smugly. *"There he goes again,"* Finnegan thought. *"Well, this waiter might have a good taste in music, but he is still a pompous arse."*

Regardless of this conclusion, Finnegan was suddenly overjoyed he didn't know any geographical markers yet and that nobody could possibly recognise and bother him... Oh, how unbelievably pleasant, after all those years spent in a town where everybody knew him.

"What?! No way..." Finnegan thought and narrowed his eyes. Oh, the horror! There came Largo and another guy. The other guy didn't look any more reassuringly credible than the beret-donning coat-wearing Largo, the amateur revolutionary.

"Finnegan?" Largo jumped merrily as he saw the Scotsman, "I'd never have thought you were such an early bird! Mind if we join you?"

"Umm," Finnegan began, trying to think of a way to get rid of Largo and his friend without being rude. Not that he had anything against Largo, he actually liked him, just not at that very moment – he'd had such fun just sitting there by himself, sipping his beer quietly, taking in the sights and sounds and smells of the new city he'd found himself in. Not to mention that after *Jakarta* Finnegan's smug waiter obviously decided to skip back to the beginning of the CD and put on *Stella* by *Infra-Red High Particle Neutron Beam*, Finnegan's favourite fusion composition on that much-loved album, involving a hefty dose of distorted guitars. Which Finnegan would love to enjoy while ordering another large beer – alone.

However, the waiter had already noticed the promising development during what had otherwise been a very quiet morning and headed towards their table nimbly in order to peddle his wares, so what was the point of trying to get out of it. Finnegan thought: *"Probably the waiter is doing this because I've seen through him, seen him for what he is... A snickering smug bastard, that's what he is, he saw that I saw through his game... And now he's getting back at me."* The fact that Finnegan and the waiter had no "game" worth of mention going on didn't catch Finnegan's attention. Apparently, Finnegan was becoming a disgruntled old man who'd always find something to grumble about even if it had all looked fine and dandy a second earlier.

"This is Ray. Ray, this is Finnegan, Amalia's friend I told you about," Largo began as they sat down. "We were quite late yesterday, right? Quite loud, true? Quite juvenile, yeah? How come you're up so early?"

"Oh, it's just... I couldn't sleep, so I went for a coffee."

"Right," Largo smiled at the sight of Finnegan's beer stein. Then he turned to face the looming waiter: "I'll actually have a coffee, for real. And milk, please. Cold milk, you hear? I still have some pretty important issues to deal with later." As if the waiter cared.

"I take one of those coffees, too," Ray said with a heavy Slavic accent, pointing at Finnegan's beer, "But give a small one, I drive," he told the waiter and lit a cigarette.

While the waiter was taking Ray and Largo's orders, Finnegan deliberated on what a fine morning it had been... Before the unfortunate turn of events spelling, without any doubt in his mind, that now he'd be forced to chat about something utterly trivial.

17. Ray Kosmick

"I was just telling Ray here about how we met yesterday," the energetic Italian revolutionary began. "Ray is a musician too, a producer, his stuff is really great."

"Oh, really?" Finnegan feigned interest quite convincingly.

"Ah, well, Largo just talk. It is very usual of him. So, you a musician too," Ray Kosmick said.

After a short pause, Finnegan continued, almost amused: "Yeah, you could say that. So you're one too."

"Ya, me too," Ray smiled sympathetically.

Finnegan took a sip of his rapidly evaporating beer.

The awkward pause that almost managed to manifest itself was interrupted by Ray rubbing his beefy hands together, declaring: "Ah, super!" He lit up as the waiter arrived and told Ray: "Sorry, sir, did you say a small beer? I seem to have mistakenly poured a large one..."

"It's OK. I handle this, no worry," Ray smiled cordially. At least he knew the waiter wasn't trying to trick him – for small beers in Slovenia were ridiculously overpriced in comparison to large ones, in terms of volume versus funds invested. Finnegan had already calculated it all while staring at the drinks list instead of looking Largo and Ray deep in the eye and engaging in what would, according to his expectations, hardly be a fascinating conversation.

"And here's a cappuccino for you," the waiter put a cup in front of Largo.

"I said coffee and cold milk... Oh, whatever, forget it."

While Largo spoke English very fluently, especially for an Italian, Ray, or rather, Žarko, struggled with it somewhat. He talked to the waiter in English just to be polite to his foreign friends – even though his foreign friends did not seem to take much notice of his selfless efforts. Žarko Kozmič, obviously, was Slovenian. Ray Kosmick was his pseudonym – because his actual name, Žarko Kozmič, was hardly cool in his line of business.

"So..." Ray began and paused to light another smoke.

"*Oh, crap, here comes the torment of small talk...*" Finnegan thought, but offered instead: "So, you're a producer? What do you work on, then?" On the outside, Finnegan wore a smile and a curious expression, while on the inside he steeled himself, ready for anything. This Ray character looked as if he might be in the polka production business – a large, hefty, beer-bellied guy pushing fifty, full cheeks, unkempt hair, rough unshaven asymmetrical face that must have seen the bottom of many a glass and the butt of many a cigarette. Finnegan's first impression of Ray was that he was a vulgar loudmouth yokel. Which was fine by Finnegan, but what he really feared was that Ray was an irritating dufus who would now bore him to bloody tears, trying to get many a polka concept across.

However, nothing could be further from the truth.

Žarko Kozmič, a.k.a. Ray Kosmick, was an artiste extraordinaire – besides playing drums, percussion, keyboards, bass, guitar, tables, chairs, floors, bottles, beer cans and any other objects he came across, he was also his own composer, producer, arranger, sound engineer, mixing and mastering engineer, fitness trainer, janitor, barber (once per month), domestic cleanliness engineer (rarely), waiter (often), cook, lyricist, screenwriter, costumes designer, set designer, roadie, and groupie. Despite the fact that the listeners of his monumental works were few and far between, Ray remained convinced he had a bit of a knack for making music. And, no, he had not recorded any hit singles yet.

Ray's undying wish was to create soundtracks for big-budget porn, and to earn a cut of those budgets, too – hence his new music project "*Ray Kosmick and His Porn Groove Crew*".

Every year Ray would attend the Venus Porn Fair in

Berlin, Germany, and tell everyone there: *"Guten Tag, ich bin Ray Kosmick und ich bin ein Porn Groove Meister,"* which about wrapped up his knowledge of German. As a rule, the porn industry professionals who had ever had the misfortune of hearing the tunes by *"Ray Kosmick and His Porn Groove Crew"* in the context of erotic films of any quality and/or subgenre soon realised that Ray's love of baroque audio drama, elaborate rhythmic embroidery, psychedelic escapades and inclination towards maximalism might not fit their productions too well. The kinder among them would then tell Ray he tended to go over the top a bit, while those among them with a perverted sense of humour usually laughed their asses off at how bizarre the action on the screen looked when observed while listening to Ray's soundtrack proposals. So until the day when Largo, Ray and Finnegan drank their morning beer in Ljubljana's Old Town, nobody had hired Ray and his co-conspirators, even though Ray was respected in certain circles as a laughing-stock: the Ed Wood of the porn groove industry.

Despite a quite lengthy (though perhaps a bit misguided) career as a musician, Ray was, of course, always completely broke. Furthermore, his *Ray Kosmick and His Porn Groove Crew* band actually mostly consisted of only himself, though he'd always write about it in the third person plural when publishing rarely sought-after pieces of information on the various "internets" (as Ray referred to the Web) dedicated to porn groove masterpieces.

When Ray wrapped up his story – his funny English, vehemently playful demeanour, amusing accent and all – Finnegan was laughing appreciatively. Oh, man, was this guy a crackpot after Finnegan's own heart. Largo seemed very happy that they'd hit it off, and he'd readily ordered another round of coffee and beer.

"So, where can I hear an example of your porn groove masterpieces?" Finnegan asked, truly intrigued by this guy's work and eager to check out whether Ray was only shooting his mouth off like so many other "artists" he knew, or if he was in fact working on something interesting.

"Actually, I have one new song on my key. Here, want to listen?" Ray offered Finn an mp3 player.

"Absolutely! What's it for?"

"What's what for? This?" Ray looked at the mp3 player. "For listening, of course," Ray looked at Finnegan funny.

"No, I mean the song, the track, what's it for, have you written it for an actual porn flick or what?"

"No, this I want to send to Italy, to porno productions house. Maybe they like it and hire me for soundtrack."

"OK, let's have a listen…"

Before pressing play, Finnegan stared into emptiness and began to imagine a nice little porn scene that the following track would go well with. Only in this way, Finn believed, could he catch at least a glimpse of Ray's creative porn groove genius – that is, apart from actually going home, putting on a random porn flick, and listening to Ray's soundtrack idea simultaneously.

Finnegan leaned back and began by – yes, how very typical – picturing two incredibly succulent and innocent young girls, aged seventeen… "No!" Finnegan scolded himself, "Fie on you!" and applied the temporal shift filter on his fantasy, so that it now involved girls aged nineteen, oh so smooth-skinned and moist-lipped, staring into each other's (beautiful!) eyes longingly, then…

Finnegan pressed play and listened to Ray Kosmick's **Bat Left the Belfry [https://soundcloud.com/ray-kosmick/ bat-left-the-belfry].**

Concentrating, Finnegan visualised the girls. In light of the beer imbibed and his usual everyday horniness it was not a tough job. An HD film of his own design rolled in his mind effortlessly.

The smooth-skinned and glossy-lipped girls (aged nineteen, to be sure) are drowning in each other's eyes. Until now they've just been best friends, but something has happened. Yes, the blonde sweetie has been hurt by her evil and pushy boyfriend, who wanted too much too soon and too rudely, too. She wouldn't give it up that easily. Not to him, anyway. Fine, enough background, let's move on to the juicy part...

OK, so the soundtrack might be a bit busy, but... Right. Let's concentrate. Let's leave the details to nitpickers.

The blonde sweetie is heartbroken, and her best friend, a black-haired (of course) nymphet consoles her... She caresses her long soft blond hair, telling her that everything will be OK, hugs her, kisses her on the spotless angel-skinned forehead innocently... Strokes her hair some more... And as she inhales the blonde's sweet scent, something seems to move in her womb, something that almost aches and pains... It gives way, and a door opens... Warmly welcoming. Here we go...

"Oh Jesus, Ray, for crying out loud!" Finnegan's face suddenly wore a tortured yet wickedly mischievous smile as the tune reached the chorus. Largo and Ray laughed, familiar with the track's peculiar sonic dimensions. Finally the forceful chorus was over.

Ohh, OK.

The blonde pulls back, slightly startled but pleasantly so, and gazes deep into her girlfriend's black eyes... She feels her heart beat and throb, and the butterflies in her stomach gather in a rabble. She opens her lips ever so slightly, breathing audibly as she trembles, overcome by what had been grief, but which is now incredibly cute submissive attraction towards her black-haired consoler. She looks up at the black-haired beauty longingly, her eyes shining with tears of desire, feeding the fire... The fire!

The beauty slowly and sensuously kisses the blonde, who sighs, breathes in deeply, tensing at first... But then she slowly melts in her girlfriend's warm embrace, so safe, so real, so true. And as they playfully take each other's temperatures with their tongues, the black nymphet caresses her blonde girlfriend's back under her silky shirt, unbuttons her bra nimbly and travels down her spine passionately, diving down between her buttocks slowly and gently, extending her fingers to seek out the incredibly soft and silky-moist treasure cove. The nymphet knocks on heaven's door and is promptly invited in. The blonde gasps and trembles as the nymphet's finger, looking forward to a fascinating spelunking expedition, gently slips...

"Holy crap!" Finn exclaimed and laughed out loud as the second chorus hit, "This track could definitely be put in a movie, but I'm not sure it's meant to accompany tender teenage lesbian sex. What is this, S&M involving meat hooks, chainsaws and sandpaper dildos?" Finnegan yelled because he still had his headphones on. All of the people who happened to be in the vicinity turned to look at the perverted Scottish hooligan. Indeed, most Slovenians understood English.

Largo and Ray giggled like schoolboys.

"Love the bridge!" Finnegan cheered loudly.

Finnegan's blonde sweetie and black-haired nymphet, offended by the insensitive frivolity coming out of Finnegan's mouth and rude sounds blasting out of his earphones, told Finnegan to go fuck himself and that they'd find someplace else to lusciously probe the insides of their virginal vaginas. As they were leaving, shuddering at the thought of having anything else to do with the vulgar Scottish bastard, Finnegan was quite sorry they were going already. But he nevertheless scoffed at them and gave them the finger, swearing that they surely weren't as virginal as they would like to appear. They were no amateurs either and most probably hadn't been nineteen in years.

"No, Finnegan," Ray said, "You don't understand. This is a song for a very artistic erotic adventure, ya, I think it's good for wet hot lesbian sex, like you maybe imagine, but the film must be made that special way. You know, more strange and bizarre erotic, not even so much everyday hardcore porno. With proper makeup and clothing. Bah, nobody can really understand. I would buy a camera and make it myself, but where can I get the girls?" Ray cackled heartily.

"I really like this," Finnegan handed the mp3 player back to Ray. "What's it called?" Finnegan inquired.

"Bat Left the Belfry," said Ray.

"Great. Maybe we can get back to it sometime, I can

just hear massive distortion guitars in the choruses, it would sound great live, too, if done properly... If you'd let us rearrange it, perhaps, and play it sometime. Excellent, I'm really impressed."

"Thank you, it means a lot," said Ray.

Finnegan suddenly felt that weird urge, that special buzz, the spark, the little something that makes artists tick: the indescribable yearning that makes them do things even if they're sure that there's no common sense in doing them. Call it the Muse, call it inspiration, call it subconsciousness, the lack of protestant work ethic or divine intervention – Finnegan abruptly felt the need to create. It must have been due to Ray's own creativity. Finn felt he wanted to put together something of his own too. His idea of fun right now was to get rid of his friends, order another beer, maybe slip inside the pub to hide in the semi-darkness, pull out his notebook and write some lyrics. But – first things first.

"So, Largo, what are those pretty important issues you're dealing with today, anyway?" Finnegan inquired carefully in order not to break the spell of male bonding, but at the same time remind Largo he had other places to be today.

"First I've got some errands to run, and in the evening Ray and I are getting together with Willit at Birman's."

"Oh, sounds great. Well..."

"Speaking of which, listen... Why don't you come, too? Willit is also a good friend, fellow artist, full of ideas. Actually Ray and Willit are always working on projects together... Never mind, you'll meet him later, he's a fellow Brit, from Birmingham I think, so that's pretty cool, right? Yeah?"

Ouch. That wasn't exactly what Finnegan had been aiming for. He wasn't sure he'd like to spend the afternoon talking to a Brit from Birmingham.

"Of course," Finnegan said pensively, and ventured: "Mind if we have the first official Cynicism Management session, too, then? Maybe before we sit down with Ray and this... Willit?" Finnegan inquired, hoping that Largo would quickly find a harmless little excuse and leave him to his pointless Sunday. All he wanted was to be left sitting there to drink more beer, write, and enjoy life without meeting anyone else that day.

But Largo was also a bit peculiar that morning, perhaps because they'd been so jovial the evening before. "Absolutely!" he said resolutely, "Today's a good day for that, actually. If we're done by nine, of course, that would be perfect. I'm meeting these guys at nine. I told you I was busy in the evenings, remember?" Largo said.

"Oh. How convenient," Finnegan sighed, but then gave in – at least he'd be able to put his creative urges to some use at the rehearsals. "Let's get cracking, then," Finnegan decided.

It was Sunday. It was a fine day to die if you were a Klingon, but if you weren't, it was a nice day to start rehearsing.

18. Coven of Bitches

The Omnipile Intelligence Agency employees were nothing to be trifled with, so the Bitches all departed for the slightly obscure but by no means very remote country of Slovenia early on Sunday morning, immediately after completing all of the bureaucratic procedures imposed on them by the OIA Agent. That involved the usual routine and standard collection of disclaimers: the Bitches had to confirm that Omnipile corporation was in no way responsible for their physical or mental health – past, present or future. They had to sign a run-of-the-mill NDA as well as an Agreement stating how much they would not be paid and under what broad range of conditions they'd even begin to owe money to Omnipile due to various penalties. They had to acknowledge an Acknowledgement that Omnipile Corporation shall by no means be held responsible for anything that might befall them or the respective subject(s) of the investigation during the course of the proceedings stipulated in the Contract on the Whole Affair, or at any time thereafter or even before that, should time travel ever be invented. The Bitches also initialled an Amendment stating that in case of their early demise or permanent disability no additional monetary penalties shall be incurred by Omnipile, reviewed a Detailed List of what they would not be reimbursed for, read an Annex on the monetary penalties payable by them should they fail to carry out their duties in the manner set out by Omnipile Corporation, and in a timely fashion as well. The Bitches also had to sign a Statement that they would carefully inventory any and all items they might require and procure with Omnipile resources during the course of this investigation, in order to hand everything over to Omnipile when their mission was complete, regardless of its outcome. They also

consented to a Consensus that they would adhere to all procedures set out in the thick Manual on the Whole Affair they
had received, and, furthermore, to any and all procedures that
may yet be specified in any thick Manuals they might receive
subsequently.

Serbian Bitch, who had toyed with a couple of neat
ideas about how to take advantage of these circumstances and
improve her own material situation on this Earth, was quite
disappointed when all the restrictions had been made clear to
her. She kept looking for loopholes, but started suspecting that
ripping off Omnipile might not be as easy as she'd imagined.

The flight arrangements that the OIA had made for
the Bitches were fine with them, especially because they felt
an urgent need to get out from under the feet of any further
Agents that could yet crawl out of the woodwork should they
waste any time whatsoever. So they all ended up in Slovenia
as soon as on Sunday at around noon. They packed light, as
their equipment had been sent by the OIA directly to their
motel where it was already waiting for them. The OIA was
definitely efficient.

From the *Letališče Jožeta Pučnika* airport, Arch Bitch
reported to the OIA Agent in charge of them, as she was
required to do by the Manual on the Whole Affair as well
as by the Statement of No Rights Whatsoever but Loads
of Responsibilities. Arch Bitch hoped that Omnipile would
provide them with some leads pointing the way towards
Finnegan Frotz, but in spite of all the pompous bull droppings
Omnipile was so full of, their Intelligence Agency seemed to
have other priorities. Just like the CIA – the agency too busy
to notice a mob of wild-eyed bearded jihad warriors suddenly
taking flight lessons, and too involved with something else to
provide a very accurate assessment of Saddam Hussein's not
so vast weapons of mass destruction arsenal.

On the phone the Agent told Arch Bitch: "Good luck
finding Mr Frotz as soon as possible. You know, for your
own good, before you face monetary penalties for not finding
Mr Frotz as soon as possible. Slovenia is very small, so that

should be a walk in the park. And next time call me on Skype, because your mobile phone bills shall not be footed by Omnipile. Godspeed!"

Arch Bitch turned to the rest of the Bitches and shrugged, inquiring: "Any ideas about how to go about finding Mr Finnegan Frotz?"

Grim Bitch rolled her eyes and sighed, implying that she was already fed up with the Whole Affair.

Another One looked the other way, wondered if they made good coffee in the airport bar, and tried to assess what the Slovenian policy on *tapas* was (once upon a time, she had loved her stay in Andalusia, Spain, where she got free food with every drink she ordered).

The Watcher rifled through her duffle bag and pretended to look for something very important in it, avoiding her boss's piercing and impatient gaze.

Serbian Bitch meditated on the chances of her getting away with purchasing a new BMW M6 Cabrio at the Corporation's expense if she claimed she needed it desperately in order to catch up with the subject(s) of their investigation.

However, Accumulator of Unwonted Locutions, who had long been known to be quite creative in times of crises, even though she was also more than a little eccentric, said: "Public entertainers are inveterately known as self-absorbed maladjusted personalities. Imaginably our subject authors compositions about himself on the World Wide Web."

"Of course!" Arch Bitch slapped her forehead. "Mr Frotz is a musician. And musicians have been known to write about themselves on the internet in third person as well as publish their own tunes that nobody wants to listen to on all the sites they can possibly find. Let's go get a coffee and google his name!" Arch Bitch almost laughed at the idea, "I'm suddenly convinced this is the best way to start looking for him," she added, thoroughly pleased with herself and with Accumulator of Unwonted Locutions's suggestion.

The Bitches dropped by the airport bar and ordered some coffee as well as, in the case of Serbian Bitch, a coffee and a slivovitz – to commemorate her visit to the Balkans, she claimed. Before Serbian Bitch could even start feeling the slightest tinge of pleasant warmth she expected the slivovitz to bestow on her, Arch Bitch had already clapped: "Got you! Thank you, Google."

As soon as she pulled out her laptop and looked up Finnegan Frotz, she found his blog titled *Epic Tales of Cynicism Management*, and after reading a few posts she already knew where to find him.

"Finnegan Frotz has formed a new band called Cynicism Management," Arch Bitch reported, evidently very proud of her detective skills. "He claims they rehearse in a place called Rock 'n' Roll Tavern, which I've already found on Google Maps. I've also scoped it out with Google Earth. It looks like Mr Frotz has caught up with certain suspicious characters we shall hereafter refer to as *His Accomplices*, and they claim to be nothing more than a simple progressive rock band. I for one do not believe that in light of the baggage we know Mr Frotz is carrying with him."

"And on such a strategically important body part, too," added Another One.

After an hour or so, the Bitches unpacked and relaxed in a little motel, officially approved by Omnipile, on the outskirts of the Slovenian capital. Arch Bitch checked out the room she shared with Accumulator of Unwonted Locutions, sniffed around the bathroom which she found was surprisingly comfy and clean, and told her crew to stand by while she thought about what to do next. She claimed she needed to meditate on their current situation while taking a nice long bath.

So, while the boss was napping in the tub, in the second room Another One, who had joined forces with Serbian Bitch and ravaged the mini-bar, seeking to relieve it of any tasty snacks, sniggered at how serious the crew of the airplane they had arrived on had been about landing in the middle of a corn field. This was typical of airport security Bitches: those pilot poseurs got on their nerves, so this line of reasoning was not at all surprising or innovative. Another One pointed out, mockingly, that all the trays had to be closed prematurely, all the seatbelts fastened far too tightly, that the pilot made an announcement in an excessively grave voice and exceedingly lousy accent, while the stewardesses could have been less official and plain. Another One thought that the airplane crew took themselves too seriously and lacked that essential bit of humour that would make flights much more enjoyable.

Serbian Bitch agreed, of course, and accused the pilots and their crews in general of acting far too businesslike and of simply putting on an act in order to justify their considerable salaries, as landing in the middle of a corn field should, in the expert opinion of the two Bitches, involve no arcane skills at all. Plus, they knew for a fact that these days planes, with the all-new state-of-the-art technology, could land themselves without any human assistance.

Yes, it was a profoundly useful debate.

The Watcher and Grim Bitch, who shared the third room, felt relieved to get out of the underground airport security complex for a change, much like all other Bitches – it almost felt like vacation. Nevertheless, they engaged in a slightly more serious discussion about the intricacies of this unexpected and certainly unusual mission.

"Well, as we all know, you seem to have what most people would call superior powers of observation at your disposal," Grim Bitch told The Watcher. "So, is there something you might have gleaned from the video feed of Finnegan, or perhaps from the OIA Agent's *PowerPoint* presentation? Because I can't shake the feeling that something more is going on here than they're letting on."

"Yeah," The Watcher agreed, "me too. I've been watching very carefully, but I can't say I managed to notice anything out of the ordinary. Maybe I was just too tired, or had too much coffee with tea. Because I get a bit of a tunnel vision sometimes when I drink tons of coffee with tea, you see, and then instead of being able to watch more carefully

I get distracted for a while, until the funny effect passes. Anyway, there was nothing worth mentioning about the OIA Agent... apart from him being a pompous jerk. But everybody can see that, and I can safely assume that about all OIA Agents without even having to look at them. "

"Anything strange or notable about Finnegan on the video?"

"Just that he checked out the toilet bowls rather carefully, and examined the ceiling more closely than people usually do. It was almost as if he suspected there were cameras everywhere, but fortunately he could not imagine how well-concealed and incredibly tiny they were. Well, maybe he's just paranoid by nature, I couldn't tell. Which doesn't matter, anyway, I don't find it very logical in either case."

"What?" Grim Bitch failed to see the point.

"If his elaborate tattoo was as damn important, meaningful and incriminating as the OIA Agent implied, why then would he willingly display it? If he suspected there were cameras in the toilet, and if his butt ornament was such a secret, he probably wouldn't have taken a dump there, it seems more likely he'd relieve himself in some nameless pub. It didn't look like an urgent bowel movement either, he seemed bored more than anything else. Bored and suspicious. Or just too curious because of boredom. Or perhaps he'd smoked a joint before coming to the airport and felt a bit paranoid, who knows. But he would surely refrain from letting such an important thing show. Speaking of which, there is also the question of the kilt."

"The kilt?" Grim Bitch raised her eyebrows, not really getting it.

"He wouldn't wear a kilt if he didn't want anyone to see the tattoo accidentally."

"Scotsmen wearing nothing under their kilts, that's just a stupid myth," Grim Bitch said, scowling.

"Really? Seriously? Because I just saw a couple of kilt-wearing Scotsmen in a pub the other day, and I could swear they were naked under there."

"How could you tell?" Grim Bitch was looking forward to the explanation.

"Well, when they shook their booties and jumped around, there was this... You know, smacking sound? Besides, their girlfriends would grab them under there and giggle a tad too naughtily. Also, occasionally I'd catch a whiff of..."

"OK, OK, fine, that's far too much information," Grim Bitch raised her arms in defence. The first signs of a barely visible smile started to show on her seldom-changing face as she told The Watcher: "But what you saw weren't your usual Scotsmen. They were obviously *drunken* Scotsmen. Wait... That's not really all that unusual..." Grim Bitch narrowed her eyes suspiciously. "Never mind. Anyway, most likely they weren't Scotsmen at all, they were totally plastered random kilt-wearing idiots in the company of random twats."

"Oh! I didn't think of that."

"You probably observed too much and thought too little," Grim Bitch actually managed a smile. This was an extremely rare incident for Grim Bitch, thus certain facial muscles of hers were shocked and awed to the point where her face would be quite sore the next day.

"Well, I also had a couple of coffees with tea, it happened in a pub, what do you expect," The Watcher admitted.

"Really, serious Scotsmen don't go around butt naked under those kilts. Actually, serious Scotsmen don't go around in kilts, period. Only drunken ones do that while attending stag parties, patriotic gatherings, certain festive occasions, wars or some other such nonsense, like parades, for example. Why Finnegan would wear it though, I wouldn't know. Probably he's just a moron. Or a bit of an eccentric. Or he's an eccentric moron, you know how these artist types are."

The Watcher chuckled, and then became worried: "Wait – but that puts a serious dent in my theory. Let me see..." The Watcher paused to think, then elaborated: "Are kilts prone to the plumber's butt phenomenon? I can't be sure, since

I've never worn one, but if they aren't... Or if they're even plumber's butt *resistant*! Then it's entirely possible Finnegan actually *did* know how important the tattoo was, and that's why he wore a kilt in the first place. With underwear, if you say so. Because it's a big tattoo, and a part of it could still show due to plumber's butt whenever he picked something up or whatever. In a kilt maybe it wouldn't, depends on how they're fixed to the waist. Ah, damn, I don't know anymore..." The Watcher looked miserable.

"Jesus, but you've surely worn a skirt, haven't you?"

"Nope, never. I hate skirts. And even if I did, I've never worn a kilt. They're bound to be different..."

"Oh, forget it, don't fret, it doesn't matter. Please, let's leave pants, skirts, kilts and plumbers' butts alone, OK? What I want to know is why would our suspect get an incriminating tattoo in the first place?" Grim Bitch asked.

"Indeed..."

"Unless he's completely unaware of its significance. Well, perhaps the numbers stamped on his posterior and the ones the rich brat is reciting are just some weird coincidence. Or this is all a pile of bollocks and Omnipile intelligence just plain old sucks. Well, be that as it may, I'm sure that the OIA knows far more than we do. They're most likely not telling us everything, so let's just leave it at that for now. Anything else?"

"Nope, not really."

"Ah, well... Say, are there any snacks in the mini-bar?"

"I think I saw some chocolates. Ah, it's nice to unwind a bit for a change," The Watcher stretched her arms.

The entire Coven of Bitches seemed to be enjoying their current situation, except for Accumulator of Unwonted Locutions, perhaps, who decided to hang out in The Watcher and Grim Bitch's room while Arch Bitch meditated, and whom nobody seemed to be terribly eager to talk to for some reason she did not understand. So she just remarked, quite indifferently, to no one in particular: "This supererogatory delay is superlatively aggravating."

At about 3 p.m., half an hour before Arch Bitch finally decided to wrap up her contemplation of untold dreamscapes, Serbian Bitch and Another One completed their mini-bar raid. Still peckish and confident that the Omnipile conglomerate would pay for it all since they'd claim they needed the goodies to facilitate their "creative thinking processes", Serbian Bitch resorted to ordering a couple of drinks and some snacks from room service, which would probably have been frowned upon by the other Bitches had they witnessed it. Even Another One was slightly worried, and she expressed her legitimate concerns to Serbian Bitch: that perhaps the evildoers at the Accounting Department of Omnipile would eventually make them pay for this, and that maybe Serbian Bitch's resolution to imbibe alcoholic beverages on duty during her first day as a top secret Omnipile agent deputy and letting Arch Bitch witness it was not such a good idea after all.

However, Serbian Bitch told Another One that she herself would pay for the damn room service if Omnipile rejected their rightful claims, and that she'd only downed a few, in accordance with the local customs, to celebrate her visit to the Balkans. Apparently she'd thought she might never visit the former Yugoslavia again. Serbian Bitch took a long thoughtful look at the beer bottle she had just emptied, cackled, and translated an inscription for Another One: "Well, I'll be... This says: Official Brewery of the Slovenian Football Team. Wow. Do you think they win very often?"

Another One laughed, and then became curious: "Wait... You understand their language?"

"I'm not an expert, but I usually get the gist, yeah," Serbian Bitch said, and then her eyes lit up with a potentially profitable idea. "Shit, maybe I could sell this talent of mine to Omnipile."

Another One agreed and expressed interest in how it was that Serbian Bitch understood Slovenian. This involved a tear-wrenching yarn which Serbian Bitch readily recited: about her traumatic childhood, a Slovenian father she hadn't known before her relocation to Slovenia, a war lasting for as

long as ten days, her family's repatriation to Serbia, the war
that would eventually result in the United States bombing
her homeland, an uncalled-for bottle of slivovitz, domestic
violence, her mother enlisting into the Serbian Army, and,
ultimately, emigration of Serbian Bitch and her newfound
Slovenian father to the United Kingdom. After Serbian
Bitch was through reminiscing, she underlined her alleged
profound familiarity with local customs, affinity towards
all things former-Yugoslav, comprehension of Slovenian
and Macedonian as well as total command of Croatian and
Serbian, languages also understood by many a Slovenian.
This would surely be extremely beneficial during the pending
investigation. She just neglected to mention out loud that she
hadn't visited Yugoslavia since she was twelve, and that she
hadn't exhibited any interest in any matters Yugoslav nor
spoke or read any Slavic languages save for an occasional
word of Serbian ever since she and her father had moved to
London in 1992.

Arch Bitch summoned the Coven for a 15:30 meeting in
the lobby of the little motel. The lobby was pleasantly cosy
and intimate, but despite its modest size it was still more
comfortable than their rooms. In a remote corner, conveniently
obscured from prying eyes by potted plants that offered
guests some privacy, stood a couple of simple but neat and
spacious tables with very comfortable cushioned sofas. Arch
Bitch, well-versed in all things related to the management
of her Bitches, had obviously scoped out that corner as soon
as they'd first entered the motel, as she now headed there
without giving it a second thought.

Even though she must have been aware that Omnipile
and its infamous OIA Agents would be breathing down her
neck, Arch Bitch seemed extraordinarily cheerful and sure of
herself as she made herself and her laptop comfortable. Her
posterior sank into one of the sofas as perfectly as if they
had always been destined to finally meet each other, and the
furniture creaked slightly in greeting. This spot in the lobby
was a part of a charming, quiet and unobtrusive bar, and Arch

Bitch readily ordered some refreshments. She did not even blink an eye when Serbian Bitch ordered the most expensive French cognac available, remarking something like how Omnipile would foot the bill. What Arch Bitch referred to as "meditation" obviously had a remarkably positive effect on her.

After all the Bitches were present, accounted for and parked safely on the sofas, Arch Bitch opened the meeting: "Well, I see we've all settled in and managed to relax a bit," she said, glancing keenly at Serbian Bitch and Another One, who kept giggling and poking each other like a couple of schoolgirls.

"Indeed, perchance we even tarry immoderately," Accumulator of Unwonted Locutions worried.

"Don't be impatient, we have to tackle this urgently... But prudently," Arch Bitch said. "No need to rush into anything. Especially since – and I hope I don't have to point this out too bluntly – we've finally gotten away from the airport underground where we've spent the last few years of our lives and where we'll most probably end up again once this is over. So I for one think we should make the most of this situation. After all, we're getting paid for this mission, and for as long as Omnipile is willing to let us enjoy some latitude, and perhaps even longitude, I see no reason not to have some fun while we're at it. For as long as we appear efficient, at least."

The Bitches nodded, obviously agreeing with the Arch Bitch's line of thought.

Arch Bitch went on: "So, without further ado, we should seek out Finnegan and his gang as quickly as possible, hopefully today, and initiate the most effective surveillance operations we can, because this is what our employers expect us to do," she said firmly and aimed a stern look in the direction of the inordinately merry Serbian Bitch. "Only then can we take control of our situation and influence the pace of the investigation. Maybe we can even stay here for a while and enjoy some well-paid time off..."

"Yeah," Serbian Bitch agreed, "if we play our cards right, we could even steer our suspects to the Croatian coast during the summer and surveil them there... You know, while enjoying the Adriatic Sea, that would be nice..."

Arch Bitch smiled indulgently. "Yeah... Look," she paused and admitted: "Frankly, I don't trust these Omnipile types much, so I would like to gather as much information as possible ASAP. Do you agree?"

Arch Bitch's gaze persisted, locked on Serbian Bitch's eyes while she was talking, so Serbian Bitch pulled herself together, wiped the teenage giggles off her face, tried to clear the mist in her eyes to the best of her abilities, and said: "Of course. I agree. I should also point out that as a former citizen of the late Yugoslavia I may be a tad more familiar with the local affairs than the rest of you. I even lived in Ljubljana for a while, so I'm familiar with the place, and I also know a thing or two about the local customs and former-Yugoslav issues. I guess that my knowledge of the Serbian language and fair understanding of Slovenian might also come in handy."

When Another One let out an unintentional titter, Serbian Bitch took advantage of the cover of the spacious table and kicked her in the shin. Another One's playfulness transformed into a resentful yelp, though she still continued chuckling afterwards, if more quietly.

The Watcher rolled her eyes, while Accumulator of Unwonted Locutions remarked: "How foretellable," she told everyone, shaking her head reproachfully at Serbian Bitch.

"Look, enough of this petty bickering," Arch Bitch said, "Granted, your awesome expertise could conceivably be put to some use. But, first things first – we're going to the stake-out and see what's going on. To the Rock 'n' Roll Tavern!"

The Bitches decided that the best way of getting around, especially with all the equipment that the OIA had delivered to their motel, would be to rent cars. However, when Arch Bitch checked in the Manual on the Whole Affair what kind of

transport arrangements had been approved, Serbian Bitch was
very disappointed when she realised that they wouldn't be
allowed to rent at least one slick black Jaguar and a luxurious
black Audi per Bitch. Omnipile only approved a single
unimposing van, and since the closest rent-a-van company
didn't have any menacing black vehicles available, the Bitches
had to come to terms with a beat-up blue Volkswagen. It
may have been less than "secret-agenty", but it was spacious,
reliable and, to the likely great satisfaction of Omnipile
Accounting Department, dirt cheap.

Why Omnipile with all of its gazillions of assets would
care about how much six of their quasi agents spent on
transport may have seemed incomprehensible to the Bitches,
but it was simply the way the Corporation conducted its
business, and this had obviously resulted in the Corporation
now being worth gazillions. One of the principles of the
Omnipile conglomerate was that it was reluctant to flaunt its
riches. Apparently, such companies sometimes liked to be
as inconspicuous as possible in order to conduct as much of
their business as they could under the radar of public opinion
and, whenever possible, behind the back of any greedy tax
administrations.

The Watcher set up the GPS and off they went.

The shadows lengthened as the summer day transformed into a late afternoon. When the blue Volkswagen van
slowed down about a hundred metres from the black and
white airbrush portrait of Jimi Hendrix, it was chirped at by
a flight of dismayed swallows, complaining that it interfered
with their traditional evening gnat hunt. Had the members
of Cynicism Management, engrossed in their first rehearsals
at the time, heard the swallows' furious complaints, their
attention might have been drawn to the van full of birds. But
at that point they were still familiarising themselves frantically with Finnegan's melancholic (and rather hypochondriac)
composition, *Life Malignant*.

The Bitches decided to park near a church on top
of a little hill overlooking Boris and Beeba's Rock 'n' Roll

Tavern in order to check out the situation without being too conspicuous.

Of course Beeba, as nosy as the next person in that suburban community, immediately noticed them from below and hoped they weren't potentially annoying patrons. When she mentioned the van to Boris, he looked through the window and muttered: "What business do they have parking up there? Oh, well, maybe some old farts from the retirement home across the river came to church again. Hope they're not coming here, I'm really not in the mood. Perhaps they'll just head to the bar over by the church. But if they come in here and ask if we serve food, just send them to the pizza place down the road," Boris told Beeba and went back to his studio where he pretended to be working on something.

For about half an hour, the Bitches sat in the van that lacked any air conditioning, sweating in the still strong late afternoon sun. Serbian Bitch and Another One, soon fed up with the droplets trickling down their spines and forming ponds in the smalls of their backs, got out of the van despite Arch Bitch's weak protests. They sat down on the curb, leaning against the van's dusty exterior, and looked at the Rock 'n' Roll Tavern below longingly, for it appeared so pleasantly cool, judging by the thick brick walls of the old house it was located in. "Fuck, I'm thirsty," panted Serbian Bitch.

Soon the rest of the Bitches also got out of the van, as Arch Bitch finally agreed that staying inside was indeed altogether crazy and useless.

"So what shall we do now?" Arch Bitch inquired as they all joined Serbian Bitch and Another One.

"No idea," The Watcher replied. "All I know is I feel like I'm being watched," she complained as a member of the aboriginal population walked by and peered at the van and the six strange ladies far too curiously for comfort. Cue in the *Duelling Banjos* theme again.

"I mean, seriously," Another One said, "Does any one here feel like a secret agent?"

"Not really. I'm tired and thirsty, even cranky in this

heat," Serbian Bitch admitted.

"I wouldn't really know where to begin in order to avoid major international incidents and disciplinary actions brought against us by Omnipile," Grim Bitch complained.

"Well," Another One surmised, "I suppose that for as long as we do it by the book they wrote, they won't object to what we're doing."

"What's that supposed to mean?" Serbian Bitch whined.

"Our taskforce should adhere to the modus operandi of our superiors and obviate any needless digressions," Accumulator of Unwonted Locutions explained.

"What's that supposed to mean?" Serbian Bitch repeated.

"It means we should stick to the procedure set out by Omnipile and not do anything stupid in order to avoid ending up in a shitstorm. I don't feel like getting on the bad side of the Omnipile Intelligence Agency. Do you?" Arch Bitch told the rest of the Bitches.

"So, what are we doing? Just sitting here?" Serbian Bitch grew restless. "Can I at least go down there and get a glass of water? Or a beer? You know, like a regular customer? I'll pretend I'm Serbian, nobody will suspect anything. Everybody around here understands Serbian, thousands of my compatriots live here."

"You know what, that's not such a bad idea. According to procedure we should first establish the whereabouts and identity of the primary subject of our investigation and confirm any potential secondary subjects without being suspected of investigating anything. I don't see how we can do that from here. Besides, I feel that this spot might not be very good for a stakeout, after all – I mean, while we have a clear view of the tavern, the people in there also have a clear view of us. And what do we say we're doing here, in a van parked by the side of a back road leading nowhere?"

Nothing much was on that hilltop but a cluster of houses, a couple of larger buildings, a bar, and, of course, a small church. Many of the buildings proudly showed off insultingly glaring facades: the Slovenian rural taste in architecture had apparently succumbed to a particularly venomous form of colour terrorism.

Churches, small or not so small, seemed to be the trademark of most Slovenian villages no matter how tiny. The Slovenian Catholic Church obviously liked to erect them on hilltops so that they appeared more imposing, and every night floodlights would light up the belfries. In a world concerned with global warming and excessive energy consumption, this was a hefty spit in the face of everything sensible, but the Slovenian clergy seemed unconcerned with the affairs of God's great Earth. Its goal – apart from fondling little children and erecting luminous phallic buildings – was to plunder and pillage while it could, just like the clergy everywhere else in the world.

While the Bitches waited, quietly and thoughtfully, for their boss to come up with a plan, it got darker. The flood-lights aimed at the belfry came on. The van, parked between the church and one of the floodlights, was now brightly illuminated against the evening sky.

When Bogomyr Yadvig pulled up at the Rock 'n' Roll Tavern's parking lot in the twilight, the shining blue Volkswagen van up on the hill caught his eye, and he wondered what all those women were doing up there. At that point the Bitches were far too busy focusing on the intricacies of their initial survey mission to even notice him. Bogomyr thought nothing more of it. He merely slipped into the tavern, hoping that Finnegan wouldn't be too upset with his absence from the first rehearsal.

19. Fergus and Fabiola

A week before the Bitches discovered the Rock 'n' Roll Tavern, Fergus found out that the men who'd kidnapped him and his sister were about to let him go in exchange for some things they needed. He took the news quite indifferently and was surprised at himself, expecting he should be at least marginally relieved. Instead he was more or less disinterested in the whole affair. Even though he was just fourteen years old, he knew that was most likely somewhat odd. Throughout the exchange, which was awfully boring and uneventful for a hostage situation, he thought about where he'd been, what he'd done, what had been done to him... But it was all so terribly confusing. Most days were a complete blur to him. What worried Fergus even more was that he didn't look forward to playing his beloved online role-playing computer games as much as he thought he would once he got back home. Of course he could hardly wait, but the complete dedication he'd felt before was somehow not all there anymore. He was afraid something was very wrong with him... but at the same time he sensed some other purpose, incredibly strong, almost like an urge to complete some mission, a quest he could not quite put into words.

Once Fergus was back in London, his father's men took him directly to what he knew had to be fancy and secret Omnipile facilities, even though everyone referred to the place as the "hospital". At least, they did so when they spoke to him. When they thought he wasn't listening, they called it "The Lab", with audible capital letters. He found that slightly disturbing, but didn't really care all that much. All he wanted was to get this over with and go home as soon as possible.

Fergus's father was waiting in the room where the boy would be staying for a while, talking to a couple of men in black suits and polka-dot ties. They fell quiet and looked up as the boy stepped through the door.

"Son! Thank god you're back!" his father spoke hastily and nervously, which was far from typical of him. Then he hugged Fergus and ruffled his hair, which was even more unlike him. In fact, it was unheard of. Fergus figured his dad must have been worried out of his mind. Either that or he'd been replaced by body snatchers while Fergus had been away.

"Where's mom?" Fergus asked.

Ferdinand Fenton seemed uneasy. "She... Well... She'd love to come, but, frankly, visitors are not allowed in here. They only let you in with a special ID, which obviously makes you a very special lad, doesn't it? A secret agent, almost!" Ferdinand smiled and Fergus smiled back at him just to make him feel better. "You'll see mom as soon as we're done here. The doctors have to check if everything is alright with you, make sure you're not ill or anything, you know. So, how do you feel, son? Are you OK?"

"Sure. Can I have my computer?"

Mr Fenton smiled. "Not right now, the doctors tell me you should rest. They need to do some tests first thing in the morning."

Fergus sighed, looked at the two men with funky ties questioningly and smirked: "What's up with the clowns? A welcome home party? Do they have IDs too?" Fergus had encountered the men with the silly ties before, and they always gave him the creeps. He would never have dared to say anything sarcastic before the kidnapping, but now he felt different somehow. Stronger. Definitely less afraid.

"Oh, them? Of course they do. Our company won't let me go anywhere without some clowns these days, I'm afraid." Mr Fenton paused and his smile waned. "Listen, son, I should get going. They're still holding your sister..." Ferdinand sighed.

"I know," Fergus muttered.

"Look, be a good boy and cooperate with the clowns, will you? They're here to help get your sister back. And listen to whatever the doctors tell you. I'll be back to check on you tomorrow. Maybe I'll bring your phone if they say it's OK, so you can talk to your mother."

Fergus nodded.

"You should get some sleep now, and in the morning try to remember everything you can and tell it to... Well, the clowns." Ferdinand managed another smile, ruffled Fergus's hair again, and left.

After the door closed behind Ferdinand, Fergus frowned and turned around to look at the goons who loomed motionlessly behind his back.

The Agents glanced at each other, then one of them glared and said slowly in a low and level voice: "Ain't ya a funny little boy. See ya tomorrow. For yer own good, if you wanna see yer mommy anytime soon, you'll tell us what went on down there in Yoman real quick. And make sure ya don't leave out nothin'."

They walked past the boy slowly and deliberately, and then the chattier Agent turned to look at Fergus again: "Try to get some shuteye before ya meet the doctors – first thing in the mornin' they're gonna prick you with needles and give ya an enema."

After the men in black closed the door behind them, Fergus could hear them laughing on the other side. The one who had been quiet snickered: "Needles and enema. You're awesome with kids."

"Well, it's true, ain't it?"

"Yuck, gotta get that image outta my head..." And their voices dwindled away.

Even after hearing the unfortunate news, Fergus remained strangely calm. "Stupid Yanks," he thought. He went to the bathroom, took a shower to wash the sands of Yoman away, brushed his teeth, and slipped straight under the covers.

Sleep would not come to him, though, and despite his apparent composure he could not stop ruminating about the last couple of weeks, trying to get a handle on it all.

He thought back long and hard.

Two weeks ago, on the fatal day when his father got the brilliant idea to take him, his boring sister Fabiola and his mom to some dump in the Middle East, Faarghuz the mighty undead priest was supposed to go on a terribly important raid with his guild, the Hordecorerz. Moolly, the tauren shaman guildmistress of the Hordecorerz, was not to be trifled with, despite her bovine name and appearance – if the guild arranged to go on a raid, they had to go on a raid, period. No lame-ass real-life obligation was more important than that.

Moolly was extremely strict with her soldiers – she demanded "utter discipline and dedication". She kept repeating this catchphrase of hers so frequently and persistently that soon she was called "udder disciplinarian" behind her back by the wittier World of Warcraft players who had the misfortune of crossing her path. Her goal was to run one of the best guilds in the game, consisting of soldiers with the most epic equipment, and this grandest of purposes was simply not attainable by putting up with any inferior scum – that is, incompetent World of Warcraft players whom she usually referred to as "n00bs" or "tards". As far as she was concerned, casual players were vermin, lowlier than worms. Moolly lived for the Hordecorerz and she wanted them to represent an excruciatingly painful thorn in the backside of their sworn enemy, their nemesis, the renowned and much larger Pwnshoppe guild of the Alliance (essentially because once upon a time, even before the first World of Warcraft expansion, those losers dared to call her guild Whordewhorers on the game forums).

Moolly was known to be so fanatical, driven and creative in the field of what she referred to as "penal measures" that some of the older and more sarcastic (usually former) members of the Hordecorerz stated this had to be because she had been introduced to far too few "penile measures" herself. Naturally, this treacherous claim was quickly picked up and regularly quoted on the forums by the Pwnshoppe, which only fuelled Moolly's profound tauren rage further. When the collo-cation "Udder Disciplinarian's Penile Measures" became the title of a cubist poem by Pwnshoppe's poet laureate, published on their blog and quoted on the forums as well as in-game, Moolly almost flipped and abruptly proved that the people who claimed she couldn't get any more rabid than she already was were wrong. Very wrong. Now, besides "utter discipline and dedication", she also demanded "absolute and unquestioning loyalty". Why people could be bothered to play with her was beyond anyone's guess – probably some players *craved* udder discipline.

So the consequence of Moolly's pathological intolerance for any signs of what she saw as lack of cooperation was that if Fergus failed to make Faarghuz show up for the raid and stand with the Hordecorerz, heal them, inflict terrible afflictions on their enemies and strike fear into the hearts of all who opposed them during their most critical quest to date, Fergus would very likely be referred to as a slacker or even – god forbid! – a n00b, while his Faarghuz would be punished in some particularly creative manner.

That was not the worst of it, though. Sheer horror would transpire if Fergus went with his dad, like he was supposed to, and failed to check in with his guildmistress for seven days – a thing like that would, in accordance with the guild charter, constitute an act of high treason and result in immediate termination – that is, removal from the guild. Furthermore, all Hordecorerz would be forbidden from communicating with the offending party ever again, so Fergus would effectively lose most of the friends he had made online in the last couple of years. By no means would Moolly put up with such insubordination. Needless to say, she obviously didn't have what normal people referred to as a 'job' or 'life', and was probably scarcely if ever seen outside of her proverbial twilit abode – or so everybody who knew her believed. Since none of the Hordecorerz had actually laid eyes on the fair Moolly in person, she could in fact be a grumpy old retired sailor man, a hairy sodomite troglodyte residing in a musty old cave with his goat and a broadband internet connection, or an eighteen-year-old cheerleader dropout with permanent pre-menstrual issues, affinity for sadism and far too much time on her hands.

Anyway, that's how utterly disastrous Fergus's day turned out to be when his father told him he was sick of his little computer game and that Fergus had better quit whining or else. (What blasphemy, to refer to Fergus's epic efforts and main preoccupation in life in such a diminutive manner!)

For the next couple of days, Fergus the pimply nerd dragged his feet like a convict on death row, mostly oblivious of anything but his incessant compulsion to jump into the skin of the formidable avatar Faarghuz again, join his comrades in battle and make his guildmistress proud. Perhaps he'd even earn a kind word, some recognition, a friendly slap on the back, maybe even catch a glimpse of her bovine attributes or attain the rank of guild officer and a piece of particularly epic gear. But he wasn't even able to check in with her, because his stupid father wouldn't let him take his laptop with him, and he'd also confiscated his iPhone. The rich bastard said that for pedagogical reasons he wouldn't pay for Fergus's roaming charges, even though his damn company *owned* their mobile phone operator, now how lame was that? Ferdinand was just an evil old fart.

So when Fergus and his family finally arrived at their reasonably fancy hotel in Yoman, the boy's eyes lit up when he saw a couple of computers in the lobby. Obviously Yomanians had managed to get their hands on some PCs despite the embargo imposed on Yoman by the United States. Probably the Chinese let them have some outdated machines. Anyway, Fergus desperately needed to let Moolly or at least her First Officer know where he was and why he couldn't join the raid when they needed Faarghuz's skills the most. It was either that or his illustrious career in the Hordecorerz would be over for good. There was no way his dad would let him use the computers, though. Ferdinand seemed intent on ruining Fergus's career and earning him a court martial. So Fergus figured he'd sneak out of their hotel suite when everyone was asleep.

In the evening Fergus got lucky. Ferdinand told his wife

Evelyn he had to go out, supposedly to inspect certain facilities too secret to define specifically. She told him she really
wanted to know what kind of 'facilities' he was 'inspecting' in
the middle of the night. He told her it was a company matter
he couldn't discuss. After which she told him: "Bollocks!" and
slammed the hotel suite door in his face.

From behind the closed door the flushed Ferdinand,
accompanied by his bodyguards who pretended not to have
an opinion on anything, yelled: "Damn it, Evelyn, I go ahead
and arrange for you and the kids to come with me, and this is
how you thank me? Aren't you the one who's always nagging
about never leaving the damn house? Didn't you want to go
on a vacation together? Evelyn, don't you dare walk away!"

Ferdinand's wife stopped halfway across the hall, turned
to the door and bellowed: "Vacation together?! What fucking
vacation together?! You're not even around! Bollocks as
always, and you know it!"

"Evelyn! Fuck…!" Ferdinand stomped his foot on the
floor. He hoped for a shocking massive boom, but the floor
was covered with fine Persian carpets and his protest sounded
like a muffled impotent plop. Obviously Iranian carpet
exporters didn't give a damn about the US embargo against
Yoman, either, to the great relief of the hotel decorators.
Behind Ferdinand's back the bodyguards were visibly amused
but they wisely refrained from even clearing their throats.

"Bollocks!" Evelyn yelled again over her shoulder as she
stormed away from the door.

All the bodyguards, including those who remained
in the hotel suite with the family, pretended to be deaf.
Ferdinand acted as if he was in a hurry to leave, because he
felt like a glaring idiot standing in front of the closed door
with four colossal men in black suits and sunglasses – a most
inappropriate fashion accessory in the dim corridor so late in
the evening. Fabiola made sure everyone noticed she thought
everyone was an asshole, picked up her luggage and theatrically marched into the room she was forced to share with her
geeky brother. Fergus, who knew this routine bickering of his

parents by heart – it always ended with his mother shouting
"Bollocks!" and storming away – only wondered whether he
might soon have a chance to sneak out. He didn't want to
check whether his mother was in on his father's plan to ruin
his life, and she probably wouldn't let him leave the room and
go to the lobby even if she wasn't. Be that as it may, he knew
Evelyn would soon take one of her sleeping pills and fall
asleep in front of the TV, while Fabiola would close the door
to their room, tell him to stay the fuck out, and do nasty girl
stuff he didn't want to know anything about. With his father
not around, their bodyguards would drink beer and play cards
in the remotest corner of the suite in order not to bother the
ill-natured Mrs Fenton and not to be pestered by those damn
spoiled brats of hers, so they wouldn't present much of a
problem.

Fergus was right. Maybe he should invest in a crystal
ball and become a fortune teller. Evelyn popped two Valiums
and a sleeping pill, obviously angry at her husband, while she
watched a thoroughly censored American comedy with Arabic
subtitles on Yoman One. When the movie ended abruptly after
just about twenty minutes (all the scenes involving sex as well
as the ones alluding to sex had been cut out by the censors,
so not all that much remained), the Yomanian Prime Minister
came on and Evelyn did not react. Fergus suspected he was
almost in the clear. Then the Yomanian Prime Minister started
yelling – judging by his intonation, demeanour and flailing
arms it must have been about something very urgent and
tragic involving the malevolent United States of America – and
Evelyn still failed to change the channel or even stir. So Fergus
knew for sure she was sound asleep. He confirmed that all of
the bodyguards were accounted for, engrossed in poker and
beer, and then snuck out of the suite.

The boy slithered slowly and stealthily down the
corridor, just as adeptly as one of his alternate characters in
World of Warcraft, a level 79 troll rogue. He was a whisper,
a shadow, the embodiment of his awesome skills – after all,
he had just eluded a bunch of mean-looking security experts!

Just as he was about to turn the corner, a female orc with an elaborate purple hairdo and a pierced nose jumped him from the other side.

When the orc wench saw what must have been a near-death experience due to an imminent heart attack on Fergus's part, she laughed so hard she had to grab her belly and bend over helplessly.

"You should have seen your face! What an absolute jerk..." she roared with laughter.

"Shut up, you moron!" said the pale Fergus when he regained some of his senses, and gasped for breath.

"It was like Harry Potter and the Premature Massive Coronary," the she-orc guffawed and added: "Which would be about time, the annoying twerp that he is."

Fergus fixed his Harry Potter glasses, calmed down somewhat, almost managed a relieved smile and panted: "Damn, Fab, you scared the shit out of me!"

"Yeah, literally, I'd say," she finally brought her giggles under control. "What the heck are you doing out here, you ninny?"

"Don't call me that. I'm going down to the lobby to use a computer. What are you doing here? What the... How did you get ahead of me?"

"Oh, don't be a jerk, I saw you were up to something from a mile away. All that snooping around, checking out if mom's passed out already, and stalking those assholes to see if they're playing poker again while dad's gone. Jeez, you're as transparent as the lace knickers hugging the asses of our father's secretaries."

"Oh, shut up," Fergus grimaced.

"And as naive as a blind puppy," Fabiola added. "I followed you when you snuck out and decided to give you a scare. I went the other way around to cut you off, there's a corridor going all the way around every floor, see? It's just that you were so damn slow because of all that stealth of yours I thought I'd lost you there for a moment. Some legendary thief you are."

"Rogue, not thief. There's a big difference..."

"Whatever. So tell me, O! great white assassin, what's this quest you're on, then?"

"I have to mail Moolly, she'll kick me out of the guild if I just vanish without saying anything."

"What a tragedy that would be," Fabiola scowled at Fergus. "What do you see in that cow, anyway?"

"Don't call her that, you know taurens are not cows."

"Whatever," Fabiola rolled her eyes, "Don't you dare take your games too seriously around me, it makes you look like a real nerd, you know that? Don't sell yourself too short," she pulled his ear and gave him a soft amicable knock on the head.

"Please don't tell mom... I'll just mail Moolly real quick and be right back, OK?"

"Don't worry, squirt, I'm bored stiff of that room and everyone in it, anyway." Fabiola rolled her eyes as melodramatically as only seventeen-year-old girls can. "Let's go, then," she barked, "Before dad's idiot agents find us here." She turned around and walked away so resolutely that the extensive Hordecorerz indoctrination kicked in and Fergus followed his orc chieftain without uttering another word.

"Hello," Fabiola smiled innocently as she walked up to the reception desk. "Could we please use the computers over there?" she said with an exaggerated British accent in an effort to set herself apart from Americans. She suspected these people might hold a grudge or two against the Yanks.

"Of course, my friend, but it cost money," the receptionist beamed.

"How much?" asked Fergus impatiently.

"Let me see... Well, you really nice children, yes, so I make a very special price, just for you, my friend. Just five dollar every half hour, yes?"

Fergus fidgeted nervously, as he didn't have any money on him. Fabiola pretended to hesitate.

"Look..." The receptionist leaned closer to the kids and lowered his voice to a whisper, telling them conspiratorially:

"I already try to help you, my friend, but maybe I can make an even more special price, just for you. But please please don't tell no one, especially my friend back there," he pointed at some men in the room behind him, "Otherwise they all just look at nakey internet girls and don't do no work anymore, OK? Let's say six dollar, but every hour, not half hour, yes? That a very very special price," the receptionist winked at them.

"Sure," Fabiola said and fished some change out of her pocket without bothering to haggle anymore, even though she knew the price was robbery in broad daylight. Fergus looked at her gratefully and they headed to the outdated PCs in the far corner of the lobby.

Regardless of what level any of their virtual role-playing game characters may have been on, their own perception attributes were obviously not high enough, because neither of them noticed two men, as stereotypically menacing as possible, glaring at them from the other side of the lobby.

Once Fergus came to terms with the sluggishness with which these computers gradually considered responding to their mouse clicks (Fabiola even voiced her suspicions that these Arab vultures had underclocked their computers in order to rip off any unsuspecting customers), he wrote an apologetic e-mail to his guildmistress and the First Officer, explaining his terrible predicament. When he was done, Fabiola pushed him aside, stating that she had to check what *Arctic Monkeys* and other interesting people were up to while they still had some time left on the computer. Just as she was about to start giggling at how George Michael got arrested yet again, and as Fergus started rubbing his forehead in order to alleviate his boredom and indignation with how Fabiola chose to waste the last minutes of their time online, something happened and darkness engulfed them.

Fergus's memories of the events in the hotel ended. He remembered sending an e-mail to Moolly, and then there was just a gaping hole. Nobody had ever told him anything about how they were kidnapped, not even the doctors in The Lab he ended up in later, after the kidnappers had exchanged him for money and insecticide. But even at the tender age of fourteen, on his first morning of captivity Fergus was old enough to assume that what he'd just woken up with had to be what he'd heard people refer to as a *monumental hangover*, so his blackout must have been chemically induced.

He figured the best thing to do first would be to whine.

"Fergy?" a disembodied voice said.

"Don't call me that..." he grunted.

"Squirt, are you all right?" he heard Fabiola worry somewhere nearby.

"My head... I feel sick," he mumbled and struggled to get his eyes open. His vision swam and he was terribly thirsty and nauseous. Somehow he managed to focus his gaze on a silhouette sitting on a bed across the dark and dusty room. Fabiola must have regained her consciousness sooner than he did. Maybe that was because she had a big butt and could handle greater quantities of drugs, he thought, but refrained from saying it out loud because she'd kick his ass. She was already sitting up on her bed, stretching wearily and wiggling her toes.

"It's so darn stuffy in here. Where are we? What happened?" Fergus asked her and rose on his elbows. He saw he was lying on another bed at the other end of a smallish room with sandstone walls and a few pieces of furniture, including a small table with two chairs near the window, a couple of nightstands and a wardrobe. What looked like rays of the rising sun pierced the darkness through a narrow crack in the curtains, slow dancing with the dust particles that swirled lazily through the air.

"I don't know," Fabiola said dejectedly. "I haven't seen anyone yet."

"Oh, jeez..." Fergus managed to sit up. "I need water." He glanced at the door.

"The door's locked," she said, "But there's a bottle of

water on your nightstand."

After Fergus quenched his thirst, he said: "Crikey, I should check my e-mail to see what Moolly says."

"Jesus fucking Christ, Fergus, how can you even think about that shit right now?"

"Don't swear."

"Oh, why the fuck not. It's not like mom's going to bitch about it, is she?"

"It's still rude."

"Oh, don't be obnoxious, you ninny," Fabiola rolled her eyes.

Fergus rolled his eyes, too, and sighed. Same old routine every day. Why was he cursed with a sister?

"What's going on here? Do you know?" he said hopefully.

"Do I look like it? Damn, you can be so silly sometimes." Fabiola paused. "I wonder what they gave us," she wondered, "When I woke up, I felt worse than the time I drank half a bottle of dad's most expensive Scotch, smoked a couple of his Cuban cigars and ate a ton of stale oysters I found in the back of the fridge. Now *that*, squirt, *that* was a monumental hangover."

Fergus retched and leaned over the bed.

"Shit, squirt, relax. I'm just saying. Please don't throw up, it'll stink in here." Fabiola got on her feet and stepped over to the window: "Let me open the window, at least. I thought I'd leave the curtains drawn while you were asleep. I know you must feel like shit. Drink some more water, the worst of it will pass in an hour or so. You'll be better soon."

Fergus grimaced and took the advice, even though it was his sister that gave it and the water was annoyingly stale and warm.

Fabiola pulled aside the curtains, opened the window, and there it was, shimmering in all its glory through the bars on the outer side: the first of quite a few sunrises over Al Awil she'd be able to enjoy. Admittedly, she didn't find the spectacle of the desert sunrise particularly wonderful that morning, but at least Fergus got some air and could breathe more easily.

"There, feel better?" she said.

Just as the boy started entertaining the thought that perhaps he wouldn't puke his guts out and drop dead after all, there was a knock on the door: "You sleep? Feel sick? You decent?" someone asked.

Fergus looked at Fabiola apprehensively, and she yelled: "No, we're having a blast in here, floating naked in our Jacuzzi, is this room service? Bring us champagne, lobster, a ton of your best caviar, and a bunch of fries with mayonnaise for the little kid over here. Thank you!" Obviously Fabiola believed she could chase away her nervousness with cocky witticisms.

Someone unlocked the door and Habib the young handsome clean-shaven Arab came in.

"Hello," Habib said cheerfully, wearing a broad smile lined with snow-white teeth, "Yes, maybe we eat lobster later, but here I bring some tea and biscuits first, my friends." He placed a silver tray on a small table by the window.

Fabiola jumped to her feet and grumbled, her fists clenched: "I'm no friend of yours! Who the fuck are you? Where are we? What the hell do you want with us?"

"Speak more nice, Miss, it is not nice for nice girl like you to speak ugly," Habib beamed.

"I don't give a fuck about what you think."

"Sit down," Habib said in a deeper voice, firmly and somewhat less cheerfully. The kids obeyed, also because they noticed a couple of stern-looking bearded Arabs standing just outside the door, armed with AK-47s and traditional jambiya daggers.

"Is this a kidnapping of some sort?" Fabiola wanted to appear as strong and unyielding as before, but her voice could no longer keep up appearances. After all, she was just a teenage girl, even though she'd be the first one to state that she was just about to turn eighteen, so she could do whatever she damn pleased.

"We not mean you harm, we honest freedom fighters."

"Sounds wonderful, good for you, I feel better already. Honest terrorists, an oxymoron in my books, but still wonderful. So what do you need us for?" Fabiola looked and sounded much more scared than she intended. Fergus just sat on his bed, sulking and peering through his Harry Potter glasses sombrely.

"You smart girl, yes? Smart ass, Americans say? I see, yes." Habib pressed his lips together. Fabiola couldn't tell whether that was a smile he was trying to suppress or anger he was reining in.

"We tell you everything in the right time," he said after a short pause, "Now I just like to say you no worry, you safe here, we just need the company of your father to give back somebody they kidnap."

"That's just great, you want me to believe my father's company kidnapped someone, and now you kidnapped us so that you can exchange us for whoever you say they took? Yeah, right! I bet you'll ransom us for a heap of cash in order to finance the little Al-Qaeda terrorist operation you've got going here." As Fabiola considered the meaning of her own words, she almost gasped. She realised the situation she and her brother found themselves in was not good... Not good at all.

As if to accentuate the point, one of the bearded guards outside the door swore and spit in the corner, frowning at Fabiola.

"You talk a lot, Miss. We no terrorist, we freedom fighter. Your company take our leader and put him in prison and torture him," Habib said firmly.

"I'm sure they did it for no reason whatsoever and now you're just trying to rescue an innocent man. Sounds like a legitimate operation. Yeah, right, some freedom fighters you are."

The bearded guard outside patted his jambiya and stammered in an accent far worse than Habib's, even: "I cut woman tongue out, but I not allowed take my jambiya out for woman."

The other soldier stroked his AK-47 lovingly: "But I can use gun on woman!"

Fergus grabbed his stomach and almost threw up. Obviously his nausea had not yet passed.

The bearded guards cracked up and looked at each other like a couple of very happy pranksters.

"They just kid around. Yes, stupid, not even funny. I sorry, my friend," Habib smiled and turned to Fergus. "I know you sick, we apologise, we no have other choice. Here, take this, make you good very soon." Habib handed Fergus a pill and passed him a fresh bottle of ice-cold water from the silver tray.

"No, don't!" Fabiola screamed at Fergus.

"Don't worry, Miss, it just aspirin. Why we poison our guests? We know you have headache, so we bring you aspirin," Habib shrugged.

Fabiola considered that for a moment. Why indeed would they poison their hostages? She glanced at the miserable Fergus who fought not to vomit.

"But I don't have to take it, right? 'Cause I feel fine already," she tested Habib.

Habib considered that for a moment, shrugged and said: "Sure, as you like, Miss."

Fabiola nodded at Fergus who gladly took the pill and washed it down with the cold water. "Ahh," he sighed with relief.

"Nice water, yes? *Oasis* mineral water, *Yomani Springs*! It nice and cold, yes? You see, Miss, my friend with funny glasses better already," Habib grinned.

"I can't wait to see if you still call him your friend once he stops feeling so sick and starts pestering you with his urgent appointments in World of Warcraft."

"World of who? What world?" Habib asked, genuinely and thoroughly ignorant.

In his bed in The Lab, two weeks after that hung-over morning in Al Awil, Fergus smiled, remembering how that morning, despite his lousy condition, a slightly unreasonable thought had crossed his mind: *"How can this man not know anything about World of Warcraft? Where the heck are we, really, in godforsaken middle of nowhere?"* Obviously, at that moment it had not yet dawned on Fergus that they really were in godforsaken middle of nowhere – in some uncharted back street in Yoman where no Google Street View cameras would appear until Fergus hit retirement age, if even then.

Tossing and turning in his bed, Fergus tried to think about the next few days, so that in the morning he could wrap up his report to the men in stupid ties as soon as possible and go home. But as he reflected on how he'd spent his days in captivity, he realised that the details got increasingly blurry with each passing day, and specific pieces of information seemed to elude him. Not because anything was wrong with him, it was just that it had all been so boring. One would think that being kidnapped would be exciting, but, heck, it had amounted to nothing more than two weeks of tear-wrenching tedium.

Fergus had had to share the room with his annoying sister, he most definitely remembered that with perfect clarity. Well, maybe that was a special kind of Yomanian torture these guys employed. After the first morning, the door was left unlocked – after all, the toilet and shower were outside, a bit further down the corridor... And the bearded Arab pranksters were always outside, anyway, guarding their room as well as keeping an eye on the bathroom door.

Fergus and Fabiola were only allowed to shower once every three days. Their captors said it was because water was scarce. Fergus liked the arrangement, but his sister called that a special kind of Yomanian torture.

The fact that they were not allowed to leave the old sandstone building even if there was nothing to do in there also contributed to constant boredom. All the rooms Fergus suspected might be interesting were always locked. Not that he was looking for anything in particular, apart from perhaps a computer room with state-of-the-art machines and a fibre optic internet connection so broadband you could fly a jumbo jet through it. He had to talk to Moolly urgently... before it was too late.

Fergus, now staring at the ceiling in The Lab, remembered how he pestered Habib constantly with that, even tried to explain to him what *Massively Multiplayer Online Role-Playing Games* were all about and how infinitely cool and impressive they were. At the time he was surprised how completely disinterested the Arab terrorist was in orcs and gnomes, but now, two weeks later, Fergus seemed to understand that terrorists were apparently more interested in large-calibre machine guns and surface-to-air missiles than epic two-handed swords.

Despite all that, one day Habib had obviously had enough and he finally took the boy into one of those locked rooms, which in fact turned out to have several terminally outdated computers in it. He let Fergus play some games while he worked on something on his own laptop. There was no internet connection, though. Still, the computers would have been a welcome diversion, were it not for the unfortunate fact that the clumsy machine Fergus was allowed to use was ancient, the games were silly and simplistic, while the boy was still plagued by his inability to get in touch with the Hordecorerz.

Fergus remembered that the next day Habib apologised for not having better games, but talked to him a bit about programming. That was surprising, as Fergus hadn't thought Habib knew anything about computers. He knew a lot, though. Apparently Fergus himself was talented as well, because after just a couple of days with Habib he seemed to understand far more about the arcane inner workings of the machines than he would ever have thought possible. His online games were suddenly no longer quite so all-important, perhaps also because he couldn't play every day and so he was getting used to not being logged in all the time.

That was about it. No torture. No political or religious propaganda. Well, except for those damn morning prayers that the guards outside their room never forgot about, how terribly annoying. Nobody wanted anything from him... Well, they *did* beg him to *please* shut up a number of times, but nobody actually cut out his tongue – though the bearded men guarding their room did caress the sheaths of their jambiyas lovingly quite often, now that he thought about it...

Oh, and Fergus also hated the food. Those damn Arabs mostly gave them vegetables, some kind of Middle-Eastern bread, tea, and biscuits, which annoyed Fabiola even more than him. She'd frequently remind Habib that he'd promised her lobster, but he'd keep saying that honest freedom fighters didn't have as much money as Osama Bin Laden, after which he'd laugh stupidly at his own pitiful joke. As far as Fergus was concerned, that about wrapped up the torture he and his sister had been subjected to.

Then, after a couple of weeks in the boring old Arab mansion, one sunny (what else was there in Yoman?) afternoon, Habib told Fergus he was going home, which did not make Fergus half as glad as he believed was appropriate.

In his bed in The Lab, Fergus turned on his stomach and started letting go, hoping these clowns in The Lab did not expect a story full of suspense, sudden twists, revelations, precious insights and impossibly useful and precise infor- mation... And even though he was still somewhat worried, doubting that what he remembered would satisfy those nitpickers, he finally managed to fall asleep.

20. Cynicism Management

The first official *Cynicism Management* rehearsal would have been fine if only Bogomyr Yadvig was there. However, he was not attending this solemn occasion "because the sun was still out", as he had said over the mobile phone (a fantastically convenient gadget for making dubious excuses).

Finnegan took a deep audible breath. Now he suddenly gleaned every conceivable aspect of how terrible it felt to find out you sucked at impersonating the "leader" of anything at all. Because if you were as unreasonable as Finnegan sometimes was, you'd soon imagine that every one of your accomplices depended on you to somehow point the way towards meaningful results. Of course, in the dimension most reasonable people refer to as "reality", Finnegan's accomplices didn't give a flying fuck at all – they just wanted him to stop whining already, get something done if he really wanted to, and if not, just go for a fucking beer and not be a pain in their collective behind.

However, Finnegan, the undying closet melancholic-romantic type (who laboured on appearing as cynical as possible), felt, in a particularly emotional manner befitting a teary-eyed teenager in a pitch-black outfit and with black fingernails, that he would be so much happier if he could just be an invisible yet influential troublemaker – not responsible for anything yet incredibly successful; not subject to any annoying publicity yet still revered. It would also be convenient if he were rich and if he didn't have to put up with any difficult bandmates. But that was just so awfully boring. He desperately needed band members he could pester. Besides, he honestly believed his current "project" was his greatest effort to date, so he had to make it work... And without his band it would just be him, his MIDI keyboard, and his utterly unimpressive laptop. Even if he painted both contraptions blood red with evil black stripes and glued infernal horns and a bunch of tentacles on them and called them Beelzebub and Yog-Sothoth, they would still be pretty impotent, especially as far as the musical audience consisting of three depressed certifiable misfits Finnegan was most probably addressing was concerned. For crying out loud, the mummified Charlie Watts and his poor excuse for a drum set, which was so pathetic that any drummer who had not been a grandpa around the time the wheel was invented would shrug away from it, both looked far more impressive than Finnegan with his little computer and his inconsequential light-weight four-octave MIDI keyboard without any *heaviness* to call their own ever would.

That made Finnegan think: by all means he had to get his hands on a hefty analogue synthesiser from the olden days. It didn't matter if the cumbersome artefact worked or not, because any software synth programmed for the purpose of emulating your random piece of analogue gear and available instantly from your local retailer or favourite torrent site would replace and outdo it a hundredfold – at least on stage, especially if he considered the profound importance of *handiness* of the gear he had to transport to his live acts. However, if the artefact was vintage, tangibly analogue (that is, wooden, reeking of mildew, huge and weighing a ton), it would be far more impressive than a boring piece of computer software nobody would be able to lay an inquisitive eye on. That was the very reason why people lugged a mellotron with them on tour: to display it onstage! Not because mellotrons couldn't be properly sampled and stuffed on a hard drive, but because they were mysterious and haunting, nostalgic and retro, large and heavy, imposing and grand... And they were made even more consequential by all the cobwebs and wormholes (in actual *wood*, not space-time), all of it hinting at history and nostalgia at its best and most intriguing. Indeed, if Steven Wilson of the *Porcupine Tree* could appreciate the sentiment, Finnegan could too: his stage rig had

to be monolithic and eerie and complicated! So he figured
he also had to invest in some random multi-coloured LED
lights that he could install around his flimsy electronics to
make the whole setup look highly complex and enigmatic,
like the bridge of the starship Enterprise... Plus some more
wires and devices and incomprehensibly complicated-looking
cryptic knobs and dials and counters and meters, everything
properly lit up in suitably mystic colours like a bunch of
satanic Christmas trees using perversely mutated fireflies as
their light source. Then Finnegan and his concert rig would
finally look like something worth paying attention to while he
performed live!

As the actual onlookers usually couldn't tell a bass
guitar from a hi-hat anyway, not even if their lives depended
on it, Finnegan figured most of them could probably be
mesmerised into adoration and blind subservience by a cheap
but seemingly high-tech set design, especially if Finnegan
somehow managed to pour buckets of blood over the whole
installation while pretending to play the damned thing in the
process.

"Oh, snap out of it," Finnegan told himself, "This is not
the time or the place for such ideas. Who cares about set design now,
first we must make this band work! We need to wring a flawless
performance out of everyone involved! We should soon be able to
play so annoyingly well that no one in their right mind will have
the nerve to call us amateurs!" swore all the beer in Finnegan.

Sadly, this honourable goal involved some leadership
skills and resolute decision-making that Finnegan had not yet
exhibited to date. Oh! the endless throes of a severely tortured
artist.

"This time around I have to establish some kind of a system,"
Finnegan told himself. Even as early as after the first semi-suc-
cessful rehearsal, he knew his band was going nowhere fast if
he failed to play his role correctly and pay absolute attention
to the workings of it all while simultaneously acting adorably
unconcerned and thus avoid being seen by his band members
as the anal retentive neurotic wreck that he really was. So he

pretended to be unconcerned that Bogomyr failed to show up at the very first band practice session they tried to organise – in spite of his own previous rambling about the importance of jam sessions and other creative gatherings. It seemed that the sun was a stronger force than Bogomyr's need to actually put the money where his mouth had been.

"OK," Finnegan said out loud to no one in particular, "maybe Bogomyr is simply not a morning person." That was nothing Finnegan had not already encountered previously. Actually, a few years ago he himself had not exactly been in the *I-wake-up-when-the-Muslims-pray-fajr* league, so who was he to judge. Admittedly, that had changed recently, when he became increasingly obsessed with the constant thought of his impending doom. That stuck in his mind and made him somewhat of a workaholic (nope, he wasn't ill or anything, he was just a bit of a hypochondriac and a realist, and he also started noticing the first grey hairs on his head... he wanted to make his time on this awful penal colony of a planet count somehow... and he was a godless son of a bitch, so he could seek no solace in the promise of pubs everlasting).

But then, at these first rehearsals, Finnegan's plot even thickened. Here he was, spilling his guts into the last project he believed he'd ever undertake, and now he had to come to terms with such mundane issues as everyone's quirks and idiosyncrasies. Why couldn't people be more agreeable? Why couldn't they refrain from exhibiting any will of their own? Finnegan supposed that was just too much to ask for.

Kip Ducker knew how to play. Very much so. But lately, despite the fact that he was a heavy metal guitarist, he started obsessing over the idea that all he wanted from life was a little bit of peace and quiet. Rock 'n' roll bands were obviously no sensible way of trying to attain that holiest of Grails. Despite that, Kip had still let himself be charmed into taking part in a rock 'n' roll band regardless of his yearning for solitude and serenity. Probably that was due to his simultaneous favourable disposition towards Viking-like rituals involving skulls full of wine spilled all over oneself while wearing a horned helmet, however inconsistent and incompatible that may seem. But, in accordance with some twisted logic even he himself failed to understand entirely, Kip had made it clear from the very beginning that putting on live shows at suspicious venues frequented by forgotten inbred cousins of village idiots was a terrible waste of time and that he'd have none of that. Neither Finnegan nor Kip knew why it was, then, that Kip strived to be a heavy metal guitarist at all, and neither did their band – for where did dubious progressive rock bands play if not in dark cellars frequented by a few miserable musicians and a pair of pompous self-appointed music connoisseurs, anyway. Furthermore, Kip kept saying that "he was thinking about not playing live much anymore, anyway, because he was getting too old". As confusing and annoying as all of this was, especially in light of the fact that otherwise the balding Kip hadn't felt the urge to say anything much, Finnegan tried to move on. He attributed Kip's existential problems to looming male menopause.

Largo Cabaleri, on the other hand, made a show of sacrificing himself for the project selflessly, and was available for rehearsals until nine that evening. That was probably also because of the entertaining encounter that had taken place in the morning. However, Largo kept emphasising that his being there was an act of a thoroughly charitable person. He also underlined maybe four or six times that he didn't believe in rehearsing all that much because rehearsing took the sincerity out of music. "Tell that to *Franz Liszt* or *Terry Bozzio*," Finnegan thought but kept his mouth shut due to his recent meditations on the urgent need to improve his skills in the field of tolerance.

Amalia was not a problem. Just give her a shot of vodka and she was happy. That was quite reassuring in Finnegan's mind. It really was: at least he could count on her being herself. She was awfully good at pretending she didn't see (or care) how complicated and irrational people were and Finnegan actually envied her. She even managed to achieve that without being too "constructive" or too "agreeable" or "sunny" or, god forbid, without referring to any "positive energy" that any and every lunatic these days always seemed to refer to when they couldn't think of any other moronic thing to say. The occasional hiccup in Amalia's performance could easily be attributed to the general chill of the first rehearsal and the absence of the missing link: the crazy Ukrainian who hated the light.

Randy, however... Hell yeah, Randy could play bass when he wanted to. But for the time being he didn't seem to want to. All he seemed to care about at the moment was having fun and rolling joints, which took a heavy toll on the fluency of Finnegan's new Machiavellian phrases written in 33/16 time. Therefore Finnegan decided to lighten up and present something easy, something *"ordinary"*, something in 7/4 and 9/4 time to his crew.

Even though Bogomyr hadn't been there to witness most of the presentation – he arrived just as they were wrapping up the first rehearsals – the band fared reasonably well, all things considered. They constructed *Touring My Backyard*, which soon bordered on presentable if not quite good by the time when Bogomyr finally joined the effort. They also started working on Life Malignant, another track brought by Finnegan with him from the incredibly optimistic streets of Kirkwall and imported to Slovenia where it strangely fit right in.

So Finnegan, actually quite happy with what they were able to scrap together on such short notice, told Kip, Amalia, Largo, Randy and Bogomyr who had just popped his head through the door that it was time to take a break and head up to Birman's for a drink. At that moment he didn't care what anyone might think of his organisational skills. Truth be told, Finnegan just had to live a little and not be such a monumental control freak: yes, their drummer might not have known *Black Page* by Frank Zappa flawlessly nor would he have been able to read the sheet music for it had he ever laid eyes on the cryptic thing. And yes, maybe their Australian guitarist wanted to tell them he wouldn't be at all happy if he was expected to breathe some much-needed life into the

Slovenian squat scene. So what.

Little did Kip know how right he was to feel that way: the Slovenian squat scene in fact consisted of two former army barracks that eight plastered punks had pinched from the terminally decomposing former Yugoslav Army long ago in order to abuse the facilities while establishing their exclusive little businesses and keep everybody else out – especially musicians who had heard of more than three chords in their lives, because such abominations had no business whatsoever anywhere in the vicinity of the three-chord punk realms.

After the first rehearsals, the band was happy to kick back, relax and enjoy a couple of beers, sandwiches, spritzers and glasses of Merlot. After a bit of a bad vibe he had blamed on lousy bourbon in the morning, Finnegan avoided whiskey for the time being, at least until Boris managed to procure a decent single-malt Scotch. Boris had promised to do so during the reckless exaltation of the previous evening, because as soon as Finnegan laid his eyes on the unseemly American booze, he started criticising it ceaselessly (even in spite of continually drinking it with beer, no less). So Boris made a stupid promise to stop Finnegan from whining. Alas, Boris was not a man who liked to go back on his word and he hated that sometimes – especially when he was expected to keep drunken promises he didn't remember making.

Speaking of Boris, he was currently nowhere to be seen. As he was only their "producer", Boris hadn't joined *Cynicism Management* for rehearsals – he was pretty sure he'd hear far too much of their "artwork" in the future. Finnegan, suspecting himself of being too loud and perhaps even a little too intense the previous evening, felt a sudden urge to check in with the guy, so he asked Beeba where her husband was.

"He had a cat in the morning, so he didn't do no work. So he must work now, in studio," Beeba explained.

"A cat? He had to take care of cats?" Finnegan frowned and turned to Amalia. "That's weird," he told her, "I've always believed I'm a very good judge of character, and I'd never peg Boris as much of a cat person. He strikes me as a barbecued lamb aficionado. You know, our kind of a guy."

"No, you don't understand," Amalia explained, adopting a bit of a teacher's attitude that must have rubbed off on her at the university where she pretended to teach English. Finnegan found that unbecoming, but her explanation was quite amusing. "Beeba means Boris had a hangover. The Slovenian word for *hangover* is... Well, something I can't remember right now, it's pretty hard to pronounce for normal people. But anyway, when you translate it literally, it means tomcat. Cute, don't you agree?"

"Quite endearing and very expressive. Yes... I can see how you can feel like a mean old tomcat after an all-night kitty hunt when you've had too much bad bourbon the previous evening. Or, should you happen to encounter such a tomcat, he might use you as a claw sharpener, which is exactly how I feel in the mornings occasionally," Finnegan elaborated.

He turned back to Beeba again: "Oh, so Boris was *tired*. What's he working on? Anything interesting?"

"He mixing *The Bottles*, that ensemble that making him nervous," Beeba said, bestowing a cute innocent smile on Finnegan.

"Oh, *The Bottles*! Yes, sure I remember. He kept mentioning them rather obsessively last night, that was quite a laugh, it was," Finnegan made another lame attempt at small talk before remembering he should keep the dialogue relatively simple for Beeba.

Beeba just smiled and went about her business of tending the bar, not minding Finnegan's gratuitous eloquence at all – the things she'd seen in her life and come to terms with would render Finnegan speechless. Too bad she couldn't communicate all that well: her wisdom and experience might have even been able to inspire some useful lyrics in Finnegan, if not a complete collection of lengthy hippy symphonies and pointless, mostly unreadable blog entries.

Finnegan stared at his beer aimlessly, not really feeling

any better after his casual and inconsequential exchange with
Beeba. He suddenly got a nasty feeling that perhaps Boris
was avoiding them, refraining from joining them this time
because Finnegan had perhaps been somewhat too tiresome
the previous evening. It all added up – ! Save for the obvious
fact that Boris didn't give a shit about Finnegan and his
tiresomeness: he just wanted to get some work done in order
to rid himself of the accursed band he'd been producing as
soon as humanly possible and then perhaps grab a weiss beer
or three. Preferably in blissful silence.

Nevertheless, it was always the same with Finnegan. He
often got in thorough personal trouble with himself and ended
up with a moral hangover. (This was also how Slovenians,
who were obviously familiar with this peculiar state of mind,
would refer to the phenomenon. However, they referred to it
in Slovenian, of course, so the phrase, if translated literally,
would mean *moral tomcat* in English. "*Now that's something
worth remembering*," Finnegan thought).

The thing with Finnegan (which he was aware of but
found almost impossible to control) was that each and every
time – no matter how solemnly he had promised himself he'd
refrain from getting too intense or too excited or too wasted –
the whole routine would always play out the same way. First
he'd get a tad lubricated. Then he'd get really loud, overly
enthusiastic and increasingly elated, feeling a sudden need to
embrace the entire world, which he often tried to accomplish
by hugging everyone, telling them he loved them, and by
imbibing more of the alcohol that the world had to offer. His
elation then became euphoria that usually surfaced around
the time his memory took a bit of a dive. Finnegan never did
anything drastic. He'd usually just shoot his mouth off ceaselessly, and perhaps finally take a Superman nap on the table
when he was at his worst.

However, in the mornings, once the euphoria had
subsided and transformed wickedly and malevolently into
abysmally bad breath, headache, thirst, and even depression
in cases of truly abusive and manic behaviour that had gone

on for several days, Finnegan would suddenly start suspecting himself of being obnoxious the previous evening; of being far too loud; of talking too much; of saying a whole lot of stupid things; of acting like an asshole; of coming up with particularly weird and idiotic ideas; of making things up as he went and of hatching highly implausible plans; of embarrassing himself and many of those around him; of being a drunken lunatic; and so on. The less he remembered, the viler he imagined he must have been. All of this, of course, was completely true, as Finnegan was right – he usually managed to do all of those things, especially make a fool of himself. However, that was it, more or less, because even though he would sometimes like to think differently, Finnegan was simply not wired to be a real troublemaker – at his worst and most annoying he was just an imbecile and then he would take a nap.

There was, however, one thing Finnegan was very wrong about: while he usually felt that everybody cared about his infantile behaviour, even wondered about it and beat himself up about it sometimes, in reality nobody gave a rat's ass about it: in the best cases they would laugh with him, while in the worst case scenarios it was more like they laughed *at* him. His self-absorbed state of mind seldom interested anyone else, as others tended to be preoccupied with their own lives.

Despite the fact that rationally Finnegan knew all of this and worked on actually seeing it that way, he still failed to shake the habit of checking in with everyone involved in one of his "previous evenings" the next day, so as to make sure everything was okay and that he hadn't been too much of an annoyance. (In reality he often *was* a major annoyance, but people either ignored such things, didn't remember, didn't care, or just wouldn't tell *him* about it – but might tell someone else in order to have a laugh).

When Finnegan finally managed to put an end to his obsessive deliberations on his own neurotic behaviour, he took an abundant gulp of his beer and looked around, trying to calm down after the intense trials of the first rehearsals and the unfortunate fact that he couldn't check in with Boris.

The shaky Scotsman saw that Ray Kosmick had already made himself comfortable at one of the tables. Ray greeted Largo far too enthusiastically, as if they hadn't seen each other for at least a decade. Apparently his pleasure meter was way up. He hung out with another character who looked like an unnaturally well-preserved relic from the 1960s, with uncannily smooth skin and a dreamy spiritual gaze that would usually be interpreted as madness by the less-than-spiritual Finnegan. The guy wore a garish hippy outfit and sported a healthy flush and long hair that must have been raven black at one time, but which was now sprinkled with countless strands of silver (despite the fact that he was obviously stoned out of his mind, this character had such a gentlemanly demeanour about him that something as mundane as *strands of grey* was out of the question). It looked like he had somehow managed to be under far less stress than Kip Ducker, who, at the sight of the old hippy's abundant silver locks, scratched his bald spot surreptitiously and muttered a couple of inaudible Australian curses under his breath.

However, something about this guy hinted at purpose-fully concealed cunning, piercing intelligence and clandestine sarcasm, so Finnegan didn't pass off the temporally displaced hippy as another new-age lunatic just yet. As he finished his beer and ordered another one, the Scotsman suddenly felt much better and more ready and willing to take on another evening. Just in time, because the hippy decided to start a conversation.

"Greetings, gentlemen and lady," Ray's silver-haired friend droned as the members of *Cynicism Management* finally started homing in on the tables after the short pause behind the bar, and kissed Amalia's hand. "And hello to you, sir," he immediately turned to Finnegan, "My name is Willit. Ray tells me you're rehearsing here. You're Amalia's old friend from Scotland, I hear?" Willit inquired cordially.

Amalia said: "Hey, Willit, what's up?" and sat down at the next table.

Largo pulled up a chair next to Ray and ordered a small

beer cheerfully.

Kip sat down opposite Amalia and told Beeba he'd like a beer and a sandwich.

Randy wasn't there at the moment: he'd slipped away when they'd walked from the rehearsal room towards the bar area in order to attend an emergency consultation with a reefer in the bushes outside.

Bogomyr automatically received his habitual glass of Merlot from Beeba and stood by the bar, waiting to sit down with Finnegan and discuss his inability to rehearse during daylight. He looked apologetic due to his absence from the rehearsals. Admittedly Finnegan, no matter how reasonable and easy-going he strived to appear, had a way of sometimes coming across as passive aggressive towards those he felt let him down in some way. Truth be told, his righteous indignation, no matter how slight and well-concealed, was definitely irritating. But this time Bogomyr obviously felt genuinely guilty, probably because he remembered his yesterday's litany about the importance of jam sessions and other creative gatherings, which he'd meant seriously, on top of everything.

"Aye... Amalia, Randy and I, we go way back," Finnegan smiled at the Englishman. "I hear you're from Birmingham?"

"That's right. I'm a kind of an artist too, though I have to make a living as a producer of reality TV shows. Yeah, I know, don't look at me like that – everybody's got to pay their bills." Willit nodded, emptying his cup of tea. "Beeba, may I have another?" he inquired.

"Black tea, with rum or with no rum?" Beeba asked.

"Do pour some rum in, dear," Willit smiled.

"Rum?" inquired Finnegan roguishly.

"Yes... It seems that some Slovenians like to drink black tea and rum during the winter, but I've extended the use of this heart-warming beverage to the rest of the year. Earl Grey with rum. I find it very convenient when I need to pull myself together."

"How incredibly inventive," Finnegan grimaced doubtfully.

"Oh, I do apologise, I bore you while you stand there...

Would you care to sit down?" Willit gestured towards the empty seat available at their table.

"I'd be happy to..." Finnegan turned around and looked at Bogomyr who was brooding over his glass of Merlot, "But first I should discuss something with Bogomyr. Talk to you later, OK?"

"Absolutely, we'll be here, right?" Willit turned towards Ray as if to confirm the plan. Ray slapped Willit's back and said: "Ya! The sister of my wife is on a visit, so they very like to be alone and don't want that I would come home too soon. They like to chat and chat and chat with no men around."

"Hey, Amalia," Finnegan turned to his most precious bandmate, who was sitting with Kip and sipping her spritzer at the next table, "I'm going to sit down over there with Bogomyr to discuss some... Strategic issues."

"Sure, hon," Amalia said, beaming, "Kip and I will have some reckless fun over here, won't we, laddie?" she leaned over the table and punched Kip in the shoulder.

"Yay," Kip cheered while yawning, raising his fist and acting like a feeble old man rather than a vicious and thoroughly reckless metalhead.

Finnegan and Bogomyr, in need of some privacy, sought refuge at the gloomy table in the remote corner of the room where the dilapidated Tinka and Stanko had tried to enjoy their drinks in peace the day before. When Tinka and Stanko came in again later – just like they did almost every day – they were extremely upset when they saw that what they thought of as "their table" had already been taken.

21. Interlude:
Life Malignant

Life Malignant was one of the tracks Finnegan had already started working on in Kirkwall. It wasn't one of his merrier tunes. It all came to him – melody as well as lyrics – when he opened his eyes wide like a madman at 4 a.m. for the third night in a row, worried that he might drop dead any second. He hated such experiences, but at least he could write funny little ditties about it.

The resulting piece was an ode to that very familiar but still unpleasant foreboding that the Grim Reaper might decide to google your name at any moment and check your Facebook wall to see what you've been up to these days and then sprinkle his shit all over it. It was about waking up in the middle of the night with a gnawingly inconvenient worm of a thought in your mind saying to you that everything had been in vain... That it was all downhill from here and you were doomed, that your heart was about to choke on itself, and that you were a good-for-nothing son of a bitch whose music sucked donkey balls.

Finnegan struggled against such bouts of anxiety by writing even more music and lyrics that sucked donkey balls. Here goes this one:

LIFE MALIGNANT
[https://soundcloud.com/cynicism-management/
life-malignant-augmented]

Every day and every weeknight
I get more cancerous
Each endeavour every stage fright
Gets me cancerous

Every weeknight
Every stage fright

Every time I close my eyes
I get more cancerous
Sometimes I get caught by surprise
And get more cancerous

Every weeknight
Is the same plight

Sleeping pills say let go
But reason murmurs don't know
It's out there stalking me
And it wants me cancerous

I'm complaining whining pining
Pondering this curse
But I go on, although declining
Shitting long-shat turds

Every weeknight
Everyday plight

On that fateful Sunday – during their first rehearsals at which Finnegan presented this fabulous tune to everyone for the first time – the band members seemed quite happy with the composition. Largo even contributed a little drum solo towards the end. Finnegan applauded, glad to see that Largo was enjoying and actually involving himself in the creative process. Kip didn't seem to care much, though, while Randy sought comfort in fumbling the ear plugs in his pocket, which could be quite beneficial to his hearing if Largo got too excited on the drums, especially the cymbals and his damn snare drums, which he hammered on like a heavyweight blacksmith on methamphetamine. Only Amalia asked what she was supposed to do while Largo had his fun. "Perform butt naked exotic dances?" proposed Bogomyr when he arrived at Boris's just after sunset.

22. Suburbia

Slovenia was infamous for its hilariously small municipalities, each one sporting its own entrepreneurial mayor –
usually a car salesman, a local eccentric with too much time on
his hands, or, in the best case scenario, the former headmaster
of the local primary school intended for some 32 kids.
However, that wasn't a rule: in 2010, a certain seaside town
in Slovenia was so advanced as to elect the first *black* mayor
in the history of the country. The man also happened to be a
doctor, of all things. For a day or two this was a notable event,
and it made *CNN* news. However, some municipalities were
even more advanced: heart surgeons ran for mayors there, and
if they were elected they doubled as officials while they still
worked in the local hospitals, operating on poor unsuspecting
patients while daydreaming about their next political move
that would ensure as much profit for themselves as possible.
Obviously Slovenian supermen could easily do many responsible jobs simultaneously, if only they could also rake in a lot
of cash and influence for being in three places at once.

Despite boasting their own mayors, armies of coffee-
swigging bureaucrats, and municipal budgets that the local
political entrepreneurs and their best pals could steal from,
many of these administrative units were inhabited by no more
than a few hundred souls. Apparently every Slovenian hamlet
aspired to constitute its own municipality. Even if that's an
exaggeration, it's not far from the truth – the two smallest
municipalities in terms of the population had around 350
people each, and seven of them had less than 1000 inhabitants.
Granted, while 270,000 people lived in the most monumental
one (the capital), 110,000 in the second largest, and about
50,000 in the third and fourth most colossal municipalities in
Slovenia, most of them were indeed inhabited by only 5,000

people, give or take a couple thousand. With the population of roughly 2.1 million, in 2010 Slovenia was divided into 210 municipalities. Now what would numerologists have to say about that?

This arrangement was justified by political wisecracks like decentralisation, equality and self-sufficiency, but to any sentient being in and around the Milky Way it was clear that the situation was the result of the fact that every Slovenian disliked his or her neighbour, every backwater parish had to be more important than the next one, and they all coveted unhindered access to the cookie jar. In any case, such fragmentation definitely failed to contribute anything to streamlining, practicality, and prudent use of the national budget. But disputes, conflicts, grudges, and jealousy between regions, cities, towns, villages, streets, street corners, families, groups and individuals were the Slovenian national sport, so this phenomenon was, more or less, just a natural state of affairs in this country.

As far as the population makeup of the microscopic rural administrative units was concerned, 95 % of them were pensioners, people with jobs in other slightly larger municipalities, destitute peasants, terminal drunks, teenage binge drinkers with suicidal tendencies, kids who would soon become teenage binge drinkers with suicidal tendencies, plus a couple of junkies and a few abominable freaks who preferred heavy metal to Alpine dancing songs. Some of the inhabitants, though, were sleazy entrepreneurs, wannabe politicians, born-again capitalists and outright thieves, in comparison with whom their role model, Del Boy from *Only Fools and Horses*, looked like a downright saint.

Slovenia was also infamous for inquisitive ladies staring out their windows (if they could see past all the plant life, of course).

"I wonder what that blue van is doing in front of the church?" the Mayor's wife remarked to no one in particular, pushing the curtain aside and peering through the window over a flowerpot brimming with the most luxuriant cascades of plenteous plants in the whole village. Or, so she liked to think – any lady of any house in Slovenia, worth anything at all, seemed to be fanatical about her excessive collection of inutile decorative flora.

The woman's husband – an exhaust pipe salesman and self-proclaimed politician, elected as the mayor of the midget municipality where the Rock 'n' Roll Tavern was located (he was the only candidate, and legally he only needed a single vote to be elected: his own) – just puffed: "Would you stop staring through the window for once? Jesus."

The Mayor's wife, who couldn't possibly tear herself from her observation post, could hardly conceal her curiosity. The Mayor, who couldn't possibly tear himself from the sports page, couldn't have cared less. But then the Mayor's wife came up with a cunning plan and said: "Maybe their exhaust pipe has burst? That van looks like it's seen better days... And it's just standing there."

The Mayor peeked at her over his newspaper and grumbled wearily: "Ha, nice try. I'm not going over there just so you can tag along and stare at strangers. Besides, it's probably just the workmen. I hear the Reverend is having some repairs done at the church. "

"But they aren't workers. They look like six strange women!"

"*Six strange women*?" the Mayor put the newspaper away, "I wonder what the Reverend's up to..."

"My, my," the Mayor's wife elaborated, leaving a lot of room for interpretation.

"Perhaps I'd better check this out then," decided the Mayor, stretched his arms, scratched his beer belly, grabbed the armrests, pushed, grunted, and plucked his considerable behind out of his beloved sofa. The reason for this sudden burst of activity was that he remembered he might as well slip out for a couple of cold ones in the bar next to the church while he was at it. After all, it had been a long late-summer Sunday, and he'd had to listen to the wife fidgeting around the house, cleaning and rearranging stuff and straightening chairs all day long out of sheer boredom, and then nagging at him for just sitting around and not helping. If he'd ever deserved a couple of cold ones, it was today.

"I'm coming with you. I should speak with the Reverend, anyway," the wife said.

"*Oh, hell, no!*" the Mayor thought, but instead muttered: "I'm sure you should," because he didn't feel like listening to even more complaints about how impossible he was.

No matter how small, every Slovenian village had a church, a couple of taverns or bars, a pizza place, and a community hall in which the local choir, folklore, and theatre group rehearsed. Every hamlet worth mentioning also boasted its own Alpine dancing songs band, while the most obligatory feature was its very own fire station with its very own firemen, at whose parties – the infamous Slovenian firefighters' merrymakings – these bands (and similar bands from the surrounding villages) would regularly perform while the firefighters and the rest of the men got drunk, pinched the gals' butts, and got into drunken brawls. The more advanced Slovenian villages also boasted their own brass bands that usually consisted of the amateur firemen doubling as amateur musicians and amateur musicians doubling as amateur firemen. Musical proficiency didn't play much of a role in any of this, and such sweetly out-of-tune bands were often even sought-after and preferred to those obnoxious fancy ensembles they had in the big cities, fie on them.

Every Slovenian village also had its local painter, local poet, local former but legendary athlete, local loose woman, local singer-songwriter, local disgruntled dipsomaniac who kept quarrelling with everyone (and, if no one suitable was in range, getting into fights with his invisible pals), local world champion of accordion (who was sometimes, but not always, the main attraction of the local Alpine dancing song band besides the half-naked local exhibitionist trollop in a quasi-traditional folk-whore outfit), as well as a few red-nosed hunters, the aforementioned drunken volunteer firemen, regular pickled civilians, and the village idiot. The same held true, of

course, of the suburban hellhole where the Bitches currently
loitered around their van and where many of the said indis-
pensable local colourful characters had urgent appointments
in the bar by the church.

As the sun was gradually getting ready to drop behind
the hills that lined the horizon, the bar near the church
was already full of stubborn characters who refrained from
frequenting Boris and Beeba's because they resented the
choice of music there. So much so that they'd rather put up
with the bar by the church, which was far more unpleasant in
the summer heat than the Rock 'n' Roll Tavern. Boris's was a
cool old townhouse with thick brick walls, while the bar by
the church was located in an oversized wooden garden shack
with a fenced beer garden covered with a plastic roof. The
roof's underside may have been overgrown with vines, but it
was plastic nevertheless. Well, whether plastic or platinum,
the whole setup was cosy when it rained, but scorching hot in
the summer sun. Naturally, the decaying wooden fence was
adorned with an abundance of potted plants, whose odorous
flowers only managed to make the place even stuffier. But,
on the other hand, the bar featured techno versions of Alpine
dancing songs as well as Slovenian covers (or insolent rip-offs)
of carefully selected Greek folk-pop masterpieces, recorded
with General MIDI sounds and sung by vulgar backwater
Slovenian songstresses whose tits showed even when they
went to their mothers' funerals. This was obviously far less
annoying to some people than Boris's incessant rock 'n' roll.
Apparently Boris had managed to perfect a very efficient
secret method of chasing away the people he didn't want to
tolerate as his customers. Admittedly, Boris didn't want *any
customers at all,* really, apart from, perhaps, a few carefully-se-
lected psychedelic lunatics, but he had to pay his bills like
everyone else. With his choice of music, Boris could at least
filter out the people unwilling to put up with rock 'n' roll (for
such characters were absolutely intolerable) before he would
even consider tolerating those who were left. At least until he
hit the jackpot and struck it rich as a musician, at which point

he'd probably shove just about everyone out the door.

The patrons of the bar near the church nodded stupidly to the idiotic 1/1 beat of a techno polka with lyrics focusing on the world-shakingly momentous issue of sturdy firemen and their long hoses. Despite the tranquil feeling that everything was right with the world, conjured up so effectively by this fine artistic achievement of a soundtrack, they grew increasingly perturbed by what six strange women of evidently foreign origins were doing standing around a blue van nobody had ever seen before. One of the red-nosed hunters saw the Mayor and his wife come out of their glaringly orange house and proposed: "Well, maybe the Mayor will know what this is all about".

The Mayor and his wife had seemingly come out for a leisurely but deliberate stroll towards the Bitches' van in order to scope out the strange visitors. Afterwards the Mayor intended to report to his electorate at the bar and enjoy a couple of ice-cold beers, whilst his wife would most likely seek out someone in order to gossip about it and get the Suburban Saga of the Mysterious Blue Van started.

When the Mayor was within earshot of the Bitches, he slowed down, raised his finger, aimed an inquisitive gaze at the sky and made a thoughtful expression, as if he'd forgotten something urgent that now had to be dealt with at once. He made an abrupt ninety-degree turn and headed towards the bar so resolutely his wife could barely keep up the pace. For a hair-raising second the Mayor even feared she might ruin his evening by accompanying him, but fortunately she slowed down, fell behind and yelled behind him: "I'm going to Jožica's, see you later!" She turned around and strode towards a violently violet house in the vicinity. The Mayor knew he was in the clear for at least a couple of hours.

The cerebrum of the village politics entered the bar. Four red-nosed hunters, two drunken volunteer firemen, the village idiot, the local world champion of accordion and his exhibitionist trollop who was currently not wearing her quasi-traditional folk-whore outfit but was (un)wrapped in sequined patches of cloth just as revealing as her stage outfit, greeted him with varying degrees of enthusiasm proportional to how giddy they already were. The others nodded in greeting – except for Stanko the disgruntled dipsomaniac who hated the Mayor for some reason that the Mayor couldn't quite put a finger on, but didn't really care about, as Stanko seemed to hate most people, including the imaginary chums of his whom he would argue with whenever he hit the bottle.

The bartender rubbed his greedy little hands and asked the Mayor: "What'll it be?"

"I'll have a cold one!" the Mayor exclaimed firmly.

The bartender smiled contentedly because he knew that resolute drinking equalled heavy drinking. The cleaning lady, perched on a rickety barstool at a small table near the entrance into the wooden shack, was nursing her coffee sullenly, all the while glancing at her cigarette that smouldered self-importantly in her ashtray and scribbling something in her notebook. She'd often stick to this routine throughout the day and until the end of the bar's opening hours, especially during the weekends, as she apparently had nothing better to do apart from waiting for people to make the mess she'd have to clean up after they'd finally gone home. She sighed wearily, because she knew that a lot of resolute drinking meant radically dirty toilets.

"So, what's up with those ladies over there?" one of the red-nosed hunters asked the Mayor who sat down at the empty table right in the middle of the hunters and the firemen in order to pay equal attention to both of the most prominent factions of his electorate.

"I'm not sure, I wanted to ask them what was going on, but they spoke English," the Mayor explained, "So I decided to come here and think about it first."

"I thought you spoke English fluently?" the tipsy exhibitionist trollop at the next table remarked innocently and smiled at the Mayor, mesmerising him with her moist cow-like gaze.

"Sure! When he brags about it on the local TV every

time he runs for mayor, he knows everything. Otherwise he doesn't know shit!" said Stanko, the local disgruntled dipso-maniac who sat alone in the far corner. The miserable geezer croaked, coughed, hawked, and launched a massive green-ish-yellow tubercular loogie into the corner flower pot. "He doesn't know shit, I tell you!" Stanko reiterated to no one in particular, and drooped his head.

"Shut the fuck up, Stanko," one of the stout young firemen told the old wreck.

"You shut up!" Stanko barked sharply, too messed up to think of a witty retort.

The Mayor was thoroughly familiar with his village and everyone in it. Even Stanko, his impotent though annoying nemesis whom no other villager liked very much, couldn't rattle him. The Mayor ignored the dilapidated saboteur routinely, employing his mayoral selective hearing. "Frankly, I'm not used to chatting in foreign languages much. Besides, I didn't want to make a lousy first impression, that's all. So I thought I'd rather ask you what you think. You know, because I might have a nice little business proposal."

Everybody looked at him eagerly except for Stanko, who hauled another lump of phlegm from the depths of his tar-ridden lungs and let it plummet to the ground with an audible plop. Stanko struggled out of his chair, got on his feet somehow, wobbled for a second as he concentrated on standing, and finally meandered out of the bar without bothering to pay for his drinks. The bartender didn't even flinch. He'd let Stanko run a tab, and Stanko was good for it – he'd always pay once per month when he received his pension, as he had no intention of getting banned from the bar nearest to his abode. The bartender also knew better than to stand in the way of Stanko's temper once Stanko was in one of his notorious moods. The bartender was glad to be rid of Stanko, too. He knew the old derelict would now fetch his wife Tinka, and together they'd wobble down the hill and get on with it at Boris's, where Tinka also cleaned the floors and toilets every forenoon before the place opened. Neither Stanko nor Tinka seemed to care if Boris kept playing his annoying rock 'n' roll bands on the stereo, as long as they could brood over their spritzers quietly at their gloomy table in the remote corner of the room.

When Stanko left the bar by the church, one of his invisible companions started bitching about that fucking idiot the Mayor, but for the time being Stanko managed to get him to shut the hell up and concentrated on walking. After about a hundred metres he regained some of his senses. He was relieved to be rid of the church-side sauna and the collection of suburban specimens sweating in it, and looked forward to a large number of cold spritzers in his dim, cool and quiet corner at Boris's where he and his wife Tinka regularly relaxed so thoroughly that they often unintentionally fell asleep there.

Another couple hundred metres further on, Stanko headed into a ramshackle house with dead grey walls that could have been white once upon a time. Apparently Stanko was not crazy about the eye-poppingly fluorescent facades that the other inhabitants of Suburbia seemed to adore so much. Either that or he couldn't be bothered by such mundane things as at least maintaining his dwelling in a reasonably passable condition, let alone investing in such criminal endeavours as painting his house poisonously pink.

The disgruntled old boozer found the door unlocked and, surprisingly, flashed a fleeting smile, glad that he wouldn't have to fish the keys out of his pockets and try to perform the very complex operation of unlocking it. He staggered inside without bothering to close the door behind him, leaned against the wall in the hallway and hollered: "Tinka! Where are you, are you home?"

"Where else would I be, you crazy old git!" she bawled from the kitchen with an audible slur and a voice of an angry crow stuck in a barrel of broken cymbals.

"Let's go for a spritzer!" Stanko was in a hurry.

"Yeah, yeah, I'm sick of working, anyway."

Tinka stubbed out her cigarette, pushed the tabloid she'd been studying aside, put her bottle of schnapps in the cabinet, stuffed the leftover salami, onions and garlic she'd been nibbling on in the fridge, grabbed her cigarettes, and went to nag at Stanko who waited in the hallway.

"You're drunk again! And you stink!"

"So are you. And so do you," Stanko cackled and grabbed her prominent behind rudely with both hands.

"Don't be vulgar, you old good-for-nothing!"

"You know you like it. Arrrr..." Stanko unwittingly impersonated a pirate and even looked like a particularly wretched one, minus a hook, a wooden leg and a parrot on his shoulder. He would have made a good one too, if his ship had happened to fly the Jolly Roger on oceans of cheap wine.

"Let's go before that Mayor fucker drinks up, I sure don't want to run into that cretin again today," Stanko begged.

"What do you have against that moron, anyway? He's just an exhaust pipe salesman, for Pete's sake," Tinka protested.

"God damn it, the very idea of him makes my blood boil. Just a salesman! Sure! If only he just sold stupid car parts. But no...! You don't realise that he's stealing from all of us, and everybody keeps voting for that retarded parasite..."

"Oh, crap, not that again..." Tinka was sick of Stanko and his constant fits of rage regarding village politics, so she said: "Let's go then, off with you!" Eager to avoid listening to more of Stanko's clamour, she struggled to look more alive and moved as nimbly as her hilarious rotund, stumpy physique allowed.

Tinka wobbled down the street like a plump little ball, her hair wildly unkempt. She was clad in seedy moth-eaten rags and bushels of bristles lined her upper lip. Stanko shuffled beside her, tall as a lamppost and just as thin, grey-haired, blurry-eyed, with yellow nicotine-stained moustache, scruffy beard and a crumpled old hat he'd just fetched from the hat rack in the hallway, and not for the sake of fashion, either – it was just that when he was drunk, he simply liked the way this mouldy headgear felt on his head. It held his brain in, somehow managed to ensure that the ground didn't sway too much, and kept his dandruff safe and his invisible pals in line. Whenever Stanko wore one of his repulsive greasy hats, it was a safe bet he was drunk.

Stanko and Tinka were a highly unusual couple, especially as far as Suburbia was concerned. What was even more unorthodox in the eyes of their fellow citizens was that despite their more or less constant intoxication, obscenity and indecency, they stuck by each other. They quarrelled constantly, but that was their hobby, their much-practiced routine, their way of getting through the day. One could almost go so far as to say they loved each other, which was far more than many of their more conventional and proper neighbours could brag about.

Be that as it may, they were still a couple of thoroughly disagreeable bastards by anyone's standards. Accordingly, as they meandered towards the blue van parked by the church, Stanko got all worked up again: "That's what the Mayor's been going on about..."

"What is? Oh, come on, screw that, not the Mayor again. Stanko, either fuck up that man, or fuck him over, or just plain old fuck him. Sometimes I have a feeling that is what you'd like to do, because you're totally obsessed with the guy."

"What the hell are you implying here?" Stanko protested.

"I'm implying that you can damn well do whatever the fuck you want, I really don't give a fuck. Just don't keep blabbering about that fat bastard and his fucking village politics," Tinka croaked in a very unladylike manner. She was loud enough to make Jožica – the resident of the violently violet house which the Mayor's wife was visiting at that very moment, fabricating the first outlines of the shocking news of the blue van and the loose women come to visit the Reverend – turn up her nose at Tinka, shake her head unappreciatively and close the window.

"You don't understand anything, woman!" Stanko went

on. "I'm sure that, as we speak, he's making plans about how
to screw us again – undoubtedly he'll come up with another
plan of how to make us earn more money for him, which he'll
then pocket without even flinching. Every time he comes into
the bar and starts lecturing everyone, it's about another one
of his business ideas. And now he's come up with something
about some foreign women..."

"What the hell are you talking about?"

"He saw these damn women and got all worked up
about it."

"What women?" Tinka waved her arms in front of
Stanko's face, getting very impatient with the old lunatic. Her
eyes were not what they used to be anymore, so she had not
yet noticed the Bitches over by the church. Her poor eyesight
may have been bad news for the floors and toilets she was
supposed to clean at Boris and Beeba's, but good news for
Tinka herself, because she was sick of looking at Suburbia but
not likely to move to the Caribbean during her lifetime.

"Jesus fucking Christ, I'm talking about the women by
the blue van over there," Stanko pointed. "Looks like they're
foreign."

"Oh, more foreigners?" Tinka raised her eyebrows,
"There have been far too many of those at Boris's lately. It's
getting so damn crowded. Boris's was so much better when
nobody but a couple of us locals ever drank there."

"Yeah, that's all we need. Fucking foreigners sitting at
our table," Stanko flailed his arms in protest.

"I know Boris needs the money, but letting all these
tourists hang out there, that's just wrong. Plain wrong," Tinka
voiced her expert opinion.

"Yeah! Foreigners. Tourists, even! Who the fuck needs
fucking tourists here!" Stanko said.

As the raggedy Stanko and rickety Tinka wobbled and
tottered past the Bitches' blue van on their way to the Rock 'n'
Roll Tavern, it looked as if the Bitches were about to get in the
van and leave. Despite that, Stanko felt the need to let them
know what he thought of their presence. Disappointed that he

couldn't insult them properly – he didn't speak any English –
he settled for telling them off in Slovenian. He turned towards
them and mumbled, as if to no one in particular, but loud
enough for them to hear it clearly, regardless of whether they
understood anything or not: "Stupid fucking tourists!"

The strange women started whispering to each other, so
he imagined he must have stirred up *some* unrest, at least.

As Stanko and Tinka swayed down the hill, the blue
van passed them by and Tinka gave them the finger, if only
to clear up and underline the point in international sign
language. At the sight of their surprised, almost appalled
faces, Stanko and Tinka started snickering. Their jubilation
sounded like broken glass and barbed wire rubbing against
the inside of a rusty bathtub.

Half an hour earlier, back in the bar by the church, the
Mayor had cleared his throat and, confirming that he had
the undivided attention of his electorate, started laying out
the complexities of their course of action as he envisioned
it. He sipped his beer, assumed a dignified posture, burped
into his hand as smoothly and discretely as he could, and
began: "Look, I know what you think about Boris and Beeba's
tavern... Actually, what we all think about it..."

"Yeah, hippies!"

"Junkies!"

"Criminals!"

"Lunatics!"

"Hooligans!"

"Gypsies," the people voiced their popular opinion.

"Let's not get hasty here. We need to be tolerant of those
who are different. You know how it is today."

"Absolutely, even hunters can no longer brag about their
trophies and achievements without pissing off some pathetic
deer hugger," grumbled one of the red-nosed hunters. "If it
were up to them animal lovers, farmers wouldn't be able to
grow anything anymore, because the deer would..."

"Right..." the Mayor interrupted the nascent lecture on wildlife management tentatively, careful not to insult the hunter. "Exactly, I agree completely. But, however we may look at it, Boris in fact manages to get many foreigners to visit here..." the Mayor proceeded.

"Yeah, hippies!"

"Junkies!"

"Criminals!"

"Lunatics!"

"Hooligans!"

"Gypsies," the voice of the people interrupted.

"Yes, unconventional clientele they may be, but nevetheless, no matter how peculiar, they're still people with money. And these foreigners are mostly musicians who get many other foreigners as well as Slovenians drop by, too. So I was thinking, why should Boris and Beeba rake in all the profit?"

The people finally started to pay attention to the mastermind hatching his ingenious scheme in their midst, but, judging by their dazed expressions, they were still somewhat confused.

The Mayor shrugged and raised his voice, employing some of his mayoral zeal in order to drive his point home in the style befitting a suburban politician/entrepreneur: "Can't you see? *Tourists*, my fellow citizens! It is *tourists* that have been visiting here lately. A lot of tourists, and frequently, too. I stop at Boris's for a cup of coffee every so often, in order to check out..."

"Those hippies?"

"Junkies?"

"Criminals?"

"Lunatics?"

"Hooligans?"

"Gypsies?!" the people gasped for their breaths.

"In order to check out what's going on! To see who's visiting. You know that Down Below the Hill is also a part of our municipality – even though it's rather backward and annoying. An important part too, since almost a quarter of

the voters live down there in that dump of a place. Boris and
Beeba are voters as well, for example, even if they haven't
voted in their entire lives. Especially not for me, now that I
think of it..." the Mayor scratched his cheek thoughtfully and
paused to think.

"Anyway," he finally proceeded, "It's true that many
of the people from Down Below the Hill are hippies, junkies,
criminals, lunatics, hooligans, and gypsies who don't even
vote. But, whenever I drop by, I also see many tourists there.
Gullible people with money. So I was thinking, why should
we let Boris be the only one to take advantage of that? There
must be *something* interesting about our town that makes all
these people come here. I'm sure it can't be just Boris's Rock
'n' Roll Tavern and those lousy concerts they organise there.
Probably it's the air, the landscape, nature, the crystal-clean
sparkling brook – well, at least when our peasants don't dump
liquid manure in it while tending to their fields – running by
our almost new road...

"Yes, I know, I know," the Mayor turned to those
malcontents in his audience who started clearing their throats,
"I know I promised I'd fix the road, and I assure you I'll take
care of that just a couple of days before my current term of
office runs out. Where was I...

"Yes. So, the brook, the sights – just look at our church
over there! Of course, you're used to seeing it every day, but
it's a splendid example of Romanesque architecture dating
back to the 12th century... At least that's what the Reverend
tells me and perhaps we should also tell this to the world.
The church also comes with a large ossuary that I've never set
foot into yet, nor do I intend to, but we could surely charge
an entrance fee to funny foreigners who may be interested
in such a thing. There is also that huge stone block in the
middle of the forest... Supposedly nobody knows how it got
there – you know, that rock our grandmothers say has healing
properties and some such nonsense? Perhaps we could call
it an Obelisk or the Hillstone, for example. Our local writer
could collect some stories about it and spin some captivating

yarns that would attract people... Maybe we could even have one of these radiesthesia experts measure its special energies and recommend it to their patients. For example, that famous mystic Dr Drago Dabić could check it out. You remember him, right? I'm sure he'd be happy to do it – for the right fee, of course..."

The Mayor was obviously on a roll. "And, have I already mentioned the inexhaustible supply of unparalleled wine and stupendous sunsets?" he said and pointed to the horizon where the sun had already disappeared behind the distant vineyards, but the sky was still painted in gaudy colours reminiscent of the local facades. "I tell you, we have a little piece of heaven here! If only we could market it properly and offer these people something amusing, something really captivating..." the Mayor mused.

The people pondered.

"You know, something original, something interesting, something that's just ours... Something that would attract tourists and make them spend as much of their money here as possible..." the Mayor brainstormed.

"Something *ethnic*!" the Head of the Folklore Society, who had a meeting with the President of the Lacework Society and Director of the Easter Egg Ornamentation Society in the corner, elaborated as a sudden spark of inspiration wreaked havoc in the haystacks of her mind, tucked away safely beneath a fake-blond perm.

"Right on!" the Mayor agreed eagerly. "Look, we have such extensive vineyards and so many winemakers around here... Our wine would be famous in such remote places as Austria if the Austrians got to know it somehow and could be persuaded to import some of it. Our lacework is beyond reproach, we have unique Shrovetide costumes that nobody else has, even if they are horribly uncomfortable and foul-smelling, and we've even invented unique Easter Egg ornaments, unheard of anywhere else in Slovenia as well as the rest of the world..."

"Hear, hear," the Head of the Lacework Society and the

Director of the Easter Egg Ornamentation Society cheered.

"We have the best deer goulash..." the Mayor decided to fire up the bar clientele some more while it looked he was on one of his winning streaks.

"Hear, hear," the red-nosed hunters agreed.

"We have the world champion of accordion..."

"Yay," the world champion of accordion and his exhibitionist trollop applauded.

"...Yes, we also have our local showgirls, just as showy as any other place in the world, perhaps even more..." the Mayor struck while the iron was hot.

The folk whore laughed heartily.

"...Not to mention our jolly pyromaniacs over there, who always manage to put out the fires they set!" the Mayor joked and the merry firemen hollered: "Hear, hear," cherishing fondly the memory of all the firefighters' merrymakings that had already taken place as well as looking forward to all the bacchanalian festivities that had yet to be organised before they dropped dead due to liver failure, clogged arteries, massive coronaries, or hypertension.

"We have our share of loose women to offer..."

A single hag cackled in the corner.

"Though they could be far younger and much stronger in numbers," the resourceful Mayor added immediately, cleverly and smoothly, so his electorate chuckled a self-important chuckle only chuckled by people kept in the loop and let in on an ingenious inside joke. Only the cleaning lady sighed tiredly and glanced at her watch, worried that this could turn into one of those evenings she'd have to write a poem about after she was done with the toilets. (She was also the local poet, but she didn't expect to be included in her Mayor's motivational speech. After all, she was, just like most poets everywhere in the world, traditionally ignored or, in the best-case scenario, misunderstood.)

The Mayor, indeed paying no heed to the village versemaker, wrapped up his performance: "And we have our unique traditional ethnic folk attire, which cannot be seen anywhere else on the face of this God-given Earth, am I right?"

"No doubt whatsoever," the Head of the Folklore Society agreed resolutely.

"So I was theorising about how to monetise the sudden influx of foreigners into our community," the Mayor abruptly employed the lingo every politician had to master and resort to when necessary. The Mayor also started explaining his plan much more quietly and conspiratorially in order to make everybody listen. Which he actually even managed to do, because Stanko the subversive saboteur had already left, and the cleaning lady bard ordered another coffee and just sat there quietly, thinking about how she would love to throw everybody out, clean out behind them, go home, feed her doggie, pour herself some milk and write a couple of verses she could present to her mates on Tuesday, because on Tuesdays she and her fellow poets and writers from the neighbouring municipalities met at Boris and Beeba's. The two aging hippies liked unorthodox artists for some unfathomable reason, so they usually even turned down their psychedelic rock 'n' roll while the artists read each other their latest crowning achievements.

"So, what's the battle plan?" inquired three of the red-nosed hunters who were also the veterans of the 1991 Slovenian Independence War. Despite its rather modest duration (it was also called the Ten-Day War), the number of veterans among the rural population in church-side bars was rather surprising, and, according to themselves, all these fearless heroes had seen breathtaking action, experienced thrilling events, and laughed in the face of terrifying dangers in order to secure the attainment of Slovenian independence. Similar claims were made by certain well-known Slovenian politicians – the Illustrious Emancipators. However, these fabled characters deserved much more credit than your ordinary cannon fodder, because at that critical point in Slovenian history they defied certain paper cuts and braved excruciating back pain in what must have been remarkably

uncomfortable office chairs by today's standards. Thus even
twenty years later they pounded their chests and furthered
their careers as professional hypocrites, liars and outright
criminals with their unprecedented wartime merits, because,
after all, they had single-handedly delivered each and every
Slovenian from the ghastly horrors of the Socialist Federal
Republic of Yugoslavia.

"Battle plan?" the Mayor paused thoughtfully. "Well...
I think we should steer the tourists away from that rock 'n'
roll pit Down Below, and show them some honest original
ethnic fun up here. Down Below they're indulging in what
they're used to at home – while up here they could get in
touch with a unique culture they don't know. You know, just
like some Slovenians – not me, mind you! – go to Chinese
restaurants, watch European films, burn Indian incense, listen
to Macedonian folk songs, practice Eastern religions, God
forbid, or learn to play funny instruments and write fake
ethnic music: to get in touch with foreign cultures, I suppose.
For whatever perverse reason they do it – I say, eat *potica*
cake and sauerkraut, play accordion, and stick to polkas and
waltzes, because that's your identity, those are your roots! –
but who am I to say. So I believe we should steal the guests
that frequent Boris's and show them a real good time, what do
you think? And, of course, I also say we should charge them
plenty for our traditional food and wine!"

The electorate nodded.

"I think we should post some guards, designate some
scouts..."

(The hunters agreed.)

"...who'd inform everyone else through the fire
department frequencies..."

(The two firemen contributed a "yay!" and readily
slammed their walkie-talkies on the table.)

"...that the loose women..."

(The corner hag cackled and cheered.)

"...should get ready to put on their traditional folklore
outfits, preferably fashioned out of lace."

(The exhibitionist trollop, Head of the Folklore Society, and President of the Lacework Society let out "yippees" in unison, even though they would otherwise by no means be associated under any other circumstances.)

"Our world champion will pull out his accordion! We'll bring out the good stuff and show those tourists some good ole ethnic fun! For a price, of course."

And so on. The Mayor worked his magic, and before the Mayor's wife, still gossiping at Jožica's, could even wrap up her Prologue to the Suburban Saga of the Blue Van, everyone in the bar next to the church except the cleaning lady, who hadn't been listening very carefully, knew every detail about the cunning tourist-trap plan and agreed with it. The plan was later set out in the Guidelines on the Development and Streamlining of a Certain Small Slovenian Suburban Municipality by the local recording clerk:

"The Certain Small Slovenian Suburban Municipality (hereinafter referred to as Municipality) shall be a tourist site. Municipality shall be a service provider in tourism. Municipality shall employ scouts from the ranks of the municipal hunters (hereinafter referred to as Scouts), who shall spot incoming tourists. Scouts shall immediately inform Municipality of any incoming tourists via the fire department radio frequencies. The needs of incoming tourists shall be met by the measures implemented in accordance with the Operation "Instant Impromptu Merrymaking". Any and all income, secured pursuant to the Guidelines on the Development and Streamlining of the Certain Slovenian Suburban Municipality, shall be transferred to the Municipal Sub-budget. The Mayor and his Commissioners shall, at their own discretion, employ the Municipal Sub-budget in order to finance the further development of the Instant Impromptu Merrymaking Operation and Municipality in general. Any surplus shall be the property of Municipality and shall be overseen by the Mayor and his Commissioners."

Translated into Terrestrial, the plan meant the following: the municipality would pay a couple of drunken hunters to keep an eye out for tourists. Once tourists arrived – like in the case of the funny-looking foreign females near the church – the villagers would react instead of just letting that parasite Boris Birman skim all the cream. The Mayor would engage the incoming tourists in a fascinating discussion of all things unique to this part of the world, while the villagers would quickly don their ethnic outfits, meet the tourists with traditional music (which unavoidably involved accordions), and offer them some traditional foods and wines. The Romanesque church, the ossuary and the giant outlandish monolith in the middle of the forest would be pointed out, tickets would be sold, and perhaps official guides in fancy uniforms could even be appointed. On a stand next to the church, memorabilia would be sold – for example, the unique Easter eggs, miniature figurines dressed in folk attire and Shrovetide costumes, lacework, Alpine dancing song albums by their world champion of accordion, and little Hillstone pendants infused with mystical energies by none other than the renowned Dr Drago Dabić himself (perhaps even different models radiating a range of energies for various purposes). At the irresistible lure of Alpine dancing songs, performed by traditional musicians (that is, the world champion of accordion, his wench and their band), the tourists would stuff themselves with potica, salami and dry-cured ham, get drunk and open their wallets, thus contributing generously to the municipal sub-budget.

"So!" the Mayor finally resolved as twilight had already concealed the hunters' red noses and the firemen's healthy flush, and the bartender had turned on a couple of discrete lights. "Now I shall go forth and see if I can interest our first tourists in what we have to offer!"

When the Mayor looked towards the church he saw, to his great disappointment, that the blue van and the six potential victims had already disappeared.

23. Operation Watering Hole: Briefing

"Hello? Pardon me?" Another One poked Arch Bitch, who seemed so hopelessly lost in her thoughts that she actually failed to see the light.

"Uh, yeah, what?" Arch Bitch pulled herself together.

"It seems we've been... Illuminated," Another One pointed discretely at the floodlight aimed at their van.

"Damn! I was thinking about what to do next and then I suddenly started enjoying the view... It's quite nice here, actually," Arch Bitch elaborated.

Grim Bitch agreed: "Yeah, it's definitely nice, but I still think we should stop hanging around and get out of here before we draw too much attention to ourselves. We've dawdled here for more than an hour! We can admire the landscape later. Let's get on with these stealthy scouting operations of ours somewhere else and preferably in a less obtrusive manner. I don't think that basking in the light of the Catholic Church is in line with the Manual on the Whole Affair."

"Who knows, has anyone actually managed to read the damn tome yet?" Serbian Bitch shrugged.

"We really seem to be a bit of a curiosity," The Watcher complained. "Especially the natives drinking in that bar over there... They keep eyeing us as if they've never seen five British Bitches and a Serbian Bitch share a van before."

"They probably haven't," Serbian Bitch said.

"Oh, I don't know," Another One wondered, "Why would they be so interested in what we're doing here?"

"Sounds like you've never visited the countryside and been stared at suspiciously by the paranoid peasant population," Serbian Bitch teased her.

"Well, OK, I see your point, perhaps we really are slightly out of place," Another One said.

Arch Bitch made up her mind: "You're right, let's go. Sorry, all the travelling and sudden loads of responsibilities seem to have worn me out a little. Before we got ourselves in this mess I'd planned on spending a quiet weekend at home."

As the Bitches were getting ready to pack their behinds back into the van, the raggedy Stanko and rickety Tinka wobbled and tottered by on their way to Boris and Beeba's, staring at the Bitches sullenly.

"*Prekleti turisti kurčevi,*" Stanko mumbled.

"What's he saying?" The Watcher turned to Serbian Bitch, "Judging by his expression and intonation I'd guess he doesn't like us much."

"He expressed his dislike of tourists, but not in such an elaborate and nerdy way as Accumulator of Unwonted Locutions could," Serbian Bitch winked.

"Pfft!" Accumulator of Unwonted Locutions failed to justify her reputation for a change.

The Bitches finally got back into the van and The Watcher drove away slowly in order not to run over the unstable and unpredictable Tinka and Stanko as they swayed down the hill. When they passed by the drunken old winos, Tinka gave them the finger, which would have seemed somewhat unusual had she been a nice venerable old lady. However, Tinka only knew nice because it rhymed with lice, only recognised venerable when she mistook it for venereal, and was not nearly as old as she was wretched. She just burped into the summer evening, looking forward to an impressive number of spritzers at Boris's, and couldn't care less about such useless matters as manners.

Even though it was already twilight, it was still humid and hot. Another One's tongue pined for a cold drink, but instead of finding refuge in Boris's oasis, which promised many a cool one, it shrivelled into a dry lump in the middle of the desert that was her mouth as the van passed the Rock 'n' Roll Tavern on its way back towards Ljubljana. Another

One looked at Serbian Bitch longingly, who, evidently quite
miserable and dizzy herself, told Arch Bitch: "Hey, don't
you think that's far enough?" She turned to The Watcher and
pointed towards a narrow gravel byway, branching off the
main road just ahead of the van and running through the trees
next to a small brook: "If you park between those trees up
there, nobody will notice us. You guys could sit by the brook,
cool off, and pretend you're just having a picnic or whatever
while Another One and I check out the situation."

"I've even noticed a little gas station across the main
street," The Watcher reported, slowing down. "We could go
get a couple of sandwiches and something to drink. What do
you think?"

"Sounds good," Arch Bitch decided. "Pull over, then."

The Watcher hung a right, pulled onto the bumpy back
road and parked the van in a convenient spot under the cover
of the trees, obscuring the Bitches from the main road and, in
particular, hiding them from the prying eyes of the snoopy
aborigines.

Arch Bitch pulled out the Manual on the Whole Affair
and together with The Watcher they inventoried the special
surveillance equipment they had with them. She soon
confirmed that using a laser microphone from such a distance,
especially through all those tree branches, was not feasible.
Even if they could see the Rock 'n' Roll Tavern from their
current stakeout spot at all. Not that it would do them any
good even if they could use the microphone, because when
they'd driven past the Rock 'n' Roll Tavern they'd caught a
glimpse of many unidentified people in there and heard loud
rock 'n' roll music playing. So it was doubtful they could
make out anything useful from that ruckus, and they couldn't
tell who was talking, anyway. First they'd have to determine
and catalogue all the voices.

Since the Manual stated that they should first confirm
the location and identity of the main subject of their investigation as well as establish who he was with, Arch Bitch
figured that Serbian Bitch's idea was actually in line with the

procedure. Or at least it was close enough.

It was soon decided that Serbian Bitch and Another One would in fact go undercover. They had already hit it off, while the others were busy or unsuitable for the job at hand: The Watcher watched, Arch Bitch supervised, Grim Bitch was too grim, and Accumulator of Unwonted Locutions was unintelligible. The Watcher, who was in charge of their spy gadgets, handed them glasses with integrated cameras and microphones as well as wireless in-ear headphones so tiny that most bald eagles couldn't spot them through binoculars.

"Holy shit, these are ugly," said Serbian Bitch as she received her new fashion accessory.

"Holy crap, I can't see anything through these," whined Another One as she took off her own prescription glasses and put on the fake ones, "And I don't have my contacts with me."

"Shut up," whispered Serbian Bitch and poked Another One in the ribs. "I don't mind holding your hand and looking stupid in these glasses, so long as we get a beer. Quickly too, I'm parched."

Arch Bitch, looking forward to a bottle of water from the nearby gas station herself, pretended not to hear Another One's complaints. She briefed her infiltration team: "OK, then. We'll codename the tavern and this current operation of ours 'Watering Hole'…"

"What's the point of that?" Grim Bitch grumbled grumpily.

"I really don't know," Arch Bitch shrugged, "The Manual on the Whole Affair sets out that we have to assign codenames to all our operations and subjects of investigation, and only use those codenames in our own internal communications as well as in our communications with Omnipile."

"It probably also states that the codenames should be as stupid as possible," Grim Bitch grumbled some more.

"But how can we name our subjects before we even know who they are?" Another One asked.

"Shut the fuck up already, will you?" Serbian Bitch hissed and stealth-poked Another One again.

"We'll just make up the bloody codenames as we go, I guess. It all seems like a bunch of baloney to me, anyway. As long as we stick to the instructions in our reports to Omnipile, we'll be fine, I suppose," Arch Bitch said. "Let's proceed with the briefing, shall we?"

The Bitches, even Accumulator of Unwonted Locutions, nodded impatiently.

"So," Arch Bitch briefed them, "Put on those glasses, turn on the cameras and microphones, and go to the tavern. We'll do a sound and video check on the way. Go in, keep a low profile, but not suspiciously low... Well, you know what I mean. Just act natural. Order a couple of drinks or something to eat, sit down somewhere out of the way, look normal, but scope out the place. Check out individual patrons and get them on video so that we can identify them and their voices... Talk to each other, so that you don't look strange, but keep quiet in case you hear anything interesting. We may get something important on tape."

"That is, on state-of-the-art solid-state disks!" The Watcher put in playfully and rubbed her hands, enjoying the high-tech toys provided by Omnipile, which she now had the chance to unwrap.

Arch Bitch could not be bothered: "Also, look around the place a bit. We'll try to figure out where to install more permanent surveillance equipment, should the OIA demand it. We'll communicate with you through your little in-ear headphones, so we'll tell you if we need you to do something else. That's about it, I suppose. Go now, good luck!"

"Understood," Serbian Bitch confirmed, slapped Another One on the back and headed towards the main road.

Another One took a step, stumbled, and would have surely rolled down a short steep slope overgrown with nettles and into the creek, high-tech glasses through which she couldn't see and wireless headphones and all, had The Watcher not noticed her instability and grabbed her in time.

"Fuck...!" Another One yelped and turned to The Watcher gratefully: "Thanks... Hell, I must remember to bring my contacts next time." She turned to Arch Bitch: "Can I at least wear my real glasses until we get to the tavern? I'll carry the surveillance glasses in my hand until then, so that you can at least check if they work. OK?"

"Fine, I suppose," Arch Bitch said. "Just be careful not to draw attention to yourself while you're in there. And don't leave the table then, if your eyesight is really that lousy. We don't need you killing yourself or breaking something and revealing the suspicious nature of your eyewear, do we."

Another One replaced the spy equipment with her own glasses and the world around her came into focus.

"How the hell did she pass the medicals..." Arch Bitch muttered to herself.

Serbian Bitch, who had ignored the commotion and was already about thirty metres away, yelled: "Hey, Bitch, are you coming or what? I'm dying of thirst over here, I mean, incredible enthusiasm for Operation Watering Hole, of course!"

24. Distressed Bodyguards

Three weeks before, several hours after the abduction of Fergus and Fabiola from the hotel lobby, the poker-playing security officers in the Fentons' hotel suite decided it was about time to wrap up their card game and get rid of the empty beer cans. It would not be long before Mr Fenton returned. He was never back before 1:30 a.m. when he went out on his top secret inspections, but he also rarely stayed out after 2:30, so usually everyone knew where they stood. It would not be terribly tragic if Ferdinand Fenton caught them playing poker for petty change and drinking a couple of lagers, as long as they did it discretely while keeping an eye on his family at all times. Mr Fenton didn't believe in riding his bodyguards too hard, because they might be less than enthusiastic to take a bullet for him or the members of his family if they hated his guts. But then again, playing cards and drinking beer on the job might not be the best of career moves, either. So, better safe than sorry.

One of the three intrepid bodyguards who stayed with Mrs Fenton and the kids that night obviously did not have a Ph.D. in quantum mechanics. He crushed the empty beer cans for no apparent reason other than the simple joy of showing them who's boss (nope, he didn't have an opinion on whether decreasing their volume effectively increased the capacity of city dumps, hence contributing to the longevity of the human population on planet Earth in any infinitesimal manner whatsoever). He dumped the garbage into a plastic bag and cursed under his breath as stale leftover beer sprinkled over his beefy paws, defiling them through the holes in the aluminium, which the bodyguard himself had just fashioned with his appetite for destruction.

The other security guard, humming a little ditty to

himself, wiped the kitchen table and put away the cards and
the chips. He suddenly found himself thinking about his wife
who'd always make him clean the table and the stove, even
though she knew he hated that. Perhaps she did it precisely
for that reason, he thought lovingly. Ah, well, he may have
hated it, but now that she was so far away he suddenly
realised he missed her terribly. It was hard being stuck in
Yoman while she was in Yorktown, Indiana. As he started
brooding about wives in general, he glanced at Mrs Fenton
and hoped she was sleeping like a log. Nobody wanted to be
in her way if she happened to wake up in the middle of the
night for some reason, not even Mr Fenton himself.

The third security expert came back from the toilet,
tiptoeing past Mrs Fenton, and startled the other two by
whispering: "Fucking hell, where are those damn spoiled brats
of theirs? They're not in their room, I checked!"

"Jesus Christ, Mr Fenton is gonna have us terminated!"

"Yeah, in the worst sense of the word."

The three bodyguards searched the hotel frantically. The
kids were nowhere to be found. The guards would have even
checked the hotel roof had it been accessible, but fortunately
it was not. Finally it dawned on them they should at least
try and ask the receptionist if he happened to see the damn
twerps. After they painstakingly described the kids, waving
their arms in the International English language, the receptionist informed them casually: "Yes, I see the girl with funny
hair and boy with silly glasses, just like you describe. They go
to computer," he pointed at the far end of the lobby.

The bodyguards checked the computers and couldn't
find anything except an article about George Michael's latest
arrest on one of the screens, which the spoiled brats had
probably been reading. That information wouldn't mean
anything at all even to Sherlock Holmes himself.

"Where are the kids now?!" the biggest and baddest
specimen of the bodyguards – the one without a Ph.D. in
particle physics – yelled as he grabbed the poor receptionist
by the collar, shaking the very life out of him.

"Hey, sir, let me go, what, you crazy? I do nothing wrong! They get sick, and two doctors take them to hospital!"

"What?! What the... What fucking doctors?!" the bodyguards were becoming desperate.

"Wait, wait, my friend, you work for mister Fenton, yes?"

"Yeah! What's it to you, motherfucker?!" The bodyguard glared at the receptionist, just about ready to punch that feigned smile out of his face.

"Wait, my friend, here is letter for mister Fenton, from doctors, you see? Here, you take... You take, read, I don't care. You give letter to Mr Fenton." The receptionist reached under the counter and handed the exasperated guard an envelope.

The bodyguard's hands shook so badly he could barely open the damn thing. Once he managed to read the letter, he became as pale as a ghost. The other two security experts leaned over his shoulder and read: "WE TAKE YOUR CHILDREN. WE SOON TELL YOU WHAT WE WANT. IF YOU CHASE US, WE RAPE THEM, SEND YOU THEIR FINGERS AND SEX ORGANS, AND KILL THEM. OR THE OTHER WAY AROUND, BUT THAT WOULD BE TOO WRONG. CHEERS, YOMANIAN LIBERATION FRONT," the note said.

"What the fuck!" the most nervous of the bodyguards screamed and was about to grab the receptionist again. "And it ain't even written in letters cut outta newspapers as it should be! It's just scrawled with a pen!"

He ran out of other ideas, so he pulled out his pistol. That always yielded some results. Since he didn't know what exactly to aim it at, he waved it around a bit, but kept looking in the general direction of the reception desk (probably because he really wanted to shoot that guy). "Fuck!" the frustrated guard yelled at the ceiling.

"I'm sorry!" the poor receptionist raised his arms in defence, "I don't know nothing, and I don't ask stupid questions. They have papers, they doctors and police, secret soldiers, rebel fighters, I don't care, I don't ask things. I am

here, nice and quiet, people check in, people check out, I do
business with people, make a very special price just for them,
take their dollar, and everyone my friend. You my friend too,
now go away!" The receptionist tried to shoo them away in a
somewhat feminine manner, but when he realised that would
not work, he turned around and shouted something angry or
urgent (who could tell the nuances?) in Arabic through the
door behind him. A few less-than-affable dark and bearded
Arab men with mobile phones, Bluetooth headsets and unfor-
giving expressions showed up. It was not likely that these
guys would start their next sentence by calling anyone their
friend.

Suddenly – and *fortunately*, as the bodyguards and
bearded Arabs started resembling twitchy-fingered cowboys
staging a Mexican standoff – a small convoy of cars pulled
up in front of the hotel. It was Ferdinand Fenton's armoured
limousine accompanied by three other pitch-black vehicles.
All of them contained gloomy men in black – a couple of them
even wore those terrible polka-dot ties. The bodyguards knew
these were agents of the Omnipile Intelligence Agency, and
they spelled especially bad news. Mr Fenton got out of the
limousine, and by the hasty way he was smoking his Cuban
cigar, the three poker-loving beer-guzzling security experts in
the lobby could tell he was already upset. Or nervous, which
would have been even scarier, because men like Fenton never
got nervous without a very good reason. The guards would
do anything to avoid pouring more gasoline on that bonfire,
and they definitely didn't want to be around when this pile
of excrement hit the proverbial fan. The cars also contained
an officer of the Omnipile Security Service – the superior
officer of the poker-loving beer-guzzling security experts –
and that man had no sense of humour whatsoever, not even
a hopelessly bad one. Therefore the bodyguards decided it
was about time they did something constructive, hatched a
cunning plan, came up with a solution, retreated, got out,
regrouped, got away, split, covered their tracks. So they
panicked.

"Holy fuck!" cursed the first security expert.

"We're screwed!" swore the second one.

"Well, fuck me!" added the third and stupidest.

Before they stated something equally creative in unison, one of them had the fortune of coming up with what he thought was a brilliant idea. He pulled a hundred-dollar bill out of his wallet, slammed it on the counter and told the receptionist: "Here. If you don't mention anythin' about this to Mr Fenton, we'll give you guys another two hundred bucks. OK?"

"Four hundred? My friend have many wife and child," the receptionist pointed at the bearded Arabs behind his back.

"Fine, damn it! And don't mention the kids! We'll tell him. Get it? You'll keep your mouth shut? All of you?"

All the Arabs nodded, including the bearded ones.

The three security experts turned around hastily and left without bothering to say goodbye, and the receptionist waved at them, the sweetest and broadest smile spreading across his face.

The men sprinted to the Fenton suite and stopped in front of the door to calm down and catch their breath. The one with the brilliant idea explained everything hastily, wheezing and panting, and as soon as they could count on being able to breathe quietly enough, they entered the room. They only hoped it would take a while before the whole of Fenton's entourage was debriefed.

The guard with the brilliant idea rummaged through his suitcase, while the other two glanced around, looking around the rooms for anything suspicious that had yet to be concealed. The first of the remaining two guards put the note from the Yomanian Liberation Front on the kitchen table. The second one grabbed the plastic bag containing the beer cans they'd forgotten to take out and chucked it over the balcony. The pool guy would curse at it in the morning.

The first guard knew where Evelyn kept her pills, so he rummaged around in her purse quietly. He fished them out and placed the bottles in plain sight, displaying them on the coffee table next to the couch she snored on. Then, on impulse, he tipped one of the bottles over and placed a couple of Valiums next to it, just to make the sight appear even more dramatic and call attention to it.

"What the fuck are you doing?" the security expert who had just dumped the beer cans over the balcony asked him, panicking.

"Just get your ass in the kitchen!" the composed bodyguard hissed angrily, followed him to the table and whispered: "I couldn't inject the bitch with sedatives, because those anal retentive forensics experts of ours would probably find the needle mark. I couldn't make her drink any sedatives, because she's passed out and I don't think she'd cooperate if I woke her up, right? But it looks like she's pretty much sedated herself, thank the Lord and all the saints, so I'm just makin' sure it's obvious, you know, like the kidnappers or terrorists or whoever the fuck took the kids didn't even have to bother with her. She didn't wake up during the commotion, and that's that."

"Say what?" inquired the stupidest bodyguard, "And what are we going to do now?"

"Just shut the fuck up and drink this shit," the man with the plan told the other two.

He poured each of them a beer (he figured that alcohol would show up when their blood was tested, they'd have to answer for that anyway, so why ruin their evening with anything else) and put in a massive dose of sedatives. They drank up and put the glasses and the empty cans on the table. It would look as if their drinks had been spiked.

When Mr Fenton finally wrapped up everything and came in, everyone was already out.

Two weeks later – a week before Operation Watering Hole – the three bodyguards became terribly worried when they heard the news: Yomanian Liberation Front had released Fergus. The boy had been recovered, quite surprisingly without any complications whatsoever, and was now located in the The Lab. The bodyguards' worst nightmare was coming true.

Of course, they didn't wish the little twerp dead, but... But the geeky fuck and his annoying sister had slipped away and got themselves kidnapped from under their very noses! If Ferdinand Fenton, their father, founder and CEO of Omnipile, knew that the kids had managed to give them the slip... That in itself would most likely result, due to gross incompetence, in their termination or at least redeployment to some inconsequential backwater post where the sun never shone. However, since they'd also lied to the Boss and made it look as if they'd been drugged by evil terrorists, they'd most likely be punished for dereliction of duty *and* gross incompetence, if not outright treason. For that they'd surely not only be fired but also *nullified*, as those characters with clownish ties from the Omnipile Intelligence Agency referred to the penalty for such transgressions. The bodyguards didn't know what exactly *nullification* was supposed to mean, but they were positive they never wanted to find out.

The unfortunate security experts ended up in this situation simply because they hadn't been able to figure out what to do exactly. They couldn't even imagine a way of getting away from Omnipile, especially not after the disastrous events in Yoman, so they just tried not to draw too much attention to themselves and waited to see what would happen, convinced that at least the kids wouldn't be back so very soon, if ever.

After the kidnapping of Mr Fenton's children, the bodyguards expected to be poked at, prodded, examined, tested, subjected to cavity searches, maybe even vivisected before they finally got fired, if they survived the wrath of the CEO at all. However, nothing like that happened. As surprising as that was, it was also a great relief. Perhaps they were lulled into a false sense of security, so that they believed everything would turn out for the best. But, in any case, they didn't even seriously consider an attempt at disappearing, as they were convinced they'd be tracked down and caught in a matter of days if not hours after the Omnipile Intelligence Agency started looking for them. And they couldn't just quit the job, either: it wasn't as simple as that if you worked for Omnipile, especially if you were privy to some very sensitive information. Even if they *could* just resign, Omnipile would keep close tabs on them.

The morning after the YLF terrorist act, the bodyguards regained consciousness in a high-tech mobile hospital which always followed the more important Omnipile officials around in case they needed medical assistance. The bodyguard without the Ph.D. in rocket science believed their plan of concealing how they'd lost the kids because they'd been too busy playing cards, drinking beer and fooling around was bulletproof. The second bodyguard – the one with a wife in Yorktown, Indiana, who, hopefully, waited for him without humping any neighbours, car salesmen, or pool cleaners – just prayed this would all blow over as soon as possible. However, the most resourceful member of the unfortunate trio – the one who'd come up with the plan in the first place – wasn't sure they'd get out of this so easily. Besides the tranquiliser, the Omnipile forensics experts would surely also find alcohol in their blood, and that would be a problem in itself.

Then there was the issue of Mrs Fenton – she might have been less outrageously sedated as the spilled pills on the coffee table suggested, and that could raise certain inconvenient questions. Fortunately for the guards, it turned out that she'd in fact popped enough pills on her own to remember nothing much after her husband left, not even the opening credits of the censored comedy with Arabic subtitles on Yoman One. She couldn't even recall that she fell asleep before the Yomanian Prime Minister started condemning the United States of America and the multinational corporations for sucking Yomanian oil and lithium reserves dry. So, due to her confusion, Mrs Evelyn Fenton was not taken very seriously by the investigators, even when she denied ever spilling the pills or leaving them on the table like that, where the kids could get to them. In any case, it was obvious she'd be unable to come up with any useful information about the kidnapping. Actually, she was unable to piece together anything much about the evening at all. Evelyn wasn't even sure where the bodyguards had been or what they'd been doing. She told the investigators that she'd been tired, her husband had pissed her off, and she was used to not noticing the bodyguards because, as far as she was concerned, they were like pieces of self-propelled furniture that always followed her husband around. Therefore she'd instructed them to leave her the fuck alone because she'd really needed some peace and quiet and that was all. Besides, this was all bollocks. Bollocks! Instead of tormenting her they should get off their lazy asses and get her children back.

Later the guards heard rumours that, strangely enough, Mr Fenton had told the investigators to back off and let the whole thing rest surprisingly quickly, and he'd forbidden the forensics to actually check the blood level in Evelyn's benzodiazepine. That, at least, was understandable – he had her, and thus his own, good name to protect.

The bodyguards, of course, were questioned thoroughly. They all stuck to their story: they admitted they'd sat in the kitchen and grabbed a couple of beers and some snacks from the mini-bar, but they'd kept a close watch on Mrs Fenton and the children at all times. There was no denying that they'd drunk some beer, because unlike Mrs Fenton's blood, theirs would surely be analysed thoroughly. Fortunately they hadn't overdone it and they'd ended up in the mobile hospital several hours after their accursed card game, so probably the tests wouldn't be too bad. They claimed Fabiola had been in the kids' room throughout the evening, and Fergus had snooped around the hotel suite for a while, then watched some TV, whined about the lack of computers, and finally gone to bed. They remembered Mrs Fenton had rested on the couch and watched TV. She must have fallen asleep, too, because they'd heard her snore... And then none of them remembered anything anymore. Next thing they knew, they were in the mobile hospital.

Mr Fenton himself was present at the interrogations, and even though the Intelligence Agency investigators seemed eager to put the bodyguards under a microscope and make them take a lie detector test just in case, Mr Fenton told them that the guards had surely been through enough and that he had no reason not to believe them. The investigators voiced their suspicions, remarking that they might have been in on the kidnapping (and stared at the guards suspiciously, even accusingly). However, the distraught CEO told them he trusted his men, who had watched over him and his family loyally for almost six years now.

The Intelligence Agency investigators, who loved turning up the heat whenever Security Service, which answered to the Intelligence Agency, made a mistake, were evidently disappointed that they would not be able to subject the bodyguards to more advanced methods of interrogation. Everyone was quite surprised at how agreeable Mr Fenton, otherwise a renowned hardliner, seemed this time. He was surely shocked by the whole affair and, naturally, concerned about his kids. The investigators found this very disappointing, so they at least took the opportunity to snarl at the bodyguards as they let them go: "We'll keep our eyes on you!"

That would most likely involve bugs and cameras and shady characters in black suits and polka-dot ties everywhere, so from then on the bodyguards refrained from discussing the previous evening, and they were also very reluctant to make any other moves.

But now Fergus was back.

They found out about it after they'd already arrived in The Lab with Mr Fenton. Ferdinand was in a hurry to see his son, so he went there to wait for the boy to arrive. Fergus's recovery was still kept secret at the time. The bodyguards' extensive training was probably the only thing that kept them from doing something stupid or even panicking. However, they were highly competent professionals, so they fled to the men's toilets, without even taking the time to contemplate that move, immediately after Mr Fenton met with a couple of OIA Agents and entered The Lab, the heavy carbon steel door slamming shut behind him. The guards didn't have clearance to enter The Lab, nor would Mr Fenton need any protection in there – the place was like Fort Knox: virtually impenetrable. So they were expected to wait outside in the lobby.

The unfortunate trio were reasonably sure there were no bugs or cameras in the toilets – after all, this was The Lab, even if it was just the lobby. Nevertheless, they checked the room thoroughly, because the last thing they needed was to be observed by those obnoxious Intelligence Agency snoops at this point.

The resourceful bodyguard confirmed that no one else occupied any of the booths, and then motioned at the other two to pull out their high-tech pocket bug sweepers and check for any surveillance bugs.

"Are we clear?" the resourceful bodyguard asked when he was sure they were indeed clear.

"Hmm, weird... What d'you make of that?" the one without a Ph.D. turned to the married bodyguard.

"Looks like there are tiny cameras inside the toilet bowls... Whatever the fuck that's for? Oh. I don't even want to imagine. Anyway, there aren't any mikes around, so we're good," analysed the married bodyguard.

"Let's make this short, or the receptionist might figure we're up to somethin'. If Fergus says anythin', which he probably will... After all, those OIA fucks will definitely squeeze every bit of information outta him, so he'll probably have to tell'em how they went down to the lobby by themselves, even if he doesn't wanna... We just say we don't remember nothin' and keep our mouths shut, OK? We only know the brat went to his room, and then – poof! We black out. They ain't gonna prove we weren't drugged by terrorists, no matter what Fergus says. Yeah, so maybe he and his sister went out later, when we were already drugged."

"We could still get fired," the chap without a Ph.D. said.

The married bodyguard just sighed and wondered

whether his wife in Yorktown, Indiana, was already screwing his brother.

"Fuck, man, I don't give a shit if we're fired or not. Right now, the way things look, I'd *love* to be fired. Let's just try to avoid gettin' *nullified*, whatever the fuck that means, OK?"

"So, no severance packages for us?"

"Only if it's severance of *our* packages, if you ask me..." the married bodyguard muttered to himself sheepishly.

25. Finnegan & Bogomyr

A week later, after Finnegan and Bogomyr sat down in the corner furthest from the people chatting and getting plastered on the other side of the semi-circular bar, Finnegan got right to the point: "So, what's the problem? What's going on between you and the sun, then?"

"It's complicated..." Bogomyr Yadvig began hesitantly, motioning at Beeba who swiftly handed him another glass of Merlot.

"Well, surprise me, I'm sure I've heard all the excuses made by people who don't feel like attending the rehearsals," Finnegan laughed loudly in order to make it clear he was joking, wrapping another one of his sarcastic remarks in the seemingly innocent gift paper of an irreproachable smile. But in fact this was just another example of Finnegan's disgusting passive aggressive attitude that he'd occasionally adopt.

"No, you don't understand, I *do* want to be at the rehearsals, it's just that I... Well... I'm allergic to the sun. I told you so yesterday! I thought I made it clear that I was an after-sunset kind of a guy."

"But are you only allergic to *our* sun or starlight in general?" Finnegan rolled his eyes, suddenly suspecting that this might have something to do with astrology, but then changed his mind, compensating for the chemically-induced mockery he was already indulging in, and hastened to say: "No, look, just kidding, sorry," Finnegan waved in front of his own face as if to ward off the thought. "What do you mean allergic? Like... Do you sneeze when you go out during the day? Get itchy spots all over? Your private parts get irritated? Or what?"

"No, it's not as simple as that. I could... Well..." Bogomyr stuttered, "As far as I know, I could very well perish."

"Very well perish," Finnegan repeated slowly, perplexed, and took a deep breath. "Do you mean you could suffocate? Is your allergy so bad...?"

"No. I could ignite," Bogomyr confessed gravely, dropping his gaze to the grimy floor tiles beneath the table, where it remained, simultaneously ashamed of itself, worried about revealing too much, and glued to the filthy stickiness thereunder. Why Bogomyr was so frank with the pale black Scotsman even he himself didn't know. For some reason he really wanted to be in this band, because he was gradually getting sick of his solo performances that no one seemed to appreciate. Probably he'd be forced to emigrate to Los Angeles or even San Francisco before finding three or four lunatics interested in an art form as complicated and complex and thoroughly meaningful, though a bit on the gay side – though he'd never admit it – as his.

"Beg your pardon?" the increasingly wide-eyed Finnegan asked. "Ignite? You mean, go up in flames? Fall victim to spontaneous human combustion? Am I getting this right or is this some kind of a Ukrainian-English language barrier that we have not yet taken into account?"

"Look, Finn... No, it's not a language barrier, I've had plenty of time to learn English, and I believe I'm able to chat in it quite well without causing major international incidents. Maybe I spice it up with a sexy Slavic accent, sure, but still. Look... I don't know how to say this exactly without sounding a bit quirky, and I don't even know why I'm telling you in the first place. But I can't keep you in the dark any longer: I'm a vampire."

After a few seconds of silence, during which Finnegan frowned and wondered whether he heard Bogomyr right or if this was one of those peculiar mental states preceding an imminent hospitalisation at the psychiatric ward, Finnegan uttered: "Are you taking the piss? Having a laugh? Pulling my leg? Are you kidding, I mean?" the Scottish artist frowned in stupefied disbelief.

"No, I mean it. Us vampires... We have yet to come clean, you know, come out of our coffins," Bogomyr chuckled, a bit clumsily, at his own wordplay efforts, "Fight for our rights, you know, much like the gay and the transsexual communities already have."

"Let's get this straight. No pun intended. You're a vampire, and daylight will kill you."

"Right."

"And you honestly believe that?"

"Not that I believe it. That's what I *am*, and that's what happens if I expose my skin to sunlight."

"Right."

"Right!" Bogomyr slammed his fist of alleged vampire descent on the table, and then finished his Merlot.

"Look." Finnegan took a deep breath and prepared himself for the worst. He went on: "Look, you don't actually believe that you're some kind of a bloodsucker, do you? Look there, you don't have any claws!"

"I do so, on my feet. I cut my toenails to points. I couldn't play my guitar with claws, though."

"But you don't have any *fangs*, mate!"

"I do so have fangs. Behold!" Bogomyr opened his mouth, bared his teeth and hissed at Finnegan.

Finnegan raised his left eyebrow, froze for a second and inspected Bogomyr's teeth attentively enough to make Bogomyr's dentist jealous. "I would hardly call those chipped and even somewhat rotten excuses for dentures fangs," Finnegan's expert opinion rolled effortlessly from his already quite lubricated mouth, "Maybe your canines are a bit on the prominent side, but they're not at all remarkable in any way."

Bogomyr sighed and dropped his gaze again. "Truth be told, I'm not a very remarkable vampire."

"You could say that again!" Finnegan laughed, "Just kidding, just kidding, of course," he raised his arms apologetically and slapped them on his knees as Bogomyr looked up disagreeably. "Sorry, I don't mean to be... You know... I don't want to be mean, but this is a bit hard for me to swallow."

"Sure, I understand," Bogomyr said and aimed a blank look at his empty glass.

Finnegan took the advantage of Bogomyr's obvious resignation and proceeded with the interrogation: "I'm still confused. Look, man, I can hardly believe you sleep in a coffin."

Bogomyr abruptly shot up on his seat, adopted a very stern expression, and stated firmly, obviously upset: "Coffin! There's a perfect example of sanguivoriphobia."

"Example of what?"

"Fear of vampires! Totally uncalled-for prejudice against vampires! Stupid and even insulting stereotypes!" Bogomyr hissed. "That's like garlic or crosses. Why the hell would I hate garlic or crosses? OK, I *do* hate fresh garlic, but only because it makes my breath stink to high heavens and the aftertaste lingers for days. But what's that shit with crosses, churches and holy water? I don't give a fuck about that, I'm not even religious. Far from it, I believe everybody who's religious should be put into a nuthouse. Us vampires are definitely not some spawn of Satan and whatnot. We may be a bit on the depressed side. We may also be partial to sinister black outfits, but so are Catholic priests... But I digress," Bogomyr smiled apologetically and continued: "I know such a revelation may be somewhat fantastic, but I'm still disappointed in you. I thought you were radically open-minded. But now I see that the next thing you'll probably be intrigued by is how I can shave and comb my hair when I can't see myself in the mirror. The stupidity of people in general never ceases to amaze me."

"I agree with you there. People are stupid. People are strange. And often – actually far too often for my taste – they're also gullible. So, since I'd really hate ending up among simpletons prone to believing whatever some crackpot tells them, I'm still trying to establish why you're fucking with me here. Because, as we speak, you're drinking red wine, which, admittedly, might be construed as a bit vampiric, perhaps... But that's not blood, far from it. You realise that, don't you?

And I've seen you eat more than a few bull testicles and
a heap of chips yesterday. So what's up with that, then?"
Finnegan managed a tired smile, suspecting that the Ukrainian
stripper might turn out to be as nutty as squirrel crap.
Which would be OK in itself, but Bogomyr was a member of
Finnegan's fabulous music project. If the Ukrainian was in
fact certifiable, that might result in more than a few problems
in the guitar department of the band. So the prying concern
was actually caused by selfishness, which wasn't very unusual
for Finnegan – a stereotypically self-absorbed self-proclaimed
artist.

Nevertheless, Bogomyr tried to explain: "I can eat
and drink anything when I feel rather optimistic. Well, not
necessarily optimistic, that would be a gross overstatement...
Perhaps we could rephrase that. I can enjoy normal food
and beverages when I don't feel so bad about the whole
affair of the universe bearing down on me. As soon as I
feel the awesome pressure of the universe lurking out there
and having it in for me, I must seek out a gullible though
preferably sexy woman and feed on her in order to survive
yet another day. Or night. That's the whole affair in a really
microscopic nutshell."

"What do you mean?" Finnegan asked, suddenly more
intrigued, "What do you mean by 'universe bearing down on
me'?"

"Well, don't you sometimes feel that the whole universe
has conspired against you, and that it wants to have you
killed?"

"Sure I do!" Finnegan could suddenly relate to the
notion. "Absolutely! Not that I feel it, I know it for a fact! The
universe is a mean old bitch and she most definitely wants me
dead. She wills itself dead, too. And whatever has ever been
or will ever have the slightest chance of being, all of that will
also eventually be destroyed."

"Entropy!" the vampire bellowed, slamming his empty
Merlot glass on the table and ordering a pint of Merlot instead
of the usual dose, "I feel threatened by entropy. The universe

is out there, stalking me, and it wants me cancerous."

Finnegan looked up, surprised.

"To explain the feeling with your own words," Bogomyr added.

"I'll be damned!" Finnegan clapped his hands in honest surprise. "The undead have registered my lyrics! Looks like I've finally managed to find a niche market for my shit. The most depressing and unlikely market, perhaps, but a market nevertheless. You know, nobody has ever quoted a line of mine in my life, as far as I know, except Amalia who is forced to learn them, poor girl. I'm flattered, I really am. Thank you for making my evening. Nobody else seems to care about lyrics these days," Finnegan said, appearing slightly heartbroken in line with his *nobody-gives-a-fuck-about-us-tortured-artists* attitude. However, he had too much beer at his fingertips to succumb to any serious negativity.

"That's not necessarily true," Bogomyr held up his index finger, which lacked the wicked claw that would befit a vampire in Finnegan's books. Instead Finnegan observed a nail that had apparently seen much biting.

"I always listen to lyrics. I write poems, too, you know," Bogomyr explained.

"No shit! Can I read some?"

"No you can't. They're in Ukrainian and they're not meant to be read by anyone," Bogomyr Yadvig said dramatically.

"Much good do they do then," Finnegan resorted to sarcasm again.

"They're personal. They're only meant for certain girls I've fed on and really liked, but even they will never ever read them."

"Okay then, I understand," Finnegan gave in, though he didn't truly understand. For as long as he remembered, he'd only known three reasons why he'd ever write a poem:

a) to impress a girl in order to get laid, which automatically entailed showing the poem to the girl in question;

b) because he was inspired and just felt like writing a

poem, after which he'd show that poem to any number of girls in order to impress them and get laid, and/or use the poem as lyrics for his music;

c) because he needed lyrics for his music, which he'd then play and sing to countless girls, hoping to impress them and get laid.

So, keeping poems, lyrics, songs, or anything else that could score him any points in the female camp, for that matter, just *personal*, was not Finnegan's thing. He could have it off with himself anytime, anywhere, and in any manner: right hand, left hand, top grip, side grip, upside-down grip, two-finger front-to-back grip, three-finger over-the-top grip, tight grip, maximum-friction or medium-friction grip, light self-administered caresses, with a condom or without, with lubricant, olive oil, in a shower, by watermelon, even sheep, had he had the notion of moving to the Scottish Highlands and breeding the woolly maggots... He could even fiddle himself through holes in the pockets of his jeans while waiting for a doctor's appointment or attending a really boring concert – and he *didn't have to read any poems* written by himself prior to that, nor did the imaginary girlfriends he imagined fornicating in his mind's eye on such occasions have to. So why in the hell would he keep such potentially useful and possibly profitable products personal?

"OK, if I understand you correctly – you can drink and eat anything if you stop feeling so abysmally depressed for a moment. Cool, I get that. It's logical, even in the realm of *humans*, not just Count Dracula."

"Don't you dare ridicule my ancestry," Bogomyr managed a tired smile. He was getting more agreeable as half of his previously procured pint of Merlot had already slid down his throat.

"So I see you don't have the blues today, congratulations," Finnegan glanced at Bogomyr's glass, laughed and picked up his beer in order to look Bogomyr Yadvig in the eye and say *Cheers*! in that fine energetic Slovenian way they had already been forced to adopt. They emptied their glasses and

Finnegan asked Beeba, who lurked behind the bar: "Can we get another round?"

After Beeba delivered the goods, Finnegan continued, dramatically: "However, let's get to the issue that gnaws at me most persistently. So, you really want me to believe you're some kind of an undead creature of the night, and that you in fact bite people and drink their blood?"

"Absolutely!" Bogomyr protested. "Obviously I bite people, I'm a vampire!"

"But…" Finnegan couldn't stop himself from laughing. "Sorry, there's no way I can swallow this. I can't picture you embracing any old victim and taking a bite."

"Suit yourself," Bogomyr Yadvig grunted, quite offended.

"Come on, Bogy," Finn grabbed Bogomyr by the shoulders and shook him. "Spit it out. Admit it. You don't actually suck people's blood."

"Of course I do!"

"No you don't."

"I do so! Well, maybe not people's blood in general. Women's blood." Bogy protested.

Finnegan stopped shaking the skinny Ukrainian and suddenly decided that Bogomyr sounded a bit homophobic for a vampire exotic dancer. He asked Bogomyr about it.

The Ukrainian stopped to consider whether Finnegan was just trying to insult him, then responded: "Look, I resent your implications!"

"Of course you do, that's why I keep implying random stuff," Finnegan snickered, "I'm just trying to figure out what this is all about. Don't you dare hold it against me. The things you've been telling me… If I didn't know better, I'd take you for another lunatic let loose on this penal colony of a world for a vacation from some cosmic loony bin. But I'm about to spend considerable amounts of time with you in a band, preferably also during daylight, so excuse me for wanting to clear this up. OK?"

"Yeah, sure."

"Fine. So, please, let's discuss vampiric homophobia before we proceed to more urgent matters."

"What do you want me to say?" Bogomyr protested. "Wouldn't you feel a bit on the gay side if you bit some stinking sweaty hairy construction worker in the neck and drunk his blood?"

"Now that I think about it," Finnegan narrowed his eyes as he imagined the scene, "I probably would. No, frankly, I think that sounds about as gay as getting a perm in pink ballet slippers and rainbow tights while *Dancing Queen* plays on the radio."

Beeba, pouring schnappses for the cranky Stanko and sulky Tinka, the old drunks who stood at the bar, suddenly succumbed to a fit of giggles. She'd witnessed outlandish debates like this before, and she rather liked them. Finnegan looked up at her, suddenly suspecting her of understanding English way better than she spoke it – and he was right.

"Exactly," Bogomyr raised his voice in order to make a point. "So, you admit you'd rather bite a voluptuous young smooth-skinned maiden, smelling of dewy mornings, bunny coats, ancient tomes of fairy tales, a sprinkle of rain during scorching summer days, who makes your mouth water as you literally hunger for her juices?"

"I suppose I do admit that."

"So, does that make you a homophobic vampire?"

"No, but it sure makes me a horny son of a bitch."

It was Bogomyr's turn to laugh. "Enough said. I just prefer the ladies and let's leave it at that."

Finnegan clapped and congratulated Bogomyr: "OK, fine. But listen," Finnegan managed to become gravely serious, "I still don't believe you're actually drinking people's blood."

Bogomyr's smile waned and his gaze dropped to the sticky grime under their corner table again.

"Look into my eyes and tell me you actually do it," Finnegan told Bogomyr.

After a lengthy pause, Bogomyr crumbled: "Well, fuck it all. To be completely honest, I don't actually drink blood. I try to keep up appearances, but I'm afraid I'm either not a very good vampire or this bloodsucking thing might as well be another one of those stereotypes I've already told you about. Sanguivoriphobia, you know."

Bogomyr let out a deep breath and became a tad teary-eyed. Had Finnegan not just witnessed him drinking a litre of Merlot in half an hour, he might have even felt sorry about prying into his personal affairs so obtrusively. However, what was done was done, so he waited, without saying a word, for Bogomyr to pull himself together and go on. It certainly looked like the Ukrainian hadn't revealed everything he wanted to get off his chest just yet.

"Frankly," Bogomyr cleared his throat, "I usually just find girls who look as nice as possible and who show any interest in me. Then I get close to them, which has never been much of a problem for me, because, as you can probably see, I'm quite a handsome guy..." Bogomyr chuckled despite his apparent despondency. "And then I bore them to death with my depressing demeanour, feeding off them. You know, I consume their good intentions and positive attitude for as long as they still have some sympathy left for me. After I'm done with them, they usually end up hating men, but I'm satiated. Some of them have even declared themselves lesbians after they'd had to put up with me for a while, so I guess I do relieve them of all their favourable inclinations towards men. All things considered, for the purpose of this debate... Yes, in the end they are nothing but husks of women that had once lived, but then met me and got fucked up and sucked dry. There, that's the most sincere description of my vampiric nature I can muster. But that's just what I am. It's in my blood and it can't be helped. I'm still afraid of the sun and pointed wooden sticks, though. And handmade toothpicks."

"Bogomyr, you *are*, I hope, aware that what you've just said actually describes most of the relationships in my life, too. And when women get totally tired of you, they most probably tell you to fuck off, right?"

"Yes, they do."

"Unbelievable. One final thing. How old are you?"

"Thirty-four."

"So you're not convinced of your incredible longevity, which would fit a vampire nicely, as far as I'm concerned?"

"Well, no, not yet. Even though I really hope that's not another one of those stupid stereotypes. Well, actually, on my more optimistic days I do hope to live for a long time, while on the more pessimistic occasions I hope to vanish without a trace as soon as possible."

"Fine, I almost understand now. You're a barrel of laughs, you really are. I'm overjoyed you're in our band, man, I love you," Finnegan opened his arms, leaned over the table, and hugged Bogomyr. Bogomyr returned the favour, suddenly feeling better as he received some attention and affection. He said: "I love you too, man, cheers," and they smacked their glasses together in that olden and much-abused Slavic fashion.

Across the bar, Amalia, who noticed the ultimate fraternisation among the key band members, laughed and slapped Kip's shoulder: "Ha! I knew they'd work it out!"

In the far corner, Finnegan pulled himself together and said: "Well then, considering everything you've just told me – why the hell do you figure sunlight will hurt you? You do realise this daylight thing of yours may be just another figment of your overactive imagination, don't you?"

"Absolutely not, I'm sure I'd be far from OK if the sun shone on me too intensely…"

"Have you ever let it?"

"Not that I know of…" Bogomyr made an effort to think about it, "I've always avoided it if I possibly could."

"Great, you must have been a really unproblematic child. What did your parents have to say about that?" Finnegan joked and picked up his beer.

"My father was not around, and my mother is a vampire, so, you know…" Bogomyr said.

After a startled pause, the tired Scotsman put his beer back on the table and smacked his forehead. He covered his eyes with both hands and succumbed to a fit of desperate giggles. When he finally managed to feign at least a marginally straight face, Finnegan gazed at his rather "special" friend, looking forward to further bizarre statements and revelations that he may yet fish from Bogomyr's seemingly limitless treasure cove of eccentricities.

"Your *mother* is a vampire? Oh, come on, really? Which Romanian castle ruin does she stalk the local peasants from as we speak?"

"Look, man, I'd really prefer not to talk about my family right now, especially not in such a perversely idiotic manner, if that's OK with you."

Bogomyr became agitated again. He almost seemed on the verge of leaving, so Finnegan figured it was best that he lay off what was evidently a very sensitive topic.

"Of course. Sorry, I see you feel strongly about this, I apologise."

Bogomyr looked at him suspiciously.

"I really do, I apologise. I'm an arsehole, what can I say? It's in my nature."

Bogomyr nodded. Finnegan, however, proceeded with the issue that currently drove too many nails in the coffin that were his daytime practice sessions with the band: "But still, I must ask: how do you suppose sunlight will harm you?"

"It burns, of course," Bogomyr replied, obviously surprised that Finnegan would ask him about things that should be pretty self-evident.

"Burns!" Finnegan spit out the word. "Of course you can get nasty sunburns, especially if you've never been out of your cellar during daylight in your life. Now that you mention it, you do look terribly pale. What I'm asking you is, would you actually die? You've never really tried it, you say. How do you know what will happen, then?""

"My mother never went out during daylight," Bogomyr explained. "She told me I'd go up in flames, burn to death, because I was a vampire, just like her, and that I was an unholy son of Satan, unworthy of walking in God's light."

"Well, fuck me with a sandpaper dildo and no lubrication whatsoever. Didn't you say you weren't religious?"

"I'm not. I'm a hardcore atheist, actually."

"Why do you believe this shit, then?"

"I don't believe any of that good and evil God and Satan crap, but I'm still a vampire. I know that for a fact. OK? My mom may have been a bit religious, but as far as vampirology goes, she knew what she was talking about. My kind may just be highly allergic to ultraviolet light for all I know, and vampires may have made up several stupid stories about supernatural phenomena over the centuries since they didn't understand any of it very well, but I surely don't want to test this out right now to gather empirical evidence just to indulge *your* sceptical ass."

"Pardon me in advance, but your mom sounds like a religious psychotic. But hey, we're not supposed to go into your family background right now," Finnegan smiled apologetically and raised his arms in defence.

Bogomyr aimed an angry stare at Finnegan, so the Scotsman decided to lay off the Ukrainian's lineage for the time being. He proceeded with his main point, though: "Oh, damn it... Look, have you *ever tried* to walk in the sun?"

"Jesus, what kind of an idiotic question is that? Of course not. Are you daft?"

At this point Finnegan started losing his sense of humour. He was getting tired of this pointless debate, so he decided to bring it to an end... gradually. He finished his drink and slammed the empty beer stein on the table: "Tell me this, then," he told Bogomyr. "When I was booking the flight from London to Ljubljana, I noticed there were no night flights. Or, at least, I couldn't find any. I looked very carefully, though, because I love night flights and I always book them whenever I possibly can. That's because I like looking at the little lights in the dark far below the airplane, and it's also convenient that not so many people hang around airports at such late hours. I also love drinking beer at airports during such journeys, but drinking beer during the day is simply not the same as doing it during the night. Nobody looks at you

funny if you carry a six pack with you while waiting for a
night flight – it is as if there was some unspoken consensus
about when it's the appropriate time to grab a pint or two.
Admittedly, this rule is somewhat more relaxed at the
airports than in, say, other public places... But, nevertheless,
everybody tends to look at you a bit funny if you too eagerly
dive straight into a good ole pint o' ale at nine in the morning.
At least, you can certainly feel some people despising your
pint, at least marginally, even if you've just flown in from
Rapa Nui with a terrible case of time lag. Yes, the Easter
Island... Speaking of Easter, the bunny..." Finnegan suddenly
hiccupped.

"No, no, wait a second, I'm getting quite sick of this,"
Bogomyr protested. "Your lines of thought just got all
squiggly." The Ukrainian tried being reasonable for a change.
He felt that he had the upper hand at the moment. "What in
the hell did you want to ask me?"

"Oh!" Finnegan lit up. "I'm sorry for digressing,
I slipped down a certain memory lane by accident," he
muttered. "I'll pull myself together. I wanted to say... I'm
damned if I know. What was it again? Shit, let me see..."

"Something about night flights, I don't know."

"Oh!" The locomotive stalled at the head of Finnegan's
train of thought suddenly coughed to life again. "Yeah. What I
was trying to say was, how did you get here then, if there are
no night flights to Ljubljana and you don't go out while the
sun is up?"

"You're a real piece of work. You should buy a stupid
hat and call yourself Inquisitor Frotz. You'd make a lousy
one, though. First of all, I came here during the winter. The
days are not so very long then, remember? Sound familiar?
Second... I flew here from Frankfurt, and there are some
evening flights to the Letališče Jožeta Pučnika airport. Look
it up if you want. Thirdly...!" Bogomyr underlined while
Finnegan tried to catch his breath, obviously surprised again
by the adverse effects of all the pestilent beverages he had
consumed. Bogomyr was on a winning streak. At least he

might succeed at drinking the annoying Scotsperson under the table.

"Well, third...!" the alleged vampire tried to continue, but then gulped down his remaining merlot and laughed: "Well, looks like I forgot the rest of my points, too."

He suddenly became very mellow, open and sincere, so he told Finnegan, who at that time seemed very preoccupied with scratching his head and aiming a glassy gaze into a remote corner: "Look, Sherlock, I admit it. I've been forced to step out during the day occasionally. But I try to do it when it's really cloudy. I put on a thick layer of special vampire-approved factor 666 sunscreen, wrap myself in tinfoil, put on a heavy trench coat, and wear welding glasses and a helmet over a tinfoil hat. You wouldn't believe how many times I've had to put up with cavity searches at airports and border crossings because the security guys thought this outfit of mine was simply too ludicrous. Not to mention the embarrassing fact that pretty girls tend to discriminate against you if you dress up like that."

Finnegan laughed drunkenly and finally managed to focus on Bogomyr: "It's good you're not allergic to aluminium, then!"

26. Ray Kosmick
and his Free Sex Revolution

At the two large tables by the entrance to Boris and Beeba's Rock 'n' Roll Tavern, opposite to the unremarkable vampire and drunken Scotsperson who kept sniggering in the remote corner, Ray, Willit, Largo, Amalia, Kip and Randy were in session.

"So," Ray Kosmick explained one of his projects passionately, "I write script for new porno film. I already have a music for it, wanna hear?" Ray asked Amalia. "Maybe you can sing for me sometime. I sent this and some other of my music to Italy if somebody want to use it in their porno or hire me for soundtrack, but then nobody answer me. Anyway, maybe I change my mind and keep it for my own master work. Beeba, can I put my new song on? It's real nice."

Beeba looked up from her cocoa and crossword puzzle, shrugged and gestured at Boris's laptop in the corner, plugged, naturally, into an amplifier and the Pub's comprehensive surround sound audio infrastructure put together by none other than the ultimate cable surgeon, Boris Birman himself. Beeba would rather have kept listening to *Pink Floyd*, but at the time she didn't feel like getting involved in highly annoying music negotiations with Mr Kosmick. She knew better than that. Ray plugged his USB stick into Boris's dedicated jukebox computer and played one of his most recent tracks, titled *I Find It Twitching* [https://soundcloud.com/ray-kosmick/i-find-it-twitching].

The beer-bellied porn groove artist returned to the table, sat down and explained: "In this my new script I write an art porno, a social... How do you call it again, Largo?"

"Socially conscious," Largo reminded the great porn screenwriter.

"Ya, a socially conscious porno," Ray nodded.

"Wow, this should be interesting," Amalia sighed.

"Sure is interesting. I can tell you all about it. In the film I propose a lot of masturbation and satisfaction with power tools," Ray gestured passionately, "but the guys from porno industry I talk to never listen to me. They always think of me some strange guy from the Balkans. Nobody listen to reason, and so year after year after year everyone keep making same crap all the time."

Willit Lonch patted his shoulder reassuringly: "I know, mate, I'm sure it's a bloody torture being such a sensitive but misunderstood and undervalued artist."

Largo's ear-to-ear smile shone from the opposite end of their table through his half-empty small beer.

Boris, who had just decided to stop mixing *The Bottles* in his studio and join everyone in the pub, suddenly became interested in the discussion, so he grabbed his weiss beer and sat down next to Kip and Amalia.

Amalia decided the topic was entertaining enough to pour some kerosene on Ray Kosmick's fire: "So, Ray, if I understand you correctly, this masterpiece of yours involves power tools in the service of art, everything packaged as a torture porn flick. How is this socially conscious? Do working-class heroes appear in it, and do they have to resort to using power tools because they don't have the money for fancy sex toys?"

"You joke, although I can put workers in, if you like see worker in action. But torture porno, no, I never mention torture," Ray flailed his arms. "I mean, pleasurable power tool use. Very pleasurable, you understand?" he winked at Amalia. "But otherwise, absolutely tools are serving art purpose. I want using Omnipile tools, with visible logos, you know, to show symbolically how today the corporations fuck you."

"How incredibly poetic," Amalia grinned. "Neat track, though," she gestured at the speakers and nodded in time to Ray's new piece.

"Yes," Ray lit up, "I think it fit nicely with my

screenplay."

"I can already see it," Willit visualised, "Dildos mounted on Omnipile reciprocal saws and power drills... Massage pads fitted on random orbit sanders and used on well-oiled buttocks... "

"Exactly," Ray concurred, "I want the world to see how on one side corporations fuck you, and also use sex to fuck you... And on the other side they make AIDS and stuff so that you can't really do nice fucking with nobody. The world need a new sex revolution, people must be free of this."

"Right on," Largo said. "Sexual revolution or any other revolution will do. Beeba, give me another small beer... Strike that, I'm having too much fun, give me two small beers."

Even Kip, sitting opposite of Amalia and following the debate with a slightly disbelieving look on his face, was intrigued: "They use sex to fuck you?" he dared to inquire.

Boris, sitting next to them, issued his trademark Muttley snicker. Then he noticed Beeba calling him over to the bar, so he sighed and tore himself away from the table reluctantly.

"Ya, of course," Ray explained patiently, glancing at Boris, then looking back at Amalia: "For example, when I was at Venus Porn Fair in Berlin..."

"Oh, god, here we go again," Largo rolled his eyes.

"Shut up, you! Your workman revolution is nothing compared to sex revolution that must come soon!" Ray turned to Kip: "At Venus Fair I see many sex product of companies owned by same Omnipile, just under different name, and they fuck people by selling a lot of expensive toys, for example like natural-sensation vaginas, self-propelled dildos, you know, who do all work alone? And I see a little strange but nice genetically engineered stimulation fish..."

"*Stimulation fish*?" Amalia's eyes widened. She was almost afraid to ask.

"Yes, genetic labs need moneys, you see, so they genet-ically make stimulation fish for men. For useful pets, see, you put fish in your bathtub, and they orally satisfy you. Nice fish with big soft slimy mouth without teeth. Or not so big, depend on the model you need. But they can swim in nice warm water and are all impatient to pleasure their master. Oral stimulation fish, they called for real. They also meant to keep in very pleasureful pools in some most classy whorehouses all around the world. I wonder what happen if they escape into the sea, suddenly all men stand in water," Ray frowned as he concentrated on picturing it all vividly.

A sudden second of silence in Ray Kosmick's corner of the pub sounded so extraordinarily outlandish even Beeba looked up from behind the bar. The awkward pause was interrupted by Kip, of all people: "Are there models for women, too?"

"Yes, they try to make special nimble-tongue fish, but that seem too strange, they say. So they tell me next year they'll be having these warm fuzzy genetically made cuddly doggies with big..."

"Oh, for crying out loud," Amalia punched him in the shoulder.

Ray laughed heartily and said, raising his arms victoriously: "Well, there you go, but you know the point I make. You see, they not only fuck you with things you don't know they fuck you with, they also even fuck you with fuck toys. And they especially fuck you by making you want to buy fuck toys they fuck you with."

"That's deep, man," Largo said, "Or is it? Who could tell, exactly..."

"Ya, I think about this a lot. I mean that, what I wanna say, ya, they make this on purpose." Once Ray got going, Ray went on and on, and he gestured wildly while he was at it, too. "On one side they use sex in every commercial, rub sex in your face, so to speak. Hidden sex, only, how do you say... What's the word again... Illusions to sex? Doesn't matter, you know what I mean, sex just so they can sell stuff. But on other side they hide sex all the time, what's that called again... Ya, censor it! And scare everyone with disease, so is really hard to get nice real sex anywhere. Much more hard than they make it look on TV."

"And the corporations have also made AIDS?" Amalia
ventured.

"Ya, of course, who else can make AIDS if not rich
company with genetic labs. If they know how to make oral
stimulation fish and always horny puppy..."

"Ray may be exaggerating, but the subject matter is
indeed fascinating," Willit Lonch interrupted, apparently
also warming up. "You'd think that today's societies would
be more enlightened and that all the puritanical neuroses,
religious fanaticism and other related childish taboo nonsense
would be a thing of the past. But in reality it's much easier to
see someone's head blown off on TV, even in the afternoon
when all the kids are watching, than being able to enjoy a
nice set of tits. Even at night, sex-related adult content is
shunned by the vast majority of television stations like the
plague. Jesus, even in the seventies and eighties, late-night
programming was kinkier! God forbid that someone would
actually go so far as to fornicate on television in broad
daylight. This nonsense even permeates into computer games:
you can shoot, dismember, run over, incinerate, behead and
disembowel everybody and every damn creature you come
across, terrestrial or otherwise, including innocent bystanders.
Meanwhile, the broads dancing in titty bars in these same
computer-generated environments have their tits or at least
their nipples censored. As if there was something so inconceivably mind-boggling about a good ole nipple that nobody
can ever be allowed to see one, while it's also about the only
sight that any slobbering mammalian infant is interested in.
Maybe that's the catch. And, while we're on the subject of sex
in computer games, every game you can possibly get laid in
only fades to a black screen when it's supposed to happen, or
only hints somehow at the action. I mean, shit, I'm not twelve
years old anymore! I want some serious bloody shagging
going on, mate! What the hell? I mean, a bloody snatch and
a tit are the first things every damn newborn babe sees and
smells and tastes, but later that's all whisked away like it's
some particularly underhanded magic trick, and replaced by

images of Dolph Lundgren caving someone's face in in every other scene. No wonder everyone's totally neurotic and kids are doing drugs and shooting each other in the face instead of screwing their brains out while they can still get it up and feel like having it off every five minutes!"

"Whoa, settle down, you crazy Brit, that Dolph Lundgren image is painfully disturbing and a tad 1980s! But, I agree, it's actually a seriously screwed-up world, and I'm sure this results in all sorts of conflicts and frustrations," Amalia said, seemingly growing a little more interested. "Besides, don't get me started about contraception, either, I mean, if they can make blowjob fish, as Ray explained so picturesquely, I'm sure it's about time they came up with something more useful than the stupid stinking condoms all men hate, and birth control pills that give women blood clots and mood swings and cancer. They could at least make pills for men. I bet it's not that hard to kill or immobilise those pesky little spermatozoa. But probably most blokes, the poor sods, couldn't be bothered popping one every morning, right? Besides, it's men who run most corporations, anyway, so why not feed a bunch of hormones to women instead."

Amalia decided to go back to the original subject and dig even deeper. So she turned to Ray again, hoping to uncover further gemstones of wisdom and partake in his seemingly inexhaustible fountain of crackpot ideas: "But tell me, Ray, why would they do that? What do these evil corporations you keep referring to hope to gain by genetically engineering sexually transmitted diseases, for example?"

"Apart from killing everyone in Africa and making room for further capitalist exploitation?" Largo proposed.

But Ray had another theory: "It's very simple. Frustration must be, what's it called... Ventilated? Let out, ya? So people let out by going to mall and buy even more stuff they fuck them with," Ray the porn groove philosopher elaborated. "They – you know, the companies, priests, those who have money – they make the situation on purpose where you can't have free love, they push you in corner, they make you frustrated, but you still need, you still want, so you just buy something for replacement. Like something for wearing, or a new telephone, or an auto, or the always horny puppy. Instead of just making sweet love to your wife or friend or neighbour or cashier at the supermarket for free."

"And so you've decided to make a film about this?" Amalia inquired.

"Of course, why not? It is excellent topic."

Willit contributed more precious artistic visions of his own: "Lots of hot lesbian sex or sex with athletic handymen if you like, involving some pretty bizarre toys made by Omnipile, not originally meant for this purpose, but adapted by the genius Ray over here. This would make the props stand out a bit, right, so everybody would see what the point is, don't you agree?"

"Yes, it would be an angry outcry against capitalism! Karl Marx meets the porn industry," Largo slammed his fist at the table.

"Karl Marx, angry about not getting hot sex for nothing, more like, so he fight for a communist sex revolution, where everyone must have sex for free, guaranteed by law," Ray cracked a smile. "Yes, we should put that in the film. We can start the new sex revolution right there. Yes, free sex revolution. Maybe when now people see how evil Omnipile is, they force companies to make cure for AIDS and every sex disease. You know, instead of making stupid product nobody needs and starting wars. Plus, as you say, maybe they finally must make free and safe and super birth control, and then people can have hot sex all the time as they like. So they no longer want so much money because they can have all the sex they want. They are no more greedy, they no longer want power, because it says in the law that everyone must have free sex. Because, you know, money and power and expensive fast autos only replace for not getting laid. Or you just want them to get you laid, because girls like money and power, too. But you see, after free sex revolution, there are sex workers paid by the state to give free sex to people who are more ugly and more fat, like me, for example," Ray winked at Amalia. "As much sex they want, ya?

So, when people are free and no longer so angry by all such tits around them they can never squeeze, they don't rape mother nature no more, because they can make sweet love to their fellow human being anytime they want. And when your friends and neighbours become more free minded, they have sex with each other and maybe even with you. For free of charge."

"Exactly, because chicks that aren't for free are also a product of the consumer society. Such behaviour should be abolished," Largo burped.

"Absolutely, mate, it's not only that prostitution should be legalised: it should be subsidised by the government. But first, before this carnal Dionysian utopia of yours is unleashed upon the Earth and capitalism finally crumbles under everyone freely humping each other for the sheer fun of it like bonobo apes, you need to find some actresses who are into it for the sake of art, not money, Ray," Willit remarked, licking his lips and glancing at Ms Winegirl.

"Don't you glare at me, you crazy old tosser," Amalia frowned at the Brit. Willit just shrugged innocently.

"Ya, tell me about it," Ray droned on, "I try to explain this to filmmaker, so I go up to people on Venus Fair, tell them *Guten Tag, ich bin Ray Kosmick und ich bin ein Porn Groove Meister*, and then try to say my ideas, but they don't listen. They never listen to me. They always think I'm just a strange crazy man from Balkans. Now after I been going to Venus Porn Fair in Berlin many many years in a row, they see me coming from far away. They start hiding that they laugh and when I want to talk, they always say they have more important thing to do."

"You really are somewhat of a weirdo, Ray. But, see, maybe those capitalists are only worried you'll unmask and dethrone them all," Willit patted Ray's broad shoulder again.

"That's right! Some day! Some day soon!" Largo raised his fist.

"Yeah, some day Ray's vision will come true and even you may get laid without paying for it," Amalia smirked at the revolutionary Italian.

27. Boris, Finnegan & Bogomyr

At a certain point during this captivating conclave, Beeba motioned to Boris, who was obviously sick of *The Bottles* and decided to take a break, to get his ass over to the bar and talk to her. At that precise moment Boris was enjoying an elaborate lecture on the fine points of female power-tool-assisted masturbation by none other than the ultimate expert, Žarko Kozmič a.k.a. Ray Kosmick. So it was not surprising that when Boris finally, grumpily, joined Beeba behind the bar, he muttered something about *damn women* under his breath.

However, Beeba must have whispered something important in Boris's ear, because he quickly became serious and thoughtful. He looked up at the remote corner table, nodded at Beeba, and made his way to Bogomyr and Finnegan. He put on a questioning expression and waited for them to acknowledge and accept his intention of joining them and starting an in-depth conversation.

Finnegan and Bogomyr became all ears: they legitimately expected this to be a very special occasion. Boris wasn't in the habit of chatting openly with people he wasn't truly comfortable with, and Finnegan doubted he'd managed to become a member of that very exclusive inner circle of Boris's best pals so soon. So this was either something sensational that Boris felt like sharing, abysmal boredom with Ray Kosmick's doctoral theses on all things pertaining to porn, a special mission at Beeba's behest, or simply a chemically-assisted cheerful disposition. It turned out it was Beeba's special mission combined with random good mood because of which Boris felt like listening to Beeba and sharing an idea with Bogomyr and Finnegan. Ray's tireless prattling had nothing to do with it this time.

Boris pulled up a chair and sat down at the end of the

table. "Hello. Well... *Na zdravje,*" Boris began and grabbed his weiss beer bottle.

"*Slainte!*" Finnegan bellowed and they drank to their health. "*And to Bogomyr's mental hygiene,*" crossed Finnegan's mind.

"So... Beeba tells me..." Boris leaned towards Finnegan and Bogomyr conspiratorially. "She says she couldn't help overhearing that Bogomyr has some kind of fear of the sun or something like that?"

Bogomyr and Finnegan looked at each other disconcertedly. They suddenly pulled themselves together and instantly seemed to sober up.

"A bit of heliophobia, yes," Bogomyr frowned.

"Well, because about a year ago I had some weird problems, too..." Boris leaned even closer to the other two, obviously trying to make sure not a word of their conversation reached the tables on the other side of the semi-circular bar, which Ray and Willit presided over. Finnegan suspected this was not because Boris wanted to keep Bogomyr's secrets to themselves, but because he wanted to restrict the information about his own embarrassing experiences to their gloomy table in the remote corner of the room. Finnegan and Bogomyr were suddenly even more curious about what Boris had to say. They waited for him to clear his throat awkwardly and get on with it.

"It all started when this strictly commercial band, *The Bottles,* started coming here. Now, I'm trying to make some money on the side with my studio, as a sound engineer and producer, you know the routine. So I said, OK, fine, I'll produce your album. They didn't seem so bad... Until things got complicated. Especially because of Niki Lipps, their singer, god damn, she's a real piece of work." Boris stared into some untold distance with dismay.

"Niki Lipps? No shit?" asked Finnegan, surprised to hear such a name in the Slovenian suburbia.

"Well, that's just her special artistic pseudonym, of course. In reality her name is Nikolina Lipušček. Not really fitting for a superstar femme fatale, is it?" Boris said, snickering.

"Does she look good, at least?" Finnegan inquired.

"Is she succulent?" Bogomyr wondered.

Boris smiled: "Well... Yeah, she definitely believes she's irresistible. And apparently most guys agree, too, though she's not my type at all, really. But she has her band wrapped around her finger, that's for sure. I don't think she lets any of them get too close, probably because she wants all of them to think it might potentially be possible to bed her, so she keeps playing the old gits indefinitely, and they can't even tell they're being manipulated. You know, occasionally she lets one of them stroke her butt playfully or brush against her boob, like, accidentally, for as long as it's all a 'joke'..." Boris made quotation marks with his fingers. "But I don't think she actually lets any of them give her the bone, really. If she ever had it off with any of them, she'd lose her hold over the others and maybe even cause the band to split up. Oh, lordie, if only!" Boris clenched his hands in a prayer and gazed at the ceiling longingly.

"I see you've given this broad a lot of thought," Finnegan laughed. Bogomyr smiled contentedly, obviously enjoying himself – finally someone else got in Finnegan's crosshairs and the alleged vampire felt relieved to be off the hook. At least for the time being.

"Sure, I've thought about it a lot. Hell, I've had to put up with her and The Bottles for far too long," Boris complained. "But that's not the point, really. After they started recording their crap, I got more and more frustrated with Niki. First it turned out that The Bottles sucked at arrangements, so I helped them work out some stuff, especially backing vocals, and then they just came to expect that from me without even thinking of paying me for it or crediting me as a co-author of the arrangements. Niki really started getting on my nerves, because her idea of singing involves screaming her head off and abusing far too many of those awful R'n'B licks, no matter what the tracks are all about."

"Oh boy, do I hate it when they wail like that," Finnegan said.

"Absolutely, it's terrible," Boris rambled on, obviously intent on pouring his wounded heart out. "Of course, then it also turned out that Niki wasn't really so very precise in terms of intonation, either, no matter how good she thinks she is. So I had to spend hours and hours tuning her, and then she'd usually demand to record a few more takes, because she hated that I'd had to tune her – which I never forget to mention to her explicitly just to let her know she's galaxies away from perfect, of course – but this only results in more tuning. By the way, did I mention that careful tuning and editing of vocals is hard work, and extremely boring, at that? You know, if you want to make it subtle and unnoticeable? It's not like that clearly audible tuning heard in so many pop songs nowadays. Or the sickening, crappy effect, heard over and over again ever since Cher recorded that damned hit of hers ages ago and used this disgusting shit in it. Because *that* kind of tuning – I think that's surely a nefarious ploy undertaken by lazy sound engineers and producers who don't want to spend the time and effort needed to record and edit their singers properly!"

"I must say your theory sounds logical to me," Finnegan agreed, having during his career as a part-time and usually unpaid music producer spent countless painful hours toiling away on vocals himself.

"Anyway," Boris went on, "Then Niki slowly got to think that fancy studio equipment and music software could do anything, so she got lazy and started relying on it far too much. Soon she'd want me to change the way her voice sounded by turning a few knobs, improve her pronunciation by using some magical plugin, and fire up a piece of software that would perfect her interpretation."

"Women!" Finnegan swore.

"Gradually I started losing sleep over it all, especially because no matter how hard I tried to explain that I wasn't quite Jesus Christ the miracle worker, Rado, Pavle, Janez and Vinko, the other members of *The Bottles*, kept backing whatever Niki came up with."

"The horny bastards," Bogomyr sniggered.

"You can say that again!" Boris agreed.

"But not you, of course, you've never considered slipping it to her, right?" Finnegan teased the desperate sound engineer.

"Oh come on, give me a break," Boris laughed. "Well, of course I *thought* about it, especially when I was drunk, because I suspected maybe something was wrong with me. Everybody else seemed to slobber over that anorexic wench all the time, and I seemed to be the only guy unable to see what all the fuss was about."

"I'll bet," Finnegan blurted out.

"Whatever. But that's not the point. What I wanted to say was…" Boris punched the giggling Bogomyr in the shoulder. "Quit it, man, I can't concentrate!"

Boris took a breath, paused to gather his thoughts, and proceeded: "The real problems started when *The Bottles*, especially Niki and Vinko, started demanding that we should include more accordions into the arrangements. Now, let me tell you, I try to be tolerant when it comes to music, but accordions I'm actually physically allergic to."

"Why? I watched some of these Slovanian Alpine dancing songs on TV and I found them hilarious. Can't you simply find humour in them? Don't you think humour belongs in music?" Finnegan dropped a quick Frank Zappa allusion on Bogomyr just to appear witty.

"I'll give you humour! It's not funny at all! Try putting up with this crap for forty years and we'll see what you think of it then," Boris rolled his eyes. "Anyway… So, at about that time, apparently because of all the stress I'd obviously had to put up with, I started losing more than just sleep."

Boris lowered his voice, glanced over his shoulder at the people across the bar who, to his relief, seemed to be – judging by Willit and Ray's flailing arms and Amalia's constant fits of laughter – engrossed in their own dramatic discussions. So Boris leaned forward again and whispered confidentially: "Honestly, first I experienced total pubic hair loss, which scared the shit out of me, not to mention the embarrassment. I had no idea what was going on or why this was happening. Then all this anxiety also translated into... Well, a little bit of an erectile dysfunction... Until finally my head hair also started falling out!" Boris's voice trembled as he stroked his long though thinning hippy locks lovingly.

"Pubic hair, erectile dysfunction, that's dreadful. But your head hair, well, that's abysmal," Finnegan said.

"Yeah, absolutely horrible," Boris agreed.

"So what happened?" inquired Bogomyr.

"Well, you see, occasionally a guy named Drago Dabić drops by. Dr Dabić, actually. You'll see him sooner or later, he lives nearby and comes here on a regular basis to drink herbal tea and listen to the concerts we organise, especially our so-called kinky psychedelic evenings. That's, you know, when Willit and Ray present their masterpieces." Boris paused, rolled his eyes and sighed. "Anyway, Drago is an expert in the occult, bioenergy, acupuncture, reiki, remote healing, voodoo, homeopathy, witchcraft, crystal therapy, astrology, numerology, astrotherapy, aromatherapy, the Seven Rays, astral projection, Atlantian healing, the Ashtar Command, angels, fairies, little green men, subterranean lizard people and pendulum-assisted magical energy identification, manipulation and application. He's also supposed to be an expert nutritionist, of course, though he's pretty fat, so I wouldn't put too much of my money on that."

"Oh, by the gods..." Finnegan rolled his eyes with obvious lack of appreciation.

"Look, it doesn't matter what you think, I don't believe any of that stuff either, with the possible exception of acupuncture."

"And why in the hell would acupuncture be any better than the rest of that quackery?" Finnegan protested.

"Come on, it's millennia-old Chinese medicine. It's been proven it works."

"Proved by whom? What scientific evidence has anyone

provided as to its effects? What documented, repeatable experiments have been carried out to date? Does any double-blind peer-reviewed research exist? What empirical evidence is there? Has it been measured properly, poked at, delved into, investigated thoroughly, explored closely, taken apart and put back together again?"

"I couldn't really say, but it's generally known..."

"Known, schmown. It's fucking placebo, that's what it is. It doesn't matter where you stick the needles, and the results will always be the same: either it'll help as placebo sometimes will, or it won't," Finnegan cursed.

"Look, it doesn't matter really. What I wanted to say..." Boris tried to explain very patiently, but Finnegan was on one of his drunken quests for the Truth. His Truth. It was one of those occasions when Finnegan felt he needed to enlighten everyone around him, regardless of whether they wanted to be enlightened or not. That was, he wanted to make them disbelieve whatever he himself disbelieved.

"Jesus, these fucking superstitious notions so many people fall for. You say acupuncture is an ancient Chinese practice, therefore it surely works. Wow, very logical, to believe in some unseen immeasurable energies that some prehistoric pre-scientific witch doctor on god knows what hallucinogenic mushrooms happened to think he stumbled upon. Not only that, then this chap also managed to develop, probably by means of divine inspiration, a complicated esoteric theory and arcane methods of how to utilise those magical forces to help others. And now people in the 21st century, when these mysterious energies still remain undetected, even though leptons and bosons and quarks have already been discovered, go on to employ this method – which is a placebo headache remedy at best – as a cure for cancer."

Boris only sighed, because Finnegan was obviously on a mission.

"Tell me this then," the Scotsman proceeded with the argument nobody was eager to hear, "There is another form of traditional Chinese medicine, which involves the ingestion of certain... errm... dubious food items in order to heal specific conditions or parts of the body. This is also ancient Chinese medicine, still in use today, and perhaps it even predates acupuncture, I wouldn't really know. So, do you also believe this form of medical practice works?"

"I don't know. I suppose. Look, I don't care, I'm not all that interested in this stuff," Boris shrugged indifferently.

"But you suppose it works. Just because it's ancient and because those Chinese charlatans still practice it today."

Boris shrugged again.

"So!" Finnegan threw up his arms and bellowed victoriously: "Why didn't you just munch on some pickled penises in order to tackle your penile dysfunction then, huh?!"

Boris sighed and stared at the floor as Finnegan's boisterous statement was first followed by sudden silence, finally interrupted by Amalia shouting across the bar: "Damn, boys, are you holding out on us? What the bloody hell are you going on about over there in the dark?"

Finnegan, suddenly aware he'd screwed up, shouted back: "We're just practicing some lines for our new theatre play. Now stop eavesdropping, will you?" The people across the room – Ray, Willit, Largo, Amalia, Kip and Randy – guffawed and then gradually seemed to go back to whatever they'd been discussing before the interruption.

When the coast was clear, Finnegan cleared his throat and said to Boris, in a somewhat subdued manner: "Sorry. I apologise. Do go on. You were saying?"

"Never mind, I'm not very touchy about the matter anymore. What do I care, after all – Dr Drago Dabić fixed it."

"He did, did he. What did he do, laid on hands? Swung a pendulum? Drew up an astrological chart? Summoned a supernatural force? Focused cosmic rays on you? Called an Atlantean angel to your aid?" Finnegan still couldn't help being excessively sarcastic.

"As I said, I would have none of that, even though Beeba wanted me to. But I agreed to acupuncture, so he gave me a series of treatments..."

"Which you undoubtedly paid for nicely..." Finnegan sighed.

"Which I got a special rock 'n' roll discount for," Boris explained and smiled. "Immediately after the first session Drago asked me if something particularly stressful was taking place in my life. Soon I realised that maybe it was *The Bottles*. You know, that those guys and that damn slut of theirs were the reason for my weird problems. After Dr Dabić was done with the therapy and I came to terms with my accursed fate as the producer of Niki Lipps, Rado, Pavle, Janez and Vinko, my troubles were gone. Drago Dabić also said something about my liver not being what it used to be, but I decided to ignore that remark. Maybe I'll let him solve that particular problem with some reiki in case I turn yellow," Boris winked and wrapped up his tale.

After a minute of silence, an ounce of feigned thought-fulness and a few sips of beer Finnegan prodded: "OK, fine, you felt better, your pubic hair grew back, your member saluted sturdily once again and your hairdo was delivered from evil. But why did you feel an urge to spin this fantastic yarn? There must be some purpose to it. You didn't just tell us this embarrassing story for the sake of entertainment, did you?"

"No, no," Boris shook his head a bit sleepily. Obviously weiss beer and longwinded tales of mishaps best forgotten were getting to him. "When Beeba heard of Bogomyr's fears that he'd melt in the sun or something like that she suggested you could go and see Dr Dabić. He's healed people of conditions far worse than yours," Boris looked at Bogomyr who seemed quite thoughtful.

"Yeah? Like what?" Bogomyr asked.

"Apart from my extreme case of psychosomatic disorder? I don't know exactly, I'm not his PR agent, man. But people talk about his achievements all the time. I don't listen to them, though, you know I don't actually pay much attention to the punters."

"Don't you know of any other examples, then?"

Bogomyr seemed interested in the whole Mr Dabić affair.

Finnegan wanted to slap him on the back and ridicule the esoteric guru he'd never met a little more, but then changed his mind. *"Actually this might be good,"* he thought. *"Maybe Dr Dabić will get these stupid notions out of Bogomyr's thick head, even if it's all just placebo or the power of suggestion or whatever. Conceivably we'll be able to rehearse like normal people and even meet in daylight. Perhaps I'd better support this idea and persuade Bogomyr to get help,"* Finnegan resolved.

Boris pondered for a while and suddenly lit up, raising a finger: "Ah! Yeah, you'd never believe it, but Drago also kind of healed our cat."

Finnegan looked up, startled: "You don't say?" He shifted his weight in his chair in anticipation, getting ready for another fascinating story.

"Yeah, when we put our pool table in, the stupid cat got all worked up about it. Dead scared of it, she was."

"And?" Finnegan eyed Boris suspiciously.

"Nothing. Beeba, god bless her simple soul, asked Drago to take a look at the damn cat when he dropped by once... He waved his hands around the dumb animal for a while, claiming he sensed what the problem was. He pulled out his pendulum, swung it around the cat and the pool table, and then told me to turn the table around and buy a new cue ball. He also mentioned my karma was slightly blemished and said I should clean the rotting marten carcasses out of the pool table and finally put the poor things to rest."

Finnegan tried really hard to keep his face from twisting into knots of laughter, but he wasn't very successful at it.

Nevertheless, Boris went on, ignoring the Scotsman: "Indeed," he said, even adding some extra gravity to his voice in order to drive his point in: "I stored the table in the attic while I was cleaning out the pool room, which took about a year or two. In the meantime, a family of martens seemed to have made their home in there. I have no clue how a couple of these critters kicked the bucket while nesting safely in the pool table. Maybe they ate something that didn't quite agree with them or dropped dead due to old age."

Suddenly Boris paused and thought for a moment.
"Wait a minute! I'll be damned," it suddenly dawned on him,
"Probably it was I who was responsible for the demise of the
martens in the pool table, after all! If I remember correctly,
I eventually noticed I had a marten infestation in my attic,
and ultimately, unable to come up with any other solution, I
decided to poison them all. The ones residing in my pool table
must have nibbled on poisoned bait as well." Boris thought
for a minute, shrugged, and droned on: "Whatever. Anyway,
the poor kitty must have had some pretty nasty experiences
with the martens, so she was terrified of the pool table. Once
I cleaned it out, turned it around and replaced the cue ball
just like Drago Dabić told me to, the stupid kitty got used to
it pretty quick. In fact, now she often sleeps on it or even slips
down into the holes when she wants to get away from it all.
Especially when she's sick of our daughter pestering her all
day long."

Finnegan was laughing quietly.

"I know what you're itching to say," Boris frowned at
Finnegan. "I'm not that stupid, you know. You're thinking...
Why turn the table around and replace the cue ball, because it
was obviously the dead martens that scared the cat."

"Right on," Finnegan taunted Boris.

"Well, first of all, I did it just to make Drago happy. He
gets upset if people don't take him seriously, you see, and
then you have to listen to his endless nagging for ages. It's
better to just humour him. Secondly, Drago also said it would
be far easier to set the table completely straight if we turned it
around... And it's cool if your pool table is nice and level. As
far as the cue ball goes... Besides it being inappropriate for the
cat for some mystical reason I decided not to ask about, it was
also chipped."

"I see, I see." Finnegan pulled himself together. "Well,
I think we should give it a shot, after all. What do you think,
Bogomyr?" Finnegan turned to Bogomyr, pretending to
support the idea.

"It's an option. Sure, maybe. I just have a couple more questions. Maybe you could clear this up for me..." Bogomyr turned to Boris.

"Sure, ask away."

"Do you think I could arrange for my first session during the night?"

"Well, I really don't know," Boris answered, "I don't think so..."

"Damn it, Bogomyr," Finnegan grew impatient, "Don't be absurd. You'll just wrap your baseball cap in tinfoil, don your special coat, smear on a thick layer of sunscreen, put on your sunglasses and off we'll go. Hell, I'll go with you and shield you with a parasol. We'll beat this together, OK, laddie?" Finnegan put his hand on Bogomyr's back supportively.

"Fine, I suppose we could try. If you'll really accompany me," all the Merlot caused Bogomyr to consent.

"Will do."

"OK, I have just one more concern then..." Bogomyr turned to Boris apprehensively and ventured: "What are the acupuncture needles made of? They're not silver or wood by any chance, are they?!"

28. Interlude:
Iniquity

By the two tables at the entrance to the Rock 'n' Roll Tavern, a considerable miracle took place: Ray Kosmick finally changed the subject and focused on something other than additional uncalled-for details about the art porn flick he was supposedly working on, to the relief of Amalia and Kip who'd already grown tired of listening to his tall tales of oral stimulation fish and always horny puppies.

"So," Ray said, "You and he, your friend there –" Ray pointed at the table in the remote corner behind his back – "You two are in a band now, yes?"

"Oh, me and Finnegan, we go way back. We've worked together for ages, already back in Scotland, of course, before I even started thinking about moving anywhere. But after I left Kirkwall we had to put our band on standby for a while, so to speak. We kept exchanging ideas, though, and working on some stuff over the internet, you know, recorded some demos, and now Finnegan's decided to join me and Randy here, so we can get on with our music."

"So you already have some songs to show? I only asking because I like to know how your songs sound. Now, I showed you mine, will you show me yours?" Ray smiled stupidly at his infantile choice of words.

"Yeah, yeah, Ray, you're a regular barrel of laughs. Well, actually, I have a couple of demos here on my iPod that we've been working on lately. Sure, I'll put something on. Beeba, could I also play a track or two, please?"

Beeba's face faded into disappointment, but after rolling her eyes and letting out a tired breath, she reconciled herself with her fate and pointed at Boris's laptop. Obviously she'd have to put up with another track or two she didn't want to hear. She reminded herself that as a flower child (or rather a slightly over-the-hill flower matron) she had to be tolerant, so she'd just focus on her crossword puzzle until Ray and Amalia were done, and then she could keep nodding by her cocoa and meditating on her much-loved sounds of the Pink Floyd's 1960s psychedelic period.

"OK, here's one of our tunes…" said Amalia, plugged in her iPod and played a track she and Finnegan had recently recorded:

INIQUITY
[https://soundcloud.com/cynicism-management/
iniquity-augmented]

Put me up and put me down
Mercy fuck me then turn around
Ready-made as I serve any whim
Then I'm disassembled
Limb from limb

Sometimes when I snap
I turn on you
You cross the line
I cross it too
I feel disdain
You feel the pain
Again

I've been had you took the piss
But made me feel I have been amiss
I'll just leave you to bleed to death
And you'll thank me as you
Gasp for breath

You are lying
So I keep prying
I swear

I will hunt you down
Won't make a sound

Abruptly I can see this might be iniquity

Maybe we could all agree
that this might truly be iniquity
This might be iniquity

"So, about what is the song?" Ray inquired.

"The usual, it's just a love song. You know, the eternal, most frequently abused and highly stereotypical, even dreary topic in pop songs – sex and love."

Ray nodded.

"Only this one," Amalia added perkily, unable to help herself, "is about two lesbian friends of mine who had a somewhat, how to put it... Tumultuous relationship."

Ray smiled enthusiastically.

"Now, these two gorgeous young lesbian friends of mine could get a little harsh with each other sometimes. They'd often fight. You know, they'd have these real, actual catfights, preferably in public so that everyone could watch? And then they'd make up and start kissing and making out in front of everyone, after which they'd have a hot lesbian shag."

Ray's eyes widened and his mouth popped open.

"No, not in front of everyone, jeez... They'd go to the toilet or home first, of course."

Ray licked his lips.

"But every once in a while one of them would fool around with a man on the side, and sometimes they'd even bring one or two or even more guys home with them to spice things up..."

"Oh, very very nice, I like!" Ray Kosmick's eyes lit up.

"Yes, I thought you would. Well, forget it, you horndog! None of the lesbians I know would even go near a bloke, especially not a sweaty unshaven heterosexual sex maniac like you!"

Amalia frowned at the laughing Ray.

"And I bet if I told you the song was about a couple of gay men I know, you'd probably be less fascinated, am I right?"

"No, I don't make such difference..."

"Come on, Ray, don't give me that. Would you cast a couple of gay men in one of your movies?"

"No, but..."

"Why not?"

"Just because it don't make me so horny, that's all. I just think it funny and unerotic if two men touch each other in sensitive places, but I don't mean nothing by it. I don't have nothing against homosexual sex, I just like it much better when it involves gay girl, not gay man. It's just how I am," Ray claimed, but became significantly less enthusiastic about the whole affair and even pretended to be offended by Amalia's insinuations.

"I'm just pulling your leg, Ray, come on. Don't fret. The track is about a pretty universal topic, and it's about no one in particular. It's just a love song, only slightly more towards the S&M end of the spectrum. It doesn't matter who exactly it's about, heterosexual couples or otherwise. You know, it tells a story of all the people who drift towards a bit of violence in their relationships, and then when one of them decides it's about time to get out, the other starts stalking the former partner, threatening to kill them. You know the routine, the usual boring stuff."

"Ah, I see." Ray remarked and avoided Amalia's gaze.

"Look, in reality Finnegan wrote the lyrics in order to piss me off. You see, Finnegan and I, we have quite a history, and there aren't many things he doesn't know about me and vice versa. So, at one point I was going out with this arsehole who used to bring out the worst in me. He lied to me, got more and more abusive, had affairs behind my back... Then one day in a bar he became jealous of some sodding waiter or something. So he grabbed me and tried to slap me around, but I kicked him in the nuts, grabbed an ashtray and punched him in the face with it. Broke his nose right there. It was pretty bad. I was totally drunk, of course. When he was down on the floor screaming and people grabbed me to stop me from doing something I'd *really* regret, I told him I'd follow him, hunt him down and finish him off."

"Oh." Ray said apprehensively and dropped his gaze.

"You seem shocked. Anyway, when I sobered up and regained my senses, I felt really bad about it, so I told Finnegan what happened. He made me promise I'd never go back to this guy again, and he wrote these lyrics right then and there so that I'd always be reminded of this."

Ray just stared at her.

Amalia laughed: "Come on, you wanker, don't take me so damn seriously, I'm just having a laugh." She slapped Ray's back and explained: "Actually the song is just a nasty inside joke Finnegan and I came up with when a friend of ours broke up with her boyfriend, who then proceeded to follow her around for a while, threatening her with a World War II pistol he happened to own."

"My, my, what friends you have... Yes, I see now. Maybe they would know about such things," Ray gestured at Stanko and Tinka, the infamous winos of Suburbia, who'd just wobbled into the pub and claimed strategic positions behind the bar.

Ray's eyes finally lit up again: "Maybe I can use this song and idea in the new porno film I make?"

29. Fergus & the Clowns

Six days ago – on Monday – Fergus was startled awake early in the morning as a couple of clowns marched into his room. He was not allowed to sleep in, and neither did the clowns cut him any slack because he was the CEO's son. Even if he were able to do such a thing, his dad wouldn't want to keep the bozos away from him, anyway.

Omnipile and its Intelligence Agency wanted to strip reality down to its very underwear and positively identify the kidnappers as well as confirm that the kidnapped had not wanted to be kidnapped in the first place. The OIA consisted of a bunch of compulsively suspicious lunatics who'd find the very roundness of Earth dubious if somebody happened to mention it during an investigation. Especially if that otherwise generally accepted fact affected Omnipile's profit margin in any adverse manner. And poor Fergus was now being scrutinised by these shady madmen.

"So," began a man in a pitch-black suit and a merry orange-polka-dot-on-a-navy-blue-background tie that should come with an epilepsy warning, "tell us about your kidnappers."

"What about them? Most of them had beards. Or a moustache. Or even both," Fergus offered this essential piece of information victoriously.

"Listen, boy," the orange-on-blue man thundered, "Let's get somethin' straight right away. We don't have the luxury of kiddin' around. You may be Ferdinand Fenton's son, and he can be the founder of this organisation a thousand times over, but let me tell ya: at this point even *he* ain't gonna stop us from doin' our job. Omnipile's the biggest and baddest transnational corporation of 'em all, and some lower life forms we usually call consumer maggots sometimes think we're an evil transnational corporation, too."

The orange-on-blue man let that sink in and leaned so close to Fergus that the poor boy could smell the stale fur on the man's tongue (with more than just a hint of garlic) and feast his eyes on a piece of bacon that must have got stuck in the Agent's teeth during breakfast.

"And you know what, boy?" the agent hissed menacingly into Fergus's face, blessing him even more generously with his exquisite breath, "Maybe they're right!"

The boy just sat there, quiet and thoughtful.

"Boo!" the OIA agent with poor oral hygiene yelled suddenly, and Fergus jumped.

The agent leaned back, laughing, and then droned on: "You know, boy, it's been so long since the Corporation's gotten so huge that now it's like it's got a life of its own. It can't simply be broken up because it's far too big for that: even your mornin' bread wouldn't be baked without us. Heck, yer toilet paper'd prolly feel like sandpaper if we didn't have our gentle luxury products with patented ass-protectin' cream setting the unattainably high standards in this department. Without our research and development in the field o' cosmetics there'd be no ingenious triple-action deodorants, protectin' you and the people around ya from the vile assertions of yer armpits for exactly 48 hours, no matter whether you play squash all day long or just kick back n' relax in the shade. So, without wastin' any more words I warn you: don't fuck with us and start talkin'!"

Fergus obeyed and ventured: "What about dental hygiene and mouthwash research? No progress worth mentioning in that department yet? Just wondering, I've had a bit of an annoying aftertaste since breakfast," he dared to remark rather tentatively.

The orange-on-blue man obviously failed to pick up on the insinuation. However, the corners of his colleague's mouth twitched and he glanced at the ceiling in order to hide his amusement with the boy's underhanded taunt.

"Look!" the orange-on-blue man pierced the boy with

an angry stare, "Stop wastin' our time with bullshit! You only speak when I ask a question, and when I do, I want all o' yer efforts invested in answerin' it. This might be yer only chance before all hell breaks loose. OK? We on the same page here?" Fergus figured that the orange-on-blue man obviously liked the sound of his own voice, as it seemed he couldn't stop talking. Fergus also thought the agent should also work on the persuasiveness and spookiness of his proverbial bad cop routine.

"Ummmm... Sure?" Fergus offered, surprised at how calm he felt despite the absurd situation he'd found himself in. He didn't even feel much indignation at the abuse, even though he was obviously the victim – not the perpetrator – of whatever these bozos thought went on here.

The second agent, obviously the designated proverbial good cop with a green-polka-dot-on-a-crimson-background tie, slapped the back of the bad cop, as if to calm him down, and took over: "Listen, kid, just describe your kidnappers in as much detail as you can. Try to think of any distinct features you may have noticed, you know, tattoos, broken teeth, golden dentures, weird jewellery or insignia, missing limbs, scars... You know, anything you think might help us identify the suspects. Remember, we have access to extensive records on terrorists. Chances are at least some of these men are in our databases. We already suspect certain anti-Omnipile elements. And don't get too intimidated by my colleague here. He's just having a bad day. OK?"

Fergus tried really hard: "They were mostly tall. They wore those white Arab frocks, you know, which are pretty loose, so I couldn't tell if they were really fat or not. Most of them had beards and bad haircuts and they smelled of exotic spices and old ashtrays. I think some of them had rotten teeth, but I'm not really a dentist."

"Listen, boy, don't ya get cute on us. Those are damn crooked terrorists we're talkin' about! The situation is urgent, dire, terrible, it's horrifyin', yer sister's still bein' hurt and raped by them, and it don't look like you wanna deliver

anythin' useful, so that we can save 'er from those evildoers!"
the bad cop got carried away.

"Look," Fergus, despite his tender age, sounded as
adult and gravely serious as possible, "I don't know what
you're getting at here, but they never harmed us, especially
not in horrible ways you're implying here. They didn't slit
our throats or anything like that. As you can very well see
for yourself, darn it. The only thing I really hated was their
food... It sucked. They only fed us exotic junk instead of
French fries and burgers. And what sucked even more was
that they had really outdated computers, so I could only play
horribly old games like Pitfall, Manic Miner, Atic Atac, and
Dig Dug. Jesus, how lame all that was, horrible sound and
graphics..."

The bad agent looked like he wanted to interrupt, but
the good cop shook his head. As if to confirm the good agent's
decision, Ferdinand Fenton, who was following the interrogation on the other side of the one-way mirror built into one
of the walls, instructed them over their in-ear headphones:
"Let him talk. We can sift through this garbage later. He's a
computer freak, it'll make him relax. And he may mention
something useful without even realising it."

"I found Elite and Mercenary slightly interesting when
I managed to get into them somehow after a while," Fergus
elaborated. "You know, after a few days when I realised I had
no choice but to come to terms with the stupid computers
which were already old when dinosaurs roamed the planet.
What else was there to do? And that's about it. How the heck
am I supposed to describe them to you? Like I've already
told you, they were just bearded Arabs. Some of them just
wore a moustache, and others, who probably liked Indian
cuisine, sometimes smelled of curry. Or do Arabs have curry,
too? I really wouldn't know. Too bad they didn't let us have
any, stingy bastards," Fergus seemed as observant as could
possibly be expected of a fourteen-year-old boy.

"Were there any clean-shaven men who spoke English
far better than the others, maybe? Well, or someone with a

recently grown moustache or beard, fluent in English? He'd probably appear smarter than the others, and he'd know his way around computers," the good agent inquired calmly.

Fergus shrugged.

"You say you had access to computers. Who gave you access, who showed 'em to ya? Did they have a special computer room?" the bad agent grunted and, to Fergus's dismay, leaned forward again, looking him in the eye.

Fergus pulled away from him and strived harder to gather his thoughts: "Just Habib."

"Habib? Who's that? What did he look like?"

"Just one of the Arabs, I don't know. He was the only one to talk to us most of the time, but he had a really bad accent. He didn't really speak English all that well at all. I think he worked on something on his computer while I played those games, but I don't know what. He had a laptop, but he sure wasn't going to let me use it, the bastard, even though I kept begging if I could send an e-mail to Moolly. And he..."

Fergus paused, suddenly unable to focus. He was so very sleepy...

"Who's Moolly?" the bad agent barked at Fergus and frowned.

Ferdinand Fenton told the agents over the headphones: "Forget the stupid Moolly character, it's one of his pals from his damn online games, it doesn't matter. I want to know about the man, the Habib guy, ask him what he was about to say. Jesus, some interrogation this is..." As Ferdinand's voice trailed away, the agents could hear him cursing about "guilds" and "raids" and "warcrafts". They obviously had no idea what he was rambling about, so they thought: "*Whatever, even the OIA can't know everything.*"

"So," the bad cop asked impatiently, "What were you gonna say?"

"What?" Fergus looked up, startled.

"You were talkin' about this guy called Habib, and before you stopped talkin', you were about to say somethin' else about him. 'And he...', you said."

"About Habib? I don't know. It was nothing, I suppose. I don't know what I meant by it. Nothing much. The whole thing was as boring as hell, that's all. Really darn boring, and I'm not kidding, either. Me and Habib, we didn't even talk about anything much, plus his English was very bad, so I didn't get what he was saying half of the time. Besides, I didn't really pay much attention. When I wasn't playing stupid Space Invaders from the previous millennium, all I kept thinking about were my computer games at home. Jeez, speaking of which, I should really get home, I must urgently go online!" The boy sighed and slumped forward on his chair, supporting his head with his hands. He refrained from mentioning World of Warcraft explicitly this time, because lately he had come to suspect that most adults, contrary to what he might think, knew nothing about it and didn't even care to know.

"Go online? Why?!" the bad agent eyed him suspiciously.

"No, goddamn it, don't ask him about that crap!" Ferdinand bellowed into their ears.

The agents glanced at each other.

"I…" Fergus began.

"Don't let him go there. Jesus wept, you'll just remind him of that Moolly twat…" Ferdinand pleaded into their ears.

"No, forget it, we don't wanna know," the good agent interrupted the boy, raising his arms in defence. "Here, take a look at this instead, please…"

The good agent pulled a photo out of a folder that lay on the desk between them: "We're especially interested in this guy." He tapped the portrait and slid it across the desk towards Fergus.

Fergus turned the photo around and saw Habib. Startled, he blurted out: "That's…" And he suddenly fell quiet.

"Yeah?" the good agent asked and the bad agent started leaning forward again.

Behind the mirror his father was eager to hear if Fergus would identify the terrorist.

"That's just some Arab chap. They all look the same to me," Fergus heard himself say, "except that this one obviously shaves."

"Listen, you worm, you ain't gonna fuck with us here! I know you recognised him, I could tell! We're extremely good at what we do! I know yer lyin' even before you know yer lyin'!" the bad agent slammed his fists on the table. The good agent's affable demeanour waned as well. He pressed his lips together, anger flashing across his face.

"You're not really a good cop, are you?" Fergus smiled at him.

"What are you hiding?" the green-on-crimson clown hissed, and for some reason his hissing made a considerably more sinister impression than the bad cop's volatile temper.

"I... Nothing," Fergus's chin dropped on his chest and he stared at the floor. "I'm not hiding anything, I just don't know what you want from me."

"You're obviously not aware of what you're dealin' with here! Are you dodgin' our questions on purpose? Obstructin' our investigation? This could lead to serious consequences, and not even your daddy, who's watching from the other room, by the way..." the supposedly good agent pointed at the one-way mirror, "Not even he will be able to help you."

"That's it. I'll talk to him," Ferdinand Fenton told them and by the click in their headphones they could tell he'd just turned off the microphone in the other room and was about to come in.

The agents sighed in disappointment.

"Remember," the formerly good agent leaned close to Fergus, reached out, held him under the chin and made him meet his gaze. This agent's breath smelled of lemon-scented roses. Fergus figured that Omnipile obviously did have a Mouthwash Department, after all, it was just that the bad agent was simply too bad to make use of it. Either that or he used garlic-flavoured mouthwash. The formerly good agent threatened: "If you don't tell your dad everything... If we're forced to interrogate you again... There'll be no more Mr Nice

Guy."

"Don't kid yourself," Fergus said, "You weren't all that nice, anyway."

Both Agents – the fake good cop as well as the real bad cop – grumbled and leaned back in their chairs reluctantly as Ferdinand Fenton stepped into the room and closed the soundproof door behind him. He was about to sit down between them, opposite Fergus, but then changed his mind and told them: "Look... Perhaps it would be best if you left us alone and let me and my son have a little heart-to-heart here, alright?"

"But –" the orange-on-blue agent started.

Mr Fenton gestured at the one-way mirror and said: "Please. You're obviously making matters worse with your intrusive poking and prodding and constant threats. I for one sure don't want to know how you're bringing up your own kids. You're making Fergus so damn nervous he can't even think straight. Right, son?" Ferdinand glanced at Fergus. Fergus kept looking at the floor. Once the agents had finally given up and left the room, Ferdinand sat down and said: "Hey, son."

"Hey, dad. Can we go home now?"

"Not just yet, I'm afraid," Ferdinand let out a tired breath.

Fergus looked at his father. "Thanks anyway, dad," he muttered, "I kind of hated those clowns. They're not much fun, really," the boy managed a smile.

"You've got that one right, they're definitely no fun at all," Ferdinand agreed. "Look, Fergus... Do you think you could try harder to remember what went on over there? Tell me everything... anything you might remember. Do you really recognise this man?" Ferdinand pointed at the picture of Habib.

Fergus suddenly felt dizzy and confused. He found it impossible to focus. "I... I don't know..." he stammered. He squeezed his eyes shut and buried his head in his hands.

Ferdinand glanced at the mirror suspiciously. He

narrowed his eyes and aimed a questioning gaze at the agents
he knew were observing the interrogation. On the other side,
the agents shrugged and shook their heads, and then remembered that the CEO couldn't see them. The green-on-crimson
agent turned on the microphone and calmly told Mr Fenton,
who had an in-ear headphone of his own: "No, we didn't give
him any drugs. At least not yet."

"What about the doc over there?" Ferdinand said out
loud, getting visibly annoyed with the whole affair.

On the other side of the mirror the Doctor, standing
in the observation room with the guards, shook his head
decisively, raising his arms in defence.

"Doc says definitely not," the agent said and paused.
"Yet," he added callously and turned off the microphone.

"Smartass," Mr Fenton muttered to himself.

"What?" Fergus seemed to pull himself together. He
wiped his face with his fingers and opened his eyes.

"Nothing," his father told him. "Just... Talking to...
Well, the clowns on the other side of that mirror. You know
they're there, what's the point of acting as if they aren't." He
looked at his son worriedly: "Is something wrong, Fergus? Are
you feeling ill?"

Fergus shrugged.

"Something on your mind?"

"I don't know. I can't think straight."

"I hope you haven't caught anything in Yoman.
Although, as far as the doctors could tell, you're all right. Are
you sure the terrorists didn't do something to you?"

"No, I told you, they never harmed us or anything. I
guess I'm just tired. I want to go home, I'm sleepy."

"I know, I understand, but I'm afraid the investigators
won't give up so easily. They can't, they're not even allowed
to. It's the rules, you know how it goes. They'll insist on
finding out everything you know first. They're looking for bits
of information even you yourself don't realise you possess.
You should try to remember, too. Any little thing, no matter
how irrelevant it might seem to you, could help us find your

sister before it's too late. Do you understand?"

Fergus nodded.

"Now, let's try to talk about something else, then, approach this from a different angle."

Mr Fenton turned the photo of Habib on its face in order not to disturb Fergus with it for the time being. "Do you know what the organisation that kidnapped you is called?" he asked the boy.

"No."

"Yomanian Liberation Front. Ring any bells?"

"No."

"They didn't mention that name around you?"

"No. They said they were freedom fighters."

"Ha! Yeah, sure, some freedom fighters. Damn terrorists, that's what they are. Freedom fighters, my ass..." Mr Fenton fumed. "Did they say what they wanted you and Fabiola for?"

"I don't know, I don't think so."

"Come on, think. Jesus, Fergus, Fabbie is still there. What are we going to do?"

"She hates it when you call her that," Fergus said.

Ferdinand Fenton was getting visibly upset: "Damn it, is that really important right now?! Jesus Christ, boy, try to tell me something useful! What happened in the beginning, when they first talked to you? What did they say? They had to have said something!"

Fergus tried hard to concentrate. The previous evening, before he'd fallen asleep, when he'd tried to visualise the events of the last couple of weeks in his mind, he'd been able to remember the first morning in Yoman quite well. So he thought about it again and suddenly remembered something. "Yeah!" it dawned on him, "Actually, after we woke up, Habib came in the room. That's the guy who could speak English a bit. Not all that well and with a funny accent too, but better than the others. He brought us fresh water and cookies. He said that Omnipile had imprisoned somebody they wanted to get back or something like that. But... Now that I think of it, why did they let *me* go and not Fabiola? Did you really put someone in prison? Did you have to let him go in order to get me back?"

Mr Fenton frowned. "No, they wanted money and some other things. They didn't say anything about their leader, at least not yet."

Fergus grimaced and fixed his father with a stern gaze, suddenly upset: "Their leader?" he raised his voice, "I didn't mention any leaders. So it's true! You really do have a man imprisoned! So all of this happened because you'd kidnapped somebody first? Because of the Company?"

"Hey, take it easy, son, what's wrong with you? What the heck do you think, that we go around and just imprison people for no good reason? Jesus! Besides, you know I can't discuss these things with you, it's top secret Corporation and government business. Several governments. We've talked about this. You know how it goes, how I can't talk about such matters, right?"

Fergus recoiled from his father.

Ferdinand reached out and held Fergus by the shoulders gently: "Come on, you know we're helping the United States, United Kingdom and the rest of the Western civilisation fight the war against terrorism. We're trying to liberate people so everyone can live in free democratic societies. We're about to bring liberty to Yoman. Omnipile will rebuild that country that's been destroyed by countless wars and religious fanaticism. We'll build schools and hospitals and roads, we'll give them a clean water supply, and we'll provide well-paid jobs to the people there. The enemy doesn't want that. These evil terrorists are afraid that their own people will get a taste of freedom, and then they won't support them anymore. They'll be able to vote, and they'll elect somebody else, somebody sensible. They'll see reason and leave the wrongful old ways behind. These are tough times, but you know I'd never ever do anything to hurt you or your sister. You know that, right?"

Fergus shrugged.

"Look, this man, the terrorists… They took you just to get back at me, because we're hot on their trail. We're about to shut them down. Matters of international security, remember?"

"Sure, dad, regular James Bond stuff, and your company helps the governments fight for human rights," the boy rasped and cleared his throat.

"That's right, we won't rest until the whole world is free."

Fergus nodded.

"But first let's concentrate on freeing your sister, OK?"

"Yeah, dad. I *am* trying, you know. It's just hard. It was all so horribly boring, same old stuff every day. We didn't talk to anyone apart from each other and that Arab, Habib. And even he didn't have much to say. He'd just bring us food and mostly make small talk in bad English. He'd just go: 'Hello, my friend, I bring nice goat milk and cookies, just for you'. You know, lame stuff like that, jeez... So I can't think of anything special. We'd just walk around the building, which was mostly empty. We'd quarrel among ourselves as usual... Eat, sleep. Go to the crapper. Take showers only every three days because of water shortage... I tried to sneak into the kitchen a couple of times to see if they had anything good in there, but the door was always locked. They probably didn't want us to steal the good stuff, the stingy bastards. Fabiola kept nagging at Habib to get us lobster, but *that* sure never happened. Damn hummus and stupid eggplant all the time, I'd give anything for a burger and fries. Speaking of which, could you get me a couple of burgers and some fries? That would be awesome!" The idea seemed to cheer Fergus up a little.

"Not right now, I'm afraid, doctors' orders. Maybe later."

"Damn..."

"Fergus, is there anything else you can think of? What else did you do?"

"Nothing much. Oh, I was allowed to play some old games, that was really nice of them..."

Ferdinand smiled wearily: "Let's not go into computer games again. You've already told us about that."

"Don't worry, I don't have much to say about it, anyway, their computers were lousy as hell. I don't think they were even PCs or Macs, if you can believe that. Not much fun, and I definitely couldn't get online with them. Unbelievable. Well, Habib had a laptop, but he wouldn't let me use it, of course."

"Was it a new one?"

"Yeah, it looked pretty nifty."

"Did you see what kind?"

"No, I didn't recognise the brand or even what operating system it was running, which is pretty weird, because I thought I knew a lot about these machines. It definitely looked wicked, I'd have loved to get my hands on it. I don't know much else, though. Habib wouldn't even let me check it out, let alone use it. He was working on something with it, but I don't know what, so don't bother asking."

"Oh, well. Fine, let's leave it at that for now. What about the building, anything unusual about it?"

"No, just a dusty old stone building. A lot of Persian carpets on the floor. Not really dirty, just a bit cluttered, you could tell there weren't any women around. Oh, and a couple of days before they let me go, I noticed a lot of big fat cockroaches, yuck... They seemed to have an infestation going on."

"Maybe the bugs got into their food supply. Well, that's not very helpful... No women, you say?"

"At least I didn't see any. Maybe they only stayed in the harem!"

Ferdinand laughed: "Are you sure they didn't just stay in the kitchen?" He soon remembered how dire the situation was and became serious again: "Ah, well, no women, that's not surprising. So, you probably didn't see anything about the building that could help us identify it?"

"Not really."

"Was it large? How many floors did it have?"

"I think it had three, at least it seemed that way when I looked through the window. We were on the second floor, and there seemed to be one more above us. But we weren't allowed to leave our floor, so I'm not completely sure."

"A window! Were you able to see through?"

"Sure. I mean, it was barred, but the gaps were wide enough for me to stick my head out. It was open most of the time, it's hot over there, you know."

"What did you see through the window, anything you can remember?"

"I..." Fergus suddenly became disoriented. He grabbed the edge of the table, breathed heavily and leaned over, resting his forehead on the back of his hand.

"Son? What's wrong?"

Fergus gasped, out of breath: "I feel sick... I think I'm going to... throw up."

"Hey, calm down, take a deep breath. What's wrong with you all of a sudden?"

"I don't know, it's just that as soon as I try to remember what I saw through the window, my head starts spinning."

"Are you afraid of heights? Is that what you're feeling, vertigo?"

"I don't know, I've never been afraid of heights before."

"Just a second. Doc?" Ferdinand looked at the mirror.

The Doctor leaned towards the microphone and turned it on: "Look, you must understand–" the doctor's voice spoke in Ferdinand's ear, "–it may not seem that way at first glance, but the boy has been through a lot. He may very well be suffering from post-traumatic stress disorder. In fact, I'd be surprised if he wasn't. So go easy on him."

"How will that get us anywhere?" Ferdinand asked the Doctor.

"I don't know. If you pry, you'll just upset him. He may even become totally withdrawn, unresponsive. He's having a hard time concentrating as it is. If I were you, I'd carry on with the indoctrination procedure, like I've already recommended."

"Not if I can help it."

"Suit yourself. Just be careful. The boy obviously has

problems. I believe you'll soon discover there's no other way."
The Doctor clicked off the microphone.

Ferdinand looked at Fergus and stroked his hair:
"Everything will be fine, the Doctor says you've been under
a lot of stress. He says we should let you rest, and we would,
too, if this wasn't such an emergency. You understand, don't
you?"

"Yeah, dad. I just don't know what else to tell you."

"Let's try something else if thinking about the view
from the window makes you dizzy, OK?" Ferdinand smiled
and patted the boy's shoulder. "Do you remember hearing
anything interesting?"

"They talked in Arabic, dad!" Fergus rolled his eyes.
"They didn't really have to keep quiet around us. But that
doesn't help us any, does it?"

"Hmm..." Ferdinand hummed.

The Doctor took the liberty of turning on the microphone again and whispering in Ferdinand's ear: "Actually it
could help, if we get on with the procedure. Under indoctrination-assisted regressive hypnosis he could most likely repeat
at least some of the things he's heard."

"Much good that would do. We'd probably just find out
what the guards gossiped about. I don't think they'd discuss
important issues with the kids listening, even if they couldn't
understand anything." Ferdinand sighed. "I'm talking to the
doc again," he told Fergus as he saw the boy looking at him
funny. "What I meant to ask you was if you've heard any
interesting noises? Something meaningful that could help us,
like trains, planes? Heavy traffic, maybe, or a muezzin?"

"A what?" Fergus raised his eyebrows.

"A... Well, a man screaming his pants off, I mean,
chanting, calling people to prayer?"

"I don't know, maybe. The guards were praying at all
crazy hours, too. How's that important?"

"I just thought if maybe any large mosques were nearby,
that could help us locate the building they kept you in."

"I... I really don't know," Fergus stammered.

Ferdinand sighed and paused for a minute, not sure about how to proceed. "Shit!" he cursed at nothing in particular and leaned against the table, scratching his forehead impatiently.

"Dad, I'm sorry, I don't know what else to tell you... I'm really really sorry we went to the lobby, I just had to send an e-mail to Moolly, it wasn't Fabiola's fault. It was my idea. This is all my fault..." Fergus buried his face in his hands and started sobbing.

"Say what?"

Fergus sniffed, wiped away some of his tears and looked at his father: "In the hotel where they kidnapped us... I snuck out of the suite, and Fabiola followed me, just for kicks. We didn't mean anything by it. We went down to the lobby because I knew they had computers there. While we sat there, I think somebody must have walked up to us from behind and put something over our noses and mouths to put us to sleep. It happened very quickly, it all just went black... I'm so sorry, dad," Fergus sobbed.

Ferdinand Fenton considered the news for a moment and consoled the miserable boy: "It's OK, son, don't worry. It's not your fault, you couldn't have known somebody was out to get you. The bodyguards were supposed to keep you safe!" Ferdinand stood up, walked around the table and hugged Fergus. He kneeled by his son and asked him softly: "Speaking of whom, where were they when this happened?"

"Upstairs in the suite. We snuck out, they didn't see us. They didn't know we went out, I'm sorry, we didn't mean to cause any problems..."

While he comforted the boy and waited for him to calm down, Ferdinand Fenton narrowed his eyes, thinking about the upcoming little chat he'd have with his intrepid bodyguards.

After a minute or two, Fergus finally stopped sobbing and Ferdinand sat down again. The Doctor on the other side observed them carefully.

"Are you alright, son? Don't worry, we'll get your sister

back, everything will be OK, you'll see."

Fergus nodded.

Ferdinand thought it might be an appropriate moment to revisit his son's favourite subject: "Listen, I didn't want to talk about computers anymore, because, frankly, I don't really understand your fascination with those little online games of yours..."

"Dad!" Fergus frowned, annoyed, implying that these were much more than little games. However, he did this more or less out of pure habit and spite, because after everything that had happened even he himself found the topic far less fascinating than before. Somehow... childish and unimportant. He feared that most of the true magic was gone for good.

"Sorry, I didn't mean to belittle your games. Actually, at this point I hope you can get back to them as soon as possible, but first let's try and get through this together."

Ferdinand paused and looked at Fergus, who sighed and nodded again.

"Fine. So, you said that this man... this Habib character... He had a laptop?"

"Yeah, what about it? I told you he wouldn't let me use it."

"Didn't you find that odd?"

"Odd? Why would I find it odd? Of course he wouldn't let me use it. I hate it if other people use my computers, too, and I don't have any top secret freedom fighter stuff on them. And no way I'd ever let anyone use any of my game accounts."

"*Terrorists*, not freedom fighters. But no, I didn't mean that. What I meant was... I find it strange that an uneducated Arab terrorist, who can barely speak English, as you say, has a state-of-the-art laptop, that's all."

"Jeez, dad, they have to come up with their *terrorist* plans somehow. You mean to tell me they do that by drawing sketches in the sand with sticks?"

"Damn, boy, when did you learn sarcasm?"

"Come on, I mean, really, aren't these guys supposed to

be swimming in oil, filthy rich?"

"Well, as far as we know, the Yomanian Liberation Front isn't exactly the wealthiest or strongest of these organisations. Never mind, I'm probably just grasping at straws here."

Fergus shrugged.

"Look," Ferdinand sighed. "The truth is, we're looking for a certain man... It's of utmost importance that we find him as soon as possible, and we suspect he might have been present in the building you'd been taken to. He may even be responsible for the kidnapping himself. Now, he's a kind of a bad guy who'd definitely carry a 'wicked', as you call it, laptop around. An extremely smart bad guy."

The boy just puffed: "I don't think there were many smart guys around there, dad. Had there been any, they would have probably figured out how to make something other than hummus for lunch."

"So you didn't see anything useful about his computer? What kind of an operating system was he using, was it English or Arabic or..."

Fergus glanced at the back of the photo of Habib on the table. "Look, I told you, I don't know anything about his damn computer, he wouldn't let me touch it!" Fergus suddenly became very upset again.

"Shit, Fergus, you must have at least peeked at the screen! Don't tell me you didn't!"

"He wouldn't show me!"

"Was he online, did they have an internet connection?"

"Fucking hell, I don't know!"

"Watch your mouth! Fuck!" Ferdinand drove his fist into his leg.

"Wait, dad," Fergus said more calmly after a couple of seconds of tense silence. "Actually, I do know that. In the beginning I kept asking if I could just check my e-mail real quick... And if I could send a message to my guild. Habib didn't even know what a guild was, duh...! At first he just ignored me and then he explained they didn't have an internet connection, anyway. I don't think he was lying, either, the place seemed like a real backwater dump. There. At least I remember *something*. Although I have no idea how *that's* going to help."

"It doesn't, really. Let's get back to Habib. His name was Habib, right?"

Fergus said: "Yeah, I told you a thousand times."

"Has anyone called him Fadil, perhaps? Maybe by accident?"

"No! Well, I don't know, do I, I couldn't make out anything they were saying. Jesus, how the heck am I supposed to tell strange Arabic names I don't recognise from other gibberish I can't understand?!" Fergus was getting red in the face again.

Ferdinand's patience was wearing thin. He tapped the back of the photo with his finger: "I saw you glancing at this before." He turned the photo around and nudged it towards Fergus. "Are you positive you haven't seen this man?"

"No! I... I mean, yes! This is just..."

"This is the man we're looking for," Mr Fenton interrupted Fergus's stammering. "His name is Fadil Dajani. He used to work for us."

Fergus took a deep breath, swayed and grabbed the table.

"What's wrong? What's going on with you?"

"I can't..." Fergus suddenly felt dizzy and he started breathing heavily again.

"Calm down, what's up with you?"

The Doctor on the other side turned on the microphone: "Stop pushing him, he's hyperventilating."

"Shut up, doc!" Ferdinand barked at the mirror, "I know my son, he just needs some discipline sometimes. His mother surely doesn't provide any!" Mr Fenton put on a stern expression and fixed the woozy Fergus with his gaze: "Enough of this! Pull yourself together! Shit, be a man! We're in a crisis here! Your sister's life is in danger!"

Ferdinand picked up the photo of Habib and shoved it in Fergus's face: "I'll ask you again: do you recognise this man? Have you seen him?"

Fergus stared at the floor, gasping for air, shaking his head emphatically.

"Look at it, goddamn it! Is this the man you call Habib?"

Fergus looked up, covered his mouth with his hand and retched. "Jesus!" the startled Ferdinand jumped from his chair. Fergus stopped convulsing – since he hadn't eaten anything, he just threw up the water he'd drunk and a lot of acid and bile, thanks to the very relaxing interrogation first carried out by the clowns and then also by his father. The boy put his arm on the table and buried his feverish face in his elbow. Ferdinand walked up to him, unsure of what to do.

The door opened and the Doctor marched in. He was obviously no longer in any mood for debates. The OIA Agents waited outside. They weren't crazy about kids in the first place, and they disliked little brats even more once they started whining and throwing up.

The Doctor motioned at Ferdinand and got him to step aside. He pulled out a syringe.

"What – !" Ferdinand Fenton protested.

"It's just a mild sedative. Stand back."

Fergus was in no shape to resist. Actually he felt strangely relieved that the ordeal was over, at least for now, and after the Doctor pricked him with the needle he was flabbergasted at how serene the drug made him in just a few seconds.

A couple of nurses rushed in with a wheelchair. Fergus, wearing a blissful smile, traced their curves dreamily and felt all fuzzy and warm inside. "Whee, daddy's company sure employs nice nurses," he mumbled.

The nice nurses winked at him, loaded him in the chair very gently and whisked him off to his room. As they helped him into his bed and tucked him in, he managed to utter a tranquil slurred "thank you". The two angels, a blond and a redheaded one, beamed a couple of sparkly smiles at him, waved from the door through a creamy wispy astral mist, and left him swimming in a warm pool of radiance. *"Mommy?"*

Fergus thought as he dozed off.

With Fergus dozing, Ferdinand, the Doctor and the two Agents headed into the room behind the mirror. Ferdinand already knew what was coming. After they'd sat down at the table, surrounded by walls covered in computer screens and other high-tech equipment, complicated-looking devices, arcane contraptions and blinking lights, the Agent with the epilepsy-inducing orange-polka-dot-on-a-navy-blue-background tie got right to the point: "Mr Fenton... I realise what you were tryin' to achieve here, it's yer son, I'm sure you must be terribly worried about him. You thought you could get through to him, but obviously it ain't gonna do no good. It's just causin' him more sufferin' than a simple indoctrination-assisted debriefin' ever would."

"I'm not going to subject my son to unnecessary experimental procedures!"

"I'd hardly call them experimental," the Doctor protested, "You're well aware of all our achievements in this field."

The orange-on-blue agent said: "And I'd hardly call 'em unnecessary. Heck, you've ordered many 'experiments', as you now call 'em, in the past yerself. Some of 'em even involved yer children, if I can remind ya. Now, it's obvious that the boy's sufferin', like the good doctor says, from an acute case of post-traumatic stress disorder. Or even a radical example of the Stockholm Syndrome."

The second Agent – the green-on-crimson one – added: "Either that or the situation's even worse. Maybe the boy's been brainwashed, or coerced somehow into keeping things from us. Maybe they threatened they'd do something really bad to your daughter if he told us anything. You know, things they mentioned in their note..."

"That's right," the first agent agreed, "Imagine how conflicted Fergus must feel if they simply told him they'd really do as the note says, you know, rape her, send us her fingers and sex organs and kill her. Or the other way aroun'."

"I know what the motherfucking note says! You have

to rub it in, don't you? You wouldn't happen to be enjoying yourself the tiniest bit, would you?! How dare you... Threaten me!" Mr Fenton's calm and composed CEO demeanour gave way to a flushed face and a bulging pulsating vein on his temple.

"It's not my intention to annoy you further by stating the obvious," the Doctor remarked benevolently, "But you should try to calm down. If you can't, I'll get you something for it, because otherwise you might give yourself a heart attack."

Mr Fenton breathed deeply and imagined a fine sunny day on lush green pastures... A sweet-scented summer breeze... He pictured himself as a happy-go-lucky shepherd, his faithful sheepdog jumping around the flock of sheep frolicking all around them... And he could almost taste barbecued lamb and a pint of ale. Ah, much better.

"Mr Fenton." the orange-on-blue clown informed him calmly, "You know that the Intelligence Agency can pull rank on ya. There are certain rules even you must abide by. I shouldn't even have to remind ya. Y'know how it works. Y'know better than anyone."

Indeed he did. He himself was the one who'd always insist on all the confidentiality clauses, non-disclosure agreements, priority objectives, waivers, special work contracts, and so on and so forth. Bureaucracy was such a convenient way of muddling things up and protecting the Company. He'd always seen to it that the rules were observed to the letter, and he himself insisted on the clear chain of command that would ensure the smooth operation of Omnipile even if he himself dropped dead or lost his mind completely. The Board of Directors had the final word and it could always veto his decisions. Chief Medical Officers, for example the Doctor in the room behind the mirror, could relieve him of active duties due to physical or mental health concerns. Furthermore, Ferdinand Fenton, the CEO, had to obey the directives of the Director of the Omnipile Security Service in all matters pertaining to security issues – even though he outranked the

Security Director, Mr Fenton had to justify any derogations from his recommendations. But not even Ferdinand Fenton outranked the Director of the Omnipile Intelligence Agency, to which the Security Service also answered, while the OIA Director himself only answered to the Board of Directors. So Mr Ferdinand Fenton, the infamous CEO of Omnipile, had to follow the orders of the OIA Director, which the OIA Director could issue with regard to the military, intelligence, and security matters at any time, should he decide such orders were necessary.

Ferdinand just sighed and drummed his fingers on the table.

"So," the agent proceeded, "you should know the Director would hate to get involved in this personally. We're all aware this is an extremely sensitive situation, involvin' some very controversial operations, to put it mildly, so I really think we should carry on as smoothly and quietly as possible. We know this is your son we're talkin' about, but I'm sure he's in no danger whatsoever. Right?" The Agent turned to the Doctor, raising his eyebrows.

"Of course not," the Doctor confirmed. "You know the procedure won't harm the boy and it can be easily undone after any information he might possess has been extracted. It's been proven a hundred times over, and you've overseen some of the procedures yourself."

"I know," Mr Fenton sighed, "But I still hate using indoctrination on my kid. Even if everything goes without a hitch, he'll hate my guts if he ever finds out. Not to mention what my wife and Fabiola would think of me."

"That's why the Security Service was strongly against you takin' yer family with ya on business trips in the first place. That's why the ongoin' infiltration operation was so... disputable. Because gettin' family members involved in any of our more sensitive projects is always a recipe for disaster. But we can't do nothin' much about it now, can we?" the second agent said.

"Yep, it seems we're outta options," the first agent drove

the point in, "Even releasin' the asset and exchangin' him for yer daughter – if that could be done successfully – wouldn't get us any information about Dr Fadil Dajani."

"I'd get my daughter back, damn it, that's my first priority!"

"You should have thought about that before," the first agent put in callously.

"Come on," the second agent intervened before Mr Fenton could pop another blood vessel, "It wasn't possible to predict that the situation would escalate in such an improbable manner. Even all of our own intelligence information failed to suggest such a radical turn of events. The fact that at this point our on-site surveillance and infiltration equipment is blacked out, that's just... Incomprehensible."

"Perhaps that very blackout is an indication of Dr Dajani's presence there," Ferdinand Fenton theorised.

"We ain't gonna be sure o' that until we debrief Fergus properly," the orange-on-blue agent concluded.

"Let's cut to the chase," the Doctor decided to put a stop to the endless discussion. "I propose that we proceed with the indoctrination-assisted debriefing immediately, as we should have done in the first place."

The Doctor turned to Ferdinand: "I'd rather have your permission and cooperation. I'd sure hate to see the orders come down from the OIA."

Ferdinand Fenton rubbed his eyes and hissed: "I guess we have no choice, do we. When do we begin?"

"I'll prep the boy immediately," the Doctor proposed. "The current situation is actually quite convenient – he's been sedated and should be asleep now. No need to move him, we can carry out the procedure in his room."

"How long till we get the first results? I hope we ain't gonna have to wait the full two weeks," the first Agent said.

"I don't think so. In my professional opinion, the boy's reactions to the interrogation weren't unusual at all. Whether he's been physically hurt or not, we shouldn't forget that the very kidnapping in itself constitutes abuse.

Psychologically speaking, the boy's suffered severe trauma. It's actually a miracle he'd been so responsive before his unavoidable breakdown. He should never have been exposed to the additional pressures of such an intrusive interrogation. Besides, let's not forget: the poor lad is only fourteen."

Ferdinand nodded.

"I think it would have been better to just sedate him and do the procedure without him knowing anything about it in the first place. However, we can still do that now. Let's proceed as always in such cases. We'll go through with the indoctrination and refrain from asking him any unnecessary questions, especially about the kidnapping. After a day or two we'll try to elicit some initial reactions, see how he responds... Since he should basically want to help us, with the assistance of the indoctrination procedure he should be able to keep his composure and start remembering his time in Yoman far more vividly very soon. Any memories he might have repressed unknowingly should resurface before the end of the first week, and then we could definitely attempt a session of regressive hypnosis, if he still doesn't remember anything useful."

"At least we'll soon know whether he's seen Dr Dajani. It definitely looked as if he had some issues with that photo," Ferdinand said.

"Very well. Are we ready to go through with this?" the Doctor asked and everyone agreed.

"Excellent," the Doctor rubbed his hands, obviously looking forward to what he'd probably call an interesting experiment. "Let's get on with it, then!"

30. Stanko & Tinka

Still smiling – which was unusual for them – the old derelicts staggered into Boris and Beeba's Rock 'n' Roll Tavern. As soon as they assessed the situation, their smiles waned almost painfully, so that they once again resembled their usual selves: alas, the place was in fact full of strangers who spoke foreign languages. To make matters worse, Stanko and Tinka's worst fear came true: their table in the remotest corner was occupied, and to their utter horror, Beeba didn't seem eager to tell the two eccentric aliens, sitting there engrossed in a conversation, to go away. Why couldn't they have their quiet little spot? Usually no one wanted to sit there, anyway.

"Hello," Beeba said as Stanko and Tinka, reluctantly, retreated to their fallback positions at the bar. "Well, I'm sorry, looks like your table is taken..."

"You don't say," Stanko growled.

"Don't be obnoxious," the plump Tinka – in accordance with the difference in their height – drove her elbow into his thigh.

Beeba smiled tiredly, ignoring Tinka's grumpy partner. She noticed he wore one of his disgusting headpieces, so she did her best to pretend he wasn't there. As far as she was concerned, her evening had been far too entertaining to get into an argument with this high-strung dipsomaniac. She also knew he'd stop being such a pest once he was too drunk to stand, so she said: "Let me give you a couple of spritzers on the house. Maybe the boys will go sit somewhere else after they're done. They're discussing something very important, but I'm sure they'll join the others over on this side of the room once they figure it all out."

"How long will that take?" the slightly less surly Tinka inquired.

"I..." Beeba started, but Stanko interrupted her coarsely: "I don't give a fuck. Fuck the spritzers! I want my table! And then I'll take the spritzers!"

Beeba swiftly changed her tactics: "You seem a bit nervous, let me buy you a couple of double schnappses, then. Why don't you just drink them here at the bar?"

"Fine!" Stanko agreed magnanimously, "But if our table isn't available soon, we're going to the pizzeria down the road."

"Just to express our discontent, I guess..." Tinka, standing on her toes, peeked over the bar, shrugged, and rolled her eyes, but Beeba knew she'd stick up for her husband no matter what. So Beeba just aimed a vacant smile at Stanko, bestowed a wink at Tinka, poured them the schnappses and hoped they'd stop pestering her.

When Boris came in half an hour later, Stanko aimed an almost hopeful glance at him, as if to plead with him to tell the imbeciles at their table to move somewhere else. However, Boris noticed Stanko's hat and gave him a wide berth on his way to Ray and Amalia's tables.

Beeba, worried that Stanko might start complaining again, let them have another two double schnappses on the house so that they'd leave her alone and she could keep on nodding by her cup of cocoa and get on with her eaves-dropping on everyone.

Beeba suddenly came up with an idea which Finnegan and Bogomyr might also benefit from, so she sent Boris over to explain it to them. When Stanko saw that now even Boris himself had joined the two despicable characters abusing his and Tinka's corner spot, he gritted his teeth in annoyance. Now they'll *never* clear out, the bastards! The disgruntled duo would have gone to the pizza place an hour ago if this hadn't involved such an annoying walk. So Stanko clenched his fist and growled and scowled until he milked another couple of double schnappses from the benevolent Beeba (Beeba, actually totally tired of the old drunks looming by the bar, quietly added the final drinks to their tab – they'd never notice, anyway, and she was sick of serving them for free).

A while later, when the track *Iniquity* by *Cynicism Management* which Amalia played ended, Ray, presiding over one of the two tables behind Stanko and Tinka, turned towards Beeba and pointed at Boris's laptop. He was obviously eager to put on more of his fabled porn groove compositions and pester innocent bystanders with them. Beeba, realising that Amalia and Ray were not yet through discussing their musical endeavours, had now come to the conclusion that this evening was turning into another one of those highly bothersome occasions she'd rather just wrap up as soon as possible and with the least amount of trouble. So she merely rolled her eyes and sighed audibly, but did not protest as the beer-bellied loudmouth self-proclaimed porn industry expert put on another recent track of his that he wanted to play for Amalia, called **Garden Gnomes** **[https:// soundcloud.com/ray-kosmick/garden-gnomes].**

Stanko clearly hated the tune, because he finally decided he was sick of waiting. In accordance with the difference in their height, he drove his elbow into Tinka's temple and started to clear out. He couldn't possibly stand putting up with anyone else sitting in his corner spot any longer.

So, after what had effectively been a sextuple schnapps, Stanko and Tinka finally left Boris and Beeba's in protest. Gradually – slowly and carefully – they squeezed themselves through the door. Stanko managed to fit his length through the vertical constraints of the exit by walking diagonally. With the aid of a good many deities with some time to spare on this side of the local galaxy cluster, Tinka managed to fit her corpulent frame through the door with an almost audible pop. She halted at the top of the three stairs leading down to the street, still holding the door open.

Ray looked up, leaned over to peek through the door, and blared in Slovenian: "Tinka! Great job! I didn't think you could do it without lubricant anymore!"

Even if she didn't understand what Ray said, Amalia laughed heartily, as it was hilariously fitting that Tinka would stage her victorious exit while *Garden Gnomes*, another immortal tune by *Ray Kosmick and his Porn Groove Crew*, played on the hi-fi. The scene was truly memorable.

However, Tinka certainly had a different outlook on the matter. "Shut the fuck up, Žarko, you fat bastard," she threw back over her shoulder, gave him the finger, and added: "And if you'd like to know, I wouldn't fuck you if yours was the last stiff dick on this planet and all the dildos had turned to putty."

"That's my girl," slurred Stanko, striving to straighten himself from the diagonal to upright position outside in the parking lot. "Shit, I should have never given up crawling on all fours..." he concluded.

After Tinka succeeded in rolling out to the parking lot, miraculously bouncing down the short flight of stairs without breaking her neck, a cockroach landed in the bird's nest of her hair. Startled, she reached into her chaotic hairdo and managed to grab the vile insect. She opened her hand in front of her eyes, and the moment she realised it was a particularly fat bug, she screamed, threw the horrid creature on the ground, and jumped on it several times just to make sure it was utterly squashed and smeared into nothing but a stain on the pavement.

Stanko, who waited for her nearby, just looked at her quizzically.

Another cockroach fell into Tinka's hair. The third one hit the tip of her nose, bounced off and landed on her belly where it desperately clung to her threadbare clothes. The fourth one touched down an inch from her foot. Tinka shrieked while trying to rake the offending creature out of her hair. She turned her head, looked up, and saw big fat insects raining down, falling, with audible plops, to the ground in a straight line slowly extending from where she stood to about ten metres further away.

Then the surreal incident came to an end, the bugs scattered in all directions, and Tinka, wheezing and panting, was the only curiosity left. Her yelping and the crazy dance she'd just performed in the parking lot might have turned a lot of heads, had there been many heads around to be turned. However, the people in the Rock 'n' Roll Tavern were too distracted and the music was too loud, while the rest of the municipality had gathered in the church-side bar and now contemplated the Mayor's priceless thoughts about tourism.

The only people who saw Tinka's unusual seizure were two women, approaching Boris's from the direction of the pizza place, the startled Randy who was smoking another joint in the bushes nearby, and Stanko, who'd grabbed his stomach and doubled over, leaning against Ray Kosmick's car and laughing so hard that the tears squirting from his eyes could kill flies in flight.

"Maybe all of this schnapps didn't quite agree with you, honey," stammered Stanko once he'd managed to bring his fits of laughter under control. He'd never noticed anything fall from the sky. Either he was too drunk to see any bugs or too sober to hallucinate.

Tinka managed to catch her breath: "Jesus, that was *weird.*"

She looked around, trying to figure out whether the cockroaches had really dropped out of thin air or if it was all just a figment of her neurons screaming for help in a flood of alcohol.

Then Tinka started to wheeze and pant some more.

Stanko grew impatient.

"Look," he said, "Enough of this crap, you're just drunk, deal with it. Now let's go, I want to grab a couple of cold spritzers in the pizza place before it closes. Maybe our table will be free later, we can check on our way back."

Tinka just nodded, muttering something incomprehensible under her breath, and followed her husband.

While slouching towards the pizzeria, the two old boozers passed the two women who'd witnessed Tinka's bouts of hysteria. Stanko and Tinka glanced at them, but Tinka was overcome by the fear that she had just experienced her first real taste of delirium tremens, so she didn't really register them. Stanko's left eye lit up with a hint of recognition, though, but he was too drunk for his right eye to confirm the left one's suspicions. He never realised he'd already seen the women when he and Tinka had passed the blue van on their way to Down Below the Hill.

Nevertheless, he heard them talk in English, surmised even more foreigners were heading towards the Rock 'n' Roll Tavern, and, because he was a disagreeable bastard, told them to fuck off. However, he also saw they were holding hands, so instead of just referring to them as "fucking tourists" again, he called them "fucking foreign dykes". This time Tinka, however, was too distracted to flip them off.

31. Operation Watering Hole: Infiltration

"Jeez, finally, I thought we'd never get going. What the hell took you so long? I'm dying of thirst here," Serbian Bitch complained as she and Another One were off.

"Sorry, I almost broke my neck back there, I really can't see shit without my glasses," Another One said apologetically.

Serbian Bitch and Another One enjoyed a pleasant little stroll through the woods. The night air was delightfully fresh among the trees and the moon was almost full, so it wasn't very dark. It was a short and relaxing walk to the main road ahead.

However, as the Bitch Scouts drew nearer to the edge of the cover of the foliage, they could see that the second part of their hike wouldn't be quite so agreeable. The road ahead was still a back road by all reasonable standards: excessively narrow, windy and riddled with holes, and with no pavement or curb to walk on comfortably. After only a foot or two, the narrow gravel bank turned into a steep slope leading down to a rather murky and thoroughly uninviting river, and there was no fence. The other side of the road was even worse: impossible to walk on safely without falling into the ditch or having a heap of nasty bushes shove their prickly branches in your face. To make matters worse, the two intensely observant Bitch Scouts had already noticed that Slovenians drove like utter maniacs. As one of these hobbyist race-car drivers whizzed past, honking the horn and displaying a rude gesture in the rear-view mirror, Serbian Bitch yelled: "Asshole!" after him. Only then did it cross her mind that the fine Serbian expression along the lines of *'jebem ti mater u dupe'*, for example, might have had a better effect in this country, though it would have left Another One in the dark concerning its exact juicy meaning. The Bitches got the message, though: they fell into formation and proceeded single file towards the Rock 'n' Roll Tavern rather swiftly, in a hurry to get off the nasty road as soon as possible.

"This reminds me of the Scottish Highlands," Another One remarked. "Narrow roads meandering around a bunch of hills, and mobs of disgruntled rustic tosspots driving like maniacs. The only difference is, here they also drive on the wrong side of the street, so let's be extra careful not to get run over, OK?"

Serbian Bitch, who had taken point, turned and barked over her shoulder: "You better concentrate on not falling into the river."

"Oh, shut up. I'm not such a spaz, so long as I can see anything. I won't put on the spy glasses until we're almost at the pub, anyway. Speaking of which, let's check if everything works while we're still out of sight. Home base, are you reading this? Over."

"Loud and clear," The Watcher told them through their miniature wireless in-ear headphones.

"Excellent... Do the cameras work? Over." Another One asked.

"Sure, though I'm only seeing dirt through yours," The Watcher told her.

"Yeah, I'm not wearing my high-tech glasses at the moment, I have them in my hand, see? Check this out!" She held up the glasses and panned them around.

"Stop screwing around with those, will you?" Serbian Bitch said. "You look like a fool. A suspicious fool, at that."

"I agree, don't wave the glasses around. You won't want to find out how much they cost if you drop and break them. I can test the camera just fine, even if it's pointed at the ground," The Watcher said over the earphones.

"OK, sure. I'll put them on once we're near our destination. Over."

"Look, stop saying 'over', damn it, we can hear everything you're saying. This is not a goddamn 1970s one-way walkie-talkie connection. Anyway, refrain from talking directly to us if it's not really necessary. You guys should be careful not to look suspicious, and remember that the Omnipile Security Service or even Intelligence Agency will most likely be reviewing these recordings. So don't kid around too much." Arch Bitch reminded them.

"Yeah, yeah…" Serbian Bitch and Another One whined in unison.

"OK," said The Watcher. "Testing the night vision camera now… Damn! It's far too bright out there, with the moon and lights and all," she told Arch Bitch who winced at the glaring screens. "Adjusting brightness… Sorry about that. Still getting used to the equipment."

"Just try not to fry anything, OK?" Arch Bitch nagged at The Watcher.

"Of course. Making a test recording of the normal video feed… Works fine… Testing the x-ray camera…"

"The x-ray camera, huh? Kinky," Serbian Bitch marvelled, wondering what range of practical uses *that* could be put to. "So we'll be able to see people naked?"

"Don't be absurd," The Watcher said. "Firstly, the images from the camera aren't projected back to the glasses unless I decide to send feedback to your head-up displays, which are integrated in the glasses. So you won't be able to abuse the cameras as you please just yet."

"We're not in complete control of our gear?"

"Not at the moment. We're currently testing stuff and I haven't given you the pocket controllers yet."

"Oh. I see," Serbian Bitch sounded a bit disappointed.

"Don't worry, I'll let you have them as soon as I'm done with the initial testing. I don't want you to mess with my calibrations right now. When I'm done setting everything up, I'll give you the controllers. You won't be able to do any harm, anyway, because all three video feeds – normal, infrared and x-ray – are being recorded simultaneously and can be reviewed later at our leisure. So it doesn't really matter which camera feed you decide to view on your head-up display, everything gets stored on the solid-state drives safely."

"Right. Whatever you say. And secondly?"

"What?"

"You said 'firstly'... What else were you going to enlighten us with?"

"Oh, yeah, and, secondly, with the x-ray camera you'll just see people's bones, pacemakers, metal things in suitcases, pipes in the walls, stuff like that."

"So you don't see a naked Another One now, if I check her out like this..." Serbian Bitch turned to Another One who walked behind her and gave her a head-to-toe look.

"No, this is not a children's toy. Contrary to popular belief –", The Watcher started explaining to the skeleton on her screen.

"Yeah, yeah, I know, come on, jeez..." Serbian Bitch stopped glaring at the smiling Another One and walked onwards, "I was just messing with you. That's perfectly fine by me, Jesus Christ, who'd want to see ugly people naked, anyway. Right, Bitch?" Serbian Bitch winked back over her shoulder. Another One rolled her eyes and sighed, pretending to be tired of everything, even though she obviously enjoyed a bit of fieldwork as well as some good old banter among friends.

"Holy shit, I mean, really!" Serbian Bitch exclaimed when she looked towards Boris and Beeba's Rock 'n' Roll Tavern looming in the distance. "Imagine witnessing the stripping of those abominations over there, for example!" Serbian Bitch motioned towards a tall thin geezer and a short plump drunken grandma, who'd just managed to wobble out to the Jimi Hendrix parking lot in front of the Rock 'n' Roll Tavern.

"Aren't those the drunken old farts from before?" Another One narrowed her eyes.

"Wow, you can really see well through your own glasses, can't you? Say, do we also have the zoom capability on here?"

"Of course." The Watcher, glad to be able to show off

what she'd already come to think of as her gadgets, fed the zoomed image back to Serbian Bitch's glasses.

"Wow, that's awesome. Phew, I feel a bit woozy. Zoom out a bit. You're making me sick. Shit, you really must let us have the controls as soon as possible. It's too weird if you're controlling the HUD. Wait... OK, yeah, that's good, leave it at double zoom."

"Got it."

Suddenly Serbian Bitch started snickering: "What's the stupid old hag doing? Did a bat get into her hair or something?" Serbian Bitch and Another One cackled as Tinka, very inappropriately for her, jumped up and down, stomping her feet like an overweight elderly contestant in a lunatic asylum kazachok championship. In a minute or two, Tinka and Stanko calmed down and started walking towards them.

"Right," said The Watcher. She turned off Serbian Bitch's HUD and said: "Time to stop fooling around now. Just proceed with your mission as planned."

"Roger. Say, Another One, put on the spy glasses now and give me your hand. We're getting close."

Another One put on the unseemly eyewear and stuffed her own glasses in her purse. Serbian Bitch took her hand and led her towards the pub.

As the drunken duo slouched towards the Bitch Scouts, the now half-blind Another One remarked: "Look at those two. Even I can see they're so plastered they can barely walk."

As the two couples passed each other, Stanko aimed an unstable cross-eyed look at the Bitches and told them resolutely: "Marš, lezbijki prekleti angležarski!" And in surprisingly smooth Slovenian too, if one takes into account that his motor skills were obviously too impaired to keep him from stumbling past them at quite a slant. The hostile old bastard was clearly very well-versed in insulting people even while his cerebellum was tripping over itself and begging his hiccupping liver for urgent assistance.

"Looks like he remembers us from before," Another One observed.

"Either that, or he hates everyone indiscriminately," Serbian Bitch theorised. "I'd use my uncanny knowledge of the Slavic languages and tell him to go screw himself, then push him into the river, but they said we should keep a low profile."

"You should also shut the hell up. These people might understand more of what you're saying than you think," Arch Bitch said in their earpieces. "From the materials I'm just reading about this place, I gather that most Slovenians under-stand English, at least to a certain degree," she said and leafed through a colourful book called *Treasures of Slovenia*.

"That probably applies to people who have seen the inside of a school at one time or another... Especially those of them who are not constantly so drunk they're seeing quadruple."

"Get serious, please, this is not a laughing matter," Arch Bitch instructed.

"I agree, but we are going to a pub, so we may as well look the part. You know, well... We can afford to be a tad cheerful, I guess."

Serbian Bitch managed to lead the way to Boris and Beeba's without Another One tripping and falling under the wheels of some Slovenian side-street kamikaze. Just as they started fixing their hair, all focused on entering the pub without drawing too much attention to themselves, a young man with ruffled hair and bloodshot eyes pushed his way from the bushes and crossed the parking lot. Somewhat startled at the sight of the Bitches, he blurted out: "Hi," but avoided looking them in the eye for too long. "Hey," said Another One. At the herbal smell that trailed after him, Serbian Bitch wondered – not seriously considering it, but just amusing herself with the concept – whether Omnipile had thought of equipping their state-of-the-art glasses with fragrance sensors.

Of course Omnipile had done that and The Watcher already proudly watched the computer analyse which strain of sinsemilla the funky character in front of them had just been smoking. "We can definitely codename this character *Herb Boy*," The Watcher jested. Arch Bitch looked at the olfactory analysis, smiled, and made a note of the codename in her logbook.

Herb Boy entered the Rock 'n' Roll Tavern and, wearing a rather cryptic lingering smile, held the door ajar for the Bitch Scouts. As Serbian Bitch and The Watcher entered, a hefty unshaven guy at the second table turned towards them, measured them from head to toe, and bellowed: "Hey, Randy, you find some nice girls in the bushes?" When he saw them holding their hands, his face lit up and he added, licking his lips: "My, my..."

Randy just sighed and rolled his eyes: "Yeah, yeah, Ray."

Another One and Serbian Bitch exchanged a wondering glance, walked around the bar, sat down at a table across the room and inspected the place.

The pub was quite small – a semi-circular bar in the middle, two large tables on one side of the room where the entrance was. Most of the people currently present in the pub sat there, immersed in a lively discourse. Another three tables stood at the far side of the room, across the bar and opposite the door. Two of these were large and well-lit, while the third spot, separated from the other two by a partition wall made of wooden lattice, was a small alcove for a maximum of four people. The nook was only illuminated by a very dim light and the small table was pushed to the grimy wall under a miniature window which would have overlooked an unkempt backyard if it hadn't been covered with a heavy curtain. The drab cloth had apparently been gathering dust and classic cigarette smoke fragrance for the better part of the last decade. The reclusive spot was obviously intended for people who wanted to enjoy some privacy.

Through the wooden lattice, Serbian Bitch discretely checked out the three men sitting and talking there, and recognised the Subject of the Investigation immediately. She winked at Another One carefully and hinted at the quite distinct pale black Scotsman of German origin, laughing in the remote corner. Another One shifted on her chair and grimaced as she peered through the lattice, struggling to make out the faces through the poorly-lit blur she registered without her prescription glasses.

"Jesus," Serbian Bitch grumbled quietly and kicked her in the shin under the table.

"Hey, stop it!" Another One yelped, "What's with you today?"

Serbian Bitch only cleared her throat, ignoring Another One's question, and aimed a friendly smile at the bored-looking Beeba in order to get her attention. Beeba, who sat behind the bar, staring at a crossword puzzle and listening in on everybody's conversations, finally caved in, met the gaze of the thirsty Serbian Bitch, worked up a smile and asked them what they wanted.

"*Pivo, molim,*" Serbian Bitch ordered a beer in Serbian, which she was sure Beeba would understand.

"*Laško ali Union?*" Beeba asked which beer Serbian Bitch would like of the two kinds most of the simpler Slovenian taverns usually sold. Sure, the fancier pubs, especially in the cities, sometimes offered a can or two of imported beer, and more recently microbreweries had become quite the rage. However, the more backward taverns usually still sold only two brands – *Union* in the red uniform, and *Laško* wearing its greens, each brewed by one of the two Slovenian industrial breweries that dominated most of the local beer market. Traditionally, the central part of Slovenia, especially its capital of Ljubljana, which every provincial yokel hated with a carefully cultivated commitment, preferred the red cans. Many other regions, especially Maribor – the second largest city in Slovenia and Ljubljana's greatest and most fanatical adversary – swore by the green ones. Some particularly inbred pubs even went so far as to carry only one of these brands and frown upon the other, in accordance with the outstanding achievements in pure and undiluted local patriotism. In certain shitholes, specifically those frequented by rabid football supporters wearing very garish, even surprisingly gay violet

colours of all the possible hues of the rainbow, you would
as a rule get suspicious sideways looks or even a shiner if
you made the mistake of ordering the red *Union* beer – they
obviously preferred the green *Laško*. On the other hand, the
opposing football fan club, its membership equally abundant
in cerebral behemoths, wore *green* colours but preferred the
red cans. To make matters worse, some years ago during the
so-called brewery war, the green beer makers had bought
out the red ones in what some people still saw as a hostile
takeover. Since then, both Slovenian industrial breweries
were owned by *Laško* until Omnipile finally gobbled them up,
effectively making the whole controversy completely inconsequential – and yet football fans and other assorted wankers
still kept losing perfectly good teeth over the farce that the
whole red vs. green or green vs. violet dispute actually was.
Indeed, Slovenia was a strange place.

Boris and Beeba's tavern, however, was run by liberal if
somewhat aging hippies who didn't give a rat's ass about the
whole thing. They sold both brands indiscriminately, and also
carried German weiss beer for good measure.

Nevertheless, the unexpected lack of elaborate beer lists
and seemingly endless selections of pale lagers, light lagers,
dark lagers, pilsners, brown ales, porters, stouts, weiss beers,
smoked beers, fruit beers, herb beers, spiced beers, wood-aged
beers, draft and bottled and canned, of all tastes and colours,
which the Bitches could expect to see in the United Kingdom,
was quite a culture shock for them. So Serbian Bitch ordered
the red bottle and Another One ordered the green one, so
they could taste both kinds (Beeba hadn't mentioned the
weiss beer that she only kept for Boris and the innermost
circle of his friends). To their marginal disappointment, the
Bitches soon figured out that both brands tasted more or less
the same – like your regular run-of-the-mill lager and with
neither of them ranking decisively towards either the positive
or negative end of the beer spectrum – but the girls were as
parched as Kalahari mushrooms, so they'd proclaim ice-cold
beer of any origin whatsoever as manna from heaven.

After a couple of rounds, however, Serbian Bitch decided she preferred *Laško* because she found it more on the bitter and heavier side, while Another One liked the slightly sweeter and seemingly lighter *Union* better.

With this leg of their journey into the enemy lair behind them and their thirst finally quenched, the Bitches leaned back, relaxed and commenced their reconnaissance operation.

32. Interlude:
The End of the Vilewood Road

The track *Garden Gnomes* by *Ray Kosmick and his Porn Groove Crew* had come to its end by the time Tinka scored a decisive victory against a couple of cocky cockroach paratroopers of unknown origin outside in the parking lot.

"Nice, yes? You like?" Ray Kosmick asked Amalia the great music critic.

Amalia, still quite impressed with how perfectly *Garden Gnomes* had underlined Tinka and Stanko's memorable exit, agreed: "Aye, Ray, very nice. I admit I can't imagine what porn flick *this* track would fit, if it isn't some kind of a bizarre sci-fi porn comedy piece featuring those genetically-engineered mutant sex pets of yours, but I sure liked it on its own, just as a track, yeah."

Ray wagged his finger at her: "I don't know if I'm happy with what you say or no, because I can very colourfully see how it would work in a beautiful fancy art porno, but I still like you like the song. Do you have any more by you and Finnegan?"

"Nah, come on, let's not overdo it," Amalia glanced at Beeba compassionately.

"You know, if Beeba let us listen to our music, we keep listening, otherwise there are Pink Floyd and Led Zeppelin waiting, and they playing all the time, all day, every day, anyway, you see."

"Even I have to agree," the psychedelic Willit Lonch at the next table agreed. "I adore the sixties as much as the next guy, but a bit of a change here and there can't possibly hurt, love."

Amalia hesitated.

"No, really, come on," Kip and Largo joined the chorus,

"Besides, we should get to know the tracks we'll soon be playing, right?"

"OK, fine, if you put it like that. I'll play another one then, if I may. Beeba, may I…"

Beeba shrugged: "Yes, play, but then when is over, I put up Janis Joplin," she decided.

"Agreed," Amalia said, stepped over to the laptop and played *The End of the Vilewood Road* from her iPod.

THE END OF THE VILEWOOD ROAD
[https://soundcloud.com/cynicism-management/
the-end-of-the-vilewood-road-augmented]

Go to the end of the Vilewood road
Where kids end up as food for foxes
Right to the end of the Vilewood road
Where garbage dreams of metal boxes

Come to the end of the Vilewood road
Let old knotted pines lure you astray
Here at the end of the Vilewood road
You'll peacefully blow your mind away

Away

Cobwebs peeling your eyes out
As you miss a roundabout
Murders crimes and tyres cut
Titties of your test drive slut

All along those Vilewood lies
Whispered by the cat's corpse eyes
Titties of your test drive slut
Complement her naked butt

Come to the end of the Vilewood road
Let old knotted pines lure you astray
Here at the end of the Vilewood road
You'll peacefully blow your mind away

Away away

As if on cue, the glassy-eyed herb-scented Randy entered the Rock 'n' Roll Tavern and held the door ajar. Willit Lonch and Ray Kosmick turned to check out the women who came in behind Randy. The horndog yokel barked and licked his lips at the sight of what he believed were a couple of lesbians, who swiftly retreated to a table on the other side of the room, as far away from the rude porn aficionado as possible.

Randy glanced at the speakers, somewhat surprised at hearing something other than the immortal sounds of the sixties, and cracked a broad appreciative smile at the sound of Finnegan and Amalia's quasi-reggae intro. After he performed a little dance just for the sake of it, he sat down next to Amalia and Kip, without saying anything, nodding to the tune.

"So," Ray interrogated Amalia after his new potential prey sat down at the other side of the bar and disappeared from his line of sight, "What's *this* lyric about?"

"First of all, mind you, this track doesn't have anything to do with sex. Just so you don't get your hopes and other things up again. But Finnegan could describe it much better, he wrote it. It's about his childhood, I gather."

Ray just kept looking at her inquisitively.

"Fine. Well, as far as he told me, it's about this stretch of woods at the end of the street where we lived as kids. You know, those irresistible places, you might remember a spot like that from your childhood, if you've ever had one..."

"Of course I remember my childhood, it was super," Ray laughed appreciatively.

"A spot, not a childhood, come on! I mean, though I do

find it truly hard to picture you as a child. Maybe it's the beer
gut that does that for you."

"Ya, and I also have a nice tickly spot, too."

"Oh, Christ, Ray, shut up already, you're starting to get
on my nerves. Anyway. You know, those special places that
attract you, lure you irresistibly, sing to you like a Siren's
song, even though you're afraid at the same time? You fear
something might be lurking there, waiting to get you, or that
something might happen to you if you go there, but you still
can't resist?"

"You mean, like the porno film shelf in the pirate video
shop on the corner of the street, which my father won't let me
see and he spank me if he catch me there?"

"Something like that, yeah," Amalia smiled, "Just that
Finnegan, when he was a kid, he had these special secret spots
of his in the forest at the end of our street, which he'd feel
drawn to all the time. Supposedly he was afraid of the forest
itself – and others must have found it scary, too, because they
did call it Vilewood – but he used to say these secret hiding
places of his were secure, he felt safe there. This way – by
always being able to run back to one of these spots – he was
one of the few kids his age who dared explore those woods."

Amalia saw Ray blinking, wrinkling his forehead and
mulling over what she was saying: "I don't know what places
you mean. Holes?"

"Foxholes, bushes, pine trees with really low branches
he could crawl under, tree branches he could climb, rocks he
could squeeze between, I'll be damned if I know them all, but
he certainly seemed to know every corner of those woods,"
she explained, and laughed: "Yeah, I agree, Finnegan was
obviously quite crazy as a child and he's even crazier now, he
is.

"Anyway, he told me it all started when he was still a
little boy and the neighbourhood bully once decided it would
be fun to drag him into the forest and scare the crap out of
him. Of course, the bully only took him there because he
was a mean bastard and he knew Finnegan was afraid of the

place. Even the bully himself was scared of it – not that he'd
ever admit this, mind you – because everyone kept telling
these children's stories, probably to keep the pesky brats
from getting lost in the damn woods or breaking their legs or
tearing their clothes in the bushes or whatever, about some
crazy man who lived in a house in the middle of the forest...
And if you happened to stumble upon the clearing where the
house stood, he'd catch you and drag you down into his cellar,
where he'd keep you in a cage before slitting your throat and
baking a pie out of your innards or whatever folks would
come up with. You know, your usual run-of-the-mill tales that
the naughty grandpa and the mischievous aunt always like to
tell children in order to make the little cherubs squirm...

"Anyway, the bully, overcoming his own fear, which was
probably not that hard to do since he was older and bigger,
dragged Finnegan deep into the woods one evening... Well,
it was just a couple hundred metres, but that can be a lot
when it's twilight and you're barely five years old and scared
shitless. The bully tripped Finnegan, forced him down to the
ground, made him lie there and told him that rabid foxes
would soon sniff him out and devour him. And if he moved a
muscle, they'd hear him and find him even sooner. Then the
sadistic little prick ran away and left Finnegan lying there.

"Finnegan, when he had overcome some of his fear,
realised that if he wanted to get out of the forest on his
own – and there was no one around to help him, so what
other choice did he have – he had to seek out hiding places
as he went, these secret spots he suddenly imagined must
have existed, where he could catch his breath for a moment
and confuse all the evil monsters, crazy old serial killer
hermits and rabid foxes that were already hot on his trail. So
he managed to find his way out of the woods by ducking,
whenever he felt too scared to go on, into one of these hiding
places he'd keep discovering as he went."

"Poor Finnegan," Ray drummed his fingers on the table.
"I think the bully maybe have a thing for Finnegan there..."
He narrowed his eyes and studied Amalia's face: "You know

much details about this. You must be pulling my foot again, I think you make this up, like in the song before. Something's not true here."

"Ah, well, OK, what can I say, you're a regular deception expert, Ray. Fine. I admit it, I was the bully. I watched the little twerp from the nearby bushes, and he really found his way home by himself. How's that?"

"Naughty!" Ray laughed and wagged his beefy finger. "Oh, and you even more naughty! You lie when you say there is no sex in the song, I hear something about titties there!" Ray suddenly cheered up and turned towards the speakers to make out the lyrics more clearly.

"Yes... I think that line might be referring to the fact that in his teens Finnegan would often drag the neighbourhood girls to that damn Vilewood forest of his. What better spot to hide in and make out than your very own trusted secret hiding places that had saved your very life more than ten years ago? Until the age of eighteen he'd definitely been there often – and even the neighbourhood bully would sometimes explore the... *Strategic spots* with him there for a while."

Amalia seemed to get lost in thought and so did Ray.

"Oh, you guys are all the same," Amalia finally wrapped up the yarn. "No matter how cute or benign a story, you just can't live without sticking a tit or two in it, can you?"

"It's no fun without tit. And even if it is, tit make it even more fun," Ray concluded.

33. Operation Watering Hole: Reconnaissance

The Watcher stared at the screens showing the video feeds from the two Bitch Scouts who had succeeded in infiltrating the very belly of the beast without a hitch. She'd set up their surveillance post on a couple of folding picnic tables they had brought with them, and the equipment was powered by heavy-duty Omnipile power generators, which relied on several patented technologies that would soon be sold for billions to third-world countries in dire need of electricity and depended on the strip mining of every conceivable metal in those same countries, some of which had once upon a time been lush green forests.

"There, you see? On Serbian Bitch's screen. That's got to be Finnegan Frotz, the subject of our investigation," The Watcher pointed out a man to the rest of the Bitches who were busy munching on snacks and drinking sodas that Grim Bitch and Accumulator of Unwonted Locutions had just fetched from the little 24/7 gas station across the main street.

The Watcher was content with Serbian Bitch's mastery of the high-tech spy spectacles: "She's got quite a knack for this, see? Acting like she's just looking around the pub, but keeping the camera on that corner table just long enough..."

"Rewind and pause, so I can confirm the ID and log it," Arch Bitch mumbled around a mouthful of sandwich. The Watcher rewound the video feed on one of the screens and paused a frame showing Finnegan chuckle through a wooden lattice. Arch Bitch compared the face of the unusually pale black man with the photos Omnipile had provided. The Watcher ran a facial recognition algorithm. It was a match. Arch Bitch entered their achievement in the logbook and promptly updated Omnipile via a satellite uplink.

"I wonder who the guys sitting with him are," Grim Bitch pointed at Bogomyr Yadvig, who sat with his back towards the screen, and Boris Birman sitting to the side, opposite the curtained window, with his right side turned towards the Bitch Scouts.

"The facial recognition algorithm produces no hits for that guy –" The Watcher pointed at Boris "– so he's probably not in the OIA database. Not yet, at least, though he will be now. And I can't run the algorithm on the back of that bloke's head, not even these gadgets are that smart," The Watcher explained.

"I'm sure we'll find out soon enough..." Arch Bitch remarked indifferently.

"Should we codename them, too?" Grim Bitch asked Arch Bitch.

It was unclear whether she was serious or sarcastic, so Arch Bitch decided to ignore her for the time being, turning to The Watcher instead: "Tell the Bitch Scouts to take it easy on the beer. Of course they're only trying to fit in," she smirked, "But let's not overdo it, I don't want the OIA to think we're unprofessional or anything."

"Go ahead and tell them yourself. Here, sit down next to me, put on your headset, here's the on/off switch for your microphone..." The Watcher explained.

Arch Bitch and The Watcher fiddled with the controls, completely smitten with all the technical possibilities, while Grim Bitch and Accumulator of Unwonted Locutions decided they'd sit down on the ground a couple of feet away. They leaned against the van, enjoying a snack and throwing pebbles into the brook.

"The unfolding exploratory operation notwithstanding, I find our respite thoroughly congenial..." Accumulator of Unwonted Locutions stretched her limbs and yawned.

"Yeah, I like slacking off a bit, too," Grim Bitch wished she had her fishing gear with her.

At the table, Arch Bitch asked: "Is there any way to focus the reception on particular speakers we want to hear?"

"Of course!" The Watcher was certainly an avid
fan of the Omnipile Gadget R&D Department. "There are
amazingly advanced microphones built into each temple arm
of the eyeglasses, near the ears, so through your high-tech
headphones you can hear pretty much what each of the Scouts
is hearing, in 3D positional audio."

"Neat..."

"But that's not all. The spyglasses also have superb
directional microphones on each side, so you can specifically
listen in on what's going on at roughly 90 degrees to the left
or right of what you're looking at. That way you don't have
to look at whoever you're eavesdropping on... There's one of
these microphones in the front, too, of course, but you have
another even fancier goodie at your disposal: a built-in laser
microphone, so that you can hear things very far away from
you, as long as they're in a clear line of sight and there's a
surface that vibrates appropriately next to the people talking.
Like glass, or canvas on a painting, even cigarette smoke
will do, even though that's hard to aim at. For example, if
you wanted to listen to some people talking behind a closed
window from a couple hundred metres away, you could
just zoom in, turn on the laser microphone, aim it at the
windowpane and hear everything they're saying with crystal
clarity."

"Unbelievable!"

"Exactly. Of course, each directional microphone can be
turned off and on individually. Everything gets recorded to
the drives simultaneously, so you can review it later, but you
can choose which audio feed to listen to in your headphones.
So can the Scouts, with those pocket controllers I haven't
given them yet."

"Awesome..."

"We also have these elastic sports bands that have
microphones and cameras built in, which you can use with the
eyeglasses to see and hear what's going on behind you. They
look pretty awful, though, so I didn't think you guys should
wear them right now. As for the glasses, well, in the technical

sense they really are the shit in all aspects, but their weight and look, jeez... They're geeky enough to put Clark Kent to shame, I can't imagine what the designers were thinking."

"Yeah. Well, I see the Scouts are settling in..."

Serbian Bitch sat with her back to the wall, facing the other end of the room where Ray Kosmick had just started flailing his arms while explaining something to Amalia Winegirl Paulin and everyone else in his vicinity. Finnegan, Bogomyr and Boris were discussing something in the corner to her right. Arch Bitch examined the situation, turned on her microphone and instructed her: "Let's hear what Mr Frotz and his unidentified companions are saying, shall we?"

The Watcher put her hands on the controls and instructed the Scouts: "Serbian Bitch, you just keep your head straight, we'll listen through the directional microphone on the right side of your glasses. Another One, you keep looking at Serbian Bitch, we'll also turn on your left microphone. Meanwhile, feel free to chat among yourselves so that you don't look suspicious, it won't affect the directional microphones."

"Hmm," analysed Arch Bitch after they'd listened to Boris, Finnegan and Bogomyr's conversation for a while, "Let's codename Finnegan's companions *Balding Hippy* and *Crackpot of the Night*."

"Agreed," concurred The Watcher, "I have a feeling that Balding Hippy is Boris, as in *'Boris And Beeba's'*," she said, referring to the ads for some concerts in the Rock 'n' Roll Tavern she had found on the internet. "And the drowsy woman serving drinks, she's most likely Beeba. I don't think even hippies like Boris and Beeba would willingly employ such a lethargic middle-aged waitress."

"We shall codename her... Ah, well, Beeba will do just fine," Arch Bitch decided.

Behind their backs, Grim Bitch rolled her eyes, stared at the moonlit sky for a moment, scratched her head, listened to crickets, yawned, and threw another pebble at the few remaining pond skaters (most of whom had already got tired of surfing the waves created by the bored Grim Bitch).

"Fine, however entertaining this rather bizarre conversation of theirs may be, it doesn't seem to have anything to do with the abduction of Mr Fenton's children," Arch Bitch concluded. "Say, why don't we listen in on what's going on across the room for a change?"

"Sure, I'm getting sick of hearing about pubic hair loss, penile dysfunctions, Drago Dabić, the demise of the martens and sun phobias, anyway," The Watcher agreed hastily, itching to test the laser microphone.

While The Watcher was telling Serbian Bitch how to focus the beam on the window behind Ray, Willit, Largo, Amalia, Kip and Randy, at the corner table Balding Hippy, Crackpot of the Night and Subject of the Investigation were wrapping up their private conversation. Boris called Drago even though it was already late – they were very good friends, and Drago Dabić was not known for turning in early. Dr Dabić agreed to see Bogomyr first thing next morning. The guys picked up their drinks and headed around the semi-circular bar and past the Bitch Scouts to join the others. Boris and Finnegan nodded at the Bitches in greeting as they walked by, but Bogomyr seemed too troubled to bother. Serbian Bitch returned the greeting.

"Excellent, now we'll be able to listen to all of them at once," The Watcher rubbed her hands. When she turned on the laser microphone it was as if she and Arch Bitch were sitting right next to them. However, the Bitches' initial fascination with the incredibly useful technology they had gotten to play with was soon replaced by the disappointment in what they heard.

It all started innocently with Finnegan remarking, as he staggered drunkenly to a chair next to Largo: "Hey, you put *Vilewood Road* on before! It's meant as a bit of a prank, it is. You know, a funny little ditty we'll probably always play last. It's got a really long instrumental part at the end, maybe a bit boring if you're not on the stage, right, and I guess it helps if you're stoned while you're listening to it..."

"Yep, it helps," interjected Randy, swaying slightly and staring at the incredibly intriguing bubbles rising from the bottom of his beer as they joined the gradually thinning crowd at the top.

"It's probably going to be the last track on the CD, so..." Finnegan apologised to no one in particular.

"I hear you mention titties, too," Ray Kosmick beamed.

"Aye, well," Finnegan smiled and burped, "It's just..."

"That's what we've just been discussing, how sex is being abused by the capital!" Largo slammed his fist on the table, pretending to be outraged. Apparently Largo and Ray, after a short digression and as three new potential victims joined them, decided to steer the conversation right back to Ray's Free Sex Revolution. They truly had one-track minds, one of them always skipping back to revolutions, and the other one always talking about sex. So a sexual revolution, that was simply too good not to revisit at least three times per average evening at Boris and Beeba's.

"Absolutely," Finnegan agreed, "Using sex to sell records, and playing music in order to have it off, isn't that what musicians have been doing since... Well, forever?"

"Sure, and it's appalling. Instead of writing socially conscious lyrics they keep abusing sex," Largo protested.

"Hey, how about socially conscious lyrics that happen to have a bit of sex in them? I don't know about you, but I don't mind a quick shag now and again."

"Bah, you're just like the rest of them," Largo smiled.

"The rest of whom? Pardon me, laddie, but I happen to have a plan. We'll abuse sex for a good cause. If you want, we can even name our future album Tit, and put a nice rack on the cover, too, but we'll do it in such a way that the irony will be obvious to anyone with half a brain."

"Will the statement be socially conscious?"

"By all means," Finnegan confirmed resolutely.

"That's something I'd like to see," Largo smiled contentedly and sipped his small beer.

"That's something you're going to see, I've just made up

my mind."

"Maybe you can join with our Free Sex Revolution," Ray Kosmick put in. Finnegan looked somewhat confused, not having participated in the fascinating debate about half an hour ago, so Ray, not exactly in the mood to repeat every-thing at that very moment (to the considerable relief of Amalia and Kip Ducker), proposed instead: "Or maybe you can write something about too little tit in the Miss World competition," Ray Kosmick proposed. "I always hate that."

"Would you care to elaborate?" Willit Lonch said very slowly, seemingly returning from a place in a galaxy far far away. He had been listening to the second part of *The End of the Vilewood Road* a little too intently for his own good, but now he registered that Ray Kosmick might unveil another one of his glamorous theses.

"Ya, sure, I explain. You know how every sexy model and singer try to sell her with her tits, right? I say, that's absolutely not fair. I mean, they all act like they'll deliver, but they never deliver. Do you ever see a sexy singer *really* show you her tit? No, you don't. You must listen and listen and listen to her wailing, but she doesn't really show any tit in the end, no matter how long you wait. They just wear, how do you call them... Those clothes you can see through?"

"See-through gowns?" Kip chuckled.

"Ya, that. And they have deep decolletage – I learn that word especially, good, no? Their tit *almost* escapes, you know, falls out, like this..." Ray demonstrated by weighing his own considerable man tits with both of his hands, "...but you *never really* see it happen. Unless they make secret 'personal' porno on purpose and put it on the internets..." Ray made the quotation marks with his fingers, "...but that's another story."

Ray's audience nodded.

"Oh! Cleavage..." Kip finally got it and smacked his forehead across the table from Amalia.

After a short pause, Willit encouraged Ray: "Do go on, mate, we all know what you're getting at here, right?" Everyone agreed, some of them amused, others gradually getting bored of Ray Kosmick's obsession with mammary glands.

"So I say, that isn't fair. I mean, if they stand there and sell shit by means of tit, then we should get the tit, right?" Ray became slightly upset.

"*Selling shit by means of tit...*" Finnegan wrote in his notebook of poetry. "Hmm, hmm," he grinned contentedly, obviously already working on the title track for the new album by *Cynicism Management*. Finnegan suddenly realised he'd somehow managed to distract the great breast guru, so he looked up and apologised: "Sorry, Ray, go on, I didn't mean to interrupt. You might have just given me an idea for some lyrics – if you'll let me use it, of course?"

"Of course you can use my wise knowledge I share with all of you, but only if I can then maybe use your song in my porno art, if it fits," Ray negotiated.

"Definitely, agreed," Finnegan and Ray shook hands.

"OK, so, where am I... Ya. So the most bad example of this – that you don't see no tit but you definitely should – are all these Miss this and Miss that competitions. What the hell? I mean, there they choose the most sexy girl, but the girls don't get butt naked. That's like buying a cat in a bag. Or a horse without looking him in the teeth. Maybe they are hiding some hideous afflictions below the dress..."

"Jesus, Ray, you're such a damn misogynist," Amalia complained.

"I am who?"

"A woman hater."

"Oh please, I don't hate women, I love them!"

"Yeah, you want to shag them, but not the less attractive ones. You're prejudiced. A bigot. A male retard."

"There you go... And you're man retard hater. Besides, I talk about beauty competitions here, not about all women, especially not about more mature women like you..." Ray smiled mischievously. Amalia punched the bigmouth in the shoulder and growled.

"So, you agree, these girls come and compete in how

sexy and seductious they look. Don't tell me you find sexy
and seductious my beer belly here..." Ray caressed his
prominent protrusion lovingly, "And you also wouldn't think
that something horrible growing out of that girl's navel would
be sexy, too. Admit it."

Finnegan and Willit laughed, and Amalia scowled.

"So I say," Ray elaborated, "that these Miss this and
that, they should first show themselves in dress, and then
topless, and then bottomless, and then full-on naked. If all
of this is on TV after the kids go to bed – and it should be,
because this is really not for children – they should also make
sweet love to each other, so that we could see how open
and nice they are and what pleasure they can bring on the
world. Not this 'I want world peace' and 'I get water for children
in Africa'. No! They should say, for example: I make love to
everyone who is lonely and sad! That would be the day! We
need some damn honesty: if your business is tit, then show me
tit, don't sell shit by means of covered tit, you lying fake. But
it never happens, they don't show any tit, ever, and they only
talk about some stupid things."

"That's so damn true, I have yet to hear a good answer
from a Miss World candidate. Or a good question, now that
I think about it, but still! They have the chance of expressing
their political views to the whole world, so they could stress
the urgency of finding some solutions to the worsening social
issues and the mounting crises of the capitalist system! They
should condemn its underhanded neo-liberal extremes and
the dire need for a new socialist agenda, but no..." Largo got
worked up again. There, that's how Ray and Largo always
ended up on the same revolutionary page.

"Bah, you expect too much, Fidel! We don't even hear
no good and funny answers to simple questions. For example,
last time I watch and they ask the Miss what is the greatest
invention in the history of human race. Now, why not say, for
example: 'Well, I say, to be honest, a dildo, so that I don't have
to tolerate such stupid twat asking such stupid questions as
you.' For example, I'm just saying, but she answer something

really stupid again, like 'Maybe a smartphone?' and then she looking at the man asking with big cow eyes and flutters with her eyelids."

In the woods about half a mile away, The Watcher and Arch Bitch looked at each other sullenly. They were gradually becoming less than amused.

"And then they ask what the miss would do to promote Slovenia," Ray Kosmick rambled on. "'Well, I say', she should say in my opinion, 'I'd shoot a fancy high-budget porno film in the world-famous Slovenian Postojna Cave, where I would very gladly shag stalactites as well as stalagmites, making no difference and no discrimination against if they are standing or hanging'. She would immediately be a superstar, starring in such awesome film. This legendary cult art porno would be showing her enjoying the magical wonders of the under-ground cave world, while for music soundtrack the best Slovenian Alpine song band would be playing its super hits behind her, jumping around in polka time with accordions and dressed only in black and white lace garter belts instead of usual folk song uniforms. Now, I tell you that would be a real famous promotion of Slovenia. Oh, and while the Slovenian Miss presented what naughty and wonderful things she can do to all interested viewers all around the world, the world-famous Slovenian human fish would crawl around her tits and bellybutton..."

"Proteus. An endemic species of cave salamander. Extremely rare," Willit Lonch interrupted and explained what Ray meant to the wide-eyed Finnegan and slightly disgusted Kip. Kip loved his steaks rare and enjoyed loads of Vegemite, but he hated seafood.

"Ya," Ray said, "Fish, lizard, whatever. We call them human fish. A funny creature, slimy, blind, almost white, and very very famous because it's really hard to find. It only lives in Postojna Cave and maybe some other stupid holes nearby, so that Slovenians keep being very proud of them, but they are good for nothing."

"Ray," sighed Amalia.

"Yes, dear?" Ray turned to her.

"You're one sick puppy, you know that?"

Outside in the woods, listening in on this conversation with decreasing zeal, The Watcher told Arch Bitch: "My thoughts exactly. Those poor Fenton kids, if these depraved individuals really had anything to do with their abduction."

"I'm afraid this could turn into a long and messy investigation," Arch Bitch sighed and added *Sick Puppy* to the growing collection of codenames scribbled in her logbook.

Ray, Finnegan, Bogomyr, Boris and Randy went into the other room to shoot some pool, and as Ray's tireless prattling faded out, suddenly an unusual calm descended on Boris and Beeba's Rock 'n' Roll Tavern. The decibels of Amalia, Willit, Largo and Kip, who remained at the tables by the door, were far inferior to Ray's passionate declamations. Besides, with Ray, one also had to take into account all the turmoil caused by everyone else who had to breathe in very deeply and invest considerable amounts of air into their statements if they wanted to outshout him in order to participate in the conversation.

Beeba, visibly relieved that the chattering had moved into the other room, was just about to relax when Stanko and Tinka, on their way back from the pizza place where they'd most likely got thrown out, opened the door. Fortunately for Beeba, Stanko hesitated at the door, waiting for Tinka who struggled to climb the horrifyingly steep and numerous three stairs leading up to the pub without succumbing to the burden of extreme alcoholic exhaustion. Beeba was able to take advantage of the delay. She rushed to the door like the wind, which was so uncharacteristic of her that everyone in the pub, including the Bitch Scouts, turned to look at what was going on.

Beeba pushed Stanko and Tinka out, telling them something in Slovenian. Despite Stanko's insistence and desperate protests, she managed to close the door and lock up behind them. She killed the lights outside and in the windows, and turned the music way down, so that *Led Zeppelin* she now played sounded like the slightest background elevator music to her dishwashing. That and the way she sighed tiredly while cleaning up the bar suggested that she wanted the punters to clear out as soon as possible. In light of this unfortunate predicament, Amalia quickly ordered another round of drinks before Beeba could resolve to throw them out. Beeba protested weakly but caved in, stressing that this would definitely be the last round. *"Damnation!"* Amalia thought, but on the other hand she figured it was for the best.

Serbian Bitch had scowled as Subject of the Investigation, Sick Puppy, Crackpot of the Night, Balding Hippy and Herb Boy had left the room. So had Arch Bitch and The Watcher, who were monitoring the developments on their spy equipment in the woods. Arch Bitch instructed the Bitch Scouts: "Another One, you stay put, you know, due to your poor eyesight and so on... We'll turn on your general 3D positional microphones, so just keep sitting with your back to the others. The music is quiet enough now and we'll be able to hear everyone without our more sophisticated gear. And you, Serbian Bitch, go to the toilet, scope the place out, and find out where the other subjects are."

Serbian Bitch turned off her laser microphone, quite relieved that she didn't have to keep aiming it at the window behind Kip Ducker on the other side of the room anymore. She wondered why it was that the laser was not influenced by even the slightest movements of her head – there was no way she could stay completely still, nor would that look very natural and inconspicuous even if it was possible – but she decided not to worry too much about the esoteric and sometimes utterly incomprehensible achievements of the Omnipile Gadget R&D Department. She stood up, walked to the bar and asked Beeba where the toilet was. Beeba pointed at the door through which the others had left and told her to go down the corridor and through the pool room.

As Serbian Bitch walked past the subjects of their investigation, looking around methodically so she'd get every corner on video, they were all too busy kicking and shaking the pool table to pay any attention to her. Even Ray seemed too engrossed in staring into the cue ball return and sticking the bumper of his stick into the hole for some reason to even notice her.

She eavesdropped on them while exploring (and using) the toilet, but found it hard to believe they had any ulterior motives – they just kept messing with the pool table, obviously trying to get something out of it. It looked like the balls might have got stuck in there. So, sadly, she didn't succeed in finding out about any secret meetings, analysing meaningful discussions, victoriously uncovering diabolical schemes, recording terrorist activities, and she could definitely not identify any hint of information with regard to what Mr Finnegan Frotz had to do with the Yomanian Liberation Front, the kidnapping of the Fenton kids, or why his posterior was adorned in such an elaborate and cryptic way.

Meanwhile, in the barroom, Another One eavesdropped carefully on what the remaining subjects of the investigation were saying. Admittedly, based on Ray's dissertation she'd just witnessed, she was doing so out of boredom more than because she believed she'd in fact hear anything useful. And her instincts were correct.

"Phew, tonight was intense," the silver-haired Willit Lonch remarked, seemingly talking to no one in particular and sipping his white wine (who would stick with tea and rum throughout an entire evening?) – an excellent sweet Riesling from the north-east of Slovenia, arguably Slovenia's best wine region.

"You mean because of Ray?" Amalia smiled. "I thought you were used to his... Well, ideas, for the lack of a better word. I was sure nothing he says can possibly surprise you any longer."

"Oh, I'm thoroughly used to his, as you put it, ideas. But even that can't quite prepare me for the insurmountable heaps of bollocks he comes up with. At least it's a fun heap!" Willit laughed, "No, but that's not what I'm talking about. What I meant was, I was a bit out there, in the sky, so to say. You'll have to send me some of that music of yours, I must say I was quite impressed with some of it, not that I can quite recall what exactly, or why, but it made pretty colours."

"Oh. Molly?"

"Don't be absurd, that new junk kids screw around with nowadays is not for the likes of me, thank you very much. I dropped some plain old LSD, just a bit of blotter paper, not a pill. But it was still rather fascinating. Many unlikely associations have popped up in my head, and for a while there I wondered whether Jesus Christ was a gerontophile."

On the other side of the table, Largo looked up and let out a surprised: "Excuse me?"

Kip and Amalia said nothing, but were already worried that an explanation was obviously going to follow. Kip put his elbows on the table and rested his chin in the palms of his hands, making himself comfortable while scratching one of his cheeks and peeking at Willit.

"Well, you see, Fidel, it's simple, really." Willit, obviously coming back from his outer space exploration, took a deep breath. "Nuns are supposed to be virgin spouses of Christ. They mostly spend their days in convents, untouched, so I assume they're waiting to finally join their husband and, I imagine, to consummate their marriage. Most of these devoted young women turn into withered old hags by the time they manage to kick the bucket, you know, especially since they're not supposed to speed up the whole process much in any entertaining way anyway – I don't believe many of them take a lot of drugs or drink themselves to death very young, or die of cholesterol overdose. Especially since heart attacks are, I'd say, mostly reserved for people who are under a lot of stress, and these dedicated women don't really strike me as such... You know, with their husband away on business all the time, so he can't bitch at them and slap them around. Anyway, once they finally get to shag the Lord, the majority of them are, well, mature, even elderly, or bloody ancient, if we're completely honest. So you see, since this suspicious arrangement had to be organised by our Lord, and if he himself has decided this is how he wants it..."

"I see," said Amalia. "Maybe it's just that the Lord likes women who belong to his own age group."

"Jesus Christ!" grumbled Grim Bitch in the night woods.

"Exactly," laughed The Watcher.

Back at the Rock 'n' Roll Tavern, on the other side of the room, Another One yawned like a starving blue whale at the sight of a crunchy cloud of krill. It was getting late. She was exhausted and tired of listening to these fruitcakes. Besides, she felt Beeba's eyes on her – Beeba was obviously trying to clear out the pub – so she was very glad when Serbian Bitch finally came back from the toilet and paid for their drinks, so they could finally leave and wrap up this rather intense day.

The Bitch Scouts left well before the others. Outside in the Jimi Hendrix parking lot they heard Arch Bitch in their tiny in-ear earphones: "OK, good job, but I have another idea. Serbian Bitch, take Another One's glasses. She'll break her neck if she wears them, anyway. Pull over by the bushes some distance up the road, where you can't be seen, and hide the glasses somewhere. Leave them aimed at the pub, so that we can see when everybody leaves and the owners go to sleep. We've received orders from the OIA to set up our more permanent surveillance equipment here as soon as possible, so we can very well do it tonight."

"Are they afraid to miss out on any additional ingenious ideas by Sick Puppy or that English guy, whoever he is?" the Bitch Scouts heard Grim Bitch ask in the background.

"There's no need for sarcasm," Arch Bitch said, "It's just that judging by Serbian Bitch's footage of the pool room, Balding Hippy is very drunk, and Beeba seems about ready to fall asleep on her feet. So this is a very convenient oppor- tunity and it would be imprudent of us not to take advantage of it. Once they're asleep, we should be able to break in and set up some cameras and microphones quickly, without much trouble. Then we'll be able to stake out the place from the motel without needing to stick around, especially not in this van or on these damn folding chairs. My butt's killing me. Oh, and, yeah, we should codename the others, too, I'll draw up another report to Omnipile while we wait. Any suggestions?"

Grim Bitch grumbled in the background: "We'll hardly be able to remember everyone as it is. Frankly, these codenames are a lousy idea."

"I disagree," The Watcher opined, "We didn't find out most of the real names of the people in there, but we already know who's who by assigning nicknames according to their appearance. Besides, it's how the OIA wants it, so it's how we should go about it."

"Whatever. But let's refrain from witticisms then and keep it simple and obvious. I propose *Psychedelic Brit, Fidel*... At least they'd already nicknamed that bloke themselves. Who else? Oh, *Quiet Guy* and *Scottish Songstress*."

"Fine by me," said Arch Bitch and jotted the codenames into her notebook.

While the Bitch Scouts walked back towards the van, the rest of the Bitches yawned and watched the screens, hoping that everybody still loitering in the pub would pack up and go home soon.

So did Beeba. Despite the profits resulting from everybody being as thirsty as they were tonight, she found evenings like this utterly exhausting. First she had to get the boys out of the pool room. Since Boris was also with them, she expected that would turn out to be quite a task, because once he really got going, Boris could, in his alcohol-induced euphoria, even go so far as to defend the customers in spite of himself. He'd usually regret that painfully the next morning, and this sometimes even resulted in a few days of abstinence from alcohol and ingestion of many an Aspirin, multivitamin and multimineral tablet as well as heaps of oranges, apples, tea with lemon, and servings of chicken soup. Although good for Boris's physical health, not even such a radical regime could alleviate his regret that he'd succumbed to his so-called "wild side" again. However, fortunately for Beeba (and perhaps also Boris), when she went to check on the boys, she saw Boris was half asleep on the pool table, while the others either shook the table, laughed, or peered down into the holes.

Oddly enough, she knew what was going on right away: "Is cat in pool? She never come out, more you scare her, more she hide," Beeba explained to the eight-ball fans while she shook Boris. When he finally managed to focus on where he was and what he was doing, she looked him in the eye and told him off in what was, for Beeba, uncharacteristically loud and angry Slovenian. The others didn't need a word of translation to understand it was time to leave.

Kip, Ray and Bogomyr's cars as well as Randy's Yugo pulled away. Kip had not had that much to drink, Randy believed that the Slovenian police were not yet in possession of portable THC tests, Bogomyr did not believe that alcohol could adversely affect vampires, while Ray drove blind drunk and just didn't give a funk.

The Bitches – all of them now, as Serbian Bitch and Another One had returned safely, without tumbling into the river or getting run over by an idiot driver – waited near the road under the cover of the trees. They heard the purr of three cars and the near-death farts of an ancient *Yugo* as the subjects of their investigation drove by their strategic position. They waited, listening to the mating calls of crickets and drunken teenagers somewhere off in the distance, until, at least according to the spy camera Serbian Bitch had left in the bushes, every light in Boris and Beeba's house went out. It was just a few minutes past midnight. Fortunately for Another One and Grim Bitch, who yawned and blinked wearily into the night, the tavern seemed to have closed quite early that night, though if somebody had asked Beeba, she'd have said it was pretty damn late as far as she was concerned. While The Watcher and Arch Bitch turned off their equipment and packed up, Serbian Bitch and Accumulator of Unwonted Locutions stared at the unfathomable multitude of stars above them. As Londoners they were definitely not used to seeing so many.

"This is nothing, really, though," Serbian Bitch told the other stargazer, "We're far too close to the city. I remember when I was a child, living in a village in Serbia that didn't even have street lights, you could see the Milky Way clearly. It looked like a streak of light across the sky."

"Yeah," Grim Bitch managed to utter between lengthy yawns, "I suppose we could almost see it here, too, if these locals weren't so crazy about lighting up every tiny chapel like a Christmas tree. What a waste of electricity."

"I didn't know you were such an environmentalist," Another One muttered.

"I'm not. I just try to be reasonable. I'm sure you find it pretty, though."

"Hey, what's your problem?!" Another One protested.

"Bitches!" Arch Bitch interrupted, "Enough of this petty bickering. I know you're all tired, but let's clean up after ourselves and get moving." In response to Serbian Bitch's resentful glance she said, as if she were reading her mind: "Yes, I for one tend to appreciate the environment, especially if it's nice and clean. And no, I couldn't care less about who has or hasn't been here, and who's responsible for littering. Just clean up this picnic spot and let's get going. We're heading out at 1:30 a.m. sharp. That should give Beeba and Balding Hippy enough time to start snoring like bears."

Fewer and fewer cars passed by, and by half past one the Suburbia was as deserted as the *Letališče Jožeta Pučnika* airport. The beat-up blue Volkswagen van drove slowly past the Rock 'n' Roll Tavern. Everything seemed dead in there. The Bitches, looking around carefully, didn't see a living soul.

This time the Watcher refrained from turning left up the hill towards the church, which shone brightly against the night sky to the profound satisfaction of the local insects, even greater happiness of the bats that dwelled in the belfry, and the occasional dismay of Stanko. One of the floodlights had the audacity to shine through his window, driving him mad on those rare occasions when he failed to drink enough to pass out successfully. The Watcher just drove on, hoping to find a place where she could park the van unnoticed.

A couple hundred metres down the road she pulled over and parked at a small bus stop in the middle of nowhere. Of course, the place was utterly deserted at this time of night. The only structure around – apart from a run-down bench, dotted with used chewing gum the kids had stuck on it – was a half-burned plastic dustbin brimming with squashed tin cans, cigarette butts, plastic bags and other junk. The bus stop was obscured from sight by thick bushes that flourished wildly, insulting any gardener's sense of proper behaviour in vegetation.

The Bitches snuck out of the van quietly.

"OK, here's the plan…"

The Bitches listened intently, finally stirred awake by the prospect of carrying out an espionage operation that was in fact more exciting than listening to Ray Kosmick's perverted fantasies, Largo Cabaleri's revolutionary tirades, Willit Lonch's drug-induced idiocies, and the never-ending woes of a thoroughly unremarkable vampire.

"The Watcher and I will stay here and keep an eye on everything," Arch Bitch outlined the strategy. "Another One, since you obviously can't wear spy glasses without tripping over something, you'll keep your own glasses. But take these night-vision binoculars and hide in the bushes where Serbian Bitch left your spy glasses. Find them and pick them up. You can use them to communicate with us. Remember, you don't have to put them on, the microphones will transmit your every whisper, just keep them close and don't forget to bring them back with you. We don't want to lose any expensive equipment, and we especially don't want anyone else to find it. Use the night-vision binoculars to watch the road. Even if you only see random cars approaching, warn everyone, so that we can avoid any unpleasant surprises.

"Serbian Bitch, you're familiar with the layout of the pub already, and you can see well, so it'll be up to you to go in. While we were waiting before, The Watcher and I had already checked the footage and decided where the most

convenient spots for our surveillance equipment are. So, once
you're inside and acclimated, we'll point out the spots on your
head-up display where you should install the microphones
and even a tiny self-cleaning camera or two."

Serbian Bitch raised an eyebrow.

"No, don't worry, we won't make you install anything
in the toilet bowls. Meanwhile, you –" Arch Bitch told Grim
Bitch, "You'll hide across from the pub, in the bushes by the
Jimi Hendrix wall on the edge of the parking lot, and watch
the house from the front, so that you can warn everyone
should any lights come on in the house or if you notice
anything else.

"And you –" Arch Bitch turned to Accumulator of
Unwanted Locutions, "You'll hide in the back yard and do the
same: keep an eye on the back of the house. And watch out for
dogs, I hope they don't have any back there. That's about it, is
everything clear?" Arch Bitch checked.

The Bitches nodded.

The Watcher handed out the equipment, including the
pocket controllers, and showed the espionage crew how everything worked.

"And here's an israel for you," The Watcher entrusted a
small tool to Serbian Bitch.

"A what?" Serbian Bitch widened her eyes.

"An israel. That's short for 'instantly self-regulating
automatic electronic lock pick'. I made that up myself. The
little gadget is a prototype, so it doesn't even have a proper
name yet. I took the liberty of coming up with something
descriptive and cute for it, so... Cool, right?"

"Sure," Serbian Bitch nodded enthusiastically. As she
envisioned what variety of doors she could open with it, her
eyes lit up so brightly that the party of irrational insects and
ravenous bats, in full swing up at the church, made a passing
swoop down to the obscure bus stop.

"You know, with any luck the name will stick, just like
laser or radar." The Watcher was as proud of the name as if
she'd invented the wondrous little gadget herself.

"Sure." Serbian Bitch couldn't care less what it was called. The only thing she could hardly wait to find out was how it worked. "You just pop this thing into any mechanical lock whatsoever, and it will promptly, as the name I gave it suggests, adjust itself and pick it. And inaudibly, too – according to the notes that came with the prototype, it lubricates the lock first, and then opens it very discreetly. It doesn't even make the noise that a proper key would. What's even more ingenious is that with an israel you can also lock the door behind you when you're done, so nobody will figure out the lock's been picked in the first place. If anything, the lock works more smoothly after you're done with it, since the israel will grease its parts. Don't worry, there's no need to understand the technology behind it, you just recharge the batteries on a regular basis and use it. Much like notebook computers or satellite phones," The Watcher winked.

Serbian Bitch eagerly pocketed the israel and asked the crew: "Shall we go, then?"

After a mostly uneventful hour or so, the Bitch infiltrators returned from a surprisingly smooth mission. All the microphones and cameras had been successfully installed. They hadn't seen a living soul. Boris and Beeba did own a tavern hound named Rex, who resided in a luxurious dog villa behind the tavern, but the old pooch was used to punters gallivanting around the place at all hours of the day and night. Even though he was not exactly a fan of strangers, Rex also knew it was useless to whine about them, so he kept any objections he might have had to himself. Serbian Bitch had only stumbled across a single problem inside the house, which resulted in the tiniest bit of commotion, but nobody had woken up. Arch Bitch and The Watcher congratulated each Bitch, and finally looked at Serbian Bitch, slightly concerned.

"Are you alright?" Arch Bitch asked her, covering her mouth and looking at her with an expression of sympathetic concern on her face.

"I'll live. But if this hasn't cost me a couple of years of my life, nothing will. I almost had a heart attack," Serbian bitch panted.

"What happened?" asked Another One. Of course, only Arch Bitch and The Watcher had seen the incident on Serbian Bitch's screen, the others hadn't been tuned into her video feed at that moment.

"I was jumped by a stupid bloody cat when I was instructed to place a bug on the bottom of the pool table," Serbian Bitch explained bitterly and used a spray The Watcher had fetched her from a first aid kit to disinfect the painful cat claw marks running across both of her cheeks.

34. Finnegan's Blog Entry No. 5

Damn, I really shouldn't be writing this right now. It'll be one of those blog posts that I type drunk and then regret in the morning. And not just because of all the typos and ludicrous sentence structures (which I'll fix tomorrow or the day after, anyway – fortunately posts can be edited, unlike embarrassing e-mails).

I only write this now because I'm too excited to just go to sleep. I feel like staying up a while longer and having another beer or two while I organise my thoughts, so it's best to write them down...

Or screw that. I'm just making this up because I want to sound nice. Nobody in their right mind is going to read this, so what the hell do I care? Fact is, THAT DAMN PORTUGUESE SLUT is in the room we're supposed to share, entertaining some fucking U.S. marine cretin. Amalia and her Deathbreath Rock 'n' Roll Bitch have already turned in, and Randy, after smoking a giant goodnight reefer, has nodded off on the couch.

So here I am, staring at my laptop in the kitchen, while Desidéria is having it off with Captain America in our room. Why the fuck didn't I grab a beer from the fridge, head on straight to my room and dump my Scottish arse on the bed while they were still watching TV, ignoring them altogether? But noooo, I had to stay in the living room with Randy long enough for them to give in to their carnal desires and slip away. And where the fuck does she find these obnoxious morons, anyhow? Sod it, the last thing I want to listen to right now is some stupid American soldier come. And even when he's done we're probably not going to be discussing Noam Chomsky anytime soon with that piece of inbred white-trash U.S. Army garbage.

Aye, you're right, I don't even know him and already I've passed judgement, but just a couple of words spoken when

312

Amalia, Randy and I finally came home from Boris and Beeba's and found Desidéria and her soldier boy necking in front of the TV in the living room were more than enough. The hardcore redneck accent and the inescapable fact of what he did for a living were more than enough for me, thank you very much. Fortunately, Desidéria dragged him off to our room before I could get into a nasty in-depth debate about U.S. foreign policy with the fucking freedom fighter, over which he'd most probably do me in.

Nevertheless, I managed to piss him off in the mere five minutes we were forced to spend together... It was rather uncalled for, perhaps: he and his Portuguese strumpet were just sitting there, nibbling at peanuts and chatting with us harmlessly before retreating to MY room. Soldier boy acted all polite and friendly as most Americans will, but there was a short news item on the TV, something about the Yomanian crisis again, and he immediately felt called upon to reveal how the American soldiers were fighting for everybody's freedom and human rights while the other nations just stood by and watched.

After that I rather miraculously managed to squeeze slavery, Hiroshima, Nagasaki, concentration camps for the Japanese, Vietnam, Nicaragua, Chile, Pinochet and the rest of South America, the Iran-Contra affair, the elusively non-existent Iraqi weapons of mass destruction, the U.S.-sponsored Israeli genocide against the Palestinians, Abu Ghraib, Guantanamo, Afghanistan, as well as Native Americans and reservations into a single sentence of carefully polished and lovingly gestated anti-American sentiment. Desidéria's dildo for the evening seemed pretty much ignorant about everything or just failed to argue his points in a rational and well-substantiated manner. Judging from the unhealthy flush that soon came over his chisel-jawed buzz-cut white Republican Christian fundamentalist face, though, he didn't much care for familiarising himself with my point of view anyway. Mercifully, Desidéria kindly decided to jump him before I could really make him unleash the murderous intent that already glimmered quite evidently in his not very sharp gaze.

Shite, if he reads this crap by any chance, I'm a dead man. So if you find me in a back alley with a couple of extra 5.56 mm holes in my poor mangled body, you'll know where to start looking for the prime suspect. Oh well, whatever. I wouldn't worry too much: the fool is probably illiterate, anyway.

As far as writing this or not writing it goes... I don't know why I'd feel bad about posting on my blog right now. I usually just regret getting involved in purposeless online quarrels that I can't quite recall in the morning, and then I look at all the stupid e-mails I've written or idiotic forum posts or whatever, and start feeling like a real arse. However, I'm currently not in a quarrelling mood.

Today was good. I'm happy with how things turned out at Boris's today, even if I got immoderately drenched again, and so I have no complaints. Well, save for the obvious invasion of my privacy by the U.S. Armed Forces, that is. And even getting plastered was worth it, you know, I have to fraternise with the band and all that. It went well, too! Bogomyr turned out to be somewhat of a loon, but I can't say I hadn't been expecting that since the day I'd laid my eyes on him for the very first time. I didn't have to wait long for him to relax and show his true colours... Which in his case didn't involve mere idiosyncrasies, but full-blown delusions. Well, at least he's loads of fun, he is. Speaking of which, I hope those lechers in my room stop forni-cating soon, I should really get some sleep. I promised Bogomyr that tomorrow morning I'd go with him to see this Drago Dabić character at the Mystic Emporium (don't ask). Dabić is obviously some kind of a charlatan healer type, who is to take a look at Bogomyr's extreme case of heliophobia. I bet that'll be something to write home about – I can hardly wait to see what outstanding examples of folly it'll involve.

Boris is a really nice guy, too. He seems to have a good sense of humour and an excellent command of the English language, so quite possibly we'll work together well. He seems to be a pretty capable producer and sound engineer, judging from a couple of tracks by his pal Ray Kosmick which Boris had mixed and produced and which Ray put on at the Tavern. And

I'm not just writing this so that we can get a special discount if Boris happens to read it!

Speaking of Ray, that guy is truly a bit of a wanker, though... Maybe I shouldn't be writing this, but what the hell, he'll never read my blog anyway. And even if he does read it, the guy's got such a bizarre sense of humour I don't think he'll mind. Besides, he knows he's a profoundly difficult character, so what else can I say? He gave me a good idea for some lyrics, though. Fortunately I carry my little notebook with me all the time, otherwise I'd surely forget. Can't even remember them now. I'll look at the notes tomorrow or the day after. Hopefully I can make out what I meant by them, because it wouldn't be the first time I had no clue what I wanted to tell myself.

So, about Ray... I'm not saying he's not fun, I mean the guy is hilarious. But if you have to listen to him for more than an hour, the way he talks – hammering you with those passionate pounding perorations of his – makes you want to hide in a quiet little corner for a while to catch your breath. While Ray's rambling, even a trip to the toilet is a much appreciated activity, since there you can at least get some respite from him. Maybe that's why Randy keeps retreating to the bushes across the street from Boris and Beeba's so often.

The rest of the guys were interesting, too. Kip Ducker is the quietest of us all, but he seems like a nice enough guy. I'll have to get to know him better. Largo can be quite a loudmouth once he gets going on about his revolutionary agenda... And I suspect that Willit Lonch, the Brit from Birmingham, might also be a colourful character, though he seemed too stoned to really shine tonight. Besides, Mr Kosmick was soaring so high that nobody else could get in more than a word or two, as everyone was too busy chuckling at his deranged theories.

There was no way anyone could get Ray to shut up for even a second, so Bogomyr, Boris, Randy and I decided to go to the other room to shoot some pool. Unfortunately, Ray decided to join us, even though his presence was highly inconvenient – due to his constant yapping as well as because we wanted to play in pairs. Even more unfortunately, it turned out that the family cat, miraculously cured of its fear of the martens by none other than Drago Dabić himself (I should post that very funny story sometime), decided to take a nap in the pool table again. Boris got really upset about it, I guess he must have been truly itching for a couple of games of eight-ball. Either that, or he'd simply had twelve weiss beers too many. He started yelling at the cat to get out, but the furry menace would have none of it, so he climbed on the table and peered into the pockets to see if he could grab it by its tail or something. Obviously he was quite tired already, because while inspecting the third or fourth hole he almost nodded off.

I suppose the ruckus we were making prompted Beeba to check up on us, so we guessed it was about time for us to leave. She confirmed our suspicions by throwing everyone out, saying something about Sundays and rest and so on.

Well I'll be damned, those animals opposite my currently unattainable bed are still at it. What the hell are they doing? One thing I can't say about the U.S. Army is that it's not bloody persistent! But that American war hero is so incredibly obnoxious it's impossible to even get horny hearing the Portuguese floozy moan, and I'm about ready to turn in. Note to self: must ask Amalia and Randy when Desidéria is clearing out. I won't be able to take much of this, especially if it's really her usual routine, as Randy and Amalia have insinuated. Shite...

Fine, I'll have one more beer and watch TV for a while, I'll turn it all the way down so that I don't disturb the snoring Rastafarian on the couch. Right, as if anything could disturb him when that relentless yelping in my room doesn't. But if they don't stop copulating soon, I'll just pretend they're not there and go to sleep, I'm getting really sick of this.

35. Interlude:
Tit

While Serbian Bitch was trying to pull the fierce and depraved nocturnal beast off her face, finally grabbing the bloodthirsty menace by the tail and sending it flying in the general direction of the toilets, Finnegan was still burning the midnight oil. He was sick of listening to Desidéria's throes of passion and tired of trying to post something witty on his blog, so he turned off his laptop in the kitchen and took another *Union* beer from the fridge (telling himself this was definitely the last one, he'd hate having too much of a hangover tomorrow).

He tiptoed to the living room, parked his tattooed posterior in the sofa, and, trying not to wake up Randy, popped open his beer as quietly as he could and turned on the TV, lowering the sound to a mere whisper. As it turned out, Randy would probably not stir even if the Portuguese sex maniac decided that the horny soldier boy wasn't enough for her and jumped the snoring bass player as well: it looked as if he had expired on the couch. This probably had something to do with the reefer of considerable length and width he had felt the urge to smoke before finally retiring to the land of highly unusual dreams.

If there was anything one could count on, it was that all around the world – from Samoa to Yoman, from Greenland to Tierra del Fuego – television sucked as intensely as a diesel-powered penis pump in one of Ray Kosmick's art porn pieces. Finnegan seriously suspected that a conspiracy of global proportions was at work involving a total lobotomy of the viewing public through the endless heaps of faeces that spewed out of these capital-sponsored propaganda shitboxes.

However, at that moment Finnegan wasn't in the mood

to jump on a train of thought which Largo "Fidel" Cabaleri constantly travelled on. No, sir, he merely wanted to be lobotomised himself, so that while he waited for the pair of fervent fornicators in his room to finally fall asleep, he wouldn't notice he was waiting.

Of course, that was just wishful thinking. Finnegan was a man of many a flaw, and one of those was that he was highly opinionated and obstinate in his convictions. Another flaw of his, made so much worse because of the first one, was that almost every time he peeked at the TV – except perhaps when he was in an extremely good mood, which didn't happen as often as it should – he would soon become infuriated by it. If there was anyone else within earshot of him at the time, his turbulent indignation as a rule manifested itself in blusterous complaints and threats, involving unsparing use of his imaginary AK-47 and fictional napalm against the targets of his anger. These were usually people or things he despised, which in practice meant just about everyone and everything, and not even *War and Peace* would be capacious enough to fit all of that in. Suffice to say that the excitable Scotsman was almost instantly driven berserk by any and all of the following:

– whatever he saw as bad taste, shitty music in particular;

– phoneys, fakers, poseurs and narcissists, especially those flaunting their egomaniacal attitude in order to promote worthless pieces of horse manure;

– irrationality, notably new age bullshit and all related quackery and superstition; "wild-eyed women" (or men), which was Finnegan's short expression for what he otherwise referred to as "thick-headed cow-eyed gullible believers in utter nonsense, full of unfounded optimism and nauseatingly sunny disposition, sporting the thoroughly idiotic notion that every cloud had a silver lining and that everything happened for a reason, whose conversations mostly revolved around astrological signs, miraculously healthy or horribly poisonous foods, various kinds of undetectable energies, and mysterious benevolent forces";

    – pseudoscientists, especially astrologists, numerologists, the whole plethora of witch doctors, clairvoyants and fortune-tellers appearing on telly and taking phone calls in particular, as well as other parasites preying on the human need to believe in something greater than themselves as well as on cancer patients;

    – religions, pseudo-religions and cults, but first and foremost creationism, Christian fundamentalism and the Roman Catholic Church in general;

    – motivational speakers, self-proclaimed quasi therapists and various self-help quacks;

    – fanaticism (especially religious or food and health nuts);

    – certain brands of extremists (especially morons who tried to climb Mount Everest in their underwear, got stuck and then pulled out in rescue operations so expensive that clean water could be provided to a bunch of African villages for at least three years with the money expended rescuing them), but not extremists such as himself;

    – social sciences experts who talked a lot but said nothing, and then wrote incomprehensible 'scientific' papers just for the sake of writing them; as well as natural sciences experts who saw themselves as inherently superior to all social sciences experts, but who wrote the same kind of purposeless 'expert' prose;

    – bureaucrats, notaries and other similar leeches;

    – yuppies, brokers, financial institutions and other promoters of greed, excessive materialism and unhinged consumption;

    – neo-liberal economists and the related shock troops trying to dismantle the welfare state;

    – capitalist swine in general as well as all other exploiters of the underdog;

    – U.S. foreign policy, domestic policy, Republicans, and Democrats;

    – Israeli policy towards the Palestinians and everyone

supporting or tolerating it;
    – the vast majority of politicians and politics in general;
    – public relations experts and spin doctors;
    – harebrained conspiracy theories and especially the imbeciles that spread them;
    – almost any kind of marketing, but most notably people who worked in advertising and called themselves *creatives*, while referring to their atrocious propaganda machines as *creative departments*;
    – and, of course, commercials and in particular so-called infomercials.

Needless to say, this effectively made it impossible for Finnegan to watch television peacefully for any length of time worth mentioning, unless he happened to stumble upon an uninterrupted rerun of *2001: A Space Oddysey* or *2010*. But in almost all cases he'd be freaking out within a minute every time he turned the accursed device on.

However, for some unfathomable reason and despite the fact that he loathed irrationality, Finnegan seemed to think that perhaps, just perhaps he'd find something pleasing on the telly this time, or at least something that wouldn't irritate him. Which was, as a rule, mission impossible.

Unfortunately for Finnegan, on that particular night, no sleepless souls were within range of his potential rambling, so, because he also hated it when people talked to themselves, he bit his lip and remained silent while the screen first flashed a news item about the Yomanian crisis, and then started showing insulting images of half-naked songstresses, filling the living room with their quiet yet still utterly abhorrent tunes. "So these Botox-ridden cock-sucking bitches are *definitely* attempting to sell shit by means of tit," Finnegan muttered against his better judgement as he remembered the verse he'd scribbled in his notebook at Boris's.

Not able to bother anyone with his rising blood pressure, the Scottish poet miraculously decided it was time to do something useful. He pulled out his notebook and started scribbling. Whenever he felt he might be at a loss for another line, he just glanced at the TV screen and the inspiration came right back – with a vengeance. A mere quarter of an hour later, after a rapid ejaculation of what he believed was a series of reasonably witty verses, he ended up with the following lyrics as well as the basic riff for what would soon become one of his favourite tracks:

TIT
[https://soundcloud.com/cynicism-management/
tit-augmented]

Tit tit tit tit

There's a tit every morning
Stalking my TV
And the girl who does the weather
Wears tits for all to see
Then some bitch pretends to sing
In a see-through gown
While I fight back stomach acid
Trying to keep it down

But holy crap I've got to see
There's a tit on my TV
I must see
I can't see
All the crap tit sells to me

Then I go and grab a beer
Promoted by a tit
I've heard beer's good for mother's milk
So I think, well, that's it
Of course the john's adorned with tits
To get me in the mood
If only they were flesh and blood
I'd grab them if I could

When they're done with selling
Shit by means of tit
They unveil a juicy butt
I like it, I admit

"There," Finnegan told himself out loud, despite his alleged lack of understanding for people who talked to themselves, "At least I'm honest enough to admit I'm as horny a bastard as any other bloke out there."

Randy's incessant snoring hesitated for a second. He moaned, adjusted his pillow, smacked his mouth, and slept on. It was getting late and Finnegan decided he was sick and tired of the Portuguese whore and her military issue dildo. It dawned on him that conceivably it was not her who'd been screaming all this time after all – not even someone as overzealous as the U.S. military could keep this up for so long. Probably the idiots had fallen asleep while watching porn!

So the sleepy Scotsman called it quits, and if they were in fact still at it, he would ignore them, plain and simple.

Quietly but resolutely, Finnegan opened the door to Desidéria's shag lair, which he had the misfortune of sharing with her, genuinely expecting to see the fornicators asleep in front of some example of Ray Kosmick's favourite industry adorning the TV screen Desidéria had at the foot of her bed.

But it was her, all right.

Finnegan stepped into the room, managed to close the door behind him, but forgot to shut his jaw that had just dropped open. He felt his heart race and another part of him stiffen readily when he saw the juicy Portuguese lass move rhythmically under the blanket that covered her naked body below her bellybutton. Her gorgeous breasts swayed as the American muff diver, exploring the succulent parts of her hidden under the blanket, ploughed her with who knows what collection of assorted machinery, only his legs sticking out in the direction of the TV, which was in fact showing porn, but with the sound turned down really low so that it wouldn't bother the rest of the household.

Desidéria opened her eyes slowly, noticed Finnegan standing breathless at the door, and fixed him with a dreamy ecstatic gaze. She whimpered, bit her lip ever so softly and gave Finnegan a naughty little smile. The poet just stood there and watched as she suddenly opened her mouth and gasped, thrust her pelvis upwards and shrieked, convulsing with orgasmic spasms as she finally came as fiercely as the ravaging armies of Attila the Hun.

The disconcerted and embarrassingly horny Finnegan took advantage of this distraction, undressed hastily while trying to conceal his saluting member, and slipped under the covers, resisting the childish urge to cover his head.

When Desidéria's earth-shattering orgasm was finally over and her screaming subsided, the thought that perhaps she could fill the role of Ray's ideal actress who was into it for the sake of art, not money, crossed Finnegan's sex-plagued mind. He gritted his teeth and clenched his fists, resenting the hell out of the American son of a whore who pushed away the covers, looked up from her dripping mound and said: "Oh! Hey. Sorry, dude, I didn't see you there..." G.I. Joe cleared his throat and pulled a couple of curly raven-black pubic hairs from between his teeth. "Hope our... Ahem... Fooling around didn't bother you too much."

36. Nullified Bodyguards

Five days ago, on Tuesday, Ferdinand Fenton's bodyguards had waited in the lobby of The Lab. They'd have been biting their nails if such childish behaviour wasn't so thoroughly inappropriate for tough men in pitch-black suits who could kill a person with a single move in a variety of spectacular and unspectacular ways. However, despite all their brawn, courage and determination, they were unusually concerned with the mood Mr Fenton would be in when he came out of The Lab.

The day before, after Fergus's first interrogation, he stepped through the thick carbon steel door dazed, absent-minded, even shocked, and the bodyguards waiting for him in the lobby were convinced their time on this Earth was running out. Something was definitely wrong, and seeing the CEO of Omnipile in such a troublesome state of mind was alarming. When one of the bodyguards decided to probe him, expressing polite concern for his son's well-being, Mr Fenton, with spine-chilling resignation, told them: "Let's just go," and brooded on without uttering another word all the way to his mansion.

On Tuesday, to the dismay of the guards, Ferdinand looked even more distraught, but this time, when they arrived at his estate, he told the guards to accompany him to his study.

"*This is it,*" the resourceful bodyguard thought.

"*We're doomed,*" the married employee of the Omnipile Security Service sighed in his mind and regretted the day he'd taken the job.

"*We're so fired,*" the one without a Ph.D. hoped against hope, still refusing to acknowledge how serious a mess they had got themselves in.

"Sit down," Ferdinand Fenton told his men, crossed

the study and slumped into his comfortable and distastefully expensive office chair. He struggled to gather his thoughts.

The day before, after reaching the decision to subject Fergus to the experimental procedure of indoctrination-assisted debriefing, he, the Doctor, and the two OIA Agents had walked into Fergus's room. At the sight of his son's blissfully sleeping face, Ferdinand Fenton felt a stab of doubt, reluctance, guilt, even fear of what might happen. He almost screamed at them, ordered them to back off, told them that he'd never subject his own son to this... But as soon as he thought about giving in to his gnawing fear – when he seriously considered opening his mouth and speaking out – the image of himself as a shepherd, enjoying a lamb barbecue and a pint of ale, re-entered his mind and he managed to push aside his doubts. He instantly felt reassured that indoctrination was the best course of action. *"Good old dependable Omnipile psych training,"* he thought in the back of his mind. *"It's OK. It's best for Fergus, anyway. Far better than letting those fucking Agents have their way with him. It'll be over soon. Everything will be fine. Nothing can go wrong. It's all good."*

The Doctor looked at Ferdinand, and the troubled CEO nodded, giving him the go-ahead. The Agents stepped aside and folded their arms on their chests. It seemed to Ferdinand that one of them wore the slightest hint of a smug smile for a fraction of a second. Ferdinand decided to ignore the OIA and focused on his son instead.

The Doctor turned on a computer terminal next to Fergus's bed, rolled up the boy's sleeve, pulled a jet injector out of a titanium briefcase, checked something on the computer monitor, and, without any hesitation, injected Fergus in the shoulder. The Doctor turned around and Ferdinand looked at him questioningly.

"That's it," the Doctor reassured him.

"How long before he wakes up?" Mr Fenton asked.

"He should be out for about six to eight hours now. When he sleeps off his sedatives, he should feel much calmer and focused than before. We'll let him rest tomorrow, but on

Wednesday we should start seeing the first signs of..."

Fergus suddenly shot up in his bed like a spring uncoiled and stared at the wall across the room unblinkingly, his mouth hanging open. Then he closed his mouth mechanically and, after a pause, stated ardently: "Six four seven three eight!" He sounded like he knew what he was talking about.

"What the..." the Doctor gasped.

The Agents, their reflexes kicking in, went for their pistols automatically and would have pulled them out, had they not, like everyone else, been forced to leave their weapons tucked away safely in the storage lockers upstairs before entering the facilities through the scanning and decontamination chamber behind the heavy steel door and taking the lift to the underground floor they were currently located on. It was impossible to smuggle anything through those scanners.

"Six four seven three eight," Fergus insisted firmly.

"What?" muttered the startled father.

"Six! Four! Seven! Three! Eight!" Fergus yelled and fell back in his bed, as if in frustrated protest.

That was what the kid had uttered on Monday, and that was all he'd had to say on Tuesday, before Ferdinand Fenton sat down with his trusted bodyguards. No amount of pastoral life imagery, lamb chops and ale could get him to let this slide. His son was virtually catatonic. It was impossible to communicate with him, and it didn't seem he had anything to say apart from those accursed numbers. Not even the Omnipile Intelligence Agency could make sense of them, and not even the Doctor knew what was happening. Nothing like this had ever happened before, and Fergus was definitely far from being the first subject to undergo the procedure. The effect of indoctrination on Fergus had been, to put it mildly, bewildering.

Ferdinand Fenton drummed his fingers on the table and frowned at the three guards.

"Time to come clean," he said.

The guards acted confused, even if they knew very well

what their boss was talking about.

"Tell me the truth, now: what exactly really happened that night in Yoman, when my kids were kidnapped?"

"What d'you mean?" the resourceful bodyguard feigned innocent surprise. "We told the Agents everythin' durin' debriefin'. But you know that, you were there."

"Humour me and take me through it again... Briefly."

"Sure, if it helps... We were in the kitchen, you know, outta the way, in order not to upset Ms Evelyn. Suddenly everythin' went black, I suppose we must've been drugged. Next thing we knew we woke up in the hospital."

"Did you leave the room at all, at any time that evening?"

"No, I don't think so. Guys?" the bodyguard turned to the other two. They shook their heads, and the married one said: "I just opened the door once, for the room service guy. We ordered some... refreshments. That was prolly how they got us."

"By putting something in your beer." Mr Fenton eyed them suspiciously, biting his lip.

"Yeah, I wonder how they managed to spike canned lager," the guard without a Ph.D. wondered. The other two glared at him, and Mr Fenton said: "They could have put something in the glasses they gave you. But it doesn't matter, does it, because you're all lying through your teeth."

"What d'you mean?" the smartest of the men shrugged, as if shocked at the accusation.

"I know all about it. Before Fergus's condition deteriorated severely, he told me he and Fabiola had gone down to the hotel lobby. I've examined the reception desk security camera footage. It was very easy to procure, the receptionist made a very special price just for me, his friend. So, what do you have to say for yourselves?"

The guards looked at each other and crumbled. The married bodyguard finally caved in started biting his nails. The one without a Ph.D. dropped his head and examined his shoes. The smartest one – Mr Fenton's favourite guard –

admitted: "OK, no reason to keep denyin' it. The kids gave us the slip. I don't know why they did it, but they can be very resourceful if they put their mind to it."

The guard offered Mr Fenton a weary smile, and Ferdinand smiled back: "Yeah, I know."

"We were playing cards in the kitchen. Ms Evelyn dozed off on the couch, and we were convinced the children were in their room. We had no reason to think they'd wanna go anywhere... Besides, we thought they knew better. We were sure they were sleepin'. So, sometime after midnight, towards one, I think, I went to the toilet and peeked in their room, you know, routinely, just to check up on them. They weren't there, so we looked everywhere and then finally ran down to the lobby, where the receptionist told us someone had kidnapped them. He gave us that note from the Yomanian Liberation Front... So we panicked. We figured we were dead, so we ran up, took some sedatives and passed out, making it look as if the kidnappers drugged us."

Ferdinand Fenton just nodded, a pained expression on his face.

"For what it's worth... I'm so sorry," the CEO's favourite bodyguard sighed.

The tortured CEO pressed a button on his desk. A minute later the large screen on the office wall showed a black OIA limo pull up at the gate. As the gate slid open and the doorman waved the limo inside, Ferdinand looked at his trusted guards for the last time: "Thanks for clearing this up. Actually, I must tell you I lied – there wasn't a single working security camera in the hotel. Well, it doesn't matter now. Incompetence, even deceit... You know that can't be tolerated, can it. Hence your immediate nullification."

The bodyguards stared at their feet.

"Lighten up, it's not as bad as it sounds... You'll just have to get in touch with your undying fascination for snow and ice."

Before the guards could even muster the nerve to look up, their destiny in the form of Agents in funky ties knocked on the door.

A couple of weeks later the bodyguard's wife in Yorktown, Indiana, turned to the postman after bestowing one of her fabled no-gag-reflex blowjobs on the poor tired fellow. "Say, Dick, d'you remember the letter from Antarctica you brought me the other day?" she asked casually, wiping around 39 million copies of the postal employee from the corner of her mouth and out of her right eye.

"Sure, you don't see Antarctic postmarks very often."

"Well, it looks like we'll have to keep foolin' aroun' for a while longer. I don't know what's up with Bill. I thought he hated the cold, but now he's sent me a letter and a video from all the way down there, sayin' that until further notice he's been transferred to an Antarctic oil rig. He says he loves the snow, and that he's always wanted to experience months of darkness and extremely modest temperatures on end. I'd complain, but the pay is awesome. Plus, since he won't be usin' any of it in that frozen hell, Omnipile is wirin' the cash to me instead. Who am I to argue, right?"

Dick nodded emphatically, looking forward to many future mail deliveries.

37. The Morning After

Monday morning was *not* very kind to Finnegan. When he'd finally fallen asleep at some ungodly hour of the night in a tottering frame of mind after the kinky incident with Desidéria and Muff Diver, all of the chatter, backslapping and unbridled optimism of the previous evening at the Rock 'n' Roll Tavern seemed to have crawled into bed with him, only to metamorphose, while he was asleep, into the very unpleasant buzz, nausea and gloom of a major hangover. Finnegan was positive his metabolism did that on purpose in order to punish him, the unworthy loser he was now convinced he was (only while the hangover lasted, of course – he'd become the same regular snotty son of a whore the minute he regained his senses). The older he got, the viler his hangovers became, as if it was all a part of some perverted scheme designed for the sole purpose of torturing him by providing constant reminders that every single day he was aging and getting closer to his imminent demise.

So instead of leaving him be and letting him doze on until the alarm on his phone went off, Finnegan's mind started hiccupping, whirring and reeling, grabbing onto bits and pieces of his consciousness while still revolving in half-sleep. Something about people talking, yapping, chattering ceaselessly, how excruciatingly annoying... A tenacious tune stuck to the bottom of his being, and he was almost awake enough to realise that Robert Plant kept singing *Whole Lotta Love* on and on without end. Then all of a sudden Finnegan caught the sight of some girl's deep dark dreamy eyes, felt exorbitant embraces, salacious palpitations and her young silky skin, tasted intoxicating kisses, drew in ambrosial smells and swam the sounds of breathless moans, slowly drifting towards the climax – !

But – the horror! A screeching ray of abrupt, physically painful consciousness punched through what had been thick veils of his vividly sensual dreams, which could no longer be maintained as the last threads of his will to squeeze his eyes shut impenetrably against the ruthless sting of the morning were severed.

"Noooo…!" his disintegrating dream mistress agonised with the final shred of substance before disappearing into nothingness forever.

"Sod it!" the now conscious Finnegan muttered into his pillow, realising it wasn't he who enjoyed the slippery slopes of the sweet Portuguese lass. Alas, it was somebody else who ploughed her blatantly in her bed across the room, stirring him awake into one of the worst hangovers he'd had for… days. He desperately needed to get out of that room.

Desidéria, the slut! Had Finnegan been able to remain stubbornly asleep – had she resolved to have it off more discretely for a change – maybe Desidéria's morning shag would have taken place without Finnegan being aware of it. No such luck. So, sick of it all, he promptly leaped out of bed, got dressed, and strolled towards the door as boldly and indifferently as he could under the circumstances. Of course, there was no way in heaven or hell he could stop himself from hesitating and turning around at the door, staring quite shamelessly and lewdly at the whorish yet gorgeous girl getting boned profusely by the American marine across the room.

While G.I. Joe on top was too busy squeezing his eyes shut and burying his face in the pillow as if in pain, obviously concentrating on not coming just yet, the gorgeous olive-skinned lassie, moaning louder and louder, met the gaze of the poor hung-over and very horny Scotsman and licked her lips, half closing her eyes in ecstasy and blessing him with another one of her naughty smiles. Finnegan forced himself to turn his back on the now quite orgasmic screams of his tormentor and walked out. He slammed the door shut violently, hoping to startle Captain America into erectile dysfunction, and rushed to the toilet. He locked the door and proceeded to do what he had to do in order not to blow a gasket. Oh! the temptress.

After Finnegan had let off the steam that urgently needed letting off, he splashed cold water on his face and dragged himself, somewhat out of breath, to the kitchen to make some tea while he waited for Bogomyr. He rummaged around the kitchen for an aspirin and gritted his teeth in annoyance, as the fornicators in his room were still at it. Unable to find any pills or ear plugs, he parked his behind on the sofa and turned on the TV, ignoring Randy the sleeping bass player, and nibbled on a couple of stale peanuts left lying about on the coffee table from the previous evening.

Finnegan was definitely not in a very jocular mood, so this morning the comical-looking Alpine dancing songs bands failed to do much for him. On the other hand, they apparently had no problem making merry couples in similarly bizarre outfits waltz, polka and cheer like a bunch of doped-out travelling freak show attractions in some grotesque movie by Federico Fellini. This time the Slovenian National Television, obviously catering to the needs of the simple folk stuck in the church-side bar in some macabre rural death trap, failed to strike the funny chord in the bitter Mr Frotz. Merely a single day after he'd seen the retards yodelling and polkaing their eyes out on the telly as adorable and bizarre in the positive sense of the words, it all started looking rather grim. In this sentiment he joined the ranks of many a serious musician as well as the majority of other sensible people in Slovenia – no wonder this country had one of the highest suicide rates in the world.

As Finnegan wallowed in his morbid deliberations, the door to Amalia's room creaked open and Amalia – her tempting geography showing impishly through transparent underwear – let Paloma Mala out. The loopy canine ran to Finnegan eagerly and bounced around him as if greeting some long-lost pal yet again. Obviously this was the dog's usual disposition. *"Mala should join the wild-eyed women's club,"* Finnegan thought.

"Hey, Finn," Amalia whimpered sleepily, rubbing her eyes and letting her underwear emphasise rather than obscure her hills and valleys, her curved outlines as well as carefully tended gardens. She yawned as if she didn't know how she looked: "Could you do me a favour?"

"Yeah, what is it?" Finnegan wanted to grumble grumpily, but only managed to sound as eager as the bouncing terrier.

"You're more of a morning person... Would you mind taking Mala out? She needs to pee and I'm still in a coma... Please? I'll make it worth your while," she smiled sleepily.

Despite his nausea, feebleness and irritability, Finnegan nodded. A short film of him finally getting laid, this time not with his roommate, popped up in his weary and currently still mostly self-loathing mind.

When Finnegan was back from his short walk with Paloma Mala the Deathbreath Rock 'n' Roll Bitch, soldier boy was already stationed in the kitchen. While Desidéria showered to wash the night and morning from her tantalising young body and get it ready for new challenges, her toy boy had obviously been making breakfast. Finnegan noticed he'd even made the tea Finnegan had forgotten about. All that military discipline was good for *something*, at least.

"Mornin'," the representative of the American armed forces greeted him cheerfully, acting as if nothing awkward had happened.

"*I guess these guys get lots of special training in indifference and disregard,*" Finnegan thought, "*It comes in handy when you must pretend you haven't just shot a bunch of civilians or bombed them to kingdom come.*" But he refrained from going down that road again.

"Morning, laddie," he said instead, and scratched the dog, trying to appear as cool and open-minded as liberal musicians such as himself were reputed to be. However, he let Paloma off the leash so she could jump on the guy and soil his pants with her dirty paws. "*Serves him right,*" Finnegan snickered in his mind, but told Paloma: "Bad girl! Go pester

Mr Jiggler over there!" and steered her in Randy's direction.

Amalia had not yet peeked out of her room, and Randy was still a corpse on the couch, even as Paloma Mala jumped up and down on him for god knows what reason. She had her own peculiar ideas about what was fun, as did the pair of fornicators. Finnegan decided he'd cut them some slack, though. What else could he do, anyway? Besides, frankly, he himself would very gladly have slipped it to the temperamental floozy, all the while professing his eternal radical support for Ray Kosmick's Free Sex Revolution if need be. So how could he honestly hold the carnal undertakings against Mr Muff Diver on the other side of the table?

"So…" Finnegan muttered as they sat down at the kitchen table. He tried to envision himself eating something, but it only made him feel as if he might barf any second now. Since Desidéria was still locked in the bathroom, that might be a considerable problem. So instead of forcing himself to eat, he decided to start the day with menthol chewing gum, a cup of tea, and a shot of vodka Amalia kept in her special nook marked "Property of professor Winegirl – do not touch!" He guessed she wouldn't hold it against him, especially in light of how happily the relieved terrier now licked Randy's arm that hung limply from the couch.

The shot coaxed his stomach into settling for a more bearable degree of nausea almost immediately.

"Well… Looks like we'll have a nice day," Finnegan tried to make some clumsy non-conversation about the weather, of all things. He was not used to chatting with chaps whose bare buttocks he had just witnessed on top of a girl he wouldn't mind ravaging himself.

Mr G.I. yawned and tried his hand at witticisms: "Yeah, looks like it. But it's very early for such a hard night, ain't it?"

"You don't know the half of it." Finnegan was not amused.

The awkward dialogue was interrupted by the doorbell. Since he despised wristwatches, Finnegan looked at his phone: "Shite, turns out it's not as early as I thought, look at the time!

That must be my ride. See you later then, laddie!" He was more than happy to leave.

Finnegan opened the door, hoping to get going immediately and preferably get away before Desidéria could come out of the shower and make him blush like a little boy who'd had a naughty peek at something forbidden (yeah, it showed, he was a *really pale* black man). But instead, Bogomyr pushed Finnegan aside, rushed into the flat, turned around, grabbed him by the shoulders and shook him violently:

"Hey, man, can you drive, I'm already freaking out here, and the sun's barely up!"

Despite what would obviously be another scorching day without a cloud in the sky, Bogomyr had wrapped himself in a heavy cloak, wore a hood over a baseball cap, and, of course, put on gloves and a huge pair of sunglasses that made him look like a demented housefly.

"Whoa, settle down, mate, I'm feeling kind of woozy..." Finnegan held up his arms in defence.

As if on cue, the alluring Portuguese roommate unlocked the bathroom door and stepped out to the hallway, wrapped in an exasperatingly small towel, flaunting an impossibly cute and sexy wet look.

"*Hei*," she chirped and frolicked towards her room.

"Fucking hell!" Finnegan slapped his forehead, squeezed his temples and gritted his teeth. He told the anxious Bogomyr to come in and proceeded to shake Randy awake.

"Hey! Wh...?! What's going on?" the bass player rubbed his bloodshot eyes and coughed, convulsing with his typical morning pulmonary distress.

"Hey, sorry to bother you, but we have a slight crisis over here... Bogomyr's freaking out, he says he can't drive."

Randy only stared into nothingness.

"We've got an appointment with Drago Dabić, remember? Bogomyr and his anxiety?"

"Oh." Randy yawned absent-mindedly. "What's that got to do with me? What time is it?"

"It's just that I'm far too hung-over to drive on the

wrong side of the road so early in the morning, I really am! Sorry, mate, but I'm feeling sick as it is. Trying to figure out my way through the city, driving on the *right* in this condition... I don't think that would be a very good idea. At least not if you'd like to avoid seeing your beloved bandmates dead. Besides, I don't think our demise would contribute much to your future fame and fortune."

Fifteen minutes later, after he'd managed to pull himself together, Randy sleepwalked towards his *Yugo*, still yawning.

"I need coffee..."

"Sorry to bother you so early, mate," Finnegan said.

At the sight of the beat-up little car Bogomyr protested and pointed at his own vehicle. It was an old *Toyota Corolla*, in an almost equally bad shape as the *Yugo*, but it did have heavily tinted windows.

"I see! Why are the windows tinted if you don't go out during the day?"

"Just in case. Besides, I hate bright lights, too," Bogomyr mumbled.

"Oh, of course," Finnegan scowled. "So, you haven't burst into flames yet?"

"Shut up," Bogomyr squealed, got in the back of the car hastily, and hunched into his coat.

Randy only grimaced and ignored the both of them, unaware of Bogomyr Yadvig's alleged vampiric lineage. That was just as well, because Bogomyr's so-called "anxiety" alone was pissing him off more than enough at such a brutal time of day.

Luckily, just like everything else in Slovenia, Dr Dabić's Mystic Emporium wasn't far away, so it was only a short ride. Bogomyr's squeamish demeanour and his obvious antipathy for daylight and sunlight in particular immediately started getting on Finnegan's nerves, even if just yesterday it had seemed hilarious. Finnegan was already fearing he'd soon regret his decision to stand by the Ukrainian guitarist stripper and help him beat these absurd delusions he had gotten into his thick head. Besides, judging by the cloak-clad nervous wreck huddling in the fetal position on the back seat, Finnegan soon started suspecting that convincing the Fundamentalist Church of Jesus Christ of Latter Day Saints to embrace monogamy would be far easier than getting Bogomyr out for an afternoon game of beach volleyball.

The bizarre trio parked their car in the thick shade of an imposing tree that seemed to provide just enough reassurance for Bogomyr to apply another coat of sunscreen, get out, and check out the situation carefully.

"I need coffee..." reiterated Randy. He coughed and looked around curiously. They were in a quiet park, with lush horse chestnut trees extending, mercifully, all the way to the entrance to the Mystic Emporium nearby. It was a lovely morning. For a brief moment Finnegan enjoyed the peace. He breathed deeply, and his morning gastrointestinal irritation almost entirely dissipated in the clean fragrance of the city outskirts – which in Slovenia, to his profound appreciation, actually meant "in the middle of nowhere".

"See? It's close. And there's tree cover all the way," Finnegan finally pointed at the elegant building about a hundred metres further down the promenade. However, as soon as Bogomyr opened his mouth again, Finnegan's irritability was back. With a vengeance.

"Did you bring a parasol? You said you'd shield me with one," Bogomyr asked nervously.

"For crying out loud... Don't push it, man! Christ, you look like a total nutcase as it is! The only thing you could wear in this weather to look even more stupid would be a fur coat over a space suit. So just stop fussing about and let's go. Jesus!"

"I don't know..."

"Shit, look there! The sun's going to peek through the leaves any second now!"

That helped.

Bogomyr moaned in distress and dashed off towards Drago Dabić's headquarters of everything esoteric, zigzagging from one bit of shade to the next. Finnegan followed.

Randy pointed a finger at the sky in exclamation, as if to say something, but his stuttering was simply too slow for the cloaked figure and his sidekick, running down the promenade like Batman and Robin on a high-speed villain chase. Randy Jiggler shrugged, sighed, checked the stash in his pocket, smiled contentedly, and headed towards the park to look for a reclusive bench where he could enjoy an intimate moment with Mary Jane. Bogomyr and Finnegan had his mobile phone number.

38. Fabiola & Habib

At an undisclosed location in Yoman, Fabiola was looking through her window, enjoying the same sunrise that gave Bogomyr the creeps and made him want to crawl out of his skin.

The days after Fergus's release had been far less irritating for Fabiola, because she no longer had to put up with her brother. However, this meant that nobody had been around to pester her all the time, and so her Middle Eastern adventure – fortunately for her, whether she was aware of it or not – had turned out to be terribly boring. She almost missed the little geek sometimes.

Perhaps it was also due to this idleness that, despite her better judgement, Habib had grown on her and she started indulging in harmless romantic fantasies involving Habib the Arab sheik and herself, an Arab princess. She knew it was childish, but she felt tingly all over as the butterflies in her stomach whispered to her that the dew materialising between her legs, beckoning her fingers to play, was a fun and highly enjoyable way to pass the time.

The Arab sheik didn't have much time for her, though. He seemed distracted and constantly preoccupied with something, so she was mostly left to herself. The guards who kept an eye on her were lousy conversationalists, so she'd spend a lot of her time reading – Habib did try hard to make her as comfortable as possible, and so he gave her a large cardboard box full of American and British novels, all of them exhibiting a surprisingly well-developed taste in contemporary literature. The princess was unaware of the Yomanian predilections towards absurdly strict censorship, but Habib made sure to explain it to her. She suspected he wanted her to know that he would be facing serious reprimands from his more fundamentalist brethren if they found out about his book collection. The trouble he'd go through in order to make her stay in the desert mansion more pleasurable...! The thought summoned a dreamy smile upon her lips, and her next idea – how the handsome Arab could make it all even more pleasurable – brought warmth to her cheeks and painted them red.

Just as she started entertaining the thought of slipping back under the covers and exploring her nether regions some more, spending the early morning in a delightful daydream, a soft knock at the door startled her away from the window. It was surely Habib.

"Come in," she chirped, too cheerfully and eagerly for her own taste.

The door creaked open and the handsome mujahid stuck his head inside: "Are you decent, my friend?"

She wished he wished she wasn't.

"Sure, what's up?"

Habib stepped into the room, carrying a silver tray, and closed the door behind him softly.

"You wake up early, enjoying another sunrise, yes?"

"Yep, just like every morning."

"Here, I bring tea," he said and put the tray with tea and cookies on the small table by the window. They sat down.

"So, what's going on, anything new?" Fabiola smiled at her kidnapper, revealing an adorable little dimple in her left cheek.

"A little. You remember the cockroach you see the other day?"

Of course she remembered. The first time she'd seen the sickening swarm of insects in the bathroom she had almost suffered a heart attack which nearly made the guards outside knock over their backgammon board and tea cups. She'd let out such a piercing shriek that no amount of evil training could have prepared the poor terrorists for it. Habib, who had been within earshot of her (as were most of inhabitants of Al Awil, Yoman), had come running. He hadn't known how else to calm her down, so he'd let her in on a little secret. He'd taken her hand, led her to a room overlooking the front of the mansion, and pointed at the window: "See there, the truck outside, it just arrive. Omnipile give us many pesticide in exchange for your brother, we know about nasty bugs. Now we finally kill them." That had done it, because there's nothing like a truckload of *OmniBug* insecticide to help you regain your composure in case of such a revolting infestation. Nevertheless, the image of the loathsome insect legion crawling out of the toilet had plagued her mind numerous times since. Imagine sitting on the toilet when it happened!

Fabiola made a disgusted face: "Sure, after that I've been terribly careful when opening that door and even more careful when lifting the toilet lid."

"We have bug problem we must talk about. Can we eat lunch together and talk?"

"You're inviting me for lunch to talk about a cockroach infestation? How's that for a date... Well, I'll have to check my schedule first."

Habib smiled: "It is serious matter."

"OK, fine, I think I'll be able to get away from my other pressing obligations and make some time around 2 p.m., how's that?"

"Good, 14:00 hours, then," Habib nodded, drank his tea and got up.

"Habib... I don't really want to make an issue out of this, but it was my eighteenth birthday yesterday."

"Really?" her Arab sheik inquired.

"Yes, really. So this might be a good opportunity to fetch that lobster you've promised. Just saying."

Habib laughed and left, waving at the princess.

When she had finished her breakfast and stopped daydreaming, Fabiola, humming to herself merrily, went to the bathroom. She lifted the lid carefully, making sure the loathsome legion was not there, then stared in the mirror. At the sight of her hair, which had been arranged into an elaborate purple hairdo three weeks ago but had since seen nothing but water, some dreadful nameless excuse for a shampoo and a comb that missed a few teeth, her merry humming gave way to annoyed complaints. She might have been kidnapped by evil men seeking to annihilate the Western civilisation, as the OIA would put it, but that didn't mean she wanted to eat lunch with Habib wearing a discoloured pale-purplish bird's nest on her head.

Frowning, the fuming Fabiola walked straight over to the two bearded men playing backgammon and smoking smelly cigarettes in the corridor. She grunted in dismay that this exotic country was obviously not cultured enough to implement some sensibly fascist anti-tobacco legislation. The vile place was in dire need of democratisation, modernisation, globalisation, transition, transformation, sanitation, hygien-isation, and enlightenment before everybody died of lung cancer or emphysema.

The princess wrinkled her nose at the guards, but addressed them politely, convinced they would not register the sarcasm: "Dear sirs... May I have a minute of your precious time?" She was mistaken.

"Ah, infidel come here especially to make joke of us! No joke, this, a serious thing," one of the guards gestured at their backgammon board.

"Sorry," the girl stuttered, "I didn't mean to insult you. I need your help desperately..."

"Maybe if you win game."

Fabiola knew how to play backgammon. She used to play it with Fergus occasionally, before he'd got sucked into the World of Warcraft, never to be heard from again. However, she had never in her life seen anyone so extremely proficient and lightning quick at it as the bored terrorist guards. She couldn't even tell if they cheated or not, that's how swiftly they made their moves. After she promptly lost five or six games in succession and they were done snick-ering at the "stupid infidel" and "ignorant imperialist", they obviously decided the best way to get rid of her would be to deliver her from her woes. So they took pity on her and led her to the kitchen, where they knocked on the door and yelled something in Arabic. An attractive woman in her mid-thirties, covered with a light headscarf, unlocked the door. The guards chattered and laughed, gesturing at the ignorant infidel while taking the opportunity to check out the cook, trying to peer under her *hijab* and through her dress. The woman rolled her eyes, shooed them away and took Fabiola's hand, leading her inside. She closed and locked the door behind them. The kitchen must have been off limits to the bearded scoundrels who rolled more cigarettes, lit up, and leaned through the window in the corridor to check out what breathtaking events were unfolding in the dusty streets below. Fabiola indeed noticed a couple of fat lobsters floating in a bucket in the corner. Finally, after all this time, something palatable was happening.

Using many hand signals and a few simple words, Fabiola communicated her troubles to the woman, who was more than happy to help – judging by her well-kept appearance, she liked solving Fabiola's hair predicament far better than whatever it was she had been doing before. So the girls enjoyed an intricate procedure involving scissors, combs, hair brushes, indigo and henna as well as some fabulous Middle-Eastern pastries which, according to the woman, the guards outside shouldn't know anything about, lest they resort to theft during the night when she was not around.

When Fabiola came back out of the kitchen, even the sweet-toothed terrorists were visibly surprised, forgetting to exhale the foul cigarette smoke. The short haircut and black hair made her so vexingly cute that the guards immediately resolved to once again take up the issue of making her wear a headscarf with Habib. They didn't understand why he hadn't made her wear the damn *hijab* in the first place – when in Yoman, she should do as Yomanians do and start looking decent already. Later, when they accompanied her to lunch, one of the guards could barely restrain himself from pinching her in the butt… *"But that would be too wrong,"* he somehow managed to tell himself, even if he knew it would have been a lot of fun.

When Fabiola heard Habib blurt out: "Well I'll be damned!" in a perfect British accent, she was as glad to have such an effect on him as she was surprised to hear him speak like that. She gave him a startled smile and he invited her to the table: "Please, milady, take a seat," he smiled back without bothering to revert to his awkward Arabic English and pulled out a chair for her gallantly.

"I'm afraid I've been forced to deceive you for a while," Habib told Fabiola and sat down opposite her. Quite uncharacteristically for a Muslim fundamentalist, he poured her a glass of wine. "It's your eighteenth birthday, after all," he offered in explanation.

After taking a sip of the sweet and exceedingly fancy *Château d'Yquem*, Fabiola pouted and told him: "Hey, you better explain yourself. What's this all about? Your accent, suddenly, and the wine... You're not trying to get me drunk and seduce me or anything, are you?"

"For a while there I thought it was I who was being seduced. I love your new look, how you did it I'll never know."

"A girl's got to have her secrets."

The door opened and her saviour from the kitchen brought in her crustacean acquaintances. She winked at Fabiola, and the princess bit her lip shyly and adoringly.

"Oh, I see," Habib said and looked at Fabiola while the woman served their luxury meal. His playful demeanour suddenly gave way to slight concern as he remembered that he should by no means get too distracted by the young girl. It was simply not appropriate for a man in his late twenties. Besides, she was the daughter of Ferdinand Fenton, the CEO of a particularly sinister corporation bent on world domination. Furthermore, they'd kidnapped the poor kid... And, by all means, he had far more urgent things to attend to.

The woman from the kitchen left and Habib decided it was about time to stop fooling around.

"Look... First of all, I'm really sorry for everything

we've done, for involving you in this at all. I know that getting you lobster and some French wine can't possibly make up for that, but perhaps it can at least convince you to hear me out."

Fabiola, rubbing her hands and helping herself to another glass of wine, surrendered: "Yes, you've been a bad boy, but I'm all ears. Don't mistake the smacking of my lips as I munch away for lack of attention. It's been a lengthy diet of hummus and cookies."

"Alright. Let me start with my name first. I'm not really Habib, it's Fadil. Fadil Dajani." Fadil paused, letting the piece of information sink in.

"Fine with me, Habib was a tad on the funny side, anyway," Fabiola mumbled around a piece of seafood.

"As you've already noticed, I'm not from here. Actually, I'm originally Palestinian, but I was born in London, where I've lived all my life. My parents emigrated from a village in the Jaffa district, which the Israelis occupied back in 1948. I have doctorates in information technology and nanotechnology, and I used to work for Omnipile."

"Is that so? Aren't you slightly young for two doctorates?"

"I was your regular child prodigy," Fadil smiled. "Now, the people who took you guys from the hotel, their organisation is called Yomanian Liberation Front. Basically the YLF was established to stand up to the imperialist appetites of the superpowers and their allies in the Middle East, and lately this organisation has mostly been trying to protect Yoman from being plundered and raped shamelessly by transnational corporations and transformed into one of their milking cows. Initially the Yomanian Liberation Front was called the Yomanian Liberation Organisation, and it looked up to and frequently supported the Palestine Liberation Organisation when it could, but then somebody figured out that the acronym, YLO, sounded a bit awkward. Members of the YLF would definitely not like to be called cowards, you see."

Fadil smiled, but the little pun was lost on the hungry

Fabiola: "Yeah, I'm listening, do go on. It's just that I don't care much for politics, nor do I know anything about it, but the food is really awesome. Thanks so much for this... Where did you get these lobsters in the middle of the desert, anyway?"

"Actually, we're located on the coast of a gorgeous sea teeming with seafood... It's just that all of the windows you're allowed to look through face the other way."

"Oh, great. That's just my luck, I suppose."

"Maybe we can go for a swim once this is all over. Al Awil can be quite charming, you'll see... Anyway, we're having quite a bit of trouble here, and not just because of the damn bug infestation. The situation is far too complicated for me to explain over lunch, so I'll just give you some documents to read. It's better this way – you seem like a very smart girl, and you might not believe me otherwise."

"Is that a compliment? I could swear that was a compliment," Fabiola blinked adoringly and looked him in the eye, her head fuzzy and her cheeks warm with grilled lobster and *Château d'Yquem*.

"Fabiola," Fadil said softly, "Another reason why I needed to talk to you is... Could you let me take a few drops of your blood? I assure you, I just need a little sample, it's for your own good. I have to check something, see if my suspicions are true. You'll only feel a tiny prick."

"Really? That's too bad... And why are you asking me so nicely? I've been abducted, you could make me do anything you want."

Dr Fadil Dajani let himself be dragged into a lingering eye contact far too suggestive, dreamy and heart-rushing for his own good. The little dimple in Fabiola's left cheek, which appeared when she smiled, drove him nuts. He let out a long breath, blinked, and tore his gaze away, trying to pull himself together and tear down the tent about to be pitched in his thobe so very embarrassingly and inappropriately.

The young princess came to the rescue of the blushing Palestinian, gracefully offering her arm so Fadil could take some of her blood. She asked apprehensively, a shade of gloom suddenly shrouding her previous playfulness: "What do you need this for? Am I ill? Is it bad?"

"No, don't worry too much. If they've done to you what I think they have, I think I already have a solution."

"They? Who's they? Does my father have something to do with this?"

"I'm really not sure, I don't have all the facts yet. But I won't lie to you any longer: maybe he does."

Fadil, formerly Habib, stared at the juicy lobster on his plate, and the crustacean underlined the accusation in a bright red colour.

39. Drago Dabić Mystic Emporium

The *Mistični center Draga Dabića* institute also went by the international-market name of *Drago Dabić Mystic Emporium*. As soon as the panting Finnegan had made it through the door, following behind the breathless Bogomyr who'd sprinted towards the building skipping from shade to shade like a frenzied hurdler, he regretted letting himself be talked into this. He cursed himself for not having got it through his thick Gaelic skull already: alcohol was bad for him! It drove him to extremes and made him do things he'd later regret. It also led him to make highly irritating promises he had to keep, as well as got him involved in dubious "projects" that only seemed utterly hilarious after he'd had twelve beers too many, but afterwards the marvellous humour of it all was unavoidably lost on him for some mysterious reason. Maybe Dr Dabić could solve this cosmic puzzle.

And now Finnegan had to deal with the issue of Bogomyr Yadvig's mental hygiene. Finnegan, a devoted adversary of irrationality, was forced to enter the very inner sanctum of the enemy. All because the day before he'd believed, for some perverted, even irrational reason, that this would be an utterly hilarious expedition. It was not.

After he and Bogomyr had managed to navigate the confusing corridors and find Dr Dabić's waiting room, they sat down. There Finnegan immediately made the grave mistake of trying to pass the time by reading some of the promotional materials at hand. His blood pressure shot through the roof as he kept reading about a vast collection of workshops in divine motivation, self-actualisation and transcendence, Tibetan sound healing, life bliss meditation, past life regression, urine therapy, divination, soul travel, clairvoyance for everyday use, chakra cleansing, lunar effects, Atlantean healing artefacts and incantations, high and low energy vibrations, personal energy shields, aura enhancement and replenishment, magic of all colours, dark forces and practical exorcism, angel-assisted heart chakra activation, angel cards, tarot cards, fairy cards, chicken-bone-based futurology, intuition enhancement, 2012 moon-cycle and planetary changes, planetary transformation, fairy spells, unicorns, deities, aliens, jinni, demons, devils and other assorted benevolent, malevolent, and very few completely indifferent supernatural creatures, and so on and so forth, until a leaflet about an upcoming lecture on the Kingdom of the Subterranean Lizard People really made his head spin with frustration and righteous indignation. Out of all these dubious workshops only the enema appreciation class managed to make him chuckle. Yes, all of the people attending these workshops should first get acquainted with enemas, Finnegan agreed, but nonetheless it made him grit his teeth. Perhaps he was in dire need of some good old transcendental meditation... Or an AK-47 with an infinite ammo cheat.

"Damn thee, despicable drink, how canst thou bring me so low!" the Scotsman muttered under his breath melodramatically, just loud enough for Bogomyr to hear him, and added: "Why the devil don't they also organise a vampirism workshop or vampire support group or something so we could get this over with in style? They seem to have everything else covered."

Bogomyr just shrugged, trying to deal with his inner vampire child and its problems.

Even though he hadn't brought Peter F. Hamilton's *Night's Dawn Trilogy* with him so he could seek solace in the fact that he wouldn't run out of reading material for another year or so, Finnegan forced himself to stop studying the accursed promotional leaflets. Unfortunately, he couldn't help looking around: it was just like a rotten tooth you can't stop probing with your tongue. Mind-boggling constructs of idiocy stared him in the eye from the bulletin boards on the walls, from the people's outfits, fashion accessories, and... Yes, their very eyes, which he did his best to avoid looking directly into.

He didn't want any trouble.

However, all of a sudden an elderly lady, cowering quietly and fiddling with her crystal pendant next to Bogomyr, made that classic mistake: she met the gaze of an extremely bored wild-eyed woman sitting opposite of her. It was just as bad as meeting the gaze of the local drunk muttering to himself at the next table while you quietly sip your beer and only wish to mind your own business: such a mishap unavoidably leads to an excruciatingly unpleasant experience.

The wild-eyed woman, as if on the lookout for such a grand opportunity, immediately pounced on the elderly lady and started rambling. After a minute or so of that it seemed that Bogomyr lightened up a tiny bit: obviously the fruitcake's litany had managed to entertain him considerably. Out of pure boredom, finally focusing on something other than his phobia for a moment, Bogomyr, who understood Slovenian well enough, began translating the gist of the crazy woman's monologue for Finnegan, whispering into his ear as she went. The poor old lady barely managed to hold on to her pendant as if for her dear life while the mental patient, whom she'd never seen before in her entire quite lengthy life, drilled into her with nefarious yarns no sentient being should ever be forced to endure.

The lunatic leaned closer to the grandma and whispered conspiratorially, but, of course, loudly enough for everyone in the waiting room to hear every word she said. Obviously she was a well-versed whisperer. Perhaps she worked in the opera as a prompter and all that sneaking around in the claustrophobic little wooden box at the edge of the stage had driven her insane.

"When I was a little girl I saved my father's life," she let everyone in on her little secret. "One day he wanted to hang himself in the bathroom, but I accidentally walked in on him. So I ran to the kitchen, fetched a knife, cut the rope and he tumbled into the bathtub. He hit it hard and loud, almost broke something, thank the Lord he didn't get hurt... But he was completely drunk and he had soiled his pants. Fortunately he was in the bathtub already, so I just undressed him and showered him right there. It was an ordeal helping him to his bed, and it was awkward, because he was naked, but I saved him. What luck mommy wasn't home, she'd kill him. Or just let him hang," the wild-eyed storyteller chortled, covering her mouth with her fingers.

"Umm..." the startled grandmother commented.

"The things that happened at home, the stories I could tell...!" the wild-eyed woman droned on, "I'd often run to the neighbours' and spend the night there. It got so bad sometimes. I don't have any family now, though," she lamented.

"Ah," the elderly lady nodded, almost relieved.

"Oh well, I have a child."

Grandma cringed.

"I used to live with this man while I studied, but he left. He had a nice steady job in the state administration, but he quit and started moonlighting as a plumber. Such a good job, respectful, too, and then suddenly a plumber. And then it was the plumber that left me. Anyway, now he lives with another woman. I'm onto them, they're doing drugs! I know all about it. They drink and they're junkies."

"Ahem."

"He'd left before I realised I was pregnant. I'd been pregnant for six months, but I didn't know! I wasn't sick or anything, but I had the runs, you know, constant diarrhoea? So I'd go to the pharmacy and they'd give me medicine for diarrhoea and it never went away. I kept having these awful-smelling liquid stools... I didn't gain any weight either. My child was so small, so very tiny, but everybody still came to look at him, and they loved him. He was the smallest... A full face, though, just like the full moon, and strong little hands. But he grew and he's normal size now. He was a Scorpio just like his daddy and even though mommy is an Aquarius. I should have known better."

"Ahem," the poor old lady contributed.

"Yes, children... I'll see my boy soon. That woman, she's

bringing him down here for a couple of days. She's reasonable enough about it, at least – the last time I saw her she admitted that blood ran thicker than water. That's true, wouldn't you agree?"

"Bad news for the child..." Bogomyr commented as he translated for Finnegan.

The weary old lady let out a trembling breath.

"A little more of this and it'll be the end of her," thought Finnegan.

"But they stole my child, they simply stole him!" the certifiable wench got upset. She no longer whispered, now she was talking out loud. "When I gave birth to him, they told me I could go home, but he had to stay in the hospital. He was too small. They told me I could visit every day, three times a day, even. You know, to cuddle and feed him. But I lived far away. And then one day I came again, and he was just gone! They stole my child, they simply stole him!"

Grandma wiped her brow with a vintage lace handkerchief and nursed her crystal pendant, probably appealing to all those benevolent supernatural creatures and energies for aid.

"Of course, I called Mr Štaubar, the lawyer, you know him? I've known him for ages, since I was a little girl. We had a greenhouse and he'd come to buy trees all the time. He loved citruses. Lemon trees, orange trees, grapefruits, kumquats, rangpur, tangerines... He liked tangerines in particular. Do you like tangerines?"

"Ahem."

"Mr Štaubar gave me a tangerine and some papers to sign and then he called the hospital, so they had to find my child immediately. They'd stolen him away from me. But soon he's coming to visit for a few days."

The trembling old lady winced and took advantage of the split-second pause to take another laborious breath.

"Yes, children... Later I worked as a part-time teacher of Italian. And I've also worked as a childcare worker, in kindergartens, you know. Back then I still lived on the Coast, and

I've been to a number of kindergartens around there, looking for a steady job. They wouldn't hire me, though, because I'm not a member of the Italian minority. Members of the Italian minority get all the jobs over there, you know? In kindergartens, schools, administration, department stores, everywhere – if you're Italian, you're set. Italian kids, too! I've seen it with my own eyes – in the kindergartens I've visited. Our children, poor things, they don't have anything. But the Italian kids!"

The deranged former childcare worker was getting thoroughly worked up about the injustice of it all.

"They have everything!" She waved her arms and almost yelled now: "They have heaps of toys, tons of Italian fairy tale books that the teachers can read from, they go to see theatre performances and puppet shows... Children's writers visit them regularly and read their works to them. But our children, poor things, they don't have anything. But the Italian children! They have free meals, and good meals, too. Tasty, high-quality food, you know. But our children, poor things, they don't have anything – and they even have to pay for whatever little they get. But their meals are tasteless, bland, musty, I've seen it, smelled it, tried it, it's just horrible. They only had to pay for lunch first, but later also for everything else, including breakfast! Not to mention that they're usually from poor families. But the Italian brats! Ha! It's incredible, listen to this: they even get crayons and books for free! It's true! I mean it, it's the absolute truth: they're just given a whole lot of crayons and books, and they get to take everything home. But our children, those poor things, they don't have anything! Just recently I went to check if anything had changed, just to see, you know. I wanted to see it all again, even though I have another job now, a really good and highly profitable job... But nothing has changed, it's still all the same, and they still won't hire me – because I'm not Italian."

"Jesus Christ and Mother Mary..." the tired old lady finally spoke.

"Yes indeed. Which reminds me of a very funny story.

Hilarious, you'll see!"

At the very thought of it, the loon laughed maniacally, tears squirting out of her eyes.

"When I was fourteen years old, my mother had a friend, a principal at the local secondary school. We'd visit him often and spend the nights at his place. My mother wasn't the only one he had, though, oh, no, not at all! He was excellent at hiding it, though: he'd even send himself telegraphs, you know, informing himself that his mother had died and whatnot. Of course, this was because he had other mistresses. And he was also a secret alcoholic. When we'd go out for lunch or something, my mother would want to order a bit of wine with roast beef or steak tartare or whatever, but he'd never drink anything but fruit juice. But at home he had all these empty bottles. My mother once asked him why he had all those empty vodka and cognac and whiskey bottles on the table, and he said he'd had company. That he'd had a bunch of friends over for a party. She knew it wasn't true, though, even if he later showed her a telegraph from one of his friends thanking him for the party. No, siree. He drank. He drank during the night in the dark, he did! When he was alone. And he was always the same, always the same, you know, because he was always drunk."

"Hmm..."

"Yes, this principal... Oh, and the funny thing was, he tickled me, he'd keep tickling me all over, and I'd laugh and laugh... Maybe you know him! He was a principal, after all! There weren't many secondary schools at the Coast back then."

"I don't know any secondary schools on the Coast," the patient old lady mustered some courage and tried to explain.

"But he's so well-known, everybody living there knows him."

"I don't know anyone on the Coast, I've never lived there," grandma was putting way too much effort for her own good into it.

"Well, where do you live, then, if you don't mind my

asking?"

"Here. I live here!" Patient or not, the old lady was becoming visibly upset.

"Oh, here! I know many people here, it's a lovely place. Maybe you'd met my aunt before she moved from the Coast..."

"I'm not from the Coast, I'm from *here*!"

"Oh, here! It's so beautiful here..."

Grandma seemed to be a reasonable woman and still sharp, despite her quiet nature, advanced age, and the crystal pendant around her neck. So she tried to manoeuvre the wild-eyed woman away from her mental hiccups: "So, what are you here for?"

"Huh?" the nutcase finally focused her wandering gaze on the old lady and took a second to take a breath.

"What are you seeing Dr Dabić for? Acupuncture? Healing bioenergy therapy?"

"Oh, no," the woman smiled eerily and even widened her wild eyes, "I'm not a patient. I'm the resident psycho-logical astrologer, hypnotherapist and intuitive life coach. My office is just across the hall over there. I have to discuss something with Dr Dabić over lunch, but I don't have any patients scheduled right now, so I'm just waiting for his lunch break. Never mind me!" the lunatic raised her arms and cracked a spooky smile at the poor old lady. Grandma nodded, grunted, got up, walked across the waiting room and sat down as far away from the psychotic astrotherapist as possible.

To ward off the revulsion Finnegan felt upon hearing this, he recited, to no one in particular, one of his silly sayings that he liked to make up sometimes. He called them "little atheist's proverbs": "Blessed are the poor in spirit, for theirs is the kingdom of heaven. In this case I'll settle for hell any day, thank you very much."

"You know, Finn," Bogomyr whispered in Finnegan's ear, "I think I've been healed. Let's just go. I'm definitely not talking to these crazy people. Vampire or human, I can handle it, OK?"

"Come on, Dr Dabić is an expert in ancient Chinese medicine, as you very well know. He's not some deranged wild-eyed woman with a rich history of abuse."

"You're kidding me, right? I know what you're really thinking about all of this and as far as I can tell, you're probably right. Let's get out of here."

"No way. Look, sticking needles in the butt still seems far more reasonable to me than astrological psychotherapy, OK? Besides, it's been a real drag coming over here, so you should at least go talk to the guy, don't you think?"

Fortunately the discussion was cut short: the door opened and Dr Dabić's assistant called Mr Yadvig. Bogomyr sighed, scowled, grumbled, whined, plucked his posterior out of the uncomfortable waiting room chair, and headed through the heavy soundproof door.

Within a minute, the wild-eyed woman focused in on Finnegan's indecision about what to do while he waited for Bogomyr. Since the patient old lady's patience seemed to have worn thin, the raving lunatic moved two chairs to her left to sit directly opposite the strangely pale black Scotsman.

"I heard you speak English?"

"You heard right." Finnegan wanted to cry. Why hadn't he just gone out to look for Randy?

"I know some English, too. It's rusty, but I manage. I'm good with languages. I used to teach Italian part-time, on the Coast..."

"No, no, no, no, no," Finnegan shook his head and raised his arms in defence.

"What?"

"Nothing," Finnegan hurried, "I don't speak Italian. Don't go there. Forget about Italians. Yes, yes," he tried desperately to change the subject, "You're good with languages, let's focus on English now," he faked a little grin, "So, are you Slovanian, from here?"

"Yeah, and you, where are you from?"

"Scotland."

"Nice! Haggis!"

"Yes... I hate haggis."

"Whiskey!"

"Aye, that's better."

"So, what are you doing here?" the loon inquired.

"Just travelling, visiting some friends."

"Have you been to the Coast yet? You know, next to Italy?"

"No, no, no, definitely not," he shook his head emphatically again, "It's my first time in Slovania. I've only been here for a couple of days."

"You have a funny way of pronouncing it. You mean *Slovenia*, no?"

"Aye, of course, Slovenia. Sorry, I keep confusing it with Slovakia, sounds about the same to me, and then I mix it up into Slovania." He regretted what he said the moment it came out of his stupid mouth.

"How can you confuse that, all foreigners do that! Slovenia is *nothing* like Slovakia, they're not even close together! It's really rude to confuse the two!"

There. The crazy lady was getting worked up again.

"Aye, well, I offer my sincerest apologies, I'll keep that in mind."

"It's funny how ignorant some foreign people are. They usually can't even find Slovenia on the map! Even Italians don't know where exactly Slovenia is, and we're their neighbouring country. Can you imagine?"

Finnegan's politeness suddenly evaporated like a lone droplet of water in the Sahara. All of a sudden he was revisited by his hangover, felt a prickling pain in his brain and a pulsing vein in his temple. He decided he was sick of it all, so he conjured up a deranged monologue of his own and launched it at the crazy bitch. He'd been planning to unleash this particular swarm of locusts on some poor unsuspecting Slovenian with an irksome knack for geography ever since Amalia had told him how upset Slovenians tended to get over this totally absurd matter. He'd even done his research

and prepared the whole pestilent tirade beforehand, just like
many of his other conversation ambushes, for example the one
involving acupuncture that he'd pestered Boris with, so this
was too good of an opportunity to pass up. Furthermore, the
wild-eyed imbecile really got on his nerves, so he even spiced
up the trap with some pure rudeness and vulgarity in order
to get rid of her as quickly as possible. "Look," he said firmly,
"Now I'm really getting sick of it all. Whatever is the problem
with you Slovanians? Are you fucking insane? What's this
obsession with geography all about? Every accursed Slovanian
keeps harassing every poor foreigner out there about the
exact location of this bloody place, and how it's different from
Slovakia... I don't care, do you hear me? Sod it!"

The woman was speechless for a change and gaped at
him open mouthed. Finnegan was on a roll and was deliberately overdoing his rant.

"After all, frankly," he thundered on, "how many of
you Slovanian natives know the difference between Great
Britain and United Kingdom, eh? Which geography nerd in
your ranks knows where the U.S. states of Idaho and New
Hampshire are located exactly, anyway? Both are bigger than
Slovania. I looked it up, and I'll tell you something you surely
don't know: Idaho is ten times bigger than your country!
Though, admittedly," Finnegan lowered his voice pensively
for a moment, "it's suspiciously empty and probably severely
inbred. But let's not digress now: I'm sure you don't know
where it is. You'd probably say: it's in North America. Sure,
just like I can say: Slovania and Slovakia are in Europe!
Shall we go on with the U.S. states? What about Vermont?
North Carolina? Arizona? Where are they? Iowa? Nebraska?
Delaware? Tennessee? Maryland? Wyoming? Oregon? Maine?
Rhode Island? Do you have any idea whatsoever? Utah?
Arkansas? Washington? New York? Massachusetts? Are you
Slovanians sure you can guess at least vaguely which side of
the whole wide North American continent these rather large
geographical entities lie on?"

The wild-eyed woman looked bewildered.

"You know – *all* of these places are probably bigger than this inconsequential patch of land of yours. So, I mean... Come on, tell me, I dare you: why am I as a disgruntled Scotsman from the Orkneys – which even some Brits probably don't know anything about – supposed to care about the exact location of every goddamn Obscuristan boasting a population of 600,000 people?"

The woman finally had nothing to say anymore. Finnegan stopped screaming, leaned back and closed his eyes, trying to ignore the students of reiki attunement to the right and graduates of the cosmic harmony vibes workshop to the left, who gazed upon him compassionately, sympathetically, and, first and foremost, condescendingly. The wild-eyed woman sighed, drawing energy and superior vibrations from the entire passive-aggressive audience that surrounded her by performing a couple of quick magical gestures and breathing exercises. She then shot up from her chair pompously. Raising her nose and establishing clearly that the excitable Scotsman was definitely beyond her therapeutic reach, she turned on her heel and strode away loftily, probably in search of some other lost soul trying desperately to worm its way through existence.

After a couple of minutes that Finnegan spent smirking, the heavy soundproof door to Drago Dabić's office opened and Bogomyr came out, carrying a rather large yellow-ish-brownish teddy bear. It looked worn but cuddly.

"What the hell's this?" Finnegan asked as they headed towards the exit.

"Dr Dabić and I talked... I told him about my problems and I also emphasised I felt I might be able to beat this on my own. So he walked around me and measured something with his pendulum... And then he gave me this teddy bear."

"What?! Why the devil..."

"It's just a safety net, you know, something to fall back on if I start feeling awfully anxious. Dr Dabić said he used to have a poodle who was terrified of fireworks, and he gave the dog this teddy bear for it. He told me he had infused the bear with protective astral energies. Well, the dog mostly just humped the bear and didn't seem to pay any attention to its protective abilities, but around every New Year, you know, when the kids start throwing those pesky fireworks around, the teddy bear became the dog's best friend, its only comfort. For as long as the fireworks kept going off, the poodle wouldn't budge, it just cuddled up against the bear in some corner and waited for the firework horror show to pass. After the dog had passed on, Dr Dabić kept the bear in his office to remind him of his late furry friend. But he said that today his pendulum indicated it was time for him to bid the spirit of his canine companion farewell. To do that, he had to give away the teddy bear, preferably to someone who might be in urgent need of its comforting and protective energies."

"And he gave the loathsome abomination to you?"

"Yeah."

"For free, I mean?"

"Well, not exactly, he sold it to me for two hundred euros, but that also included the fee for the session, of course, as well as the protective incantations he had infused the bear with."

"Awesome! It seems that dog sperm and cosmic energies cost some serious cash. He charged you two hundred euros for half an hour of pendulum bullshit and a raggedy old stuffed animal! Actually, no, not only raggedy and old: formerly exposed to serial sexual abuse by a horny poodle! Well, I hope he'd washed it, at least, the sodding fake-ass charlatan... And, if you haven't noticed, stuffing is coming out of its tail, which I'm sure had been chewed on by that horny mutt of his!"

Bogomyr wasn't listening to Finnegan anymore. As they neared the exit, the only thing he registered was the late-summer sunshine outside, and all he heard now was what the teddy bear kept promising when he squeezed it to his chest. It comforted the poor recovering heliophobe in a deep melodic bear voice: "I luv ya. I luv ya," it chanted.

40. Interlude:
Whence She Came

"Bogomyr, please stop squeezing that bear," Finnegan pleaded as the teddy bear said "I luv ya" for the twelfth time. "It's pretty damn disconcerting. I'm sure your stuffed pal can keep you safe even if it doesn't talk all the time."

"Yeah, yeah," Bogomyr grumbled. He seemed far more composed and calm in the presence of his fuzzy friend. Mr Dabić's quick solution seemed to be working, and that was good enough for Finnegan. He didn't care whether this was because Bogomyr Yadvig believed in indiscernible otherworldly energies, or simply because the stinking toy had cost two hundred euros. However, no matter how happy Finnegan was about the rapid improvement, he was already sick and tired of listening to the bear. It was also a superbly embarrassing companion, especially in the presence of the ladies – and Finnegan had glimpsed some pretty attractive ones down the corridor, standing around in a small group near the exit. When he and Bogomyr walked by, Finnegan noticed them gathering in front of a certain door and obviously waiting to be let in. Seconds later Bogomyr and Finnegan passed a particularly flamboyant and snazzy bimbo in her late twenties. She was obviously heading towards the group, because smiling artificially she chirped a "hello" in an irritatingly high-pitched voice and, waving a frisky little wave, hopped around like a silly puppy. She was wearing excessive makeup, her eyebrows were all plucked out and new ones drawn as thin black lines in the middle of her forehead, and she was drenched in reeking perfume. Finnegan's eyes and especially his nose were immediately drawn to and offended by the posh little tramp, and as they neared the exit he could smell whence she came, her scent trailing after her.

"God, what stench," Finnegan growled. "I'm sure we could track it all the way back to her flat. I suppose she might be quite fuckable, though, if she scrubbed off all the makeup and perfume and kept her mouth shut."

"Let's try following the scent for real then, just for kicks," Bogomyr proposed, suddenly feeling playfully mischievous.

The almost visible oily wisps of the trollop's pungent perfume hung in the air cartoonishly, leading them through the entrance. When they stepped outside, Finnegan was surprised at how calm Bogomyr was – apparently the bear was in fact helping him. Bloody expensive as it was, it better do its job.

It was a calm windless day, and they could still smell the woman. Maybe Bogomyr, as a recovering vampire, was even more adept at this: he readily led them to the park and abruptly dived into some thick bushes. Finnegan considered cursing and telling Bogomyr not to be a jerk – he didn't want to poke his eyes out with brambles – but he felt somewhat roguish himself. The scent seemed to lead through a virtually invisible narrow path, winding through the shrubbery where the branches parted a little, barely enough to let a grown man through. One had to know where the path was to navigate it – or follow the smell. After a minute or two the two shrub divers emerged in a tiny clearing, just large enough to lie down in, surrounded by almost impenetrable shrubbery on all sides. The scent was still hanging in the air a tad more thickly here. Finnegan could still detect it distinctly. The little clearing reminded him of one of his "secret spots" he knew in a certain forest back home as a kid.

The two bloodhounds looked around and found some trampled grass, a used condom, and white lace panties, which someone had obviously flung beneath the branches, and which the owner hadn't bothered to pick up after what had obviously been a nice open-air shag.

Finnegan and Bogomyr laughed. Both of them felt as horny as naughty little boys who had spied something forbidden as they thought of the vulgar tart walking past them in the corridor and smiling at everybody, while under her dress she was evidently not wearing any panties over her freshly ploughed snatch.

"This makes for a good story about lust and perversion with a creepy ending. What did the sign on the door they were waiting at say? Did you see?" the nosy Scotsman asked Bogomyr.

"Yeah," the Ukrainian guffawed, "Sex Addicts Anonymous."

Bogomyr handed the anti-phobia bear to the chuckling Finnegan, lay on the grass and reached under the bush. He pulled out the soft moist panties, got up and put them on the stuffed toy. "There," he told the teddy bear, "that'll keep the stuffing from falling out of your tail. I hereby dub thee Bear in Underwear!"

They got out of the bushes and called Randy to ask him where he was. As he saw them coming, Randy stubbed out a joint and flicked the butt in the general direction of a massive horse chestnut tree near the bench where he had been meditating. He looked at the couple of wankers coming towards him, winced and blinked at Bogomyr's companion: "What the hell's that?"

"That's Bear in Underwear. He's my friend and he keeps me safe from the sun."

"I luv ya," said the bear.

"I won't even ask."

They got in the car. This time Bogomyr, testing his newfound courage, wanted to sit in the front. However, he claimed he still had to see how he fared when they pulled out of the shade, so he didn't want to drive himself. Finnegan, on the other hand, was still concerned about the unconventional Slovenian habit of driving on the right. So it was up to the stoned Randy to drive once again.

To prevent the sun from hurting him when it pushed its evil scorching rays through the windshield, Bogomyr put his stuffed friend under the seatbelt, so that it rested safely on his chest when he fastened it. It looked ludicrous.

"Just for the record," Randy turned to Bogomyr and Bear in Underwear on his right, "If the cops pull me over now and take me away for a blood test because of you, I'll kill you."

A couple of weeks later, Finnegan wrote the following ditty, inspired by the events that had transpired that day:

WHENCE SHE CAME
[https://soundcloud.com/cynicism-management/
whence-she-came-augmented]

From whence she came?
It was easy to detect
Wisping pungent air, traces trailing
From whence she came?
Whiffs of heavily lagging scent
Remnants slowly fading
Like a bitch in heat
All made up flawless painted glossed
Lined groomed tanned and flossed
They always knew
From whence she came

From whence she came?
She'd be nice for some action
Short of mental interaction
From whence she came?
She would serve for some blowin'
'Cause a mouthful is a mouth shut

When they came

They came

When they came
I heard a scream through the ceiling
And I nursed a gnawing feeling
That by the time her skin got peeled away
What was left of her was bloody insane

41. Operation Watering Hole: Analysis

"That's weird," The Watcher said.

The Bitches were spending the day in their motel, following what went on at the Rock 'n' Roll Tavern and analysing the surveillance materials gathered the day before. Already early in the morning, they'd set up the equipment in The Watcher's lair, which made Grim Bitch, her lairmate, even grimmer. Now she could barely find a spot to sit down let alone enjoy some peace and quiet in what had already been an impractical room, too small for two people to share comfortably for an extended period of time, even before they'd filled it with gadgets and computers. To make matters worse, now Arch Bitch was constantly hanging around, too, looking over The Watcher's shoulder.

"What's weird?" Arch Bitch asked.

Grim Bitch pulled a book out of her duffel bag and locked herself in the bathroom. Earlier, when she'd realised what mess their room would soon turn into, she'd proposed swapping with Arch Bitch, because even putting up with Accumulator of Unwonted Locution's atrocious vocabulary seemed more entertaining than listening to The Watcher and Arch Bitch analyse the audio and video feed from the Rock 'n' Roll Tavern all day long. However, Arch Bitch wasn't keen on that, of course, the cunning Bitch that she was – she preferred a quiet room she could retreat to whenever she didn't feel like spying on drunken rockers anymore. Besides, Accumulator of Unwonted Locution had also said: "I do express my regret and hope to exculpate myself in your eyes, but Arch Bitch and I have priorly detailed the division of our abode as well as assigned and congested the storage capacities of our furniture. I would not derive pleasure from supernumerary laborious relocations during our sojourn – I hope you can empathise with my reservations. Conceivably we can share subsequent accommodations hereafter."

Thus Grim Bitch resorted to reading comic fantasy literature in the john for extended periods of time. It was better than putting up with the two surveillance zealots outside, even if her legs and even buttocks kept falling asleep on the toilet.

"Nothing is happening at Boris and Beeba's at the moment. Boris is still in bed, their daughter is in school, and Beeba has gone out," The Watcher explained. "So instead of monitoring what their silly cat is currently up to, I've been reviewing yesterday's footage... And I noticed something really strange about the video of that old woman, you remember, the one doing that jig in the parking lot?"

"Sure," Arch Bitch smiled.

"Look here..." The Watcher showed her the zoomed-in video recorded by Serbian Bitch.

"What? It's just that drunken old hag jumping around like a deranged bullfrog."

"Right. Now check this out."

The Watcher switched the same footage into infrared mode, and suddenly an unidentified flying object passing slowly over the parking lot became visible.

"See that? Something flying over the nasty old couple? Whitish-magenta, that means it's quite warm. And it's dropping something, you see?"

The UFO dropped a number of small, apparently cooler objects, which, dropping to the ground and scattering in all directions, turned from orange to yellow to green to blue and then gradually faded to black as they cooled off.

"What the devil is that?!" Arch Bitch gasped.

"I tried zooming in on that flying object and clearing up the image... Here," The Watcher brought up the processed image. It looked like a small plane of some sort.

"What's this all about? Counterintelligence, maybe?"

"Countering what? Us?" The Watcher asked.

"Sure. Maybe it's Slovenian counterintelligence."

"Don't be absurd, Slovenia is not very likely to have access to such equipment. Sure, it's a member of the NATO, but such equipment must be terribly expensive. It seems to be some kind of a spy drone, cloaked so that it can't be seen in the visible spectrum of the human eye."

"What is it then? Does it belong to some terrorist organisation these people we're investigating are working with?"

"I considered that too," The Watcher said, "But as soon as I found out about it, I sent an inquiry to Omnipile, uploaded the shots and everything, of course, just like we're supposed to do. Here's what they wrote back." The Watcher brought up an encrypted e-mail from Omnipile on one of the screens:

```
From: Field Agent Division, OIA
To: Field Agent Group "Coven of Bitches"
Subject: Re: UFO detected
Classification: Organisation Confidential

Dear Field Agent Group "Coven of
Bitches",
You are hereby instructed to disregard
any further sightings of "UFO", as
you refer to the phenomenon in your
original inquiry. You shall cease and
desist from investigating this matter in
the future.
See attachment for clarification of
the nature of the UFO. You shall wipe
the attachment to this e-mail with
our Secure Encryption and Wiping Agent
(SEWAge™, v7.2) within two hours of the
receipt of this e-mail.
Be advised that the knowledge and
all footage of the UFO must be treated
in accordance with the Confidentiality
```

Agreement, constituting a part of and annexed to the Contract on the Whole Affair. All procedures set out in the Manual on the Whole Affair shall be observed. The penalties in case of any information leaks, especially – God forbid – online publication and dissemination shall be pursued to the fullest extent of Omnipile internal regulations and shall result in the immediate termination of Field Agent Group "Coven of Bitches" and nullification of all its members.

P.S.: Despite the awkwardness of the situation, your resourcefulness and diligence, which enabled the detection of the UFO, has been noted by the OIA Field Agent HQ.

Cheers, Field Agent HQ, OIA

"Hey, it almost sounds like they commended us for our competence in the end there," Arch Bitch smiled cheerfully. "Maybe they'll give us a raise."

"Yeah, but I'm not so crazy about it all. The very mention of *nullification* chills me to the bone."

"Me too. It sounds ominous. It's best if we never learn what they mean by it."

"I looked it up in the Manual. In the chapter Definition of Terms, the following is written under nullification: 'Disciplinary sanction under Omnipile's internal regulations, applied in case of most serious offences, depriving the subject of nullification of continued self-determined existence indefinitely. Appeals against nullification shall not delay its execution, and the execution shall render the free will of the subject of nullification null and void'."

"Great," Arch Bitch said and shuddered, "I told you it sounded sinister. Let's change the subject, shall we? So, what's in the attachment?"

"Was. What was in the attachment. I received the e-mail
while you were in the shower. You took your sweet time in
there again, so I sewaged it before I forgot and ended up
terminated and nullified."

"Damn. That's too bad. What did it say?"

"It was a confidential promo leaflet from the Omnipile
Weapons R&D Department, you know, the stuff they
include in the annual weapons catalogues they send to
NATO members and U.S. allies, like Israel and Saudi Arabia,
for example. The UFO was obviously an experimental
prototype, a stealth unmanned aerial vehicle employing
cloaking technology and vertical thrust capability. Seriously
mind-bending stuff. The whole plane is covered in miniature
sensors and projectors, recording whatever should be seen
from one side of the plane and projecting it on the other
side. That renders the plane virtually invisible to the naked
human eye. For example, if the plane passes between your
point of view and some objects or whatever on the other
side, it projects those exact objects to the side you're looking
at, so you only see whatever you'd see if the plane wasn't
in the way. Thus it keeps blending into its background in
real time. The only thing you could notice if you knew the
plane was there and looked really hard would be a kind of
a shimmering, you know, like hot air? Fancy, right? And it
has vertical thrust capability just like the Harrier airplane,
for example, only it's a lot smaller. This allows it to fly along
really slowly, deploying its payload and performing tasks with
maximum efficiency and accuracy. The engines are state-of-
the-art secret technology, and they're very quiet."

"Bad news for evil terrorists," Arch Bitch concluded.

"And Palestinians, should the Israelis decide to buy
some of these," The Watcher put in. "You don't even want to
know about the mass murder implements you can mount on
them. But for now I'm more concerned about what the plane
is doing here. I don't like it at all. What's Omnipile up to? So I
zoomed in on one of those little things it was dropping to the

parking lot, take a look..."

A processed image of something that looked like a yellow-green cockroach on the thermographic camera appeared on one of the screens.

"An insect? The plane was deploying insects?" Arch Bitch grimaced.

"Looks like it. Too bad they were only so bright and easily visible while they were still warm from the interior of the plane. As they cool off, they get much harder to notice. Like all insects, they too take on the temperature of their surroundings. But now check this out."

The watcher clicked something, and one of the monitors started showing a jerky video.

"Jeez, that makes my head spin. What is it?"

"It's the footage from Another One's glasses, while she was carrying them in her hand, remember? It's hard to look at, of course, because she's not focusing on anything, but she's unwittingly recording stuff she'd hardly look at otherwise."

Arch Bitch nodded.

"Check this out," The Watcher pointed at the screen. "She carried the glasses by her side, pointing at the ground all the time. I hoped she'd catch one of these... There!" The Watcher paused the image. It showed one of the cockroaches just before it dived into the tall grass near Boris and Beeba's Rock 'n' Roll Tavern.

"Oh my god, that's huge."

"Yep, as far as I could tell by its morphology, you know, by comparing it to the pictures on the internet, it appears to be a Madagascar hissing cockroach. They can grow up to ten centimetres, or four inches. This one is small, though, only around six centimetres."

"Yuck, six centimetres," Arch Bitch shuddered, "I hate bugs. What the hell was Omnipile doing bombing the place with plump hissing cockroaches from Africa?"

"I wouldn't know. I'd love to take a look at one, though... Not that the OIA would let me do it. Remember, *'we shall cease and desist from investigating this matter in the future'*."

"Didn't they only mean the spy plane by that? You haven't actually mentioned the bugs yet, have you?"

"No, I haven't, really..." The Watcher said, shrugging.

"Then don't mention them," Arch Bitch winked, "And if we get our hands on one, you can check it out first and only then report it, if you feel you have to. Yuck," she shuddered again, "though I definitely wouldn't want to get my hands on one. Disgusting..."

"There's one more thing," The Watcher said, her voice graver now and her face sullen.

"Sounds like trouble."

"Yeah, it's very... disturbing. Check this out."

She showed Arch Bitch the video Serbian Bitch took when they tested the x-ray camera and Serbian Bitch looked at Another One.

The Watcher paused the x-ray footage at the frame showing a small white dot near the middle of Another One's back, just beneath her shoulder blade.

"See that?"

"Yeah, she's got something there. What is it?"

"I checked it out, it's a subcutaneous chip."

"What does it do?"

"Transmits data. Surprisingly easy to decode, obviously it's just a tracking and identification device."

"I still don't like it... When has she signed up for that?"

"I'm not sure she has. Because, look here..." The Watcher picked up a pair of spy glasses, activated them, projected the video feed from the glasses on one of the monitors, and switched them to x-ray mode. She pointed them at herself first, and sure enough, she had a chip, too. Then she aimed the glasses, snickering in spite of the grave situation, through the bathroom wall. The screen displayed Grim Bitch's skeleton sitting on the toilet, studying the newest novel by Christopher Moore. The dot was hard to make out through all that mess of wires and pipes and bones, but it was there.

Arch Bitch nodded: "OK, I get the point. What about me?"

There it was, as plain as day.

"I don't remember getting one of these," Arch Bitch protested. "I definitely haven't agreed to anything like it. I don't even remember being stung in the back."

"Neither do I. I doubt any of us do, but I'm sure we all have the chips. Maybe it's just a safety precaution, but it's really horrible of them to inject us with implants without letting us know. Shit, maybe every airport security worker has one, perhaps they injected us during one of our medicals! We should be careful, and try to find out more about what's going on, I don't like it at all. Now you definitely don't have to think you're crazy if you feel you're being followed..."

The Watcher suddenly shut her mouth and looked around suspiciously.

"What is it?" Arch Bitch shrugged.

The Watcher put her finger on her lips and pulled out her the incredibly advanced signal scanner, courtesy of Omnipile Gadget R&D Department. After walking around the room, confirming that the only signals going in or out were harmless wireless network connections and GPS data from their implants, she said: "I just freaked out there for a second, I thought they might be listening to us."

"And?"

"It seems we're OK for now, the implants are only trans-mitting our location, the same as when I'd checked before, but better safe than sorry. And I definitely don't know what else these implants are capable of, so let's keep our mouths shut. We should be very careful about where we discuss this and what we say, and we should always check the rooms with the scanner before doing anything stupid. We should also be extremely careful about what we say and do during the mission, because I have to keep uploading everything to the OIA. So we should really be on our toes from here on in."

Arch Bitch frowned: "How the hell did we end up in this situation? It's creeping me out. Pardon my French, but I'm starting to hate these sodding Omnipile bastards, I really am. I only took the stinking job because of the money."

42. Monday Confidential

It was already late afternoon when Fabiola returned to her quarters. She closed the door and leaned against it. Looking dreamily towards the window and listening to the exotic sounds of Al Awil below, she thought of verses from the Song of Solomon that frequently crossed her mind – at their own initiative, it seemed – whenever she thought of Habib... oops, Fadil: *"Thy teeth are like a flock of sheep that are even shorn, which came up from the washing; whereof every one bear twins, and none is barren among them. Thy lips are like a thread of scarlet, and thy speech is comely..."* Sadly, Dr Fadil Dajani had told her – in a comely manner, but still – that he'd had urgent work to do, and he'd refrained from kissing her good night... oops, good afternoon.

Fabiola Fenton immediately hated herself for even seriously considering such a thing and blamed the whole issue on the wine she'd had during lunch. The man was about ten years older than her! But he was so cute... How perfectly awkward.

To get the fair Palestinian out of her mind, Fabiola opened the curtains to let some afternoon desert sun in. She had nothing better to do, anyway, so she made herself comfortable on her bed and started studying the documents Fadil had given her. The printouts of journal entries and e-mails were arranged from oldest to newest.

Dr Fadil Dajani's Private Journal Entry
At the today's meeting of the R&D Departments we unveiled our research group's first series of working proto-types of multi-purpose nanorobots. The scope of application of these programmable microscopic machines is simply staggering. The presentation was a great success. It looks

*like all our hard work is finally going to pay off. Hopefully
I'll be promoted to a position with a more lucrative salary as
well a better health and dental plan...*

From: Mr Rupert Doors, Director of the OIA
To: Mr Ferdinand Fenton, CEO
CC: Board of Directors
Subject: Priority of nanotechnology
research
Classification: Top Secret

   In light of Dr Fadil's presentation earlier today I must reiterate
that several competitors of ours have
recently made considerable progress
towards the practical application
of nanorobotics in humans [refer to
attached reports from the Industrial
Espionage Department of the OIA].
We should make nanobot development &
practical application our top priority
immediately. All documents attached are
to be SEWAged™.

From: Mr Rupert Doors, Director of the
OIA
To: Mr Ferdinand Fenton, CEO
Subject: Nanorobots/Public Opinion
Management
Classification: Top Secret

   Ferdinand, I know it's probably too
early to consider this, but maybe these
nanobots of Fadil's could be useful

for further development of our Public
Opinion Management and Crowd Control
project? Let's keep Dr Dajani out
of this for the time being, though.
Currently we can't be sure of how
reliable he is.

From: Mr Ferdinand Fenton, CEO
To: All R&D Departments
Subject: Application of nanorobots
Classification: Organisation Secret

In the attachment I am sending the
Heads of all our R&D Departments the
initial information about the new
series of nanorobot prototypes by Dr
Fadil Dajani's Nanorobotics Group at
the Robotics R&D Department. Review the
documentation and get back to me with
ideas for potential application in your
Departments. All documents attached are
to be SEWAged™.

From: Mr Ferdinand Fenton, CEO
To: Dr Fadil Dajani, Nanorobotics/
Robotics R&D
Subject: Application of nanorobots
Classification: Organisation Confidential

I was very impressed with your
presentation of functional nanorobots
yesterday. After reviewing your documentation I am confident your technology

could soon be put into practical use.
We want to focus on their use in humans
first - because we're looking forward
to saving many lives with what I hope
will be incredibly impressive results in
the medical field, of course. Therefore
I feel you should definitely have more
latitude and resources at your disposal
to ensure prompt and continuous progress
in this field. Get back to me with your
ideas about practical application in
humans as soon as possible. Prioritise
fields of application in terms of how
long the development of working prototypes in certain areas of research
would take, with the aim of ensuring
breakthroughs in the field of medicine
and biochemistry as soon as possible. I
expect you to outline a few ideas for
me, based on your professional opinions
- guesstimates acceptable - so that
we can decide how to prioritise and
allocate our resources.

From: Dr Fadil Dajani, Nanorobotics/
Robotics R&D
To: Mr Ferdinand Fenton, CEO
Subject: RE: Application of nanorobots
Classification: Organisation Confidential

  Here are some applications of
nanotechnology in humans, organised by
R&D Departments in order of how long I
predict development would take. These
are informed guesses, further research

is needed. I will only sum up a few
ideas here. I'll send more concrete and
detailed analyses as well as estimated
time and resources needed to produce
the first functional prototypes for safe
use in humans as soon as possible.

1) Chemistry Department

- using nanites for the manipulation
of chemicals at the molecular level.
Chemicals manipulated in this manner
do not differ from "naturally" occurring
ones, so this is already feasible at
this point

- nanite-assisted synthesis of organic
and inorganic compounds

- replication of organic and inorganic
compounds

2) Food and Drink & Biochemical
Department

- using nanites to change the
molecular structure of foods. By the
way, nanites not interfering with any
biochemical process in the body itself
will just pass through the digestive
tract like any other inert inorganic
matter. Foods with various properties
could be engineered through direct
manipulation at the molecular level.
For example, chewing gum with prolonged
flavour intensity could be made, or even
chewing gum developed to alter its
flavour while you chew it. Ultimately
programmable flavour sequence chewing gum
could be made

- nanite-assisted production of food
(vat-grown meat)

- using nanites for long-term food

preservation (microbe elimination)
- using nanites to keep beer cool (by reducing the kinetic energy of atoms and molecules)
The possibilities are almost endless!
3) Pharmaceutical Department
- nanites could be used against virtually any disease, and also as safe permanent (until deactivation) contraception without any side effects, vaccines, etc.
4) Medical Department
- all kinds of enhancements – strength, even intelligence, brain power, retention, memory capacity, eyesight (and all other senses), agility, etc.
- eradication of unwanted microor-ganisms and anything else, including but not limited to cancer cells
5) Genetic Engineering Department
- direct manipulation of DNA
- eradication of genetic diseases
- manipulation of genetic traits
6) Biorobotics Department
- cybernetic implants, bionano-technology, artificial intelligence, self-replicating cybernetic organisms, self-directed mutation
7) Weapons Department
- I would rather not elaborate on this, but the applications are obvious. The potential of this technology is staggering, but so are the possibil-ities for abuse. I sincerely hope the technology can be used for good rather than evil… I cannot stress this enough!

See attachment for additional analyses
and projections. We are still working
on more concepts and ideas. Feel free
to let me know if you would like a
detailed analysis of a certain application I have not yet covered, I'll be
happy to provide any information I have
available at this time.

Dr Fadil Dajani's Private Journal Entry

*As of today and until further notice I've been promoted
to Head of Nanotechnology Group at the Food and Drink
R&D Department. We've been authorised to come up with
permanently cold beer immediately. It's good to know we'll
be focusing on the most important goals first!*

*The salary is great, and so is the dental plan. I can finally
get my teeth fixed! However, I can't shake a bit of a bad
feeling about this... I'm sure by now every head of Omnipile
R&D Department has dreamed up innumerable ways of how
to abuse the technology. Fortunately my security clearance
level prevents me from checking what the Weapons R&D
Department has come up with already. With my knowledge
and connections in the Information Technology R&D
Department I could most likely get my hands on all the
sensitive information, but I really don't need to know. I
don't want to know.*

From: Public Relations Department
To: Mr Ferdinand Fenton, CEO
Subject: Use of nanotechnology in
advertising
Classification: Organisation Secret

We came up with an idea how to
use nanobots to make people buy our
products. See attachment. All documents
attached are to be SEWAged™.

From: Mr Ferdinand Fenton, CEO
To: Mr Rupert Doors, Director of the
OIA
Subject: Current status of POM&CC
programme
Classification: Top Secret

Rupert, please have the guys at the
OIA Archives send me a short overview
of our Public Opinion Management &
Crowd Control (POM&CC) experiments.
I should refresh my memory, and of
course I don't keep any files on that
project, not even encrypted ones, on my
computer. The unconscionable employees
at the Advertising R&D Department have
come up with some appalling but useful
ideas. Perhaps we could transfer Dr
Fadil Dajani to Advertising R&D after
he's completed his current assignment
at the Food and Drink R&D. That way
he could be manipulated into working
on the POM&CC programme without even
realising it, just in case he should
encounter any inconvenient ethical
dilemmas. Based on my communication with
him I suspect that could in fact be the
case, regardless of the persuasion effect
of abundant monetary compensation.

From: the OIA Archives, on behalf of Mr
Doors
To: Mr Ferdinand Fenton, CEO
Subject: RE: Current status of POM&CC
programme
Classification: Top Secret

Here is a short summary of the
Public Opinion Management & Crowd
Control programme. Details are in the
attachment.
The Public Opinion Management & Crowd
Control programme (politically correct
expression for mind-control experiments) first started in the 1930s. Since
according to popular opinion lunar
cycles have an effect on human behaviour,
large-scale secret mind-control experiments have been carried out only during
full moons, so that any adverse effects
or peculiar incidents could be blamed
on lunar effects. Since then the OIA has
promoted references to lunar effects in
the media. The programme has included
experiments with chemicals, telepathy,
psychological techniques, mass hypnosis,
mass hallucinations, TV preachers,
religious congregations, infomercials,
subliminal messages encoded into TV
broadcasts, ads and superbly annoying
jingles, lowering the IQ of the general
population by means of mass media and
popular culture, etc.
Many experiments have yielded results,
especially the plan to lower the IQ of

the general population by means of mass media and popular culture, but there is still much room for improvement.

All documents attached are to be SEWAged™.

From: Mr Ferdinand Fenton, CEO
To: Dr Fadil Dajani, Head of Food and Drink R&D
Subject: Nanorobots in information technology?
Classification: Organisation Confidential

Congratulations on your incredible progress in the field of nanite-processed food and drink, especially melt-free ice cream and permanently cool beverages. However, I think the rest of the Food and Drink R&D team can take it from here. We need your expertise for our next priority project: use of nanorobots in information technology, especially voluntary nanobot implants in humans for communication purposes. See details in the attachment. All documents attached are to be SEWAged™.

Dr Fadil Dajani's Private Journal Entry

I've accepted the latest promotion. The salary is even better, even though it's not an executive position. I was happy to focus solely on research and leave bureaucracy to others. I thought it would be a nice change to join my friends at the Information Technology R&D Department.

But even though I'm working in the Communication Technologies Group, which is a part of the Information Technology R&D Department, I've become increasingly worried about the implications of our research. So I poked around a bit on my own and found out our data is being sent to that obnoxious Advertising Technologies Group at the Public Relations Department. Great, that's all we need: adverts via implanted communication devices!

All these high-level security clearances are creeping me out. I think I should start encrypting my journal entries, just in case...

Damnation: now I am become Advertiser, the Destroyer of Good Taste.

43. Finnegan's Blog Entry No. 6

I was looking forward to going to Boris's today and working on some new material I've been carrying around in my head recently, but it turned out that the Rock 'n' Roll Tavern was closed on Mondays. So Randy, Bogomyr and I soon figured out that none of us had anything meaningful to do today. Bogomyr had the whole day, anyway – before his miraculous recovery from his bizarre fear of sunlight he'd only been able to go out after sunset, so his whole life had revolved around that, including his jobs. Admittedly, the demand for male exotic dancers was pretty nonexistent before midnight, anyway. As far as Randy was concerned, though, there wasn't much work for self-proclaimed bringers of the English spoken word unto the aboriginal population of Slovenia during the summer. (I'm spelling Slovenia correctly now, I apologise for all the "Slovanias" in my previous posts. However, I'll just leave that as it is. I don't feel like correcting everything. Anyway, I'll probably never misspell Slovenia again thanks to an incident involving a certain wild-eyed woman at the Mystic Emporium that I'd rather not go into right now.)

Bogomyr, proud of his achievements in the field of mental health, decided it would be fun to celebrate his newfound tolerance for sunlight by inviting us for pizza (which seems to be Slovenia's national food: there's at least one pizza place in every village). However, Bogomyr Yadvig wouldn't be himself if he didn't complicate things, so he decided to invite the whole band. Then Kip didn't pick up the phone, Amalia claimed she was on a diet, and Largo said he was already having lunch at Ray's in the afternoon. Ten minutes later Bogomyr got a call from Ray Kosmick, who invited the three of us as well. Great. As if listening to Ray's prattling for hours yesterday was not enough. And – what joy! – Willit Lonch would also be there. Now, don't get me wrong, I don't have anything against these colourful characters, but they can be a little intense. Why did we all need to hang out on what seemed to be turning into a perfectly relaxing Monday?

As far as I can recall, I've always disliked visiting people in their homes. I just don't like being in other people's dwellings very much and I hate sleeping over even more – for numerous reasons I don't feel like elaborating about right now. I simply like my privacy and I hate invading the privacy of others just as much. Therefore I wasn't exactly crazy about this lunch, but Bogomyr and Randy seemed eager to go – they said Ray's wife was a superb cook. So, since I had to be happy if the band was happy, what the hell... How bad could it be?

Oh, it was bad. First of all, I, of course, had forgotten all about the barely conscious warning about slippers Randy had given me the other morning, and I walked into Ray's flat in my shoes. Judging by the pained expression on his wife's face as I trampled on their precious Persian rug in my sneakers, which, admittedly, had seen better days, Randy hadn't been exaggerating – Slovenians really *did* mind if you didn't take your shoes off. So I went back into the hallway to make amends, and they offered me some slippers from their extensive collection of the vile things.

Now, what I dislike even more than hanging out in people's homes is putting their footwear on. I saw that Randy and Bogomyr also headed into the living room in their socks, so I took a pass on the slippers and did the same. Funny: Slovenians will bitch about sneakers, but won't mind if you leave smelly sticky sweaty foot stains all over their parquet and spruce up their precious rug with the fragrance while you're at it. It was embarrassing to me, though, because I was sure everyone could smell it. Hopefully they thought it was Bogomyr or Randy.

Or Ray, who wasn't wearing slippers, either. Oh, how the guy rambled on again... Though this time Willit, Largo and Bogomyr got equally incensed about everything – and, believe me, you don't want me to elaborate. I could hardly wait to get out of there. However, it turned out that the discussion indulged in by these lunatics gave me another idea for some more riveting lyrics, so I very happily looked forward to going home and working on the idea instead of listening to their preposterous debates any further.

44. Interlude:
Four-Circle Penile Substitute

The insanity of Slovenian drivers was an issue of
some note, while the Slovenian average Joe – or, as these
were referred to in Slovenia, the average *Janez* – could easily
succumb to a pathological obsession with cars that was
actually a rather widespread phenomenon locally. The quality
of the Slovenian car fleet was also surprising, especially if one
takes into account that their wages, unlike their prices, lagged
behind the old European Union countries considerably.

Discussing traffic and bad drivers was also a Slovenian
pastime, and this debate also sprang up over the lunch at
Ray's. This time Randy started it all by telling Ray: "But mate,
you Slovenians really drive like idiots. Hell, on our way over
here I stopped at a yellow light like any sensible driver would.
Suddenly this moron decides to overtake us and runs the red
light, hanging a right in front of us and almost killing a couple
pedestrians in the process. What an imbecile..."

"That's for you driving like my grandma, especially after
smoking a grass and making poor man nervous," Ray said.

"Don't be absurd..."

"Was it a fancy car?" Largo probed.

"Aye, actually it was, a huge *Audi*, I think".

"Of course it was," the Triestine revolutionary nodded,
"The members of the four-circle club are the most infamous
morons. Many Slovenians drive like total nutcases, and I'm
sure each one of them thinks they're the best driver in the
world. But the cocky yuppies who drive the most expensive
cars are the worst. If you're driving on the motorway, passing
a bunch of trucks, and some fuckwad catches up with you,
blinks wildly and tries to push you under a truck, you can be
pretty sure it's an *Audi*. Used to be *BMW*s and the occasional

386

Mercedes, too, but lately it's mostly *Audis* for some reason. Probably in the eyes of the Slovenian yuppies that car's the shit."

"I've heard quite a lot about the lunacy of Slovenian drivers already, and I haven't been here very long. What the hell's their problem?" Finnegan asked casually, trying to contribute a little something to the discussion, even if he seemed in a bit of a hurry to get the lunch over with and leave. Like foreigners often will, he'd had a bit of a run-in with Ray's wife about taking his shoes off and putting on communal slippers. Ray's wife had a thing about the expensive Persian rug Ray had brought back from a visit to Teheran years ago, and the only creature who was allowed to defile it was their annoying little Chihuahua who'd decided long ago that the rug was the best surface to throw up on whenever it had indigestion.

Largo seemed to have given the Slovenian obsession with cars quite a lot of thought: "I think it's all a result of the new capitalist mentality. In the former Yugoslavia most Slovenians had the same cars, either a *Fiat 101* or a *Fiat 128* or later a *Yugo*. Those were produced by a certain Yugoslav car and weapons factory, and everyone had to wait in line for the new ones (especially at times when weapons were a priority). Cars must have therefore been a source of great frustration for Slovenian men who wanted a nice set of wheels as well as the status that went with that. After all, they'd see all these nice cars in Austria and Italy every time they'd cross the border to buy stuff that was in great demand in Yugoslavia at certain times, like coffee and chocolate and jeans and leather jackets.

"With the onset of capitalism and transition into a free market economy, the first thing that the majority of Slovenian families invested in was a nice car, which, by definition, had to be better than their neighbour's. Then their neighbours followed suit, and so on. This still goes on today. Furthermore, thirty years ago families owned half a car, and now everyone with a driver's licence has one.

"Now, the *Mercedes* was often a status symbol of the

migrant workers earning their money in Germany in the time
of the former Yugoslavia. But as far as Audis and BMWs go,
they're the trademark cars of the new Slovenian entrepreneurs
and capitalist exploiters, who are almost to a man egoma-
niacs and sociopaths. You can imagine how such people drive
– they're all-important, they always come first, they see the
road as their own property, and everyone else is only there
for the sole reason of annoying the shit out of their majestic
and bloated selves. Since in our modern society a downright
epidemic of narcissism seems to be taking place before our
very eyes, I'm not at all surprised that traffic has turned into
a source of great frustration as well as a seriously dangerous
affair. Plus, I think that most of these unconscionable capitalist
pigs have the tiniest dicks and they compensate by fucking
people over and by buying fancy cars. I'm pretty sure that the
son of a bitch who lives near my flat and is always cruising
around the narrow streets of this already extremely crowded
city in a Hummer is not quite right in the head or in the pants,
wouldn't you agree?"

Increasingly bored, Finnegan was extremely happy when
they finally bid the Kosmick (or Kozmič) household farewell.
But even if listening to this enlightening monologue was hard
on his body and soul, Finnegan intended to use it as a source
of inspiration for a new track he called *Four-Circle Penile
Substitute*. He could hardly wait to begin – he hated throwing
away any inspiration whatsoever (who knew when he'd feel
inspired for the very last time?). Alas, despite his best intentions, Finnegan didn't actually finish the lyrics until a couple
of weeks later.

FOUR-CIRCLE PENILE SUBSTITUTE
**[https://soundcloud.com/cynicism-management/
four-circle-penile-substitute-augmented]**

*Such display of sound and vision
I've got what it takes
No indecision*

I don't make mistakes
I own highways roads and side streets
Alleys know my name
With utter precision
I'm driving them insane

I'm the smartest smoothest best
Way above you and all the rest
I stop for no one
I am like the wind possessed
Every day I rub and polish
That which makes me me
All I can wish for
And everyone can see

All my life I wanted these four circles
Greeting me each day, greeting me each day
All my life I wanted these four circles
Taking me away, taking me away

Then one day some stupid cunt
Dares to make me swerve
I stop for no one
Damn she's got some nerve
Then the circles of my life
Get stamped into my head
Now I'm the greatest
Even though I'm dead

On their return home, Amalia's Rock 'n' Roll Bitch greeted Randy, Bogomyr and Finnegan as enthusiastically as always. She looked like she might suffer a heart attack any second due to her incredible elation. However, she was soon back to chasing something unseen all around the flat, not stopping to lick the newcomers as she usually did. Bogomyr decided he'd stay until sunset, just in case – he claimed that driving during the day was much harder than simply tolerating daylight.

Finnegan's cheerfulness and artistic zeal waned, though, when he stepped into the living room and noticed that Desidéria's playmate was still there. He and the Portuguese nymphet had made themselves rudely comfortable on the couch, even if they refrained from fornicating in plain sight (for the time being). So Randy, Finnegan and Bogomyr joined Amalia in the kitchen, where she sat behind the table, sipping a glass of cognac and reading a book.

"Say, darling... Is your dog delusional? Look at her go..." Finnegan pointed at the crackpot terrier who kept poking her schnozzle behind the wardrobe, sniffing and sneezing.

"Yep, I'm afraid Mala can be somewhat peculiar and a tad crazy. I believe the anaesthesia she had as a small puppy wasn't very good for her," Amalia explained absent-mindedly before going back to her book.

It looked as if nobody was in a particularly chatty mood, so Finnegan grabbed a beer, sat down next to Amalia and pulled out his little notebook. He worked on his new lyric idea for a while, but couldn't concentrate, especially not with the accursed TV yapping about the ongoing Yomanian crisis. As if it weren't bloody obvious that the Capital was up to its old tricks again.

Suddenly Finnegan put down his notebook and turned to Amalia: "Look, I've been meaning to ask you... Not that I want to be a pain in the butt or anything, but when is she leaving?" he whispered, hinting at the Portuguese lass spread all over the couch with her soldier boy.

"Hmmm?" Amalia looked up from her book.

"Desidéria! You said she'd move out, but she's still here, and her nocturnal pursuit of carnal knowledge is getting rather tiresome, if you get my drift," Finnegan whined impatiently.

"I have no idea," Amalia shrugged and looked at Randy

questioningly.

"Oh, I don't know. How would I know?" Randy jumped when he noticed his sister eyeing him.

"Randy! She was your roommate!"

"But I don't know what's going on with her. The fact that we used to share a room doesn't mean I understand her or Portuguese all of a sudden."

"Don't start with that again. Take care of it, I'm getting sick of it all. *Comprende*?"

Randy grumbled, turned towards the living room and said: "Dessy? Could you come over here for a moment, please?"

Desidéria untangled herself from her companion, got up surprisingly quickly, and promptly hopped towards the table.

"*Hei*," she chirped, blessing everyone with a playful smile.

"Look... We were just wondering... When are you leaving?"

The Portuguese nymphomaniac frowned.

"Aren't you supposed to be moving out? You know..."

Desidéria grimaced angrily, yelled at Randy in Portuguese (judging by the sound and intonation, she must have said something rude), and belted him. Twice. Hard.

Captain America rushed towards the commotion as if to her rescue: "Hey, babe, what's goin' on?"

He put his arm around her shoulders, perhaps to console her, but she seemed to take it the wrong way, because she whirled around and slapped him, too. She was very good at it. No wonder: she'd also used Finnegan for target practice, so it must have been her hobby.

The cursing Desidéria pushed the soldier towards the door, barely giving him the chance to pick up his things. Yelling something which most likely meant "screw you, too, and don't bother coming back", she threw him out of the apartment.

Without bothering to shake her booty as she normally did, Desidéria then stormed into the room she was sharing so selflessly with the amused-looking Scotsman and slammed the door.

"Shit, Dessy's really hard to communicate with. That's why I don't like to do it," Randy shrugged and started rolling a joint.

At first Finnegan revelled in the fact that G.I. Joe was gone. But when he went to bed – quite early that evening, for a change – he realised that listening to Desidéria sobbing was even more disconcerting than putting up with her yelps of passion. It was very sexy, too – the horny Scotsman could hardly keep himself from attempting to console her, which most likely would have provoked another outburst of needless violence.

45. Tuesday Confidential

Early on Tuesday, Fadil's knocking stirred Fabiola awake. She refrained from watching the sunrise that morning because she'd been burning the midnight oil, pondering the documents Fadil had given her.

"All right, all right," Fabiola scolded the door. She preferred waking up on her own. "Come in," she said after she hastily put on a light summer dress. Fadil entered, carrying his laptop.

During breakfast Fabiola was curious: "So, what's up? Did you find anything in my blood?"

"Actually, yes, but it's nothing to worry about, really. It's just very... how should I put it... Annoying? Nope, that doesn't seem to cover it. I'd rather not elaborate right now, but I'll explain after we're done, if you could just bear with me for a while longer?"

Since he had brought some fabulous Middle-Eastern pastries for breakfast that day – the woman in the kitchen had apparently taken a liking to her – Fabiola felt lenient towards Dr Dajani. She nodded, nibbling on the fascinating sweets, a cluster of crumbs enjoying the view from the corner of her mouth. Even though it was early, she was as cute as a button.

Fadil did his best to ignore that: "I'll try something here, it might seem a bit weird. But if I'm right you'll soon feel some discomfort and cramps in your belly, and you'll most likely have to spend the next few hours in the restroom."

She gave him a funny look: "Sounds awesome."

"Well, that's why I've brought you some reading material," he smiled and handed her more printouts from his laptop case. He cleared his side of the small table, took out the laptop and turned it on. "OK," he told Fabiola, "Are you ready?"

Fabiola wiped her mouth, putting a sudden tragic end
to the gathering of the crumbs, and nodded, raising a slightly
annoyed eyebrow: "Yeah, whatever it is you're doing."

Fadil pressed *Enter*, the laptop beeped, and he
confirmed: "Alright. That's it. See you when you're done." He
packed up the laptop and got up to leave.

"Wait, what's this all about?"

"I'll explain when you're... Done," Fadil smiled
sheepishly.

"But I don't feel anything."

"You will in a minute, make no mistake. Better get going
before you do."

"Stop messing around with me... Oh. Darn. You're
not kidding, are you," Fabiola grimaced and grabbed the
documents, very much intrigued by what they might say. She
also snatched the novel she'd been reading from the nightstand, just in case – the few pages of secret documents alone
might not be enough where she was going. Waving at Fadil,
she rushed through the door and hurried to the bathroom.
By the time she got there, it was too urgent a matter to worry
about the loathsome legion much.

```
From: Dr Fadil Dajani, Communication
Tech
To: Mr Ferdinand Fenton, CEO
Subject: RE: Comm nanobot introduction
procedure
Classification: Organisation Secret


  As per your inquiry, I'm sending
you a rough outline of the comm
nanobot introduction and stabilisation
procedure.
  INTRODUCTION AND STABILISATION:
  Comm nanobots may be injected or
ingested orally. Before a fully
functional communication link is estab-
```

lished, they must replicate in sufficient
numbers and stabilise themselves in the
brain and nervous system. Replication
and stabilisation takes roughly 14
days (minus two to four days in case
of injection). Successful replication
and stabilisation depends on the introduction of a sufficient initial number of
nanobots.

However, the initial effects are
sometimes noticeable as soon as within
the first two days and the link may
function to a certain degree from the
third day on, especially if the subject
is a calm and eager participant (the
correlation established on the basis
of experiments on chimpanzees – you
wouldn't believe how quickly they were
able to make use of the link to get
bananas). As a rule, within a fortnight
the link will be completely stable and
functional, and no further large-scale
replication will be necessary.

DEACTIVATION AND EJECTION

Communication nanorobots may be
deactivated via the user interface. In
this case the nanites will shut down
in accordance with the built-in safety
protocols and flush themselves out of
the system.

The built-in safety protocols will
also activate in case of any malfunc-
tions, which will also result in an
immediate ejection from the system

[See details in the attachment.
Summary: in case of deactivation or
malfunction, nanites will be excreted

from the body by what will look like
acute diarrhoea, but the liquid stool
will in fact be the result of several
ejections of nanites and nanite-re-
lated matter. The excretion will begin
immediately after the activation of the
safety measure and last between one and
three hours].

MAINTANENCE AND UPDATES

As individual nanites deactivate
themselves due to wear and tear, more
are replicated in their stead, but the
built-in safety protocols will keep
their number in check. Therefore no
"physical" maintenance is required and
theoretically the link should remain in
operation indefinitely (the complete set
of nanites only deactivates when the
host dies).

The firmware of the communication
nanorobots (of course, including those
already stabilised and fully functional)
can be updated as new features are
developed.

From: Mr Ferdinand Fenton, CEO
To: Dr Fadil Dajani, Communication Tech
CC: Board of Directors
Subject: Large-scale human testing
Classification: Organisation Secret

The Board of Directors has decided
to push forward the large-scale human
testing on volunteers as planned. An
experimental division of the Omnipile

Security Forces has already applied for
the programme.

From: Board of Directors
To: Mr Ferdinand Fenton, CEO
CC: Indoctrination Department
CC: Counter-indoctrination Department
Subject: Establishment of new
Departments
Classification: Top Secret
  As you all know, two new Departments
have been established under the auspices
of the OIA:
  - Indoctrination Department, which
will oversee all public opinion
management and crowd control procedures
involving the so-called "indocrination
nanites" in the future;
  - Counter-indoctrination Department,
which will detect and prevent any
attempts at mind control undertaken by
the enemy.
  These Departments shall answer
directly to the OIA Director.
  The existence of these new Departments
shall be classified as Top Secret until
further notice, and all the correspon-
dence shall be handled by the Director
of the OIA in their name.

From: Indoctrination Department
To: Mr Rupert Doors, Director of the
OIA

Subject: Small-scale test ready
Classification: Top Secret

We're happy to report that the first
independent small-scale human testing
of the technology provided by the
Advertising Technologies Group at the
Public Relations Department may begin.
We are also looking forward to
receiving the results from other
research groups conducting their own
tests. The OIA should ensure that as
many independent tests as possible are
conducted. All data with regard to
"indoctrination nanites" must be shared
with the Indoctrination and Counter-
indoctrination Departments immediately,
so that we can collate the data and
streamline Omnipile's efforts. Dominance
in this field must be ensured by all
means!

Dr Fadil Dajani's Private Journal Entry

*I grow increasingly concerned about the situation I
find myself in. I don't want to sound like some crackpot
conspiracy theorist, but this technology we're working on
could easily be abused for horrible purposes, like extremely
efficient (and unnoticeable to the subject!) suggestion
and persuasion, memory implantation, memory scanning,
directed hallucinations, direct control of physical functions,
remote incapacitation/death, psychological and mental
reprogramming, and, when perfected, even full-blown mind
control. Fortunately I still have plenty of time to hardwire
a means of remotely triggering a self-destruct mechanism
into all nanobots before any functional prototypes are tested*

*on humans for the first time. I must build in a plug that
can be pulled, and hide it so nobody can find and disable it!
Which they won't be able to do if they don't know it's there.
So until I'm sure what I'm dealing with, I'll keep it a secret,
just in case. I'll do it immediately, and send a sealed copy of
the documentation to my lawyer, so that it becomes public
knowledge in case I die under suspicious circumstances.*

*OK, I'm probably a paranoid moron, but I'll sleep better
this way.*

*If I only think back to how overjoyed I used to be about
the progress of our research, and how monstrous it all seems
now... I'll document my misgivings and send them to the
CEO and Board of Directors. Mr Ferdinand Fenton seems
like a relatively reasonable man. We should at least take
the time to think this over very carefully and ensure that
extremely rigorous controls and abuse-prevention mechanisms have been put in place before unleashing this potential
doomsday plague upon the world.*

From: Mr Ferdinand Fenton, CEO
To: Mr Rupert Doors, Director of the
OIA
Subject: Use of nanites in POM&CC
Classification: Top Secret

Rupert, you have also received Dr
Dajani's document detailing a number
of abominable uses the public opinion
management and crowd control technology
could be put to. I must admit it gives
me pause. Perhaps Dr Fadil Dajani is
right: we should have foolproof abuse
prevention systems in place before we
even consider testing this. Aren't we
getting ahead of ourselves here?

From: Mr Rupert Doors, Director of the
OIA
To: Mr Ferdinand Fenton, CEO
Subject: RE: Use of nanites in POM&CC
Classification: Top Secret

  Nope, we're not.

From: Mr Rupert Doors, Director of the
OIA
To: Mr Ferdinand Fenton, CEO
Subject: A drink?
Classification: Public/Unclassified

  Drop by for a glass of Scotch in
my office after work. It's been a long
couple of months… I just have one more
meeting. Something seems to be happening
in the Middle East again. Afterwards
I'm free over the weekend for a change.

From: Mr Rupert Doors, Director of the
OIA
To: Mr Ferdinand Fenton, CEO
CC: Board of Directors
Subject: Large-scale indoctrination
experiment
Classification: Top Secret

As of now our first priority is to address the Yomanian crisis as soon as possible. See attachment for details. All documents attached should most definitely be SEWAged™.

From: Mr Ferdinand Fenton, CEO
To: Dr Fadil Dajani, Communication Tech
CC: Counter-indoctrination Department
Subject: RE: Comm nanobot introduction procedure
Classification: Top Secret

Make sure the nanites are ready for large-scale human testing as soon as possible. You may have seen in the media that a crisis is brewing in Yoman. We should prevent the enemy from developing a working prototype before we do, and experiments are essential if we're to develop effective counter-measures.

From: Mr Ferdinand Fenton, CEO
To: Dr Fadil Dajani, Communication Tech
Subject: Personal message
Classification: Organisation Internal

Unfortunately the decisions with regard to your priorities are no longer mine to make.

Dr Fadil Dajani's Private Journal Entry

   Even though Mr Ferdinand Fenton's initial response to my concerns had been positive, it seems that later he decided to push for immediate large-scale human testing. I'm afraid the pressure from the Board of Directors and those madmen at the OIA was too much for anyone to stand up against. Or perhaps it was even an order – even the CEO answers to the OIA in military, intelligence and security matters, and it seems pretty clear that the OIA has made our technology about that. Hell, I'm sure they've already come up with plenty of devious ideas about how to weaponise it.

   I've got myself in more mess than I can handle, so after Mr Fenton kindly explained that the decisions were no longer his to make, I sent him my letter of resignation, letting him know that under the circumstances I could no longer work on this due to ethical reasons. Fortunately Mr Fenton seems to have some sympathy for me. He refused to accept my resignation, but offered me a way out instead: a spot on the international scientific team heading to Yoman soon. This way I'd no longer be responsible for the experiments, and I could use my extensive knowledge in the area for something good: preventing the technology from falling into the wrong hands. Imagine terrorists getting their hands on mind-control nanites or nanoweaponry?

```
From: Mr Ferdinand Fenton, CEO
To: Dr Fadil Dajani, Head of Inspection
Team
Subject: Yomanian nanotechnology crisis
Classification: Organisation Secret

   Congratulations, you've been promoted
to Head of the Nanotechnology Inspection
Team, which is to head to Yoman
```

shortly. Be advised that the team and
all its operations are to be kept in
the strictest of confidence for the
time being so as to avoid a global
panic at the possibility of a terrorist
attack with nanoweaponry. Your primary
objective will be to determine the
presence and source of nanotechnology in
Yoman. Officially the team is a part of a
humanitarian disaster relief operation.

From: Omnipile Public Relations
Department
To: undisclosed-recepients:;
Subject: Scientific team
Classification: Public/Unclassified

  Omnipile has appointed several of its
leading experts in the field of genet-
ically-modified crops to a scientific
team heading to Yoman shortly. Omnipile
itself will cover the expenses of the
humanitarian disaster relief operation.
See attachments for detailed information
and pretty pictures.

Dr Fadil Dajani's Private Journal Entry

*Yoman is not half as bad as I was afraid it would be. I
definitely sleep better now that I know I'm doing something
useful. No nanotechnology of foreign origin has been
detected yet in the samples provided to us by the field
agents. Of course, hopefully we won't detect any.*

From: Weapons R&D Department
To: Mr Rupert Doors, Director of the
OIA
Subject: Nanoweaponry Group
Classification: Top Secret

  We're glad to report that the
Nanoweaponry Group at the Weapons R&D
Department has become fully operational.
It is currently focusing on developing concepts necessary for many new
fascinating and useful applications of
nanotechnology. We can already taste
a whole lot of victories for the good
guys!

From: Indoctrination Department
To: Mr Rupert Doors, Director of the
OIA
Subject: Indoctrination of the scientific
team
Classification: Top Secret

  Ready to indoctrinate the
Nanotechnology Inspection Team. Please
confirm and authorise.

46. Fadil's Story: Part One

"Does this mean I had these… tiny robots inside of me?" Fabiola frowned at Fadil after wrapping up her lengthy appointment with the restroom.

"In a way, yes, but not like you think."

"Was it some kind of mind control? I don't feel any different now… Bloody hell, did my father have something to do with this? That's impossible, I can't believe it."

"It's alright, calm down. No, your mind wasn't influenced in any way. Please, sit down and let me explain. Here, have a drink. It'll help settle your stomach."

Fabiola took the glass of Scotch Fadil offered her and sat down, glancing at the drink and then peering at Fadil suspiciously.

"I think everyone who's old enough to vote can handle a little drink. It'll take the edge off. And no," he laughed as she narrowed her eyes suspiciously, "I don't intend to get you drunk and take advantage of you."

She sipped her drink and told him: "Too bad."

"Come on, stop fooling around."

"I'm old enough to vote and drink, but not old enough to fool around?" Fabiola teased the Palestinian.

"I mean, we've got serious things to discuss."

"Fine. So, tell me, does my dad have anything to do with this?"

"Let me start at the beginning."

Fabiola nodded.

"So, as you've probably read in the documents I gave you, before I went to Yoman with the Nanotechnology Inspection Team, I built a reset code into all the nanites, just in case something went wrong and we'd have to reprogramme or deactivate them. When the code is communicated, the nanites reset themselves and wait for new orders for exactly two minutes. If the transmission of new orders doesn't start within 120 seconds, the nanites shut down. I've also left a so-called hidden backdoor access for myself, so that I can connect to any Omnipile nanobots developed and replicated on the basis of my design without anyone else knowing. And it looks like that wasn't a bad idea at all, if I may say so myself. Of course, I've never informed Omnipile of this, so hopefully they're still unaware.

"After all that I joined the scientific team that was about to be deployed to Yoman. At the time I still thought the Yomanian crisis was real and that I was in fact looking for unknown and unregistered nanotechnology, even nanoweaponry... As time went by, though, I came to suspect that I might have been a little naive, but I tried to keep a low profile. I certainly didn't want to piss off the Corporation. Frankly, I've never thought of myself as anything like a freedom fighter or revolutionary or anything like that. I still don't.

"But then all of a sudden we were told we'd have to take anti-malaria pills. Suddenly we were in danger of contracting malaria? In the middle of the desert? I took the damn pill – they made damn sure all of us scientists swallowed them – but later that evening, when the air was clear, I scanned myself, and, just as I feared, we'd all been given Omnipile mind-control nanites. Third or fourth generation. By the look of it they'd been working hard on developing and perfecting them, but fortunately my backdoor access and reset code still worked as intended. I reset the vile things replicating in my body and flushed them out. But I wouldn't be able to pretend for long – in two weeks at the latest they'd realise I haven't been indoctrinated. Even worse: since the link wouldn't work, they'd probably suspect something was wrong within a week or so. I had to do something. I had to know why they wanted to mind control us! So I accessed the OIA network back home by means of my nanite backdoor... You see, nanites are constantly sending and receiving data from HQ, and I've been able to use that link to access certain information, for example the e-mail archives, in order to figure out what to do and how to get out of this. That's how I got my hands on the documents you've been reading. I considered disabling all the nanites, but I couldn't do that without going through the mainframe, which is located in The Lab. Unfortunately, the mainframe can't be accessed remotely from anywhere, because it's obviously not connected to the internet. Even the nanite link is useless, because the mainframe only establishes a one-way satellite downlink with all or some of the nanites in case of a general firmware patch or new instructions, and then closes it again. So it can only be reached either directly at The Lab or through one of the terminals linked to it via the Omnipile intranet. I don't have access to such a terminal, of course, and there aren't many people who do – I only know the Director of the OIA has it. So does your father, of course, and apart from them only the Board of Directors have access. So simply disabling all the Omnipile nanites in existence at that time and going public with the whole affair was not an option.

"Going public without disabling the nanites first, though, or just disabling some of the nanites... That would only give Omnipile the chance of finding and disabling my backdoor access and reset code, thus..."

"Fadil," Fabiola sighed, "I don't speak Geekish very well, OK? You must have mistaken me for my brother. Spare me the technical stuff and just get to the point, will you?"

"Alright, I'll try to keep it short... Maybe this'll help: I also found this document in Rupert Doors's inbox. It makes for an interesting read. Check this out before I explain further."

Fadil handed another printed e-mail to Fabiola.

From: Indoctrination Department
To: Mr Rupert Doors, Director of the
OIA

Subject: Our Diabolical Plan
Classification: Top Secret

OUR DIABOLICAL PLAN
by the OIA Indoctrination Department
 As we all know, the development of
fully functional mind-control nanites is
imminent. If we don't do it, one of our
competitors will, and the first corporation to succeed in producing fully
functional indoctrination nanites and
especially a means of disseminating
them on a massive scale will secure for
itself a vast advantage over everyone
else.
 Currently the successful reproduction
of nanites in a human host still
depends on a sufficient number of nanites
initially introduced. In practice that
impedes any massive-scale testing on
involuntary subjects, for example by
introducing nanites into the food chain
or water supply or disseminating them
as airborne particles. Nevertheless,
massive-scale testing is of crucial
importance, and in order to stay a few
steps ahead of the competition, we need
to carry it out before somebody else
does. The fate of the world and the
future balance of power most definitely
depends on it! So we've come up with a
plan.
 We need a small isolated country.
Yoman seems convenient: with proper PR
and media propaganda, we could declare
it a "rogue state". Yoman has been
under embargo from the United States

for decades as it is, so it makes
a perfect target. We could create a
crisis, famine perhaps, or engineer an
epidemic of some suitable affliction and
send relief teams there to inoculate
the population. Of course, the vaccine
would contain nanites. When the entire
population has been indoctrinated,
we'll test the efficiency of the indoctrination by making the people organise
democratic elections and vote for the
right candidate, who will then entrust
us with Yomanian natural resources, hand
over their gold reserves and pension
funds, sell off their most successful
companies for petty change, take out
colossal loans that they'll never be
able to repay, start adhering to the
austerity measures imposed by the IMF,
the World Bank, the Omnipile Economic
Council and other benevolent institu-
tions, and so on. Yomanians can finally
start working in Omnipile factories for
minimum wages and be ecstatic about it,
too. We can transform the rest of Yoman
into a paradise for tourists (Yoman has
great beaches). Fast food chains can
finally replace hummus and falafel shops,
the bazaars can be made into tourist
trinket factories, and our Corporation
can finally take over the entire state.

If all that works, we should be able
to ensure that Omnipile is the first
corporation to successfully introduce
its nanites to the rest of the global
population in some way, maybe by
putting them in yogurt and chewing gum,

```
otherwise somebody else will surely do
it anyway. What if an evil Arab country
should succeed first, or Iran, the
Russians, the Chinese, or North Korea?
Massive-scale indoctrination cannot be
avoided in the long run, so it's best
that the forces of good should do it
first.
  Maybe we could cook up a deadly flu
pandemic and vaccinate everyone?
Cheers, Indoctrination Dept.
```

"Horrible," Fabiola said. "I really hope my dad's been kept in the dark. I'll never talk to him again if he was in on it. But wait – they haven't pulled it off yet, have they?"

"Oh, they're trying, alright. The whole world is currently listening to hysterical news reports about the so-called Yomanian crisis. First Omnipile shipped several containers worth of inmates from their privately-owned prisons in the United States here, then staged a jailbreak and accused Yoman of harbouring criminals. To their dismay, though, those damn do-gooders at the United Nations as well as some prover-bially inert European Union bureaucrats stalled their efforts. They seem to be somewhat allergic to such tricks after that CIA stunt with weapons of mass destruction in Iraq and the situation in Afghanistan, where Omnipile and other similar corporations have been making a killing by rebuilding the infrastructure they've demolished themselves."

"Fadil," Fabiola sighed, "I'm not into politics much, either. OK, I believe you when you say it's some kind of a horrible conspiracy, and I've never liked Omnipile's Fashion Department either, so I'm not a big supporter of the company, but can you just fast forward to more concrete issues, if you please? Thank you!"

"I'll try, but it's complicated. Let's see… Omnipile needed a really good reason to totally isolate Yoman so they could carry out their massive-scale mind-control experiment on the Yomanians. Finally they decided that the best way would be to accuse Yoman of possessing nanoweaponry. That way they'd let the world know about its existence and terrify everyone into supporting its own nanoweaponry research as well as so-called counter-indoctrination activities. Of course, Yoman has never had any such technology, and Omnipile didn't want to plant anything experimental anywhere for fear of it actually getting into somebody else's hands. So they came up with an elegant solution: they'd send a scientific team to Yoman – that's us... They'd indoctrinate us... And then they could make us say anything. Some of us might even admit we'd been working for Yoman all along. Be that as it may, they'd create enough of a smoke screen to create panic. Then they'd close the borders, occupy Yoman, put in motion a controlled epidemic and vaccination programme, and thus effectively establish total control over an entire sovereign nation within a couple of months. Fortunately this plan hasn't been implemented yet because I got away. Unless they neutralise me somehow, I could blow the whole thing wide open just by revealing what I know right now. They certainly can't afford that to happen before they've found a way to indoctrinate people on a massive scale."

"Jesus... So how did you get out of it?" Fabiola's cockiness and sense of humour seemed to have dissolved as the big picture was finally beginning to dawn on her.

"I had to act fast. I knew my days were numbered, so I used my knowledge of computers as well as my family connections in Palestine to get in touch with the Yomanian Liberation Front. These YLF guys are not stupid and they knew what Omnipile stood for, even if they had no idea about just how monstrous the whole plan actually was. They believed Omnipile – just like other corporations as well as the entire Western civilisation – had just been out to get the Yomanian oil and lithium and diamonds and so on. I promised to provide the YLF with the evidence of the entire operation and a means to overthrow Omnipile by making the world aware of what horrible things these corporations are capable

of. Finally – almost miraculously – I was contacted by the
YLF leader himself. I sent him some of my files and told him
I had a means of disabling the nanites permanently, but that
I wasn't ready to divulge that information just yet. I told him
that if I got caught and this information got out prematurely,
the last chance of stopping Omnipile could be lost forever. I
promised the YLF I'd share all the evidence and assured them
we'd figure out how to deal with the situation, but first they
had to get me out of that place. I had to get away from the
Corporation immediately."

"And they got you out."

"Yes. A Yomanian Liberation Front resistance cell
rescued me. I gave them the copies of the files as promised,
and we arranged a personal meeting with their leader at
the Al Awil bazaar in order to figure out how to proceed.
Meanwhile, Omnipile were terribly upset by my disap-
pearance – they didn't know exactly what was going on yet,
but they were afraid I might reveal sensitive information to
the Yomanians or someone else. So they've put a lid on their
diabolical plan, at least for the time being. They must have
tried to activate the nanite link that should have become at
least partially functional within a week, and when it did
not start responding, they must have become aware that
something was wrong. Then the OIA found out about our
meeting somehow. We suspect they have a mole in the YLF
somewhere, but if that's true, he or she must be in another
cell – because otherwise this place would already have
been stormed by the Omnipile Special Forces. Fortunately,
individual resistance cells within the YLF don't know the exact
locations of other cells, for precisely that reason – to contain
the potential infiltration of individual cells.

"Anyway, it looks like Omnipile found out that the
leader of the YLF, who fortunately also didn't know the
whereabouts of each individual cell for the same security
reasons, had been in contact with me. So they abducted him
in order to find out where I was. They captured him at the
bazaar on the very day when we were supposed to meet.

Looks to me like they weren't aware of the meeting that was about to take place, otherwise they'd surely have tried to take us both at once. It was a damn close call..."

Fadil paused, thinking. He took a deep breath and poured himself a splash of Scotch. Obviously he too needed to take an edge off.

Fabiola let out an annoyed grunt: "I realise this is a serious and complicated issue, and you still haven't told me why I had to spend hours in the toilet, obviously leaking these creepy microscopic machines of yours. I also understand you've been through a lot and, to make matters worse, my father seems to be involved in it. Still... I don't want to sound insensitive... But could we continue this discussion over lunch? Because the death of the crummy little robots and listening to matters of such formidable importance has made me very hungry. I could also use another glass of that fancy French wine you tried to seduce me with yesterday to help put things into better perspective. Could we continue this conversation over an early candlelight dinner?"

47. Interlude:
Right Humpster

Miraculously even Largo Cabaleri had nothing against some good old rehearsals and a wee jam session on Tuesday. It was summertime and the living was easy: even revolutionaries had to unwind occasionally.

Cynicism Management kept developing what they'd begun working on, and this time it was all starting to sound much better now that Bogomyr Yadvig was finally able to rehearse during the day. Soon everybody was used to Bear in Underwear sitting on his *Mesa Boogie* amp and stopped eyeing the stuffed animal suspiciously. *"Whatever floats Bogomyr's boat,"* they thought.

After the band had wrapped up the rehearsals as well as the subsequent jam session and proceeded to their regular spots behind their favourite table by the entrance to the Rock 'n' Roll Tavern, they noticed that the place was unusually lively that day. It would even have been crowded if *The Bottles,* who had obviously been pestering the grim-looking Boris, weren't just leaving. Finnegan stepped into the pub in time to check out the infamous Niki Lipps, the tit of *The Bottles.* She really lacked much of a rack to speak of, as she was in fact an anorexic wench. Boris had not exaggerated. Nevertheless, she seemed to have a certain mysterious sex appeal at her command, because the members of her band actually did hop and jump around her like eager puppies. "Must be special pheromones that only work on antiquated gentlemen who are enduring their end-of-life crises," Finnegan figured, as Niki's bandmates were all senior members of the society. Niki Lipps (in her late twenties) had a mouth which was undoubtedly capable of breathing life into the limpest of the limp – as well as big eyes that conveyed a false impression of a helpless wounded creature in need of protection (and perhaps some good ole boning). She was definitely capable of wrapping her band around her finger easily, no matter how emaciated and sour and prickly and obviously manipulative she was. The very presence and potential accessibility of tight and relatively young strategic anatomical parts was too much for the geriatric league of central Slovenia to resist.

To Boris's visible relief, *The Bottles* soon left and he was able to sit down with *Cynicism Management*. Beeba strolled over to their table to ask everyone what they'd like to drink, taking the opportunity to tell them, in her awkward but excited English, that on Sunday night she had once again heard her dead first husband walk around the house. Even the cat must have witnessed the apparition, she claimed: she'd heard it hissing and meowing and running around hysterically in the dead of the night. Boris just rolled his eyes at the ceiling and sighed. Obviously the manifestations of Beeba's dead husband were one of Beeba's favourite and Boris's most detested topics.

In the motel, The Watcher looked away from her monitor and glanced at Arch Bitch with a slightly worried expression on her face, realising that Beeba might be referring to the nocturnal battle of Serbian Bitch versus the ferocious cat lurking in the pool table. However, since nobody back at the Rock 'n' Roll Tavern bothered to take Beeba seriously, Arch Bitch just shrugged and let it go.

At the next table, in the corner which Willit, Ray and Largo usually presided over, three women sat that evening. Boris explained they were the local poetry club. This time it was the cleaning lady's turn – the one who worked in the bar by the church, where she also composed her greatest works of literary art – to present her latest masterpieces.

"The following is a series of poems dedicated to Billbee, my dearest little doggie whom I love very much," she said and Bogomyr translated for the curious band. "I wrote these in English," the cleaning lady declared, "because I'm currently working on some material with which I hope to penetrate the

English-speaking market. Don't be surprised, we all know
how hard it is in Slovenia. For example, as some of you
probably know, I've published four poetry collections already,
one of them with the financial support of the Municipality of
Ljubljana... While my fourth collection was even co-financed
by the Ministry of Culture. Still, I haven't yet earned a single
dime, in spite of all my dedication and tireless work. Actually
it's been quite the reverse: I've had to pay my publisher for
each and every copy I've given to my friends, and I've had to
cover all the expenses for my first two self-published collections. Appalling. So here's the first series of my poems in
English. Perhaps I'll be able to sell them in Hollywood or to
Dolly Parton at some point, who knows?"

The cleaning lady's two chums smiled knowingly,
while the cleaning lady prepared to read some of her work.
"To Billbee, my mongrel mutt... She may be nothing but a
hound dog, but she's my best friend. First, the prologue," she
announced:

EVERY POET NEEDS A MUSE
and I have a hairy one with horrific breath
and legs unshaven

The cleaning lady's two chums chortled and clapped.
The cleaning lady turned the page:

CONSTRICTION BUSINESS
The distance, Billbee, that I have to keep from you
is as important as the love that I feel, too —
'cause in the morning your breath smells stale
as stale as it does all day long
and at the thought of whiskers lining
your smelly dungpit of a snout
my face grows sad, dilapidated, pale
for the sensation of projectile vomiting
comes onto me quite strong.

The two fellow poets laughed and clapped again.

Finnegan leaned towards Amalia and whispered in her ear: "I thought this would be an evening of Vogon poetry, but actually it's almost entertaining!"

"I shall now proceed with a collection of haikus. The first one is written from Billbee's point of view," the poet explained and read on:

HAIKU No. 1

Cats across the street.
I dash, she screams, but I have
selective hearing.

"Here is another one, dealing with existential matters:"

HAIKU No. 2

In goes ambrosia –
uncanny transmutation –
out goes excrement.

Smiles of appreciation.

"And now a victorious haiku from my point of view," the poet announced:

HAIKU No. 3

Almond eyes nose black.
Undivided attention.
I'm the steakholder.

After some appreciative nodding, the cleaning lady proceeded with the following number:

THAT EMPTY BOWL

That empty bowl
is there for a reason –
it's not that time of day
when it's your munching season

Everyone laughed and the cleaning lady seemed happy to announce the grand finale:

RIGHT HUMPSTER
Right, humpster!
Do your nasty thing!
Be what you are!
Let the frolicking begin!

After witnessing this crowning achievement, Amalia, both impressed and inspired, turned to the poet and asked her: "Funny stuff you've got there, I like it, congratulations. Say, could I borrow the last one and use it as a chorus for some lyrics? You see, this is my band..." she pointed to the band members around her. "I also have a dog and for a while now I've wanted to write some lyrics about those terrible turd-by-starlight experiences, you know, when your dog stuffs itself with bones, for instance, and then in the middle of the night it's suddenly desperate to take a dump?"

The poetess smiled and nodded.

"You know that horrible experience when you have to take the dog out at three a.m. and wait until it kindly does its thing?"

"Absolutely."

"OK, so I've been thinking about this for a while, and your poem fits it so perfectly. Could I use it?"

"Of course," the cleaning lady said. "See?" she turned to her fellow poets. "Almost as soon as I decided to enter the English-speaking market, things started looking up. This certainly isn't Hollywood yet, or even a jingle in a lucrative dog food commercial, but it's a start!"

And so it came to pass that Amalia Winegirl Paulin wrote Right Humpster, right then and there, using the poem by the cleaning lady working in the Suburbia's church-side bar as the chorus. Who knows how famous Paloma Mala the Deathbreath Rock 'n' Roll Bitch (as well as Billbee, the mongrel of unknown origin) might become thanks to it?

RIGHT HUMPSTER
**[https://soundcloud.com/cynicism-management/
right-humpster-augmented]**

Right, Humpster!
Do your nasty thing!
Be what you are!
Let the frolicking begin!

Her bulging eyes at three a.m.
I really wish I'd give a damn
My eyelids kiss
My upper lip
Indeed this is a vile routine

She's watery eyed like frogs in heat
Ignoring me, my every plead
When bonecrumbed dump
Spills everywhere
Repugnant, yes! But it's the end

48. Operation Watering Hole: Data Theft

"Looks like another exciting evening," The Watcher said as she saw, to her dismay, Willit Lonch and Ray Kosmick enter the Rock 'n' Roll Tavern shortly after the creation of the hit single *Right Humpster* by *Cynicism Management*, featuring lyrics by Amalia Wingirl and an unnamed cleaning lady.

The Watcher let out a tired grunt as Willit Lonch immediately began to theorise about how modern societies were so disturbed that a new science he called Psychotherapy of Culture needed to be invented. Fortunately, though, a priority message from Omnipile came through that very moment, so the Bitches could mute the audio feed on Mr Lonch's prattling.

"Yikes," The Watcher blurted out and turned to Arch Bitch as she noticed the call coming in, "the OIA Agent in charge of our group wants to talk to you over a secure connection."

"Darn, what now? Oh okay, put him through," Arch Bitch grumbled.

"Hello," an Agent wearing a shockingly mundane black-and-white chequered tie appeared on the screen.

"Jeez," Grim Bitch, lying on her bed reading but occasionally peeking at the screen nevertheless, muttered in the background, "The Agents have changed their tie design. Something must be very wrong at Omnipile."

"Is the connection secure, am I only talking to the Bitches? Who's chattering back there?" the Agent peered from the screen as if he wanted to see off camera. The Watcher picked up her laptop and panned the camera around the room.

"Yes, it's just me, Arch Bitch and Grim Bitch listening at

the moment, as you can see."

"Good. So, it looks like the Subject of the Investigation
and His Accomplices are at Balding Hippy and Beeba's hospitality industry establishment at the moment. Since the time in
Slovenia is just half past seven in the evening, our experts in
leisure activities and recreational alcoholism predict that they
are going to stay put for at least another three and a half to
four hours. That presents us with a window of opportunity we
shouldn't ignore. Are you ready for some immediate action in
the field?"

"Of course, every Bitch is accounted for and ready to
go," Arch Bitch confirmed.

"Very well. Here's the plan. It's essential that we figure
out the connection between the number tattooed on Mr Frotz's
posterior and the one recited over and over by Mr Fenton's
son. Until now we have discovered nothing, so the connection
hasn't been proven, but it simply looks like too much of a
coincidence. The surveillance, however entertaining it may be,
has also not turned up anything useful.

"Apart from the fact that Finnegan Frotz seems to hate
Israeli foreign policy in the Middle East – at least, that's what
we've gleaned from his blog and some of his other online
activities – he doesn't seem to have any connection to the
Middle East at all, let alone the YLF specifically. But maybe
it's just that he's really good at concealing his real agenda.
So it would be extremely convenient for us if we got all the
information from all of the computers he's been using. We
have already hacked the laptop he uses to access the internet
and found nothing useful – just a couple of texts, admittedly
odd but obviously inconsequential, and some music nobody
in their right mind would want to listen to. Oh, and a couple
of fabulously kinky pictures of Scottish Songstress, apparently
taken a few years ago.

"However, based on our surveillance information
we know that Herb Boy has a stationary computer in their
apartment, which is not connected to the internet. This might
be due to Herb Boy's general paranoia or perhaps even

concrete fear of malware, but conceivably sensitive files might be stored on that machine, music-related or otherwise, and we've seen Finnegan's also been working on it. We want all of the information stored in it."

Arch Bitch nodded, wondering how they could possibly know all that, but decided to let it go. She was already worried about what was obviously going to follow.

"We have confirmed that currently the apartment is empty. That..." the Agent cleared his throat "...fine energetic roommate of theirs has also gone out, so currently no one's there. Take the portable data leech and a 10 TB solid state drive, that should be more than enough. Just plug the leech into a USB port, connect it to the SSD and turn on the machine. The handy little gadget will automatically bypass any passwords and copy all the data on Herb Boy's hard drives directly to the SSD. He will never notice any tampering, as long as you don't spill coffee on his keyboard or something like that."

Apparently the chequered-tie Agent liked to spice up his briefings with lame attempts at jokes.

"Sure, I've already tested the device, it's quite wonderful. But don't you also want us to bug the apartment while we're there?" The Watcher raised an eyebrow, somewhat surprised.

"You don't have to worry about that for now. It's already been bugged with our experimental self-propelled infiltration and surveillance equipment. We don't want to risk the installation of more permanent equipment at the moment, because unfortunately we don't know the whereabouts of the... erm... that nice roommate of theirs, so be careful, she may return any time. Better post a Bitch outside to warn the one in the apartment in case she comes back." the Agent smiled.

"That's just great," Grim Bitch mumbled in the background.

"Are we clear? Run along now and upload the information to us as soon as your mission is completed. We'll be watching."

The Watcher shuddered and raised an eyebrow: "Understood. Bye."

"I wonder if Randy has any interesting pictures of his former roommate on his computer..." the Agent grinned at someone off camera just before he clicked end call.

Half an hour later, after confirming nobody was home, Serbian Bitch used an israel to get into the apartment. She sneakily closed the door behind her and squinted into the twilit corridor. The place smelled of burned ganja and stale cigarette smoke and could easily be a student pad just by the unkempt look of it.

Suddenly Serbian Bitch got an eerie feeling and glimpsed something moving about in the living room. She tiptoed to the door and leaned through, peering into the living room carefully. There was a sudden noise, as if something had skittered over the parquet, a pause... And then a shadow dashed from under the table and, rushing directly towards Serbian Bitch, leapt at her. Serbian Bitch yelped, instinctively covering her face, her throat, her heart pumping wildly in her chest and a flashback of the vicious monster and its razor-sharp claws at Boris and Beeba's rushing through her mind.

However, it was just Paloma Mala, the Deathbreath Rock 'n' Roll bitch, eager to greet and lick another of her long-lost pals, jump all over her, and perhaps convince her to magically conjure up a snack.

"Jesus fucking Christ, I almost kicked the bucket right there," Serbian Bitch told the other Bitches watching from the van parked outside and pushed her spy glasses back into place. Relieved, she scratched the buffoonish Irish Soft-Coated Wheaten Terrier behind the ear.

"You're a nice doggie! Yes you are! Yes you are! Though you could use some breath mints," she told Mala and gave her a pat on the butt to shoo her away while hastily looking around for Randy's computer. She found it and plugged in the data leech, turned on the computer, and a beep confirmed it was working.

As she waited for the leech to get on with it, Serbian Bitch took a look around the flat. Paloma seemed to have calmed down, taking no further interest in her visitor. Instead she went back to doing whatever she'd been doing before her visitor came in, which involved running around the flat and chasing something. Suddenly Paloma pounced on something like a cat, trying to catch whatever it was with her paws. Curious, Serbian Bitch stepped over to the dog who seemed to have killed one of those hissing cockroaches The Watcher had noticed near Rock 'n' Roll Tavern. The blonde terrier bitch, after realising the bug was very much dead, was off again now, seemingly chasing after a livelier specimen. Serbian Bitch was inches away from blurting out "Well, I'll be damned. Do you see this? It's one of those roaches", but fortunately she remembered what the Bitches had agreed on the other day about being on their toes constantly when it came to Omnipile.

Therefore Serbian Bitch, acting as if she didn't know what the deal was, uttered: "Yuck! What a hefty bug!"

"It figures they'd have cockroaches, the whole building could definitely use a little bit of a makeover," The Watcher said.

Serbian Bitch kneeled down to look at the vile insect. "Gross," she cringed and made sure to look away before snatching the bug secretly and sticking it in her pocket. "Oh, looks like the leech is almost done," she said, stood up casually and walked towards the computer.

The Watcher turned off the audio recording on their side and let out a long breath, obviously relieved: "For a second there I thought she'd say something incriminating," Arch Bitch said.

"Me too," The Watcher agreed. "I think she managed to grab the thing, though. Can't wait to see what it is."

Serbian Bitch wrapped up her data procurement operation, turned off the computer, scratched Mala behind the ear again and left without anyone seeing her, locking the door behind her.

Several hours later, The Watcher completed her

examination of the cockroach corpse.

"As I suspected," The Watcher said, "These bugs must be what the Agent referred to as *experimental self-propelled infiltration and surveillance equipment.* Watch this…"

She put an image from their portable electron microscope on one of the screens. It clearly showed microscopic robots of some sort.

"I've heard and read a lot about nanorobots, but I thought the technology was still in the domain of science fiction. I've never believed I'd get to see them in action so soon, maybe not at all during my lifetime. But this seems to be it. The cockroach is full of them. They're inert, though. Obviously they deactivate themselves when the organism they've been controlling dies. Which is just as well, otherwise they could still be transmitting an audio and video stream back to the OIA via a satellite uplink.

"Now, obviously the OIA deploys these cockroaches using that cloaked drone of theirs. After they're transported to strategic locations, these bugs can go anywhere. They can't exactly fly but can climb pretty much anything, including smooth glass. It's evident they've been genetically engineered, because apart from their usual organs they've obviously had additional sensory capabilities grafted onto them. Most probably Omnipile chose this species because the Madagascar hissing cockroaches are large enough for additional sensory organs. Looks like the nanorobots, apart from controlling the creatures, are also used to encode sensory input into a data stream that the OIA can decode as video, audio and other kinds of information. These roaches work quite similar to our spy glasses, but they're… Well, yeah, that's what they are, self-propelled spy glasses."

The Bitches stared at the monitors. None of them were amused. Serbian Bitch immediately kneeled and looked under the bed, while Another One peered into corners uneasily. Grim Bitch started scratching herself nervously.

"I've already scanned the room for incoming or outgoing signals, and fortunately there are none." The Watcher said reassuringly. "At least none that I could detect. We better be careful, though."

"This is getting more and more sinister," Arch Bitch declared.

"And rebarbative," Accumulator of Unwonted Locutions added.

Meanwhile, Amalia, Randy and Finnegan returned home. Although they were unusually early that evening, the OIA experts in leisure activities and recreational alcoholism were right on the money: they hadn't gotten back until about a quarter past eleven and nobody noticed anything out of the ordinary. Amalia may have had a fleeting feeling that the lock opened unusually smoothly, and Paloma Mala seemed to be uncharacteristically low on her jumping and frolicking energy, having been chasing big fat bugs all day long, but that was all.

Finnegan was tired, so he decided to turn in before Desidéria had the chance to show up with another boyfriend and introduce him to the warm hospitality of her inner sanctum. He drifted off but was stirred half awake when his Portuguese nemesis came in quietly at about midnight and tiptoed to her bed without turning on the light. Automatically, he muttered "*hei*" absent-mindedly, his face towards the wall and back towards her. "*Hei*," she whispered. He heard her sit on her bed across the room and sigh quietly. After a couple of minutes she turned on her discrete little bedside lamp, got up again and started taking off her clothes. Finnegan, despite his better judgement, turned over in his bed, clearing his throat quietly as if in his sleep, and tried not to peek. Of course, he failed.

There she was, facing the door, undressing in semi-darkness. She unbuttoned her pants, opened the zipper and shook them off. As she leaned over to hang her jeans on the back of the chair at the foot of her bed, her thong grinned naughtily at Finnegan, who almost whined in dismay like a dog in heat. Then Desidéria took off her T-shirt and her bra, leaned over again and put that on the chair as well. At the sight of her breasts Finnegan's mouth watered. He swallowed hard but kept peeking. She took another T-shirt – a far more comfortable one – that was on the bed, put it on and slipped under the covers. She reached under the sheet and took off the thong, pulling it from beneath the covers and flinging it in the general direction of the chair. Obviously she slept in nothing but her socks and a big old T-shirt when she slept alone. If she had company, she slept naked.

Suddenly she turned her head, looked at Finnegan looking at her, and smiled roguishly. She turned on her side and looked him straight in the eye. Finnegan wanted to look away, to squeeze his eyelids shut and pretend he was asleep, but it was too late for that. She knew he'd been watching. After a minute or two she pulled away her blanket and sat up in bed facing Finnegan, nothing but the very large T-shirt covering the entrance to her most private domain. Slowly she got up and took a tentative step towards Finnegan's bed. She stood a couple of inches from him, assuming a shy girlish posture, and he could smell a hint of her sweet juiciness.

As she started to climb into his bed, the bewildered Scotsman shot up and dashed towards the door.

"*Hey!*" Desidéria seemed to protest, as this time the hey did not sound like another chirpy hei. She ran after the fugitive, following him through the living room where Randy, without reacting to the silly roommates, was smoking a spliff and staring, glassy-eyed, at the TV screen showing a late-night *Pink Panther* cartoon. The Portuguese pursuer failed to catch her prey: Finnegan sought refuge in Amalia's bedroom and slammed the door in Desidéria's face.

Desidéria, fuming, turned around, assumed a strategic position between the unresponsive Randy and the cartoon that seemed to fascinate him so, and drove her foot, clad in a teal sock, into his thigh.

"Hey! Wh...?! What's going on?" the startled bass player stuttered, glancing at her indifferently, and coughed.

Desidéria grimaced angrily, gave him the finger and stormed back into her room, which now lacked a certain Scotsman.

Randy shrugged, finished his joint and turned off the TV.

Sudden silence came over the apartment, but the few experimental self-propelled infiltration and surveillance bugs that had managed to survive the onslaught of the terrifying terrier nevertheless successfully recorded stifled giggles, spilling like the gentlest tune written for muffled chimes and xylophone, from Amalia's room.

49. Fadil's Story: Part Two

"Ah, that's better. Sitting on the throne and squeezing out those mini machines leaves you famished," said Fabiola after she ate something. It wasn't exactly a candlelight dinner at a fancy French restaurant, but she was so hungry she wouldn't have even flinched at the sight of frog legs and snails if it were.

"Yeah, I know," said Fadil.

"Oh. Of course you do."

After a couple of minutes of focusing on nothing but food, Fabiola demanded: "OK, so please tell me what those things were doing inside me if they weren't those persuasion robots or whatever it is you call 'em."

"Indoctrination nanites. Well, actually we could say you *did* have a certain type of a mind-controlling nanite inside you, but it wasn't you they were controlling."

Fabiola's fork hung in the air in front of her mouth: "What do you mean?" she scowled.

Fadil hesitated. "I guess there's no easy way to say this during dinner. Finish your meal first."

"Oh, sod it! Just get on with it, I'm a big girl," Fabiola grumbled.

"Fine then. So you know that bug infestation we had..."

Fabiola nodded and kept on eating despite the disgust she felt at the mere thought of the cockroach army. She hated to appear weak and childish. "Yes, I've been wondering about that," Fabiola looked Fadil in the eye, "What was that all about? And why did you release Fergus? It couldn't have been just because you needed a ton of pesticide."

Fadil wavered, unsure of how to explain everything.

"Look," Fabiola stabbed a piece of fried eggplant with

her fork, "I'm getting tired of this. Just go ahead and tell me everything already."

"I'm worried you'll take it the wrong way..." Fadil fretted.

"First of all, I can handle it. Second of all, how am I going to take it the wrong way? I've been *kidnapped* after all, for fuck's sake! Stop treating me like a damn child and spit it out. I promise I'll just eat, drink, listen, and I won't even interrupt you until you're done. Otherwise this will take forever and I really don't feel like spending all night talking to you about this. It's been a fucking exhausting day. So do we have a deal?"

"Alright then, first things first..." Fadil poured himself another Scotch, gathered his thoughts and tried his best to clear up the situation.

"The first thing I did when I got here was set up a so-called interdiction field, covering this building and a perimeter of approximately two kilometres around it. I'd just recently perfected it. It was going to be my contribution to the rigorous control and abuse-prevention mechanisms I'd proposed to Omnipile before they rejected my concerns and decided to send me to Yoman. I'd kept the technology to myself, just in case. It's basically like a firewall that prevents any data from passing through the perimeter. It also prevents nanites inside it from transmitting or receiving data from outside. This way I ensured that any nanites located inside the field were severed from the outside world. The interdiction field doesn't actually kill the nanites, it only prevents any information from getting in or out. It also warns me immediately of the presence of any signals attempting to get out through the field, while also detecting any nanites within it. When I first turned it on, I didn't detect anything apart from the nanites I had brought with me. In the absence of any mind-controlled individuals within the perimeter, I knew there weren't any *involuntary* moles among the YLF men in this resistance cell, at least. I couldn't be sure about voluntary ones, but since we hadn't been taken out by the Omnipile

Security Service yet, I guess it was safe to assume the cell was clean.

"However, I decided not to continuously transmit a reset code so as to immediately disable any nanites entering the field. That would just cause too many problems. First of all, I don't want anyone to know about my secret weapon until the time is right... And secondly, I needed certain nanites to work: I took advantage of my backdoor and nanite data link so I could get some information from Omnipile, at the very least. The interdiction field only allows my data mining nanites to connect to the satellite link whenever I need them to and blocks all others. I needed to have confidence in my security measures if I wanted to sleep ever again. As it turned out, everything worked just fine, as you'll see.

"So, I've already told you that Omnipile, trying desperately to find me, abducted the YLF leader. I'm sure they indoctrinated him immediately. Fortunately he doesn't know our location, but they've tried to exchange him for me, of course. They even sent a video of him trying to persuade the YLF to do that, but by then I'd already explained about the nanites and shown them documents to prove what I told them. They understood that their leader wasn't going to be who he was supposed to be. The YLF's rejection of the exchange must have pissed off Omnipile royally.

"In the meantime, I started looking for ways to access the Omnipile mainframe in order to simultaneously reset all the nanites currently in existence via the central satellite downlink. The task seems almost hopeless, because I'd have to gain physical access to either the mainframe – which I don't think can be done since it's located in The Lab, so it could as well be on the Moon – or I could try to find some way to get to one of the terminals connected to it, which would probably prove to be just as impossible. As I told you before, the only men I know have access to these terminals are your father and the director of the Omnipile Intelligence Agency. These people are, as you know, notoriously well guarded and the terminals themselves are located at secure locations in their own homes, where the level of security is easily on par with The Lab itself. According to the information I've been able to dig up, the Board of Directors has another terminal in the meeting room at The Lab, but that's just as impossible to gain access to as the mainframe itself.

"But then out of nowhere we got lucky: it seems Mr Fenton wanted to keep up the image of the Corporation in the media. So, to further the propaganda by means of which Omnipile is attempting to isolate Yoman completely from the rest of the world as we speak, he made a personal appearance in Yoman and visited the so-called humanitarian disaster relief centre as well as the scientific team operating here. That's my former team, now indoctrinated, minus me, of course. Also... To show how confident he was in the abilities of the Omnipile Security Forces to the media, Mr Fenton brought his family with him. At least that's what we thought then."

Fadil watched Fabiola's reactions carefully, but she just zipped her lips with her fingers and kept looking at him curiously. Fadil puffed tiredly, rubbed his eyes and continued: "The YLF got wind of what the CEO of Omnipile – your dad – was up to, and I had an idea... It was too good of an opportunity to pass up, so we came up with a plan to kidnap you and your brother. I'm really sorry, but there was no other way. Besides, that was before I got to know you."

Fabiola just kept staring at Fadil without saying a word.

"Well, fortunately it all went according to plan. Actually, the plan went too smoothly for my taste, so I was even more suspicious than usual. It turned out I was right to be careful, because as soon as you were brought here that night, all drugged out, the interdiction field sounded the alarm. I found both you and Fergus had subcutaneous chips on you. Nothing fancy, just tracking and identification devices. They weren't able to transmit anything through the interdiction field, of course, so I just extracted and destroyed them while you were still unconscious. I believed they were probably standard safety measures for high-ranking Omnipile executives and their families. Despite the fact that my interdiction field worked perfectly, we decided to move to another location immediately. Just a precaution – but the tracking devices only stopped transmitting two kilometres from our former base of operations, and I was too paranoid to be happy with that. Fortunately though, the YLF cells have access to lots of places such as this. So we moved here – which turned out for the best: it's closer to the coast so it's not as damn stuffy as our previous hideout, it's more spacious, and it has a better kitchen. Once you get to know the cook, that is, otherwise I gather she feeds the stalest cookies and cheapest tea to those she thinks of as infidel imperialists.

"Anyway, I digress. It turned out that the subcutaneous chips were not all there was to it – the scanner also showed both of you had nanites in your bodies, including your blood stream. I found that odd – what purpose could that serve? They were definitely not the pure mind-control type I was used to seeing, but were still largely based on my own work. More precisely, on my second-generation communication nanorobots, so I knew they were Omnipile technology. I confirmed that the reset code worked on them as originally intended. However, at that point there wasn't anything establishing any data links or communication streams with the outside world. They were practically dormant and therefore not dangerous, even without my firewall. I suspected they'd been combined with some form of bionanotechnology and I'm not an expert in that, so I thought there might be some medical reason. Therefore I refrained from simply deactivating them before I fully understood what they were.

"As far as my plan for you guys… I thought I'd use Omnipile's own weapons against the Corporation. So on that first morning – remember, when Fergus had a headache – I brought you a so-called aspirin, which you didn't want to take?"

Fabiola glared at him angrily now, but still she refrained from speaking. She was indeed very stubborn once she made up her mind. Fadil could no longer avoid telling her the truth.

"Well, those were my own mind-control nanites, I'm

afraid. I wanted to use them on both of you. Of course, I knew there was no danger. They'd been thoroughly tested and I knew how to deactivate them. If my plan worked, they'd all be deactivated, anyway. When you refused to take the pill, I figured what the hell, one of you would be enough and we'd still have a hostage left, just in case. The plan was simple... I uploaded so much computer knowledge into Fergus that he'll probably be able to skip university altogether and go straight to being rich..."

Fadil's attempt at defusing the situation at least partially did not register with Fabiola, who now eyed him angrily, her lips pressed together tightly.

"Then we sent him home. A Trojan horse, so to speak. The nanites actually don't affect him a whole lot. They do prevent him from revealing any useful information about me, the YLF, or our present location to anyone, though, and he probably feels a strong urge to get home as soon as possible. Afterwards, whenever he's all by himself and for reasons he won't even understand, he'll feel an uncontrollable craving go to your father's terminal at home, which is, as far as I know from the files I've managed to dig up on the issue, located in his office. With all the knowledge Fergus has been given, he should be able to easily use the terminal to access the mainframe and instruct it to flash all the nanites with a simple sequence of numbers – the reset code. At that very moment, all the nanites in existence should stop functioning and I'll finally be able to make all the evidence public. This would definitely stop Omnipile right in their tracks, at least until some foolproof safety measures, strict controls and monitoring are established to deal with all the nanotechnology that's bound to appear in the future."

Fadil stopped talking and waited. Fabiola was still silent. "So?" he said, "Do you hate me?"

Fabiola raised her eyebrows: "You're not done yet. What were those things inside us?"

"Oh, that! Yeah, I forgot about that. As I said, at first I didn't know what those nanites were for. For all I knew, they could have been vital to your health or something. They definitely didn't seem harmful as they were more or less inactive. Even if they weren't dormant I knew they couldn't send or receive information from outside due to my handy little interdiction field, right? Admittedly, after my initial failure to figure out what exactly their function was, I became too preoccupied with my work with Fergus and following the progress he made to worry about them much.

"Then, on the very first day after your arrival, more nanites started appearing on my scanner. Just tiny clusters of them, but still I almost freaked out in the beginning because I didn't know what the hell was going on. I checked and rechecked and no signals were coming in or going out, and the clusters didn't move around much. So I thought maybe they were trace nanites from your body and that you excreted them unknowingly or something.

"Which is *exactly* what you did. A couple of days later my scanner went crazy, indicating that these clusters started bursting apart and tiny little dots started running around. As if a bunch of nanites suddenly decided to throw a party. This stirred up quite a commotion in the mansion as we strived to figure out what these dots on our scanners were, though you wouldn't have noticed anything, of course. We made damn sure to keep you in the dark about everything, though. Soon we caught a 'dot' and it was one of those accursed cockroaches, which you familiarised yourself with a couple of days later, right?

"Anyway, the nanites were *inside* the roaches and I finally figured out that the bugs were some form of spy equipment. I panicked – how the hell did they find us? Why weren't the OSS forces here already? I did some research using my nanite data link and I found a few references to *experimental self-propelled infiltration and surveillance equipment*, which is obviously what these damn insects are. Unfortunately I haven't been able to find any detailed technical specifications and elaborations about them yet. They must be new and experimental, probably the first products of the new

Nanoweaponry Group or Indoctrination Department or god knows what dubious experts they have working with nanotechnology now. I certainly don't want to dig too deep. The last thing I want is to draw the attention of the OSS, the OIA, or anyone at the Information Technology Department to the nanite data link I'm using to access the information I desperately need.

"The whole issue was driving me nuts, but soon I put two and two together. When I figured it out, I needed to confirm I was right. Fortunately, the interdiction field prevented the roaches from transmitting anything, so essentially they were just bugs and nothing more. Fat fancy bugs, expensive technology, sure... But without the data link they were quite useless and completely disorganised. But still I didn't want to tell you these things and drag you into anything before I was absolutely sure about it."

Fabiola looked at him sideways and rolled her eyes: "Oh, come on, first you kidnap us, then you brainwash my brother, and now you suddenly don't want to drag me into this? Just be a man and admit it: you're a manipulative bastard. Sure, I can also see things from your perspective, thanks to all the documents and explanations, but you're still a bastard. So don't give me this 'I-didn't-want-to-get-you-involved' shit."

"You're right. I apologise. But honestly, I didn't want to just... You know... Tell you awful things that might just turn out to be my paranoid delusions, or perform any more procedures on you without your knowledge and consent. I was feeling guilty as it was. Frankly, the fact that we had to kidnap you, extract the chips while you were sleeping and use your brother in such a way was more than enough for me... Besides, I've grown to... Well, I just like you, that's all."

Fabiola and Fadil looked at each other for a few long seconds, and then Fabiola kicked him in the leg under the table: "Go on. Wrap this up, you brute. I knew I shouldn't have said anything."

"Right," Fadil got startled. "Well, the roaches kept multiplying and I finally thought of another thing we could use in exchange for your brother apart from a big chunk of cash: a truckload of OmniBug insecticide. Initially the bugs were just a minor nuisance, but then it turned into a full-blown infestation. You've seen them, so you know. We had to get rid of them, regardless of whether they were functional or not, or at least diminish their numbers until I got all my facts straight.

"Naturally, the insecticide didn't work on them. Of course it wouldn't, how stupid of me – the bugs were the product of Omnipile Genetic Engineering and Bionanotechnology Departments and of course they'd be immune to Omnipile's own insecticides. They're probably the only insects in existence immune to that poison. And even if the insecticide worked and they had all dropped dead, more of them would have kept appearing until we ran out of it. You see, what I figured out about these bugs that were suddenly everywhere... It was Fergus and you who brought them here. Those maniacs at Omnipile put a large number of bioengineered oothecae – that's tiny containers of insect eggs – inside your digestive tract. The purpose of the nanites inside you was to control the locations of these egg containers within your body, so that they'd stay put until needed. In practice, these nanites of yours saw to it that the oothecae stayed in safe areas within your intestines, so that they wouldn't be digested or trigger a response from your immune system or cause you any discomfort or anything like that. They would just stay in place, inert, and then at the right moment – whenever you'd go to the toilet, you know, for a number two – one or two oothecae would be ushered towards, erm... The rear exit."

Fadil even went so far as to smile, and Fabiola sighed and rolled her eyes adoringly.

"Right..." he said, "So, basically, every time you guys went to the toilet, you also excreted a couple of oothecae. These egg cases would then pop open in the sewers and tiny nanite-controlled cockroaches would hatch. However, the ones that hatched here found themselves inside the interdiction field, so they were completely disorganised due to their inability to establish a satellite link with the base. Hence the uncontrolled multiplication. Had they worked properly, they most likely would have stayed out of sight and their numbers would have been kept in check.

"Before deactivating those pesky little buggers, I familiarised myself with their software, of course, to get to know what our enemy was up to and all that. Well, my enemy, anyway. What was interesting was that normally the bugs are supposed to home in on a predetermined location and stay within a certain distance of it at all times. In other words, they're assigned a target and an exact distance they're allowed to stray from the target is also specified. That keeps them from crawling everywhere and anywhere, leaving trace evidence of the technology lying around. If they do stray too far from their zone of operations for any reason, or if something happens to carry them away, the nanites deactivate the bugs as well as themselves. This seems like quite a reasonable precaution.

"However, in your case their programming was a little different: the target of your bugs was you and Fergus was obviously the target of his bugs."

"Why's that?" Fabiola blurted out.

"The roaches determine their location in relation to their central network, their central command, if you will: the network of nanites inside you and Fergus. Of course, in your case they were still able to communicate among themselves and with the central network, even inside the interdiction field. The firewall only kept them from establishing any connections with the outside world. It's all very logical. The purpose of these insect eggs was obviously this: whenever you'd go to the toilet, one or two oothecae would also be excreted and a few bugs would hatch. If you were moved and they were left behind, they'd die off and new ones would hatch at the next location. I tested this: the bugs died when I took them further than some five hundred metres from you. Fergus's bugs must have all dropped dead the moment we let him go. So they operated only for as long as he stayed within range. Logical: Omnipile didn't want evidence littering every toilet between here and wherever you've been since they'd implanted them."

"The bastards! That's... That's what those alleged medical checkups at The Lab must have been for! This and the chips! They told us they just needed to vaccinate us because we were going to an exotic country with our father!" Fabiola was enraged.

"Yeah, could be. Anyway, after I'd figured everything out, I took a sample of your blood – just to test the reset code on a few live specimens and check if it worked properly. To make sure that you wouldn't be harmed. Then I sent your nanites the reset code via a wireless connection and as soon as they all deactivated, the roaches all around the mansion died off too – because for them the target, that's you – no longer existed."

"But why did they put these things inside us?"

"To find out where I was, obviously, so they could get me back or kill me. No, I don't think they'll kill me, they probably want me alive, to indoctrinate me before proceeding again with their plan. They must suspect I have a way of deactivating the nanites by now and they'll surely want to know what it is. They definitely made sure we swallowed their pills, and when after two weeks my link was still inactive... They must have realised I'd reversed the indoctrination process somehow.

"There, that about wraps it up, more or less. There's just one more thing I really don't want to tell you, but I have no other choice."

"Absolutely!" Fabiola flung the fork she'd been fiddling with at the table. It bounced off it, fell to the floor, and slid under the couch, where it joined an impressive collection of dust and Madagascar hissing cockroach corpses. "Why did they put these things inside us?!"

"Exactly. I asked myself the same question. It turns out that the counter-counter-intelligence service of the OIA was feeding information to the YLF, probably through the same mole that betrayed the location of the YLF leader. They wanted to make sure we knew where you and your family were going to be, fed us the whole plan, everything. It was a setup from the start. I'm sorry, Fabiola... But your father knew about it all along. It was his idea. He and that bastard Rupert Doors, the Director of the OIA. They arranged it all."

"Impossible! My dad would never do that to me! He would never...!"

"I know such betrayal hurts like hell... I've experienced it myself. But if it makes you feel any better, he must have been terribly worried about you. They did have the subcutaneous tracking devices installed, they couldn't have known the signal could possibly be interrupted. They surely thought they had everything under control. But, do you see now what I meant when I said I didn't want to tell you anything until I was absolutely certain it was true?"

This didn't make Fabiola feel any better. Her lovely eyes brimmed with tears, but she bit her lip and intercepted the treacherous droplets before they could possibly trickle down her cheek. She trapped them in her sleeve and gritted her teeth, trembling ever so slightly.

Fadil took the last document from his laptop case – a printout of the communications between Mr Fenton and Mr Doors about the matter – and handed it to Fabiola. He didn't want to do that: he yearned to hug her, console her, tell her everything would be all right... But he believed that such a move would be horrendously inappropriate at this point. Instead he decided to put his trust in Fabiola's capacity for processing information rationally. She just needed to sleep on it.

50. Interlude:
Bad Bad Boy

Finnegan woke up around 4 a.m. in Amalia's bed. "*Oh, the splendour of her body, the heavenly scent of her skin... Bah, pull yourself together!*" he thought as he got out of bed and headed to the toilet to take a leak.

In the back of his mind a tiny little thought gnawed at him. He struggled to keep it at bay, but it kept poking away at him from its dark confines: "*Somebody's watching.*"

Finnegan was very familiar with that little thought: he felt it every time he happened to take a puff of Randy's space herbs. He hated the feeling so much that lately he'd been avoiding any puffs whatsoever. Now the annoyingly elusive paranoia was back again, but this time it had made its nasty appearance when Finnegan was more or less sober, minus those four or five beers he'd had the evening before. He sighed heavily as he sat on the toilet, refraining from aiming at the toilet bowl from the standing position for the sake of... What, some kind of nocturnal male pride? As he directed a tired unfocused gaze into the almost total darkness, only a little flame flickering in the gas boiler in the corner, he could swear he almost glimpsed something skittering across the tiles. He instantly worried whether something might be seriously wrong with him.

He shuddered, stood up, flushed the toilet, and hurried back to Amalia's bed, trying not to register what seemed to be something strange lurking just beyond the edge of his vision. He shook his head violently and rubbed his eyes, and what had to be figments of his imagination were mercifully gone. "*It must be one of those 4 a.m. issues of mine,*" Finnegan thought and slipped back under the covers to seek solace in the warmth of his rekindled flame, his rediscovered companion, his love restored. He basked in these fuzzy thoughts and tried to concentrate on all the wonderful and mouth-watering attributes of Amalia, who was snoring ever so gently next to him.

However, the image of himself ending up in the loony bin persisted just below the surface of all the pleasantries he was trying to focus on, and Finnegan soon found himself thinking about an old deranged acquaintance of theirs from Kirkwall, who was most certainly certifiable. Finnegan figured even his 4 a.m. issues were not as bad as that.

This bloke – Bran was his name – would always turn into a serious menace and become virtually impossible to put up with when he drank. On the other hand, he was only horribly depressing during his bouts of sobriety. Bran was famous – and not merely locally, at that – for his despicable demeanour and deplorable attitude towards life, the universe and everything else, but apart from that he was mostly harmless. Still, most people avoided him because he was such an utter killjoy. His appearance prophesied the end of any party regardless of how merry it had been, as if he were a particularly menacing comet or ominous solar eclipse foretelling the imminent arrival of the Black Death. However, somehow Finnegan and Amalia would still frequently end up tolerating the disgruntled malcontent for whatever reason, probably also because they enjoyed making up all kinds of spooky stories about him. Indeed, Bran was picture-perfect for such mischief: he wore huge thick spectacles, sometimes referred to as "rapist glasses", and had very real issues with his elderly mother. It wasn't a particularly vast leap of the imagination to picture him driving a serial killer van or tending to a little children's shoe collection in his cellar.

So in the time before Finnegan finally drifted off an hour later – just as the birds outside reached the peak of their rather overzealous salute to another summer morning – he found himself giggling and replaying *Bad Bad Boy*, one of their more disturbing songs, in his mind. It was inspired by Bran, and Finnegan, Amalia and Randy had jammed on it a few of times back in Kirkwall. It was yet to be revealed to the other members of Cynicism Management, though.

BAD BAD BOY
**[https://soundcloud.com/cynicism-management/
bad-bad-boy-augmented]**

I've been a bad bad boy

All the wants that I may have
Tremble at my mother's stare
I implore her to desist
This thing she does

I've been watching her grow old
Never penetrated, cold
I have never even grasped
The sin

I've been a bad bad boy
Got little hamster legs in my secret drawer
Therefore I hide till I can hide no more
I've been a bad bad boy
I have her visit my mind
Make her my own whore
Therefore I loathe
Till I can loathe no more

I grow older she grows old
I've been hiding things untold
It's been years and I am
Unrepentant

But she steals the cellar key
I make her stay eternally
Now I love her quietly
She's watching

I've been a bad bad boy
My little hamster legs I carry in my pockets
I no longer run 'cause I can run no more
I've been a bad bad boy
Those children's shoes
In my cellar locker
They're all just for you
So you can love me too

Bad bad boy

51. Wow, How Annoying!

Fabiola was convinced that she wouldn't be able to fall asleep that night, but around midnight she finally drifted off. Her dreams were plagued by insect infestations, infernal micro-machines, and disturbing images of her father. Fadil was right to have given her some breathing room the previous evening – had he said anything else other than "good night" at that point, she would have gladly kicked him in the nuts. Now that she had woken up refreshed, she was seeing things more clearly, though.

She got dressed and headed towards Fadil's office. The guards were still posted outside her room, but they had a good idea what was going on. She must have still been wearing a dangerously volatile expression, because they stayed well out of her way and just tailed her at a safe distance of three or four metres.

"Come in," shouted Fadil as she knocked on his door. She entered and the guards stayed outside. Visibly relieved, they pulled out their backgammon board and rolled a couple of cigarettes.

"I read this damn thing," Fabiola said as she walked up to Fadil. He sat at his desk, scratching his head as he stared into his computer screen. With disgust and loathing, she tossed the printed document which detailed the elaborate abuse of Fergus and herself for the alleged good of the Western civilisation onto his desk. Fadil turned and looked at her.

"What if I don't believe any of it? You could have made it all up!" Fabiola accused her kidnapper.

"Why would I do that?"

"I don't know... To establish control over me, to gain my trust while you were waiting for the right moment to

exchange me for money or whatever it is you're doing here!"
Fabiola flailed her arms. "You got a lot of money for Fergus,
didn't you?"

"Sure. We had to make a plausible demand in order to
send him home."

"You could have demanded that they hand over that
prisoner, that leader of yours."

"Well, not a leader of mine, the YLF leader. We did
demand that, actually, but Omnipile started complicating
things. I think they were still under the impression that they
would have some leverage over the YLF as long as they held
on to their leader. You know, they didn't want to exchange
him for you – they wanted to exchange him for me. So, since
I wanted to get Fergus home as soon as possible, we backed
off a little in order to wrap up the negotiations immediately.
We told them fine – that they could have Fergus for some
serious cash and as a sign of our goodwill and all, but not
you. They'd have to give up the YLF leader for you. They went
for that almost immediately and later on it crossed my mind
that we should have asked for a lot more money. I think we
were lucky they didn't get really suspicious, because I got the
feeling they thought we asked for too little."

"You could still be making all of this up."

"But I'm not. Look, you've read the documents. You see
the stamps and stationary and signatures on some of them,
don't you? You do recognise your father's signature, right?
Apart from that, I also have access to a couple of videos
of successful indoctrinations, if you'd like to see them. It
looks like they have some sort of programme going on in
Antarctica." Fadil showed her the contents of a folder that
contained the videos.

"I don't care. They could all be fake..." Fabiola began
and then paused abruptly. "Wait, what's that file?" she
pointed to one of them.

"I have no idea," Fadil admitted.

"Those are the names of our bodyguards. I know those
jerks! Play that."

Fadil played the video. The three bodyguards whom Fabiola had known for years stated that they were ecstatic about having been transferred to an Antarctic oil rig and then went on and on about how they loved the snow and how they enjoyed the frozen wastes. Then the video showed them frolicking outside, throwing snowballs at each other and singing Jingle Bells over and over again like a bunch of madmen.

"They love snow?!" Fabiola almost laughed. "What the hell?"

"From what I know of the enclosed documents, the video you're seeing shows some members of Omnipile staff who have done something so wrong as to deserve the disciplinary action called *nullification*. These videos are sent to their families as a way of explaining where their nearest and dearest are. Beats your everyday death sentences or, to use an overused euphemism, *disappearances* and the complications such procedures entail, right? Besides, these people in fact do serious work on oil rigs and actually earn their pay checks, even if they don't know why they're so happy about it all of a sudden. Based on what we can see here it could even be argued that they really do love their newfound purpose in life. I wish I was as happy doing what I do. Damn, I wonder what horrible form of lobotomy nullification meant before mind-control nanites... Anyway, the guards in question seem to have pissed off your father royally," Fadil looked amused.

"Yeah, probably because we got away from them. We slipped down to the lobby to check our e-mail," Fabiola smiled a little, summoning up the small dimple in her left cheek that made Fadil squirm.

"That's when the YLF took you. According to our original plan, one of our operatives posing as room service was supposed to take out everybody in your hotel suite with knockout gas. But then they saw you both in the lobby without any of your guards around, and so they just snatched you there. Later on I thought that Mr Fenton must have taken care of that, to avoid any possibility of an armed conflict in the hotel. Looks like it was just coincidence after all, though."

Fabiola clicked back to the beginning of the video and watched it again. On seeing the guards throwing snowballs at each other, she grumbled calmly but almost disappointedly: "They love snow, my ass. The only thing these guys loved was chicks in bikinis, beer, poker, strip clubs, fancy cars, lack of any real work for months on end, and fat pay checks. Sure, they'd probably snap you like a twig in a second. They were well-trained. But other than working out in the gym or wasting ammo at the gun range, which they were happy to do whether they were being paid for it or not, they were essentially a bunch of slackers. I haven't seen any of them break a sweat in years, except when they were 'guarding' us at the swimming pool or pumping iron. And now they've signed up for a tour of duty on an oil rig? In Antarctica? No bloody way. I guess you're not lying, after all."

"Most definitely not."

"Alright, fine. Fuck my dad. I knew he was a bastard. I'm old enough to realise that nobody can be that filthy rich and a good guy at the same time, right? So, how do we do it? How do we access the mainframe then and liberate the crews of many an Antarctic oil rig, by the look of it?" Fabiola revolutionised.

"I don't know. I really thought Fergus would have pulled this off by now. Something must have gone wrong... I've been thinking about this for days, and I've just had a most troubling thought. They must have debriefed Fergus, right? Interrogated him? What if they found it suspicious that he couldn't tell them anything useful? Which he wouldn't, given the mental block that my nanites would have put up if he had tried to communicate any sensitive information... They might have figured he was keeping something from them for some reason, so they could have given him a second dose of indoctrination nanites, not realising he was already indoctrinated. As I was saying, the interdiction field is all my own technology which I hadn't shared with Omnipile, so they certainly wouldn't have anything like that in place to warn them. Besides, they know that they're the only corporation that's actually already using nanites at this point, so they'll surely think they're quite safe from any similar technology being used against them. So they could definitely have tried to indoctrinate the boy to peer inside his mind and see if there was any additional information in there, even the kind he was unaware of. I'm just running some simulations here on my own equipment as we speak, and I'm more and more convinced that a second indoctrination would certainly lead to a conflict between the two sets of indoctrination nanites. These early generations of nanites are not programmed to deal with that kind of a situation, so probably they'd end up in a kind of a stalemate and the person affected would find it extremely hard to function with any normality. The conflict between nanites could lead to temporary impairment or even shutdown of the higher cognitive functions, a kind of a temporary catatonia, perhaps."

"Why don't you try to get some information on Fergus, find out what's happened to him since he got back home?" Fabiola shrugged.

"Of course, let me try. I've just come up with this scenario, my simulation is still running. OK, let's see... Connection established... Now, where should I look? I'm trying not to abuse my backdoor access too much. You know, this is one of the few advantages we have. If they figure it out, we're screwed..." Fadil rambled on while he was unconsciously covering up the fact that he didn't know where to look. But still, he had to be the one to save the day while Fabiola was watching.

"Try the Medical Department in The Lab," Fabiola was the one to actually save the day. "My dad's always bitching about the doctors there and how important they think they are. If there were some strange affliction which appeared to be a medical issue affecting Fergus, those mad scientists would surely be working on it."

"You're right, wait..." Fadil brought up some of the medical files from The Lab.

"God, what a mess. I suppose those doctors suffer from a serious lack of organisational skills," Fabiola grumbled at the sight of the chaotic collection of files on the server.

Fadil suddenly jumped, pale as a whiteboard: "Jesus! What the hell..."

"What's wrong?"

"This title! No, no, no... This can't be..."

Fadil opened a file titled *64738.doc* and, after skimming through it hastily, let out a sigh of thorough relief.

"God, for a moment there I thought we were finished. That my plan had been ruined. You see, the title of this file... This sequence of numbers... That's the reset code."

"Six four seven three eight?"

"Yep. That's the reset code I've built into the nanites. For a second I thought they figured it out. Fortunately it looks like it's something Fergus has been obsessing about, and thank god they don't know what the hell it is. For now, anyway. We should act quickly, though..."

Indeed, nine days ago, on Monday, Fergus's mind darkened as a new collection of mind-control nanorobots started replicating in his brain and nervous system. Fergus shocked his father, the agents and the Doctor by reciting the numbers after suddenly jerking awake from his slumber. His cerebral cortex struggled to make sense of the conflicting instructions firing throughout its neurons, and then the brain, striving to prevent damage, partially shut down. All that Fergus felt after that was an urge to get home, within range of his bed and his computer, and all he could think about was a sequence of five numbers. That, incidentally, was also all he could say: the five little words for the five little numbers.

On Thursday the doctors gave up. They told Ferdinand Fenton that before they did anything else, they'd have to wait the full two weeks for the indoctrination nanites to fully replicate and stabilise within the boy. Only then would they be able to run reliable diagnostics and see what was going on. Until then it was pointless to keep the boy in The Lab. So they released Fergus from the hospital ward in The Lab and Mr

Fenton took him home. There Fergus seemed to calm down somewhat, at least at first. His parents kept him in his room and Ferdinand posted guards outside his door. For a fleeting moment Fergus almost seemed glad when he first laid eyes on his computer. After fiddling around with his computer games for a couple of hours, though, he became agitated again. He ran to the window and shouted "six – four – seven – three – eight!" at a bunch of paparazzi lurking in the garden, who were trying to get a story on anything related to the kidnapping of the Fenton kids: how was the CEO taking it? Has his wife shed any tears yet? Was there any hope for their daughter? What hellish brainwashing techniques had Fergus endured at the hands of the evil terrorists?! Do tears exist that have not yet been shed?

After Fergus's protestations, the windows in his room were all nailed shut. Since then he was confined to his room at all times, except when he had to go to the bathroom. Not that the boy wanted to get out: all he did was stare at his favourite online computer game, seemingly doing nothing at all other than muttering the accursed five numbers under his breath and feeling constantly frustrated for some reason.

"I see," Fabiola said after reading everything there was to read about the unfortunate fate of her brother. "Why don't you send me back too? Exchange me for the YLF leader, and I'll get to the bloody terminal."

"Look... I'm not going to say I haven't considered that, because I'm not going to lie to you anymore, ever. But I don't want to do that. First of all because you'd undoubtedly be put through the same ordeal, as they'd definitely indoctrinate you as well... And there's no sense in sending you back without indoctrinating and programming you with all the knowledge and expertise you'd need. You'd never be able to figure out how to access the mainframe without it. Not that I'm belittling your knowledge of computers by any means, I wouldn't imply that..."

"Jesus, Fadil, I know. I know, you're right. As I told you before: I don't speak bloody geekish. And I don't mind not speaking it, either, I find it mind-bogglingly boring," Fabiola frowned at the awkward Palestinian.

"Yeah, it can be rather dull," Fadil smiled at her. "And secondly, subjectively speaking..." Fadil made a slightly dramatic pause that Fabiola didn't exactly appreciate because she immediately suspected him of being somewhat of a charmer with a lot of experience in impressing women, "I really don't want to put you in any unnecessary danger, OK?"

"But of course, my prince," her flair for sarcasm kicked in. "If we all get mind-controlled, let's get mind-controlled together, right? Sure. Stop getting cheesy on me and let's figure out how to get my brother to... Ah..."

Suddenly Fabiola, even if she liked to poke at Fadil's weaknesses and embarrass him, thought of something.

"Computer game?!" she blurted out.

"What?" Fadil was at a loss.

"The report on my brother's mental state we've just read... It said he played a computer game in his room, you know, at home?"

"Yeah, what of it?"

"Get me a credit card, please. Do you have a decent internet connection here?"

"Of course, I've got a state-of-the-art satellite link. What's this all about?"

Fabiola accessed her Battle.net account, downloaded and installed World of Warcraft on Fadil's computer, and after a couple of hours of setting up the entire parallel universe she logged in. The expenses of reactivating Fabiola's old account were covered by an anonymous Yomanian, since it seemed it wouldn't have been very prudent to use Mr Fadil Dajani's credit card.

Fabiola's level 37 female orc shaman shook off thick layers of sand dust which the wind blowing in from the Barrens had deposited on her while she had been asleep for ages next to an open window of an inn in the orc capital of Ogrimmar. The shaman hadn't moved a virtual muscle ever since Fabiola had grown tired of the game, which had taken place about the same time her brother had started exhibiting the telltale signs of extreme obsession with it. Fabiola knew Fergus's guildmistress, though. She used to be a member of the Hordecorerz, but only for a couple of months, until she came to realise such loyalties could get pretty annoying and surreal very quickly. This was an acquaintance she'd never have expected to prove useful in her entire life. It's funny, the absurd turns life can take sometimes.

"`/tell Moolly Hey, Moo :) /huggles`", Fabiola typed.

"`/reply Favielle! /hugs Hey, wht u doin here? long time no c :))`", the fabled guildmistress typed on her side of the massive multiplayer online role-playing game universe.

"`Just lookin for my bro. Urgent stuff. Seen him?`"

"`sec... Ya... U back from that strange country yet? He sent me mail from somepl0Ooooooops , sorry, fighting, justa sec....`"

A couple of minutes passed.

"`Moolly? u there?`"

"`sec`"

A couple of minutes passed.

"`It's kind of urgent, death in the family.`"

"`Oh! I'm so sorry. Just a sec, brb`"

A couple of minutes passed.

"`had to finish the fight and tell teh guild to wait up, we're raidin. Yea, your bro sent an email worryin about his rank and all. Look, maybe I shouldve cut him sum slack lol I hope hes OK`"

"`Yeah, he takes the game so seriously, you know how little boys are.`"

"`roflmao ya I hav eone at home, my hubby :))`"

"lol"

"I guess your bro logged in, cause he
left the guild, i was surprised by that
really ... let me se the timestamp"

"OK"

"Yea on thursday he left the guild,
didn't say nuthin, I just saw he resigned.
THought maybe he was angry, I roleplayed a
tough commander and reprimended him by email
fgor not raidin… sorry but you know how it
is, raiding is serious stuff, i hav to keep a
tight ship"

"No, he has other problems, like real
life, I think… Can't find him on his usual
toons, not even Faarguz… Need to speak to
him urgently," Fabiola was growing impatient.

"Oh sure!1 Before he left the guild he
plyaed an alt named Loopy alot, Madward says
he saw him on auction channel in IF yellin
some numbers or something Oh, yea Switters
saw him too, he says it was weird, he sent
him a tell and he replied with that number
of his is he OK?"

"Sure. Look, thanks, Moo, I'm in a hurry,
need to find him. Appreciate this a lot, cya,
OK? I owe you a dwarven ale, cool? :)"

"hehe cool cya hope u find ur bro /hugs
luv ya!!!!!!1111"

Five minutes later Favielle, as soon as she arrived in the
dwarven capital of Ironforge, contacted a character who went
by the name of Loopy. Everybody thought Loopy was quite
obnoxious: he'd spammed all the available chat channels in
Ironforge with his mathematical mantra, which got him on
everybody's ignore lists. Loopy, a ridiculous-looking level 42
gnome warlock, was the only member of his own guild, called
Six-Four-Seven-Three-Eight, and he wore the tag proudly
beneath his name.

Fabiola and Fadil, who followed Fabiola's progress carefully and wondered at the cartoonish splendour and apparent fun of the game, found out that Fergus was indeed still alive and well, but incapable of typing anything save for "64738", "six four seven three eight" or any combination of the two (or asserting that same assertion via the built-in voice chat).

"Wow, how annoying!" declared Fabiola.

"Indeed," Fadil agreed.

52. Ferdinand & Rupert

At around noon, the Director of the OIA Rupert Doors dropped by Ferdinand Fenton's office. The time for official e-correspondence and beating around the bush had come to an end. Ferdinand poured them each a glass of Japanese single-malt whisky and Rupert lit a Cuban cigar. It was never too early or too late for the big boys to sit down and talk serious business.

"I must say, I'm growing increasingly worried about the progress of our diabolical plan," Rupert said through the foul-smelling mist his cigar had conjured up in front of his face. "The indoctrination of the YLF leader hasn't revealed anything useful about the whereabouts of that treacherous bastard Dr Fadil Dajani."

"Yes, and Fergus didn't tell us anything, either. Jesus, what a mess this is. The Doctor tells me he suspects there might be a second set of nanites at work inside the boy, but he says he can't run reliable diagnostics and won't be able to do anything until the full replication and initialisation process is completed. So we'll have to wait a fortnight. But a second set of nanites? If it's true, then it must be Dr Dajani's doing, there's no other possibility. I'm sure our plan worked – the kids were definitely taken by the terrorist cell protecting Fadil, just as we planned. At least our counter-counter-intelligence did that right. But the kids' locator chips didn't make a peep after being deactivated a few hours after the abduction. We're pretty sure they were extracted. The damn bugs do work as intended, see, because Fergus was still seeding them when he came back, yet the ones deposited at the target location haven't been reporting back to us for some reason."

"Maybe the terrorists are hiding in caves too far under-ground or something. Look, any way we look at this, we're

456

running out of time. Our friends in high places in the cabal of benevolent and democratic Western superpowers are getting nervous. If we release the information about the possibility that Yoman may have access to nanoweaponry, they might start pushing for an immediate military intervention, and we're not quite ready to carry out a full-scale indoctrination yet. We're in no position to fuck around anymore. We're in danger of losing all trace of Dr Dajani. If we can't find him immediately and either recover or terminate him, who can tell what crap he might reveal to the public before we're able to ensure world domination for ourselves. My god, who knows what he could do with the nanites if in fact he has access to them. Imagine if anyone found out that our leading nanotechnology scientist joined a terrorist organisation and delivered that technology into their hands!" Rupert said and puffed on his cigar nervously.

"Indeed. And that's not all that worries me. I've reviewed the footage of the scientists' indoctrination more than once, and it's been confirmed with absolute certainty that Dr Fadil Dajani had been indoctrinated together with everybody else in that compound. How is it possible, then, that he's not responding? Not only does he have access to indoctrination nanites and unsurpassed knowledge of them, he has apparently also come up with a way of countering them."

"Either that or he's dead."

"Yeah, we wish. Anyway, Dr Dajani might be able to somehow undo everything we've strived for and prevent us from succeeding. Not only that, he could use our own weapon against us, cause serious financial damage... Even, heaven forbid, loosen our grip on the global economy!" Ferdinand said morosely.

Both men scratched their foreheads absent-mindedly. Such an infernal fate was almost as unimaginable as it was unacceptable. They washed away the sour taste in their mouths with a splash of perversely expensive whiskey.

"My data forensics experts sent their preliminary report," Mr Doors sighed.

"Oh, about the stuff on that pothead bass player's computer? Hell, now *that*, I'm sure, has been a fucking stab in the dark, I would think."

"I'm afraid so, just as we'd feared. However, that number, it's just too much of a coincidence."

"I guess... Did they find anything at all?"

"Nothing. A lot of information on marijuana growing. We could take Herb Boy's botany manuals with us in case everything goes to hell and we have to pack up and hide out on a desert island somewhere," Rupert Doors laughed and puffed at his cigar.

"Stop screwing around, I'm not in the mood. Anything else?"

"Yep, some porn, nothing too bizarre. A lot of pirated software, mostly music applications and a heap of games, but even I play pirated solitaire on my computer. We could probably make his life miserable because of that if we wanted to, but I don't see why. Other than the fact that the guy is getting on my nerves, why even bother? He's obviously just a total slacker – just like my son, now that I think of it."

At the mention of offspring, Ferdinand Fenton cringed: "Alright, I get it, but did he have anything remotely suspicious on his computer?"

"Well, there's this highly annoying music. There seems to be a lot of stuff that he, Scottish Songstress and the Subject of the Investigation, Mr Finnegan Frotz himself, have been collaborating on over the internet. I see you're about to roll your eyes and dismiss all of it, but we – my data forensics experts and I – doubt that anyone would want to produce or even, god forbid, listen to such music for the fun of it. The lyrics are also rather unorthodox, by the way – not one straight love song, no allusions to meaningless sex, and no optimistic drinking ditties. Can you imagine? One of my data experts who has some experience with music tells me that the rhythmical structures of the songs are also highly unusual. She also says that such silly structures in combination with preposterous melodies as well as the very peculiar lyrics on top of all that couldn't by any means be invented with actual listeners in mind. So we've theorised that maybe sensitive information has been encoded into the lyrics or the musical structure somehow.

"So we've forwarded the whole collection of tunes to our Musicology Department. Sadly they informed us that for the last forty years or so the only thing they've really worked on have been recipes for the ghastliest of jingles for our Advertising Department. The only other Musicology Department project worth mentioning was the insidious plan they'd drawn up for our record labels: how to keep recycling the same shit endlessly as new generations of children and teenagers continue to be our most promising and continual consumers with a seemingly inexhaustible purchasing power and a very short attention span. So effectively Omnipile-owned record labels just continue to re-sell the same shit over and over again to new generations of consumers every few years, subject to patented Omnipile algorithms, while actively and purposefully ignoring and even obstructing any unpredictable new developments in the field of popular music and thus effectively destroying any kind of innovation.

"But I digress, I'm afraid I've been listening to our musicologists' crap for too long and snorted way too much of their coke while I was at it. I talk too much. Anyway, we'll have to find and hire trustworthy external experts to check out these suspicious so-called Cynicism Management tunes, I'm afraid."

Ferdinand Fenton had already emptied his glass, but refrained from pouring himself another. After work he had to run back home and check whether Fergus was showing any signs of snapping out of his peculiar state. Ferdinand knew that Mr Rupert Doors, who, to Ferdinand's relief, finally stubbed out his damned cigar, wouldn't have had anything against another whisky. He didn't offer him one, though: "Anything else? I have to get back to work, I'm afraid."

"Oh, yeah, just one more thing," Mr Doors grunted as he got up, eyeing the bottle of exquisite liquor disappointedly.

"That stupid dog in Finnegan's apartment killed almost every damn bug of ours! The fucking mongrel... So the apartment has been left with very little coverage. I'm sending you an order for our field agent taskforce to sign, if you don't mind."

"Sure, what order?"

"I'll order the Bitches to bug their flat. I mean, with more permanent equipment which the dog won't be able to devour. Long shot or not, I don't want us to miss anything important. If we could only find out what the connection between Finnegan Frotz and Dr Fadil Dajani is... Furthermore, I'll tell our surveillance guys to start intervening in the actions of our field agents with direct orders if they need to. I don't care anymore if they know we're watching. We're running out of options. The time for political correctness, unnecessary pleasantries and other assorted bullshit covered by the fairy-tale term 'common decency' is over."

53. The Sound Solution,
or Interlude:
TV Turns On You

"So I was right. Damn! Those idiots *did* try to indoctrinate your brother," Fadil barked as he watched Loopy
say "6 four 7 3 eight" on the computer screen for the
umpteenth time.

"This is useless," Fabiola covered her eyes with her
hands and growled in frustration. She sighed and explained:
"He let me join his guild... But I can't get anything out of
him except for those damn numbers. I think he must have
recognised me, because he's making his character dance with
me and hug me and stuff like that, but he won't communicate.
It's funny – he must be okay to some degree, because he's able
to log in and type commands and so on. It's just that he can't
tell me anything but the stupid numbers."

"It must be a really strange nanobot error of some sort,
either software or hardware. Probably software. Fergus is
trying to communicate the number to the nanites, I guess,
but for some reason one set of nanites or the combination
of the two are blocking him from completing his mission or
from saying anything else to anyone. It's impossible to know
why this is happening without examining him up close and
running proper diagnostics, but the nanobots are clearly
malfunctioning."

"Shit... It doesn't matter why he is as he is, does it? We
just have to reset his nanites. But how? Maybe I should just
phone him and tell him to snap out of it," Fabiola grumbled.

"Yeah..." Lost in his thoughts, Fadil drummed his
fingers on the desk. Fabiola, disheartened, gave up on Fergus
for the time being and logged out of the game. It was too

461

disturbing to see him like this.

"Wait..." Fadil held a finger in front of his nose, "I might have an idea. I've researched these damn spy bugs in detail, and I might be able to use their communication protocols to get in touch with other spy roaches on the network and access their data. If there is just one bug near Fergus, I might be able to make it connect to his nanites and forward the reset code through it!"

"Why don't you simply take control of his computer and use his wireless connection?"

"I tried hacking your father's home computer days ago. As I expected, though, he's had the newest firewalls and security systems installed. Stuff that even beats my own expertise and equipment. My friends from the Information Technology Department must be constantly and promptly upgrading his system. I don't have the capability of getting through all those security measures blindly without the risk of triggering an alarm. If they catch me, they could figure out what I've been up to. But I can get through to the spy roaches by means of my backdoor nanobot access – after all, they *are* controlled by my nanites."

"Why would there be any bugs hanging out in Fergus's room?" Fabiola made a disbelieving as well as slightly disgusted face.

"Oh, I don't know. Perhaps they're monitoring him. Or maybe he's still excreting them and now they're all over your house, crawling around in your underwear drawer."

"Shut up!" Fabiola punched the joker in the shoulder, "And don't be absurd."

"Look, I know it's a silly idea, but it can't hurt to try and it won't take long."

Dr Fadil Dajani stared at his computer screen for a while and quickly managed to establish a connection with the experimental self-propelled infiltration and surveillance equipment.

"That's weird," Fadil muttered after a short while. "Currently very few locations are designated as targets for the spy roaches. Apparently they are indeed completely new and experimental, otherwise I'm sure we'd be seeing swarms of them at work all over the world, if I know Omnipile as well as I think I do. Most probably they haven't yet officially cleared them for widespread use, and by the look of this there aren't any bugs anywhere near your house, unfortunately." Fadil stared at his computer screen. "There are some signals coming from several Omnipile facilities, I guess they're running tests or doing who knows what... Oh, that's interesting! There are a couple of roaches transmitting from Mr Rupert Doors's house, wow, the Director of the OIA himself, let's see..."

An image of a living room seen from a glass tank appeared on the screen. Someone – probably Mrs Doors – rested on the couch, nibbling on popcorn and watching soaps on a huge plasma TV. Another cockroach seemed to be hiding under the bed in the bedroom.

"Wow, full of suspense," Fabiola joked.

"Yeah, intense. Let me check the related e-mails... Bah, it looks like we've finally figured out why the geniuses at Omnipile chose the Madagascar hissing cockroaches for this job. Yeah, first of all, they're big enough... Secondly, they don't stink... And, thirdly, since people also keep this species as pets, they can be passed off as such. So among other uses they can set them up at home and peer into their own living rooms. Looks like our friend Rupert here is spying on his wife. Some international intrigue this is turning out to be, he's a regular man of mystery," Fadil sighed. He left the secrets of the Doors household alone and kept checking for more spy roaches.

"There seem to be just a few small groups operating in the United States, most of them around Washington D.C., to be precise," he droned on slowly, staring at the screen and pushing his mouse around the mouse pad, "But I don't think that's got anything to do with our situation. We won't waste time with that right now...

"Ah, there, of course. A large number of roaches are operating in the Yomanian government building and at the Prime Minister's home, of course. Apart from that there's a single group currently at work in Moscow... And that's about it, it would seem.

"Hey, what's this?" Fadil lit up suddenly. "As many as eight groups operating in Slovenia, some little country near Italy! And one of these groups has recently sounded an alarm, let me see... It looks like something has wiped out almost every roach in the group named *Flat*, whatever that means. The other groups operating nearby are named *Pub*, *SikPuppi*, *Crackpot*, *QuietGuy*, *Brit* and *Fidel*. Let me pull up the communications archives... Holy crap, gigabytes upon gigabytes of audio and video and heaps of texts. I think the main problem that Omnipile will have with these roaches when the Corporation gives in to its desire to control and monitor everyone will be how to employ armies of people large enough to sift through all this garbage. It's like searching for meaningful information through billions of pointless e-mail exchanges. The next department to receive a heap of resources, such as the Nanotechnology Department currently does, will most probably be the Artificial Intelligence Department and their Virtual Pencil Pusher project."

"Fadil," Fabiola sighed, "we're getting dangerously close to Geekland again. What are we looking at here?"

"Just a sec, I'll run a keyword search. What should I search for... Alright, let's try 'Fergus', 'Fabiola', 'Dajani', 'Fadil', 'kidnapping', 'abduction', and my magical number first..."

Fadil typed in the keywords and searched through the text. "Indeed, there it is... I found some e-mails which seem relevant, finally, going to and coming from Slovenia... Let's check this out."

Fadil and Fabiola browsed through a briefing on the kidnapping of the Fenton children and an abundance of information on a character named Finnegan Frotz, his elaborate tattoo, his band, and a field agent taskforce referred to as *Coven of Bitches*.

"Well I'll be damned," Fadil swore, "This guy has my reset code tattooed on his ass?! How bizarre is that?

Fortunately nobody seems to know what it means. Not yet, anyway. Well, it's not a random and completely unheard-of sequence of numbers, though – in a certain computer programming language, too ancient for you to know anything about…"

"Hey!" Fabiola snapped her fingers in front of Fadil's face. "Geekland, remember? Let's focus on the job, shall we? How can we take advantage of what we know now?"

Fadil scratched his head and pondered. "Hmmm…" It seemed that was all he had to say.

Fabiola grabbed Fadil's mouse and played a track by Cynicism Management. All of the fabulous musical compositions recovered from Randy's computer were in the archives. It was one of the tracks already recorded by Randy, Finnegan and Amalia during one of their so-called "online collaborations".

TV TURNS ON YOU
[https://soundcloud.com/cynicism-management/
tv-turns-on-you-augmented]

I can't wait to flush my face
In flickers of the human race
All of this I may despise
But it sustains my dreary life
Need some genuine heartfelt screams
To liven up my stillborn dreams
I need some blood I need some pain
I need to think that I'm still sane

I'm so bored, I want more
Need some gore, need some gore

TV turned on me
I can almost see now

I turn it on
'Cause it turns me off

As I cease to be
It turns on me

Madness greed blood screeching tearing
Never subside no retreat no
Shelter inside all because of
Hatred fear wrath I've seen all the
Liars tell lies sold-out assholes
Anger bursts out misdirected
Preachers spread blight murder all the
Sense that we might have left out there

Omens portend we are failing
Massacred and entrails trailing
Final dead end we are nearing
Pestilence dread disappearing
Poisoned this place killed bystanders
Utter disgrace parasitic
Malice! We waste good intentions
Straying so far from redemption
Doomed

Anger bursts out misdirected
Preachers spread blight unsuspected
Omens portend we are failing
Utter disgrace parasitic
Liars tell lies sold-out assholes
Sense that we might have things left there
Malice! We waste good intentions
Straying so far from redemption
What a relief this can't happen
Ever to me, I just watch some
TV

It was a rather lengthy song. Fadil rolled his eyes – it wasn't his cup of tea. Fabiola listened for a while, nodding to the heavy guitar riffs, thinking, and then brainstormed out loud: "Let's see. We've got agents investigating a rock band consisting of a bunch of loons who have nothing to do with you, even though the OIA seems to think you're connected somehow because of that number of yours. They seem to be harmless weirdoes and pretty inconsequential, nobody's even heard of them… Though I find their tracks quite interesting, I must say." She smiled and waved the sign of the horns in front of Fadil's nose. "I know, my taste in music is slightly unconventional, so who am I to say."

"Yeah, and apparently the OIA is obsessing about the possibility that something might be encoded in the music these guys make…" Fadil suddenly stiffened, his mouth hanging open, and stared into some unknown distance.

"Fadil?" Fabiola raised an eyebrow.

"That's it!" It must have been one of his eureka moments. "Shit, we could… That's it, we could do it! We could do what those bastards at the OIA have been worrying about all along, and it would be quite simple, too!"

"What is it? What's going on?"

"Sorry if I venture into the realm geekdom again," the excited Fadil blabbered hastily. "Look, the nanites are capable of receiving information in a number of ways, which have been put in place so that we can give them instructions, update them with new software, and so on and so forth. Usually this is done via a wireless computer connection, or, in case of large-scale updates, a satellite link. But we've also added another intuitive and very handy way of instructing the nanobots: they can receive messages via one's sense of hearing. The purpose of that was to provide an option to command the intra-body nanites within ourselves orally, so that we can simply tell them what to do… Though proper codes or encoded signals need to be used to prevent accidental instructions, obviously. That's been implemented to provide the foundations for the most natural of interfaces, so that we can control the nanites without needing computers all the time, like when we are out in the field and so on. It was foresight, to provide a platform for future functionality. The feature is not fully functional yet, so nanites cannot actually understand plain spoken language or anything like that at this time, but we could use their existing sound detection capability to get an audio-encoded system message across by means of..."

"Yeah, yeah, I suppose I get the gist of it, so what? Does that mean you can just order the damn machines to shut down by telling them to do so?"

"Essentially, yes! I could encode the numbers as a sound wave in a way that they'll understand! Something similar to how computer programmes used to be stored on audio tapes once upon a time."

"Audio tapes? What're you talking about, old chap?" Fabiola laughed and poked Fadil in the ribs.

"Yeah, yeah, I know, ancient history. Anyway, I can turn the reset code into an audio signal. The nanites inside anyone who hears that audio signal should reset, pausing for new orders for two minutes and, when there aren't any, shut down and flush out. Shit, we could broadcast this over the radio, TV, internet streams even..."

"Ha!" Fabiola slapped her knee, "TV Turns On You, what a bizarrely well-fitting title! That's bloody marvellous!"

"But how to reset every nanite on the planet at the same time..." Fadil narrowed his eyes.

"Why complicate things so much? What you're basically saying is, if I understand you correctly, that I could also play this reset signal for Fergus over the in-game voice chat or send him an mp3, and he'd be OK, right? Then he could just proceed with the original plan."

"Shit, girl, you're a genius!"

A couple of hours later Fergus heard an annoying sound in his headphones: *the nanite reset signal* **[https://soundcloud. com/cynicism-management/nanite-reset-signal].**

Suddenly his mind started clearing up and he could focus on a message from Favielle – his beloved Fabbie – screaming at him from the guild chat window:

"HEY, YOU SQUIRT, PAY ATTENTION, WILL
YA?! This is your sis, Fabiola. You
have exactly 2 minutes to read this, so
hurry. You'll be yourself again shortly.
But you'll have a bad case of diarrhoea
for a couple of hours. Don't worry,
it's all good, I'll explain everything. DON'T SAY ANYTHING TO ANYONE,
YOU HEAR?! This is EXTREMELY IMPORTANT!
Just pretend you still can't talk!!!
When you're done soiling the toilet,
hurry back, I'll be waiting for you in
WoW. Love you!! P.S.: grab something to
read, you'll be stuck in the crapper
for a while."

54. Operation Watering Hole: Home Invasion

"I'm getting sick of this." Serbian Bitch complained to Another One as for the second time in two days they walked towards the apartment where half of the Cynicism Management band members lived. "We've only been working as secret agents for four days and it's already turning out to be total crap. I've been told that the vast majority of field agents are either despondent drunks or they pop Prozac every morning. I'm no longer surprised about that. You'd think it would be a far more spectacular job, a calling considerably more purposeful and consequential than listening in on a bunch of depressing conversations and sneaking around people's apartments, scratching their silly and smelly though admittedly cute n' cuddly dog behind its ear."

"Really! Would you rather more excitement in the form of a bloodthirsty cat while breaking and entering somebody's pub?" Another One took the opportunity to have a little laugh at Serbian Bitch's expense.

"Oh, come on now, you know what I mean," Serbian Bitch grumbled and touched the slowly-healing claw marks on her face. "This job got highly annoying surprisingly quickly and I think it would be a lot more entertaining if those creepy OIA stalkers weren't breathing down our necks, looking so dead serious and judgemental all the time. They're making me nervous."

"I hear you," Another One sighed as they kept walking through the colourful streets of the Ljubljana's Old Town.

Meanwhile, back in Yoman, Fabiola and Fadil were waiting for Fergus to do his business and return from the restroom. While World of Warcraft was running on Fadil's laptop, showing Loopy with an *"away from keyboard"* tag under his name, Fadil and Fabiola kept monitoring the data streams that the bugs were transmitting from Slovenia. Suddenly Fadil noticed another connection pop up. Out of curiosity he tuned in.

"This one's called *Bitches*. Let's see..." It was the same communication protocol as the spy roaches, but this time it looked like the transmission was coming from some form of eyewear – a helmet or glasses or even contact lenses – making use of the same communication nanotechnology Fadil was very familiar with.

"Well, here we are," said Arch Bitch, "I'll wait out here and watch the street, just like last time," Another One said and found herself a comfortable spot in a nearby pub – the one where the smug waiter who liked music for conceited intellectuals worked. Another One didn't care for the music, but she did enjoy the pleasant wooden tables lining the pavement in front of the pub: a cosy setting, cool beer, and a good view of everything that went on up and down the busy narrow main street of the Old Town.

Serbian Bitch headed towards the apartment, avoiding some loser on the staircase whose eyes she felt on her bum as she walked by, and let herself in with her precious israel again. This time she was prepared for the imminent appearance of the excessively friendly dog. Actually, she was almost looking forward to it. After Paloma Mala collected the entrance fee in the form of an intense jumping and petting session, she left Serbian Bitch alone and went to check if anything had miraculously materialised in her food bowl in the meantime. When she saw that nothing had, she fetched her rubber chicken from under the coffee table in the living room so as to satisfy her chewing cravings with that instead.

Serbian Bitch headed into the kitchen to install one of their tiny microphones. "That'll probably do, open that cupboard," The Watcher said in her ear.

Serbian Bitch agreed and looked around inside. Some corn flakes, soy sauce, booze, and something called *Čokolino* (she smiled at the sight, remembering the tasty chocolaty gunk from the now deceased Yugoslavia – it seemed to have outlived the country where it had been invented).

"Where do you want the microphone, then?" Serbian Bitch asked. "Oh, what's this?" she asked as an instant message from the OIA Agent in charge of the Bitches appeared on her head-up display, in glaring matrix-green monochrome letters on black background, screaming: "Check whatever's in the corner marked *'Property of professor Winegirl'*."

"Why are you typing all over my HUD all of a sudden?" Serbian Bitch asked The Watcher. She was hearing commotion over her headphones.

"Shit!" The Watcher blurted out in the motel, obviously shocked at seeing the green message appear on the screen that displayed the video feed from Serbian Bitch.

"What is it?" Arch Bitch scowled.

"They're watching the audio and video feed from our spy glasses in real time!"

"But I thought you had to send them data after every mission!"

"Yeah... It turns out that maybe the data uploading was just supposed to make us think we had some control over what they saw and heard. They've been watching us in real time all along. Weren't you?!" The Watcher yelled into the microphone. "How nice of you to let us know!"

After a short pause another message appeared: "We didn't think it was necessary, you might have objected or felt too much pressure if you knew. Now you know. Just proceed with the mission."

"Why the heck are you writing this? Don't you have a microphone, damn it?" The Watcher barked with righteous indignation.

She heard a click as an audio connection was established: "I thought it would be more ominous this way. I have a flair for the dramatic, you see," the Agent said into the ears of all the Bitches.

In the background somebody else laughed.

"Fine, now you know," the Agent droned on calmly. "Look, don't feel so bad about it – we don't care if we see you going to the toilet or picking your noses. We don't even give a damn if you talk about us behind our backs. You just need to get the job done or my boss will castrate me. Oops, maybe I shouldn't have said that. He's probably watching us, too, if he's not spying on someone else. Whatever, you should just get used to how this works. Now stop dawdling and get on with your mission."

Serbian Bitch was too busy dealing with this revelation while peering into the special nook marked *"Property of professor Winegirl – do not touch!"* to notice the sudden extreme excitement of the Deathbreath Rock 'n' Roll Bitch, who darted into the hallway merrily. As Serbian Bitch, standing on her toes, stuck her hand behind Amalia's vodka bottle and felt around, checking whether something incriminating might be stashed in the back of the cupboard, somebody grabbed her from behind.

On his screen in London, the Agent heard Serbian Bitch yelp. The picture rolled as her spy glasses tumbled to the floor. They lay there showing two pairs of feet dancing wildly for a few seconds, and then somebody tackled Serbian Bitch. She fell onto her back. Someone turned her over, squashing her claw-marked cheek against the floor beside her spy glasses. A man knelt on her back and tied her hands expertly with a belt. After he disabled and immobilised her, he picked her up and sat her on one of the kitchen chairs. The glasses kept transmitting the sound and image of her and the man from the waist down. He pulled up a chair and sat down, facing her.

On Fadil's laptop in Yoman, Loopy's *"away from keyboard"* status cleared and the little gnome came alive.

"Fergus is back!" Fabiola cheered.

"Excellent! Let's fill him in on the situation," Fadil said. "He'll remember everything that happened while he was under the influence of the nanites. His memories should be intact, including his computer knowledge. So this shouldn't take too long. He already knows what he's supposed to do and why, all of the neural pathways are still there, it's just that he's no longer influenced by the nanites, he's in command of himself again."

Fabiola initiated a video chat with Fergus. Meanwhile, Fadil kept one eye on the other monitor to see what was going on with the Bitches. Fergus was promptly briefed by his sister, whose hair, in his opinion, looked much better now – he hadn't appreciated her wild-purple phase and found it stupid and childish. He was overjoyed at the sight of her.

Fergus and his sister might have had their differences, but he trusted her implicitly. He took the news that his father and the OIA had planned the kidnapping better than expected and said that after what he'd experienced during the inter-rogation and indoctrination in The Lab, he wasn't surprised at all. "You should have been there. I'm not sure we can blame dad for everything, though," he told Fabiola, almost whispering so the guards posted outside wouldn't hear him. "It looks like he isn't the big boss we thought he was, he had to listen to those secret agents and the Doctor. But he was also there with them when I woke up and when they gave me more of those creepy machines. He didn't say anything, he just let them do it. I'll be glad to put a stop to all those nanobots, they stink! OK, maybe not the ones that Habib gave me, I kind of like all the computer stuff I know now," Fergus's eyes sparkled as he catalogued the unsurpassed geek heaven which had been etched into his mind.

"Looks like traditional schools are coming to an end. That's too bad," Fabiola rubbed her hands and smiled happily. "Did anyone notice anything strange about you? The guards... Or anyone else?"

"Nope," Fergus whispered, "They all think I'm still, you

know… Confused."

"Awesome!"

They closed the video chat and Fergus logged on to Faarghuz the mighty undead priest to await further instructions like a good soldier.

Fifteen minutes later, Finnegan's phone rang at the Rock 'n' Roll Tavern: "Hei," Desidéria chirped into his ear and passed the phone to someone else.

The man in the kitchen, eyeing his prisoner suspiciously, said: "Finn? It's Chuck. Yeah, Dessy's 'toy boy', thank you very much. Look, come home, I caught a burglar in yer kitchen, red-handed, so to speak. Nah, I'm not kiddin'. I was waitin' on the stairway for Dessy to come home, you know, to find out why she threw me out like she did, to make up, maybe… Yeah, I agree, she's quite a 'colourful character', you've got that right…" Chuck glanced at Desidéria standing nearby. "Sure. Hell yeah! Well, listen, so there I am, sittin' on the stairs in the lobby, waitin'. This chick walks right by me and for some reason I check out where she's g… No, she's not particularly good-lookin', but she's got a great figure, tight ass, that's why, yeah," Chuck smiled at Serbian Bitch but thought better of it when he noticed that Désideria was giving him the evil eye. "So she walked by without payin' any attention to me, but I kinda was watching where she went out of pure boredom, y'know, and then I saw her open yer door with some lock pick thingy. Nope, never saw the 'bird', as you put it, before. Yeah, I did. I went in, snuck up behind her and brought her down with my awesome U.S. Marine Corps skills… She fought back, too, the bitch. Yeah. Yeah, I got 'er here, I called Dessy up, told 'er about it, and she came home as soon as she could. Of course, yeah, I didn't have yer number myself. Yeah, she had all yer numbers, Amalia, you, Randy, and that crazy dude who dropped by the other day. Yeah, Bogomyr. Alright, see ya soon, bye."

In Yoman, Fadil and Fabiola exchanged amused glances. "Looks like we might finally get to meet the Coven of Bitches in person. The situation doesn't look good, though. Omnipile's Security Service forces will surely intervene immediately... Wait, this might be a good opportunity to make a diversion for Fergus!" Fadil said.

"What do you mean?"

"Fergus is confined to his room and guarded at all times, right? So, if we want him to gain access to your dad's terminal unnoticed, we'll need to get his guards out of the way. We'll need to provide some kind of cover for him, something he can tell them, a reason why he's better all of a sudden, something to make your dad leave him alone and call off the guards..." Fadil said, scheming, his ability to come up with cunning plans shifting gears like a desperate Formula One driver entering a life-or-death lap. "We could sever the Bitches' connections and convince them they need to hide. Finnegan and his guys, too. The more trouble Omnipile has finding them, the more the OSS and the OIA will look in the wrong direction and then we can mount a surprise offensive back home. The Bitches and the band shouldn't resist or run too much, though, we don't want anyone to get injured or even killed, we just need to create enough chaos to distract the OIA... How to contact Finnegan immediately... That's it, through the Bitches, and we better do that right now! Finnegan should be talking to Serbian Bitch in less than half an hour."

"Won't the OIA see you contacting them? You know, through the video feeds and everything?"

"That's precisely what I want. I'll relay our communications through the bugs," Fadil said, hammering on his keyboard and poking at his mouse. "OK, here, these look like fun, the roach group called *Fidel*. If the diversion reminds the OIA of communist revolutions for any reason at all, that'll make them freak out even more. To them and to the Bitches it will appear that my signal is coming from Ljubljana. I'll even introduce myself, that should make the OSS and the OIA jump and deploy their forces within the next couple hours. In the meantime, Fergus should be able to end this before they even begin to figure out what's going on and start suspecting I'm nowhere near Ljubljana. They'll believe I'm there, too, they're actually expecting me to be in contact with Finnegan because of that tattoo."

"My my, you're very good at this for a geeky scientist."

"I read a lot of pulp fiction..." Fadil remarked absent-mindedly as he hammered on the keyboard and connected to the spy roaches in Largo's flat. Since Largo was not into vacuuming and disinfecting his abode all that much, their numbers were highly stable and their connection strong. "Let's see what trouble we can stir up."

An extreme close-up of Fadil appeared on The Watcher's computer screen. The startled OIA Agents back in London struggled to make sense of it. "Hello," the face told the Bitches at the motel, "I'm Dr Fadil Dajani." The Lab went to red alert immediately.

About twenty minutes after making contact with them, The Watcher and Arch Bitch, biting their nails in their little motel, decided that it was time to make a decision. At the thought of oil rigs in Antarctica, which Fadil told them about with a naughty little smile lining his lips, they agreed it would be best to avoid the OIA for the time being. Fadil then started shutting down some of the connections, and to the extreme fury of the OIA Agents back in London, certain vital video and audio feeds started disappearing.

Back in the apartment, Serbian Bitch pondered what to tell the curious Finnegan, frowning Amalia and glassy-eyed Randy who had just arrived. To her great relief – although she didn't know what was going on at that point – the doorbell rang. It turned out to be Another One, who started telling Finnegan that the situation was extremely urgent and persuaded him to put on Serbian Bitch's spy glasses. Through the head-up display, Dr Fadil Dajani told Finnegan and the others that they needed to leave the apartment immediately. A description of his elaborate tattoo and the footage of his bum from the airport toilet removed any remaining doubts about whether he should do what Fadil said or not. "Oi! So that's how it looks? Kinky..." Finnegan blurted out at the sight of his posterior.

The Bitches, Finnegan, Amalia and Randy retreated to the smug waiter pub below their apartment to talk things over. They agreed with Fadil that it wouldn't be prudent to run too far and tempt the OIA and OSS Agents to use excessive force, but the pub was so stupidly close to their apartment that it would almost assuredly make a very unlikely hiding place. The Agents should be kept busy for a while. At the same time it was a public place, so if the foreign paramilitary forces finally found them there, it wouldn't be easy for them to do anything too drastic. The three bandmates and the Bitches were soon joined by Kip Ducker, who was too worried about the burglary to stay at Boris and Beeba's with Bogomyr, Largo and the others – though maybe his concern was just a convenient excuse to get out and not have to listen to all the endless idiotic prattle at Boris's anymore.

Fabiola joined Fadil behind his monitor. Now that Fadil had shut down all the unwanted connections and the OIA was in the dark, he was busy explaining the situation through The Watcher's fancy laptop. At the sight of their bleak demeanour, Fabiola popped her face in front of Fadil's camera and told the band: "Hey, why won't you guys lighten up, maybe you'll get famous after this. Every cloud has a silver lining, you know."

Finnegan gloomily responded with one of his little atheist's proverbs: "I don't agree. As far as I'm concerned, every cloud with a silver lining more likely has ulterior motives. Try explaining your silver lining theory to pancreatic cancer patients."

Fabiola laughed, taking an immediate liking to the ascending rock star.

"Oh! I have an idea," Largo proposed out of the blue.

"Perhaps we could use the nanites to bring about a new communist revolution, perhaps even a slightly improved version this time? You know, maybe we could make future politicians understand Karl Marx and the struggle of their fellow human beings, albeit belonging to a slightly different social stratum, without resorting to the unusually persistent impulse to line their pockets and abuse their power once they seize control?"

"Largo... You're just being naive," Finnegan said. "Sure, quite similarly I've also toyed with the idea that perhaps we could mind-control everyone on the planet to listen to our songs. But do you think that would be fun at all? If such an unlikely scenario would actually become reality – you know, if everyone started listening to us – we would, for all intents and purposes, be playing pop."

Finnegan pronounced the word "pop" with such poppy Ps that his indignation was clear even to the smug waiter, who was loitering on the other side of the pub and daydreaming about which song he could punish his guests with next.

"And if we suddenly found ourselves playing pop," Finnegan went on, "we'd have to create something new so we wouldn't end up resembling everyone else. So we're better off sticking with doing the music we like rather than worry about being adored by the masses. In any case, being adored by the masses is thoroughly overrated, anyway. Apart from the money, that is, but I for one prefer being adored by a sexy lass with an urge to make her cunny available to me at all times, regardless of whatever any masses might think of anything."

Largo wasn't sure if he understood what Finnegan was on about, but applying the general concept expressed by the wordy Scotsman to his socialist endeavours he was able to come up with at least one positive consequence of capitalist exploitation: if nobody ever exploited anyone, it could become sort of difficult to keep the permanent revolution going...

After some lengthy discussion and a bit of careful planning, Finnegan called in some favours at Radio Kirkwall. Then he also phoned Bogomyr, explained what was going on, and told everyone still drinking beer at the Rock 'n' Roll Tavern to migrate to another drinking establishment before the proverbial shit hit the fan.

Almost as soon as Finnegan hung up, they all noticed through the windows a number of unsavoury characters, running around outside the smug waiter pub and barely concealing their bullet-proof vests and particularly deadly-looking handguns.

55. The Chase

The first place the hefty Security Forces chaps stormed was, of course, Largo "Fidel" Cabaleri's bachelor's pad. To their utter disappointment, Dr Fadil Dajani was not there, and neither was anyone else who might scream *"viva la revolución"* and sing *The Internationale* while they were dragging him or her out of there while zealously using instruments of pain induction on their softest spots.

Back at the *Cynicism Management* abode, the mighty Chuck, happy that everyone else had gone out, was about to be compensated for the courage and heroism he'd displayed in the recent Battle of the Kitchen. Desidéria had slipped into the bathroom with some new lingerie and toys she'd just brought from the local sex shop, hinting that she was about to do something real special for him as a reward for being such a hunk. So Chuck put a porn flick on Desidéria's TV and then peeled off his clothes, letting them fall to the floor before making himself comfortable on her bed.

Just about the time when he started clenching his fists, trying to keep his hands from his little private that saluted at the highly intriguing plot unwinding on the TV screen as well as at the promise of the imminent appearance of the silky-soft and endlessly succulent Desidéria, he heard something that sounded like a squad of special forces tearing the door off its hinges and charging into the apartment. His Marine Corps training kicking in instantly, G.I. Chuck jumped from the bed and peeked through the bedroom door keyhole just in time to see a mountain of a man with a deadly-looking weapon Chuck had never seen before yell "clear!" from the kitchen. The intrepid marine knew when it was time to retreat and regroup. He grabbed his phone, his wallet and some clothes from the chair and took immediate evasive action by leaping through

the bedroom window butt naked. He only realised too late that
the bunch of clothes he had been able to snatch up from the
chair before fleeing had only consisted of Desidérias oversize
T-shirt, a push-up bra, and a pair of pink lace knickers.

Ten minutes later, after they had thrown Desidéria, clad
in nothing but her terrycloth bathrobe and with her hair still
wet, into their menacing black van, the hefty Omnipile Security
Service chaps were loitering in the street in front of the pub.
They probably wouldn't have found Finnegan, Amalia, Randy
and the six Bitches, had one of them not popped inside to take
a leak. As the enforcer was about to ask the smug waiter where
the restroom was, his mouth dropped open as he noticed their
quarry acting all innocent in the far corner.

"How pronouncedly baleful," Accumulator of Unwonted
Locutions stated as the OSS forces asked them to kindly get
into the van. Kip Ducker, who'd been to the toilet himself in
the meantime, came out just in time to see the agents search
everyone and confiscate their phones and laptops. He was such
an unassuming guy that nobody paid any attention to him, so
he just sat at the bar and blended in with the walls until the
Omnipile Security Forces cleared out of the bar. In the same
way – wearing his invisibility cloak – he left the pub and got
into his car without anyone noticing him.

Kip followed the van to the outskirts of the city without
being spotted. It wasn't much of an achievement: the van's
British driver, newly arrived in Slovenia, struggled to keep his
cool, meandering down what was, for him, the wrong side of
the street. He drove like Ray Kosmick's grandma, while around
him all sorts of crazy Slovenian race car drivers were throwing
apocalyptic fits and suffering a series of nervous breakdowns,
which distracted and annoyed the Brit even more. Kip, although
Australian himself, had already gotten used to putting up with
the local maniacs as well as to driving on the right by then.

The van drove through a tall wrought iron driveway
gate. Kip parked his car out of sight and called Largo. No
answer. They must have got him, too. Kip tried Bogomyr, and,
to his relief, the unremarkable vampire picked up. He sounded

completely out of breath.

"Jesus..." he panted over the phone, "You won't... believe this, mate... Ah... Jeez... Just wait a second, will you... Gotta... catch my breath..." Bogomyr wheezed and panted like a broken locomotive for a couple of minutes before he was able to talk:

"Hell, man, that was intense," he told Kip. "Whoa, I'm really not in very good shape, it's about time I put a stop to this full-time nightlife of mine... Where are you, are you OK?"

"Yeah, they took everyone else away, but they didn't see me."

"Wow, you're lucky."

"What happened to you?"

"Well, we were just hanging out here at Boris's minding our own business when the phone rang. It was Finnegan and he told us the whole story. We decided to go up to the bar by the church, you know, to prevent those fucks from catching us right away, and, more importantly, to be in a public place when they found us so no one would get hurt. Just like you did. Boris's wasn't really much of a public place, you know, we were the only people there today. But..."

But things went wrong. Another one of those menacing black vans – the one that had been sent to Largo's apartment earlier – approached just as Largo, Bogomyr, Ray and Willit stepped out to the Jimi Hendrix parking lot all casual and actually looking forward to a drink somewhere else for a change. The driver slammed on the breaks and a mob of hefty men, eager to make up for their failure to beat the crap out of someone at Largo's earlier, pulled out their tasers, stun batons and similar discomfort-inducing implements, and jumped out of the van. As they leapt out in the direction of the Jimi Hendrix graffito, the startled tipsy quartet sobered up immediately and, not particularly eager to experience the wrath of the goons, dashed off and up the hill towards the village. If they could at least reach some people before the vicious security persons caught up with them, maybe their pursuers would be forced to get in touch with their gentler sides.

From their lookout spots, the drunken hunters who had

been designated to keep an eye out for tourists noticed a bunch
of people fitting that description running up the hill towards
the bar by the church. To the hunters, these prospective targets
looked terrifically thirsty and eager to get to where they were
going. So they sounded the tourist alarm.

By the time the breathless quarry with the OSS forces
on their heels reached the top of the hill, they were intercepted by a crowd of villagers in ethnic outfits. The sound of
accordions filled the air, blessing Down Below the Hill with
the merriest of Alpine dancing songs. Apple strudel, potica,
prosciutto and other assorted mouth-watering cured meats
were on display, wine and schnapps being poured, and tickets
to the Romanesque church, the ossuary and the Hillstone
monolith being offered. The Mayor awaited the guests with
open arms next to the stands peddling – as the villagers had
planned – a broad range of memorabilia. Sadly, the first four
guests tried to push their way through the villagers, while
the larger, stronger and more fit-looking tourists in menacing
militaristic outfits jumped the leading quartet. The accordions coughed and lost their breath, the half-naked local
exhibitionist trollop in her quasi-traditional folk-whore outfit
screamed, and the strange guests knocked over the memorabilia stands. Bogomyr was somehow able to take advantage
of the pandemonium and vanish amidst the rain of unique
Easter eggs, miniature figurines dressed in folk attire and
Shrovetide costumes, lacework, Alpine dancing song albums by
the local world champion of accordion, and the little Hillstone
pendants, infused with mystical energies by none other than Dr
Drago Dabić himself. He dashed across the nearby graveyard,
zigzagging between the gravestones, finding some comfort
and confidence in the close proximity of coffins. Just before
he reached the woods on the other side, a peculiar gravestone
briefly caught his eye. It belonged – at least that was what it
said – to some woman named Amalija Pavlin, née Vajngerl, who
died in 1889. *"How bizarre is that?"* the fleeing reformed vampire
thought. *"Maybe Amalia's lineage can in fact be traced back to this
country, just like she suspected."*

However, Bogomyr quickly put off thinking about irrelevant trivialities so as to focus on vanishing among the trees.

"How the hell did you manage to get away?" Kip asked on the phone.

"It's just a little old magic trick I learned as a creature of the night – you just turn into mist and dissipate."

"Ah, one of those tricks you do in your late-night exotic dance performances?"

"Well, something like that, yeah. Man, if all those weird people hadn't been gathered there for whatever reason so that all hell broke loose, I'd never have got away," Bogomyr nodded with the phone against his ear, leaning against the giant outlandish monolith in the middle of the forest. Omnipile Security hadn't caught him. Maybe he had the mysterious powers of the Hillstone to thank. "Let's wait till the air is clear, OK? Talk to you later," Bogomyr said and put his phone away.

Five minutes later the phone rang again. It was an unknown number, but Bogomyr decided to pick up anyway.

"Hey, man! Chuck here. I don't know if you remember me, Dessy's friend?" Chuck whispered, hiding behind a dumpster in a back alley. "Yeah, her 'toy boy', thank you very much. Listen, they took Dessy... How can I explain this... Oh. What d'you mean you know? Is that so? Shit, you have to fill me in, man, I ain't got a fuckin' clue what's up. No. Yeah, dude, I'm in deep shit here. You gotta help me out. I didn't know who else to call. Thank god Des gave me your number earlier when I needed to call Finn... Yeah, when I caught the burglar. Listen, I kinda like the girl, and I let 'er down real bad back there, I gotta make up for it... Yeah, of course I wanna bang her again, what do you think?!"

A wino shuffled by, a soggy cigarette hanging from the corner of his mouth. He gave Chuck a cross-eyed look, coughed, let out a raspy snicker, and said something in Slovenian. The message he meant to convey to the U.S. marine, who currently looked nothing like a soldier nor understood a word of it, was the following: "Nice outfit, darling! Celebrating summer, eh? Love is in the air and all that, eh?"

56. Captive

"This feels odd... But still, it's kind of nice! I must admit that when I left Portugal I thought I'd be able to learn foreign languages pretty quickly. Turns out I was right," Desidéria chirped.

"Yeah, it's a funny feeling. I have no problem either speaking or thinking in English now. I'm sure I could even write without even a hint of dyslexia," Beeba smiled.

"Yeah, superb! Now I'll be able to communicate with the English-speaking adult film market without any problem at all," Ray said. "I wonder if Omnipile might also hook me up with some German, I could use that at the Venus Porn Fair in Berlin. Italian would be very handy, too."

Everyone now being held captive in a large house on the outskirts of Ljubljana that belonged to the Omnipile Intelligence Agency had been injected with nanites almost as soon as they were herded through the door.

Back at The Lab, the technicians overseeing the procedure remotely immediately noticed a surprising side effect of indoctrinating foreigners: everybody suddenly spoke English. Perhaps it was because the operating system of the communication and indoctrination nanites had not yet been localised into any other languages yet, so the first thing the nanites did was to simply teach their hosts the language.

Be that as it may, the technicians decided that perhaps they should address this issue before they turned the whole population of Yoman into new consumers of English literature. "Not that Omnipile-owned publishing houses would mind new markets, especially in view of the crisis that book publishing is currently in," one of the technicians said, "However, due to this side effect it might be fairly easy to figure out who among foreigners who hadn't generally spoken

486

English very fluently has been indoctrinated."

Everyone who'd been caught in their net – all the Bitches, Finnegan, Amalia, Randy, Largo, Willit, Ray, Desidéria, even Boris and Beeba – was being held prisoner in a large room with military-style bunk beds, some ordinary tables and chairs, a small separate bathroom, and another small toilet for emergencies. Three walls were solid concrete, and the floor was imitation stone laminate. The neon lights and lack of any windows or sounds suggested the place must have been a soundproof basement, although – fortunately for those who'd arrived in more liberal summer style clothing – it wasn't too chilly, just pleasantly cool. The fourth wall and the door, though, consisted of iron bars. Probably that was so that the prisoners would appreciate their situation while the guard posted on the other side of the bars at all times had, apart from his desk lined with security monitors, an unobstructed view of the room except for the bathroom and additional toilet cubicle... Which he could, unbeknownst to his involuntary guests, observe on his monitors, though.

Arch Bitch wondered how in the hell Omnipile could have had access to such a rather conveniently-equipped facility so quickly. It wouldn't have been a terrible shock to her to learn that Omnipile had these kinds of so-called "business embassies" all over the world, or that each one of them had a basement like this, just for those times when their "business partners" were in need of some persuasion.

"They could've at least let you take some clothes," Beeba said to Desidéria, who sat legs crossed in the corner wrapped in nothing but her bathrobe.

Ray chuckled and tried to peer under the terrycloth: "Nah, that's alright. Looks like they didn't mind her choice of garment and neither do I."

Desidéria glared at him and contemplated whether she should liven things up by engaging in another superior-accuracy supersonic-speed slapping session, but decided to get up resolutely and make a show out of her distaste for the vulgar beer-bellied porn expert. Walking away from Ray in protest, she joined Randy instead, who, sitting on his bunk in the opposite corner, looked rather lost.

"Hey, Randy," she chirped.

"Hey! Wh...?! What's going on?" he looked at her and coughed.

"Mind if I sit down?"

"No, of course..." he moved over and made some room for her on his bed.

"Look... Now that we can finally communicate, I'd like to talk to you," she smiled shyly.

"Yeah... Of course, what's up?" Randy couldn't help noticing how absolutely adorable and fresh she appeared in her bathrobe despite her recent unlawful and violent arrest by the Omnipile Security Forces.

"I need to take advantage of my new linguistic ability and explain something to you just in case I wake up tomorrow only to discover I've forgotten English for some reason. So, to quit beating around the bush... Randy, I love you!"

"What are you talking about?"

"Look, I know you probably don't remember, because your memory doesn't seem to be what it was once upon a time, but when we met that evening in that bar, just a few days after I'd arrived in Ljubljana, it seemed like we had fallen for each other right away. It was real love at first sight. That had never happened to me before, but it was all for real. At least from my perspective. You see, I didn't know how to speak English back then, but I could understand it just fine. But that evening you somehow... Miraculously, it was like you could understand me, too. Yes, now that I think of it, back then it appeared like you understood me really well, even if later on you frequently claimed you had no idea what I was going on about. That's strange, now that I think about it...

"Anyway, despite all our communication problems I managed somehow to get through to you and explain that I'd love to go home with you, but I wanted to take it easy because I hadn't had much experience with men. But you professed your eternal love for me, told me you'd do anything for me, swore you'd marry me and father my children... You wanted me to move in with you right then and there. Well, you were so darn cute and I was so hopelessly naive that I believed you. I hadn't even unpacked at the apartment I was staying at then, and I didn't much like the place anyway. It was as small and damp and musty as it was expensive. So we went to pick up my things and there I was all of a sudden, in your room as your roommate, and before you know it – like, in a minute or two – poof! My virtue was a thing of the past. I found sex awesome, though, and couldn't get enough of it," she smiled adoringly and blushed.

Randy wanted to say something, but Desidéria put her finger on his lips. She wanted to finish what she had to say first. "Anyway," she went on, "Naive as I was, I hadn't noticed you must have been plastered and stoned out of your mind. God only knows what you were on that night. It was great, though. I couldn't get enough of you and your little randy rod – that's what you called it..." She glanced at his crotch and Randy looked around embarrassed, checking to see if anyone happened to be listening. Many of their fellow prisoners were indeed doing precisely that – what else was there to do – and on the nearby bed Amalia and Finnegan were cracking up like a couple of hysterical teenagers.

"And you..." Desidéria bit her lip and blushed, "You couldn't get enough of me and we kept at it all night, only falling asleep after the sun was already up. You must have gone to the toilet while I was asleep, because when I woke up, you were snoring away in the other bed across the room. I thought maybe you just needed some space – the bed we'd been cuddling up on wasn't exactly king size. But when you woke up, you didn't seem to know me at all!"

"Oh!" Randy blurted out. "Erm..."

"Yeah, it seemed you'd forgotten all about our engagement and eternal love and all that. I don't think you were even aware we'd had sex."

"No, no, I remember that, of course. I think. But... Is that how it happened? Well, I remember Amalia and I'd been looking for a roommate. The flat's expensive, so we needed someone else to share the expenses with. So, as I remember it, we met, took a liking to each other, and I invited you to... You know, become my roommate. One thing I don't remember must have led to others I don't recall, and I may have been somewhat out of it, you know... Confused. Especially the next morning, because I didn't remember anything much... Besides, I couldn't understand a word you were saying! You realise how confusing that was, right?"

"Oh, god, you're such a loser. I must say I wasn't exactly thrilled about the way you acted that morning. Actually I felt you were just a plain old bastard. But still, after that... All those other boyfriends of mine and so on... That was only because I wanted to make you jealous! Well, that and, frankly, because I simply can't get enough hot sex. But it was mostly to make you jealous, to make you love me again. I'd much prefer having all that sex with you, though."

"Really?!"

"Absolutely, it's you I wanted all along! Jesus, you're such a jerk!" she turned towards Randy and put her hands on her hips theatrically, parting her bathrobe enough for him to catch a glimpse of her irresistible feminine attributes.

"If you say so..." Randy Jiggler submitted.

"So, what are we going to do about it?" the Portuguese lass inquired.

"I don't know..." the insecure bass player muttered indecisively.

"But I do!" Desidéria decided, grabbed Randy and kissed him passionately. Randy's little randy rod came to attention right away and the room and everyone else around them seemed to magically disappear.

Finnegan panted and decided it was time for another one of his little atheist's proverbs. "Blessed are the meek, for they shall inherit the Earth. Does that mean everybody else will get relocated to some other less annoying piece of real estate?" he inquired of the mysterious powers of the universe and rolled his eyes theatrically.

After Randy and Desidéria had returned from the bathroom not even two minutes later, the guard, his cheeks rather flushed, eyed them enviously. For a second or two, Randy rummaged through his pockets in search of some post-coital Mary Jane for him and his rekindled flame, having forgotten that his stash had been confiscated by a couple of hefty men who were now sitting stoned under a tree behind the secluded makeshift prison, enjoying the multitude of stars above them immensely. They didn't seem to care about the mating calls and drunken songs of horny teenagers, echoing far away in the distance. For once they weren't so utterly obsessed with giving their best to their job. Instead they sailed upon the gentle summer night breeze, sang along with the crickets, and enjoyed a wonderfully colourful cascade of thoughts far more entertaining and intriguing than the usual. It was a liberating feeling for them... One they hadn't experienced in quite a while.

57. Interlude:
Herbal Haze

Randy's romantic conquests, or rather, romantic capitulations and achievements in the field of roommate acquisition inspired Finnegan and Amalia. Actually, the newest development entertained them so profoundly that they couldn't see any other alternative but to dedicate a song to Randy. Besides, writing something helped pass the time. They worked away on the lyrics with enthusiasm while Randy and Desidéria, spent after their precious minute in the bathroom, napped in each other's arms on Randy's bunk. "Who knows what's going to happen next, maybe we won't get another chance to tease a band member by dedicating a song to them," Amalia and Finnegan thought.

HERBAL HAZE
[https://soundcloud.com/cynicism-management/
herbal-haze-augmented]

Welcome dear tainted dawn
Are you to stay here long?
I plan to stay away
From your big brother day

Hello my trusted friend
Ready to make amends?
I'm yearning for your touch
Why cope with drudgery much?

And while I listen to them breathing
I want to see them fast receding
Longing for its touch

I know I don't want too much

Lead the day
And get sick get sick of it
Speed the day
There's much so much of it
Free the day
Roll it up and shrug it off
Heed your way
Feel it calling
Herbal haze became my face

58. The Bear Affair

"There," Kip pointed at the large three-storey house surrounded by a tall iron fence. Through the binoculars Chuck had grabbed after Kip had taken him back home to change after his embarrassing back-alley incident, they watched a couple of broad-shouldered and quite unpleasant-looking chaps guarding the gate.

"If I don't get Dessy outta there, she'll probably hold it against me," Chuck whined.

"You mean, she might not hold anything of hers against anything of yours anymore, at least not for a while, now that you've jumped through the window in pink knickers and left her in the bathroom to the tender mercies of those brutes over there," Bogomyr teased from the back seat.

"Oh, shut up. What else was I supposed to do?"

"I know, I know, just kidding. If you hadn't got your naked butt out of there, you'd be a prisoner too. You might even have been injured or severely killed, had you given them any trouble."

"Damn, what a mess," Kip hissed in frustration, giving the steering wheel an angry squeeze while very uncharacteristically for him rambling on: "I hate this, it's so fucking stressful. I knew I shouldn't get involved with another rock 'n' roll band. Every time I do, I regret it. It always gets me in trouble and I start feeling pressured, you know, physically." Kip touched his bald spot. "Usually it's just all the stress from playing concerts and all the obligatory sex and drugs and booze and hot teenage nymphomaniac groupies forcing themselves on me, and then I start worrying about my health 'cause it takes forever to mellow out after all that strain, but this..." he pointed at the house guarded by the private paramilitary, "This easily takes the biscuit. It's heavier by far than anything I've ever seen in my life, and I've seen lots of shit. This fucking tension..." Kip rested his hand on his rumbling acidic belly.

"That's not tension, it's hunger, we've been here all night," Chuck grumbled. He was glad to see that after a long and fantastically uneventful stakeout, even Kip had overcome his reluctance to speak out. Yet, in spite of all the open communication, the threesome still hadn't come up with a workable plan.

"Come on, guys, we gotta do somethin', what do you say?" Chuck urged them.

"Sure, I'll just walk up to those guys over there and kick them in the nuts, and then we'll just crash the car through the closed driveway gate made of inch-thick steel bars. We'll bust in there, kick everybody's ass, and get our friends out just like that. How's that for a cunning idea?" Bogomyr barked.

"I luv ya," said Bear in Underwear as Bogomyr unconsciously squeezed the toy a little too frantically. A couple of kids walking by on their way to school looked sideways at the suspicious-looking uncle Bogomyr and the disturbing-looking teddy bear clad in white lace panties that sat in his lap.

"Hmm," Kip hummed, fiddling with his phone.

"Sorry, I just feel a lot safer with my fuzzy friend around, who are you to judge...?"

"What? No, I don't give a rat's ass about your unconventional relationship with Bear in Underwear. I've just got an idea. Do you think all those security guys are mind-controlled? I'd do that if I was their boss. It would seem like a very convenient way of ensuring discipline."

Kip brooded, tapping his fingers on the steering wheel. "I have the mp3 file with the reset code that Dr Dajani sent to all of our phones just in case right here," he waved his phone. "I think we could try resetting the guards. Can't hurt to try."

Bogomyr got upset: "Are you insane? I have no desire to walk up to those two robocops over there to play an annoying screeching sound for them off my phone, especially when I'm not sure they're mind-controlled at all... What would I tell

them? 'Hey, chaps, listen to this, it really rocks'? And even if
it turns out they've got those mini robots crawling out of their
ears, they'd supposedly have exactly two minutes to knock my
teeth in, wouldn't they, which I'm sure they'd be more than
happy to do, too, by the look of them. Shit, these guys look
like they mean business," Bogomyr shuddered and passed the
binoculars back to Chuck.

"I agree," Kip said, "That's why I've hatched a cunning
plan…" He opened the door and readily fetched a tool case
from the trunk.

"I'm panicking already," Bogomyr wheezed and
squeezed his teddy bear.

"I luv ya," claimed the bear, and Kip, getting back inside
and behind the wheel, said: "Yep, the bear happens to be an
instrumental part of my scheme."

"What the hell are you talking about?"

"We can replace that nerve-wracking message of his
with the reset code and bribe one of these school kids to play
it for the guards."

Bogomyr laughed: "I can't believe the silly ideas
brewing unceremoniously inside that bald head of yours!"

"Stop fucking around, just hand me the stupid bear,"
Kip said grumpily and added: "And take the bloody knickers
off!"

"How are you going to get my poor teddy to play the
code?" Bogomyr fretted, "And, more importantly, will he still
love me after?"

"Don't worry about that, mate. I happen to be the
best stuffed animal engineer in Alice Springs." Kip Ducker
drummed his fingers on his tool case.

"A what?" Bogomyr and Chuck asked in unison.

"A fucking teddy bear repairman. Now leave me alone
and let me do this."

A little kid walked up to the two goons guarding the
gate. The guards towered over the freckled roguish-looking

boy, an oversize and obviously heavy school bag on his narrow shoulders and a scruffy teddy bear in his arms, and worried immediately that this might spell trouble. One of the men subconsciously caressed his stun baton, while the other tickled his taser and rumbled: "Move along, squirt!"

The boy just gazed up at them innocently with his big sad eyes, sucked on his thumb and squeezed the teddy bear to his chest. The guards grimaced at what sounded like agonised screams of a tortured rodent coming out of the depths of the teddy bear's guts. After about six seconds the hideous screeching was over. The child stopped sucking on his thumb, turned on his heel and marched off.

The guards watched him go. Glancing at each other with their foreheads wrinkled in annoyance, they shrugged and refocused on their job, which consisted of populating their doorman's booth, appearing menacing and acting deadly for no good reason. Two minutes later, though, the deadliness gave way to unexpected panic and an utter urgency to find a toilet.

The guards darted through the gate and disappeared into the building without even bothering to close the gate or look back, while Bogomyr was thanking the kid in Slovenian and handing him a banknote through the rear car window.

"A twenty, eh? How about a bonus for efficiency?" the boy said and twisted the bear's already shabby arm. Some stuffing fell out of the teddy's tail, which was now exposed because Kip had insisted that the women's panties covering the bear's bottom might attract too much attention.

After Bogomyr gave the boy another twenty euros, the brat thrust the bear into Bogomyr's desperate embrace and said: "Not exactly the jackpot, but it'll buy me some cigarettes and beer. See you later, bozos!" the boy waved and headed in the opposite direction of the school, cackling naughtily.

A few minutes later Bogomyr, Kip and Chuck reached the small doorman's booth next to the driveway gate. Chuck, well-versed in these things, quickly figured out how the interphone worked and promptly made the receptionist and everyone else he could reach flee to the restrooms. The place was already running low on toilets and everyone was conveniently distracted, including the people who hadn't yet heard the signal as well as those few clueless secretaries who hadn't even been indoctrinated. Chuck told Kip and Bogomyr to sit this one out in the booth and wait until he let them know the air was clear, and then proceeded to sneak across the yard. So as not to appear hostile, he refrained from pulling out the tear gas spray he stored in his pocket, but kept it close to hand just to feel safer. He'd always resented the fact that U.S. marines weren't allowed to walk around with their M16s in their free time.

Chuck secured the entrance expertly and confirmed that the small lobby was deserted. As he expected, there was an internal PA system at the reception desk. A couple of minutes later the reset code was blaring from every speaker which had until then played the same obnoxious patented relaxation muzak, but also from all the hideously sounding but extremely loud horn loudspeakers mounted outside, which were there solely to potentially sound the alarm. Within a couple of minutes, every victim of nanobot mind control inside the building and within 500 metres of the facilities had been afflicted with a horrible case of projectile diarrhoea, except, that is, for the people in the soundproof basement – the prisoners and the single guard. So Chuck let Kip and Bogomyr know it was now safe to join him.

Meanwhile, due to extraordinarily urgent bowel movements, nobody bothered to contact the unaffected dungeon guard through his in-ear headphones, though on his security monitors, showing a panorama of views from several cameras mounted throughout the building, he watched people running around in panic. The guard tried to reach his bosses and the reception desk on the interphone but nobody answered, leaving him to wonder what the hell was going on.

The guard then decided to leave his post and headed through the door. Out of nowhere and to his considerable shock, he ended up in a very special circle of hell, reserved perhaps for gluttons and sinners who'd died of food poisoning. Everyone seemed to be experiencing terrible stomach cramps. Since all the toilets were already in use, those who were not particularly shy were using flower pots, urinals, trash cans and closets. Some of the more unfortunate and indecisive victims of the inexplicable outbreak had soiled their pants, while most of the rest, for the lack of other options, had run outside to answer the call of nature in the same way as their ancient ancestors. Nobody paid any attention to Kip, Randy and Chuck – and even if someone might have, they had far more pressing issues on their mind.

On the ground floor the intrepid trio mostly saw offices and it seemed obvious to them that the first and second floors would probably be reserved for the higher-ranking staff. Therefore the rescuers proceeded towards the basement, where they all thought the prisoners would most likely be kept: what other place more suitable than the dungeons.

They slipped unnoticed through the foul-smelling pandemonium and walked down a corridor towards the stairs. As soon as they started descending, they ran straight into the one unaffected guard who was climbing the stairs towards them. Chuck, well-versed in such matters, noticed the guard long before the guard noticed Chuck: the guard was too busy staring at all the suffering people in disbelief. Desidéria's marine – instinctively and without hesitating even for a split second to wonder if the guard was deaf, immune, or not indoctrinated in the first place – ambushed the poor clueless fellow on top of the stairs and punched his lights out before the guard could even make a peep. Chuck tied him up and tried to lock him in the janitor's closet, but the room was already occupied by a wide-eyed individual sitting on a mop bucket with his pants around his ankles who implored Chuck to "close the motherfucking door already". So Chuck just dragged the unconscious guard into a quiet corner, searched his pockets and took his weapons and some keys he thought might come in handy. Then the intruders resumed their rescue mission.

The prisoners were overjoyed at the sight of them.

As soon as Chuck opened the iron bar door with the guard's keys, he saw Desidéria, who seemed to have just woken up next to Randy. Chuck ran up to her, hugged her and held her tight, not even registering Randy who had also stirred awake, coughing like a tuberculosis patient. After Randy finally got his breath back, he said: "Wh...?! What's going on?"

"Randy, you should really come up with a better opening line. That one's getting really old really fast," Finnegan rolled his eyes.

Kip told everybody: "Listen, we have to get out of here immediately and find a place with lots of toilets."

"And hurry, for Pete's sake, before someone regains their senses!" Bogomyr urged them anxiously, but this time refrained from giving Bear in Underwear a squeeze: such a mistake would have had a disastrous effect on the rescued prisoners.

Accumulator of Unwonted Locutions stared at Bogomyr and informed The Watcher enthusiastically: "Oh! It's that titillating ecdysiast! What a cavalier!"

"I think you'd better tell *him* that," The Watcher raised an eyebrow.

"Jesus!" Amalia said later, after they were all sitting together in a huge shopping mall that had a large selection of restaurants, pubs, as well as an appropriately extensive collection of restrooms. "What would we have done if the basement hadn't been soundproofed? God!"

"You'd just have had to come to terms with the embarrassment, wouldn't you," Kip said. "Everyone got enough reading material?" They nodded. "OK, then," Kip held up his phone, "Listen to this and run!"

59. Faarghuz

Radio Kirkwall played the first track by *Cynicism Management*, with the reset code as an introduction, at seven o'clock in the morning or about an hour before all hell broke loose in Omnipile's "business embassy" in Slovenia. After that it did the same every hour throughout the day. The radio station soon received several calls concerning its appalling choice of music and the state of its owners' mental health. However, Radio Kirkwall was a small station and owned by a close friend of Finnegan's who owed Finnegan a few favours, so he kept playing Finnegan's tracks until further notice. Finnegan hadn't really bothered to explain why all the tracks had the same annoying 6-second introduction – he just claimed the whole thing was part of an elaborate art installation.

Fergus had waited until the radio started airing the tracks before he opened the door to his room and started hastily and excitedly explaining to the guards that he felt better and that they should call his dad immediately.

Ferdinand Fenton arrived promptly, some shaving cream still on his cheeks.

"Dad!" Fergus ran towards him and gave him a hug.

"Son! What... How..."

"I don't know, dad, it was really weird... There I was, playing my game on the computer and listening to the radio, the same stream I always listen to. There was an unusual song with an even stranger introduction by some band called Cynicism Management..."

"Cynicism Management!?" Ferdinand jumped. He recognised the name, of course.

"Yeah, what of it?" Fergus shrugged innocently.

"Nothing. And? What happened then?"

"I don't know. First I noticed I was able to focus on the song for a change... Rather than just think about those strange numbers, I mean... And then all of a sudden my mind just cleared and that was it. Suddenly I could speak again, and I feel all better."

"Wh... What radio station did you say it was?" Mr Fenton stuttered.

"Radio Kirkwall. You know, the one I always listen to?"

"That's the first time I've heard of it, but if you say so... Kirkwall?!" he remembered Finnegan was from up there.

Ferdinand Fenton called The Lab immediately, telling them to check what was going on with Radio Kirkwall. He hung up, put the phone in his pocket and hugged his son. Then he grabbed him by the shoulders, shook him and asked, overjoyed: "So you're fine? You're really OK? No more numbers and confusion?"

"Nope. I remember the numbers for sure, but I have no idea what they mean. I had a terrible urge to tell them to the world, I don't know why, but I just couldn't bring myself to say anything else. A strange feeling. It really sucked," Fergus looked at his father with profound sadness in his eyes.

"What's wrong, Fergy?"

"Oh, nothing, dad. I'm just tired as hell, I haven't slept properly for days... Even when I managed to fall asleep, all I'd dream about was that stupid number. I hated that so much I've been up for ages." Fergus yawned. "I'll get some rest and talk to you when you're home from work, OK?"

"Of course, son, thank god you're OK. The Doctor will have to examine you thoroughly..."

"Sure, but please, not now. I'm so tired I could go to sleep right here in the corridor."

"OK, I understand," Ferdinand stroked his hair.

"Oh, and dad... Tell the guards they can go away now, I'm sure they're sick of sticking around," Fergus gestured at the men shuffling their feet nearby. "I know they're here for my own good, but I'm fine now, I won't pester anyone else with that number anymore."

"Are you sure you don't want them around just in case...?"

"Dad, please. They're making me nervous, I can't even go to the toilet without them watching me. I'm fine, I promise, I just need to get some rest."

The negotiations were interrupted by Ferdinand's phone. It was Rupert Doors. "Sorry, son, I've got to take this... Yeah? What? Shit... Holy shit... I'm coming right away."

Ferdinand turned to Fergus: "Sorry, Fergus, an emergency at The Lab. OK, get some sleep and I'll talk to you later. You two –" Ferdinand nodded at the guards, "Come with me. See you as soon as I get back, son! Great to see you're OK. Sleep tight!"

"Bye, dad! Have fun at work!"

Fergus narrowed his eyes as his father and the pesky guards left. He heard Ferdinand yell into the phone as he walked down the corridor: "What's going on there, I can't hear you... OK, better. So our Media Monitoring Department forwarded a copy of the track aired at around 7 a.m.? Great. What? It breaks the connection? How's that even possible, god damn it... Shit, what if it airs on the BBC, too..." His voice dwindled away.

The Lab was in a state of emergency. First there was the Radio Kirkwall affair. The experts in The Lab had soon figured out what the signal that the radio kept playing was about. They tested it on a couple of security guards, members of the volunteer experimental division of the Security Forces, and they were soon moaning and groaning in toilet cubicles, attesting to its effects.

Just as Mr Doors considered dispatching the Security Forces to Kirkwall and shutting down the radio, even more dire news started trickling in from the business embassy in Slovenia where Finnegan, his cohorts and the compromised field agents had been imprisoned. It looked like somebody had broken in, most likely using the same anti-nanite audio signal, and freed them all.

While everyone else was panicking, desperately trying to figure out what was going on, the Omnipile Public Relations Department immediately initiated a rabid propaganda campaign whose goal was to convince the international community of Yomanian involvement in a range of experiments with the next generation means of infiltration, espionage, as well as weapons of mass destruction, of course. As proof, they revealed that a number of bioengineered Madagascar hissing cockroaches, undoubtedly of Yomanian design, had just been discovered in Yoman, Washington D.C., and Moscow. It appeared that the bugs had been bioengineered by terrorists, Omnipile claimed, because even the *OmniBug* insecticide, which was notorious for killing every possible species of bug and beetle under the sun, couldn't harm them. The spy roaches must have been the work of a certain scientist who'd recently gone rogue in Yoman and was now suspected of joining the Yomanian Liberation Front, a known terrorist organisation. The villainous nanotechnology expert of depraved Palestinian lineage must have had a personal agenda, because he'd also arranged for the recent kidnapping of his former boss's children. The American government took the situation under advisement and would promptly draw up plans for a series of surgical strikes using the so-called daisy cutter bombs and a few hundred strategically placed mini-nukes, as well as a logistical plan for a potential full-scale military intervention in Yoman.

In the meantime, Fabiola informed her brother that the diversion worked like a charm: everyone seemed either to be running around like a headless chicken or meditating in whatever came even close to resembling a restroom. Fergus seemed to have all the time he needed – so without any undue haste or pressure and so as to avoid making any mistakes, he went down to the kitchen to eat something first. The ejection of the nanites had made him very hungry, but he'd waited until those accursed guards had finally made themselves scarce before leaving his room.

Fergus's mother was overjoyed that he was feeling better, and while the housemaid was preparing his favourite breakfast, Fergus had a look around to establish the where-abouts of the remaining bodyguards so that nobody would surprise him or get in his way when he proceeded with the operation. After Fergus had wolfed down everything the housemaid served him and a couple of desserts besides, he simply headed up to his father's study nonchalantly, as relaxed and indifferent as if it was just another day (perhaps also because he'd been in there countless times, snooping around). He needed the security code to open the door, but what kind of a geek or nosy kid would he have been if he hadn't known it for years. His father had never bothered to change it – not only because he had forgotten how to do it, but also because its only purpose was to keep any nosy guards out. Other sorts of uninvited guests would never get into the house alive without an army at their disposal, anyway, and even then the break-in would turn into a medium-scale war.

After slipping inside unobserved, Fergus closed the door behind him. He walked past his father's desktop computer, heading straight towards an ancient-looking terminal on a forgotten dusty table in the corner. Its dirty 13-inch green monochrome CRT monitor was such a massive turn-off that Fergus would never even have considered touching it before, let alone suspected that this was a direct gateway to one of the most powerful supercomputers currently in existence. He'd always thought that it was some old machine of his father's that he kept around out of nostalgia or as a souvenir. Of course, all of the terminals with access to Omnipile's otherwise isolated central supercomputer had been purpose-fully designed in such a manner, so that nobody in their right mind would think they were anything but antiquated relics, XT PCs. The designers had actually gone so far as to make the machines boot into MS-DOS 3.21, something that would convince any potential unauthorised users that they were looking at a museum piece. And even had they known the truth, they wouldn't have known what to do with it.

Fergus, however, *did* know, thanks to the nanobot intel provided by Dr Fadil Dajani.

Back in The Lab, Ferdinand Fenton frowned. After several experiments with some formerly mind-controlled guards, a suspicion crossed his mind: if Fergus had been reset at 7 a.m. and had come to him immediately, why hadn't he spent the next few hours on the crapper?

Just as Ferdinand considered calling home and checking in on his son, his head spun momentarily and he *felt* something happen – something that made him feel very peculiar, disoriented and slightly nauseous. *"Something isn't right,"* he thought. *"Fergus... Fabiola... Why did I bring them with me to Yoman? Was I fucking insane? Holy shit, what's going on?"*

Two minutes later, a vast number of Omnipile employees, politicians, businessmen, journalists, celebrities, and other renowned individuals from all walks of life were simultaneously afflicted by terribly urgent cases of projectile diarrhoea. It turned out that planet Earth simply didn't have enough toilets available to keep up with the demise of the New World Order. One of those who joined the poor souls bound to spend their next several hours in the john was none other than Mr Ferdinand Fenton himself, but unlike the majority of people who were stuck cursing and staring at walls with nothing to keep them occupied, Ferdinand didn't crave any kind of distraction. He was preoccupied instead with trying to make sense of it all. How had it all started? Who had done this? Would he ever find out?

Mr Fenton fished his mobile phone out of his pocket and spent the next hour or so talking to the Members of the Board and finally even his prime suspect: Mr Rupert Doors himself. Mr Rupert Doors, however, bored him with ten minutes worth of bragging about the ingenuity of his idea to install a heated leather toilet seat in the private restroom in his office and praising his habit of taking his mobile phone everywhere with him.

Apparently nobody in fact managed Omnipile: it was staffed by mind-controlled drones. So who the hell was really in charge?! That question would give Ferdinand Fenton an ulcer before long.

When all was said and done, Mr Ferdinand Fenton walked out of The Lab without saying a word to anyone and headed straight home. When he got there, the house was empty. The guards told him that his wife and Fergus had packed their bags and departed without leaving a message.

Ferdinand headed straight up to his study. From the corridor he saw that the door was open. His heart racing, Ferdinand stormed into the room. There he saw that someone had switched on the terminal in the corner. He walked over and leaned against the small table. The monochrome monitor displayed the following message in retro green letters: "Satellite link established. Transferring data, please wait... Data transfer complete. Satellite link closed." An underscore cursor blinked indifferently into his bewildered face.

The CEO, feeling as if something was staring at his back, turned around and looked at the triple monitor on his desk. On each and every screen he saw a screenshot of something that looked like one of those cartoon characters from the game Fergus liked to play so much. Ferdinand sighed and looked more closely at what was, unbeknownst to him, a mighty and well-known – at least in his own circles – undead priest. He noticed a name tag over the character's head. It said "Faarghuz".

60. 6-4-7-3-8

Even before visibly relieved people finally started to
emerge from the actual or improvised johns all around the
world, Omnipile – acting as if it were a sentient entity with
a mind of its own – had begun spreading rumours that
Yomanian terrorists had just carried out a large-scale attack
against the Western superpowers by infecting many of its
politicians, businessmen, journalists, celebrities and other
important people with a particularly vile nanoweapon, causing
a pandemic of acute diarrhoea. This horrible affliction could
bring the economy to its knees as it spread and everybody
wound up in the crapper. But to the profound relief of the
Western civilisation, Omnipile had managed to figure out
how to shut down the technology. The Corporation had used
its supercomputer to infect all of the invading self-replicating
nanites with a computer virus and destroy the nanobots as
well as the pesky espionage cockroaches mentioned in the
earlier propaganda materials.

A few days later, Omnipile Headquarters also started
issuing official statements and presenting evidence in support
of their claims. The Corporation had been able to counter the
terrorist diarrhoea-inducing nanoweapon attack so quickly
and efficiently because it was in fact their own scientist gone
rogue who was behind these attacks – the very same culprit
who had given the terrorists the bioengineered cockroaches.
He had used Omnipile's own technology against the global
population, but fortunately Omnipile's own scientists were
familiar with it as well.

Omnipile then released the photo of this now infamous
terrorist doctor who had to be found and neutralised urgently.
For this purpose they used a generic photoshopped face of
a prototypical bearded terrorist. The Corporation would

then have the option to either eliminate almost any bearded bloke with a brownish complexion or make sure this non-existent person would never be found, so that everyone would keep looking for him forever. On the other hand, the OIA might bring him up again sometime in the future, should it happen to find itself in need of some exceptionally positive propaganda. Of course, in that case the face wouldn't matter, because his executioners would burn the body and dump the ashes at sea so as to avoid making a martyr out of him as well as prevent him from being raised from the dead.

Supported by a so-called Restroom Coalition of nation states, Omnipile then deployed several nanotechnology inspection teams to Yoman. Within weeks, Yoman was occupied by well-meaning and better-armed troops whose pretended aim was to bless that part of the world with peace, stability, democracy, prosperity (for the select few) and jobs (grossly underpaid, for everyone else). The first resounding success of the Restroom Coalition was the discovery and prompt neutralisation of the not quite so infamous but still renowned terrorist for whom the bearded terrorist doctor, the inventor of the nanobot attack, had worked: the leader of the Yomanian Liberation Front. The clueless man, even more bewildered and useless now that he was no longer indoctrinated, wasn't so globally important that anyone would worry about him too much. So rather than executing him quietly and spreading his ashes very thinly over a large area, Omnipile simply had a few members of the Western-sponsored Democratic Army of Yoman hang him on TV instead and dump him in a ditch.

Meanwhile, the very confused and voraciously hungry Omnipile scientists who'd been stationed in Yoman, clueless about anything that had happened, were shipped back home and told that they'd also been guinea pigs for the infernal experiments of the evil doctor.

Nevertheless, the good people of Omnipile were terribly pained when those treacherous bastards at WikiLeaks released a heap of falsified materials supporting all kinds of crazy conspiracy theories. Omnipile hadn't quite expected that even lowlifes such as Yomanian terrorists who sought to undermine the Western way of life would stoop to such an abysmal level. The Corporation was to suffer immensely due to many an insane insinuation, paranoid delusion, and wild accusation. Damage estimates were in the billions, not to mention the most horrible setback the Corporation had to come to terms with: the demise of its master plan to pre-emptively pacify and/or neutralise all evil forces around the world.

After everything had blown over – as the media focused its attention on the liberation of Yoman by the Restroom Coalition and on the critically-acclaimed termination of the YLF leader – Omnipile though, having removed itself from the prying eyes of the media and the general public, had come to an agreement with Dr Fadil Dajani to refrain from persecuting him. Supposedly now that everyone was nanite-free, extremely rigorous nanotechnology controls and abuse-prevention mechanisms would be put in place, and Dr Dajani was more than welcome to join the effort to make the use of nanotechnology safe in the future. Fadil was glad to hear this, but apart from that he was unable to muster much sympathy for Omnipile. He refused to keep working for them, but for as long as they left him and Fabiola alone, he agreed not to bother them, either. As far as he was concerned, he had deactivated all known existing nanites and published all of the evidence he had gathered. That was all he could do at that point, and it was enough of a win in his books: Dr Dajani believed (and was certainly correct in his assumption) that the Corporation was much too dangerous to stay on its radar.

Naturally, the Board of Directors relieved the founder and CEO of Omnipile Mr Ferdinand Fenton, blaming him for everything he could possibly be blamed for. After the frantic Restroom Day, Ferdinand was never again the same. For weeks after his golden-parachute dismissal, he rolled around on his bed and living room couch alone, purposeless, and depressed.

As for his wife Evelyn, she had disappeared with

Fergus on that fateful day. A couple of days later her lawyer, a strikingly handsome and perversely young fellow, showed up on Ferdinand's doorstep and informed him that his wife wanted a divorce and that she was planning to relocate to the Cayman Islands. The handsome young divorce lawyer went on to tell Ferdinand that Evelyn had been surprised to find out that a small import-export company had apparently already been established by Ferdinand in her name there, and that it must have been doing fabulously well because it had an astronomical amount of cash in its accounts. So while Evelyn waited for the divorce papers to go through – so she could also take half of what Ferdinand hadn't yet deposited in the Caymans – the young lawyer would watch over her there. "You know, help her run the company and teach her surfing," the young man smirked.

On hearing the news, Mr Fenton gave the lawyer a blank stare and slammed the door in his face. His nascent ulcer came a-knocking as the lithium for his future pacemaker battery started being dug out of the bowels of Mother Earth.

The only thing that made Ferdinand feel slightly better was an e-mail he received a couple of days later. The e-mail itself was blank, but in the attachment he found a screenshot of Faarghuz and Favielle from World of Warcraft. On it Favielle said, in a comic-book bubble: "Whatever happened, you're still our father. So we're just letting you know we're OK. Maybe we'll see you later, maybe not, but if we do, it'll be on our terms. Until then – if you want to talk to any of us ever again, mom included – please don't try to find us and don't even THINK about sending your goons after us or Fadil or anyone else. Bye for now, Fabiola & Fergus."

On a magnificent beach in some tropical heaven far, far away, Fabiola drew in a hasty breath and moaned slightly as Dr Fadil Dajani touched her gently in a strategically important place. He whispered: "You're not... You know... A virgin by any chance, are you?"

"What are you, daft?" Fabiola laughed. "Don't be absurd, what do you think I am, an Arab princess or something?"

Fadil kissed the little dimple which appeared on her left cheek when she smiled.

Antarctic oil rigs were becoming a little less crowded after the larger part of their employees came to the realisation that they didn't love snow after all. Omnipile had no choice but to replace most of the staff, but the number of reliable people desperate enough to take a job there was limited, so the whole operation had to be scaled down considerably. The Corporation gritted its teeth in annoyance, suffering severe financial losses as its capacity for the constant destruction of the Antartic environment was temporarily reduced. The situation even resulted in violence as a certain former employee of the Omnipile-owned Antarctic Oil Rigs, Inc., returned home to Yorktown, Indiana unannounced and found a certain postman in his bedroom. The employee's Omnipile insurance grudgingly covered the poor postman's hospital bill just to make it all go away.

The Bitches understandably harboured a grudge against their employers. However, upon receiving *substantial* monetary compensation, they were able to get in touch with their forgiving and forgetting sides. Most of them saw reason in that, especially now that the indoctrination nanotechnology threat was over and nobody was mind-controlled anymore: all the heinous corruption people would be involved in as of that moment would be completely voluntary. Since comfortable work in the surveillance tunnels underneath the airport control tower was hard to come by in a world beset by constant crises and recession, most of the Bitches agreed to go back to their original jobs – with higher wages and consid-erable bonuses, of course. All of them returned to that life with the exception of Serbian Bitch and, more surprisingly, Accumulator of Unwonted Locutions.

Serbian Bitch decided to stay in Slovenia and reconnect with her Balkan heritage. She started collaborating with Willit Lonch on their first project: the *Toilet Chronicles* reality show. They'd had a lot of time to chat during their imprisonment at the business embassy and it seemed they'd hit it off. Besides, the recent events were a good omen: in light of what had just happened, all kinds of target audiences around the world would surely have a newfound appreciation for scatological humour.

As for Accumulator of Unwonted Locutions, sick and tired of being misunderstood, she opted to join the ranks of outstanding linguists working on the next edition of the World's Most Comprehensive Thesaurus.

Žarko Kozmič a.k.a. Ray Kosmick kept trying to pry his way into the porn industry. After publishing **Bat Left the Belfry**, his first EP, he started working on several new immortal porn groove compositions such as *Weapons of Mass Attraction, New Year Steve, Harrowed Be Thy Name, Handling the Bush, Librarian Girl, Toying With Yours*, a track in the Croatian language without any lyrics called Poput zečeva, and a cheesy composition that he called Lovable Deformities (which he'd written right after Amalia had called him a prejudiced male retard, which still stung). He eventually finished many of these tracks and published them on the first full-length album by *Ray Kosmick and His Porn Groove Crew*, titled **Something for Nothing.**

Meanwhile, Amalia and Finnegan had gone on a romantic vacation to an undisclosed Greek island, where they found temporary respite from evil corporations as well as from their band – which, to their profound relief, chose not to accompany them. Instead, they enjoyed this time away

on their own: Randy and Desidéria retreated to a secluded
wood cabin where they smoked lots of pot while pursuing the
outer limits of carnal pleasure and perilous sexual positions;
Largo decided to drop in on his family and co-revolution-
aries in Trieste; while Kip and Bogomyr attended a jazz
guitar workshop together. Kip wanted to come to terms with
growing older and find out how other balding guitarists
managed to cope with their receding hairlines – and what
better place for that than a jazz workshop. Bogomyr was
more or less just keeping Kip company and finding out how
marvellous and enjoyable daylight could be, even in the
company of exasperatingly enlightened but still elaborately
boring no-nonsense musicians who took themselves way too
seriously.

After an evening made memorable by devouring a ton of
lobster, quaffing a cistern of carefully selected wine, washing
it all down with an overabundance of ouzo and then spicing it
all up with even more copious amounts of hot sex, enjoyed by
the former lovers who'd known each other very well for a long
time but were just now rekindling their lust for each other,
Amalia turned Finnegan on his stomach, kneeled over him
naked and gave him a little massage while they waited for his
nether region to start showing signs of life again. Her eyes
then were drawn to the elaborate tattoo on his bum.

"Hey, Finn, I completely forgot to ask you," Amalia said,
"What the heck does this infamous tattoo of yours stand for,
anyway? I mean, what's this damn number over here – the
stupid digits which caused all this trouble in the first place?"

"Oh. Ah... Well, that's a rather silly story."

"As are all your epic yarns. Come on, tell me anyway."

"All right then. Well, one day I found myself in
Glasgow... That was during one of our so-called 'breaks',
mind you, so don't you dare hold this against me!" Finnegan
struggled to turn his head like an owl to look at Amalia. He
saw her narrow her gaze from the corner of his eyes.

"Go on, you horndog," she encouraged him.

"Right. There I was, after a little gig in some pub, and

everyone had already gone home. It was one of those magical nights, though, when I let myself become somewhat nostalgic, you know how it is, so I got drunk. So did this girl a couple of barstools away. The pub owner wanted to get rid of us and close up, and we were the only punters still pestering him for another drink. One thing led to another and we ended up at this girl's place. After she humped my brains out, we drank some more. It turned out she was a tattoo artist. A melancholic tattoo artist, at that. So there we were, yapping about tattoos and melancholy and nostalgia, and soon we were on a trip down the memory lane, discussing the olden days all emotional and teary-eyed, the usual routine. So I told her I was fucking sick of this endless nostalgia of mine, that it drove me nuts and sucked the life out of me. 'Sod the old times', I said and then added: 'If I could.'

"So the girl got a great idea. 'I'll give you a tattoo of the most nostalgic thing we can possibly think of,' she said. 'You know, something symbolic of everything we should leave behind'. And I said: 'Excellent! I'm totally fed up with nostalgia and melancholy and depression and cynicism and bitterness. I'd like to send it all where the light don't shine'. So she said: 'Awesome, that's a damn good idea, and a damn good spot, too! We can tattoo the symbols on your bum, you know, so it'll all go where the light don't shine. Even better: you can leave it all behind you and fart on it.'

"Then we talked about the most nostalgic stuff from our childhood we could come up with. We were the same age, actually, same generation, you know? Pretty weird."

Finnegan paused for a second. "No, that's not really weird at all, a lot of people were born in 1976, I suppose. Whatever. Anyway, we both agreed that the discovery of heavy metal was one of the turning points in our lives, so we had to put that in the tattoo... And then I remembered my old Commodore 64 computer, which had been my ticket into the wonderful world of electronic music and, you know, making music with a computer in general, as well as playing computer games. Well, she didn't quite agree, because she was a Spectrum 48k fan, fie on her, but at least she could appreciate the nostalgia conjured up by thinking of that magical first computer she'd had as a child."

Amalia and Finnegan sat on the bed now and Finnegan poured them more ouzo. He warmed up and Amalia seemed to like the story.

"There we were, discussing a highly complex project: how do we combine a symbol of heavy metal and something reminiscent of the Commodore 64 computer? Sure, heavy metal was not a very difficult task. We decided to go with a pentagram and the Goat, obviously. Then she said: 'Do you want the number of the Beast with that, you know, 666?' And I went: 'Sure!' And she said: 'But crap, I don't know where to put that so that it looks good. I can't put it where the points of the pentagram touch the circle, you know, there are only three digits in 666.' For sure!" Finnegan chuckled. "We were plastered, did I mention that?"

"Anyway, then I thought about it a little and came up with an idea. We needed five digits, and we also needed a symbol for the Commodore 64 computer. So I told her to use 6, 4, 7, 3 and 8. SYS 64738 is an instruction in C64 basic, used to reset the machine, you know, as if you turned it off and on again. I knew the number by heart because I'd used it dozens of times every damn day for years as a kid when I played around with that endearing little machine. It still has meaning for me."

Amalia laughed.

"Don't look at me like that, and don't try to use it as a password for my stage laptop, either, you hear me?!" Finnegan frowned at Amalia.

"So that's it?" she snickered.

"Yeah. What more do you want? Oh, and when I told my one-night tattoo artist the number, she quite liked it, too – I mean, after she'd rolled it around in her head for a minute. She said that 6+4+7+3+8+5 amounted to 33, and if you multiplied that by 2, you got 66. 'Fascinating, right?' she said, 'Because that's almost 666.'" She was into numerology a bit, you see.

"I kind of looked at her funny – you know how I am and what I think about numerology – and genuinely intrigued, I asked her: 'Where the hell did you get the 5 in the end?' 'Well,' she said, 'that's because there are five digits in your original number.' So I asked: 'And where did you get the 2 to multiply it with?' 'Oh,' she explained, 'Obviously 2 is the logical number after the series 6-4-7-3-8'. And that was that. I suppose that's how insane people and numerologists operate. They can get any result they want if they toss the numbers here and there as they please. OK, well, maybe my tattoo artist wasn't insane, I should remind you that we were drunk like skunks. She gave me the tattoo and then we went to sleep. I left in the morning and that was that. I actually never had a good look at the tattoo back there. After all, the nice girl who gave it to me told me not to. I must say, now that Fadil has shown it to me, it seems that she did a damn good job, all things – and the state we were in – considered."

Amalia let out a deep breath, shook her head and rolled her eyes: "So this – this idiotic series of events which can only happen to a very special jerk such as yourself – this is why a gargantuan evil Corporation was after us?"

"Yeah, I guess Dr Dajani appreciates Commodore 64 computers, too. At least he isn't a member of the Spectrum camp."

Elsewhere, Desidéria apologised to her unfortunate U.S. Army hero and explained the situation (fortunately everyone retained their fluency in the English language, even after the nanites had been flushed out). Desidéria made her apology after she let him make love to her one last time for the old times' sake, which she hadn't kept from the absolute love of her life, Randy Jiggler. She'd told Randy this was how it had to be. He had shrugged and said: "Cool, do whatever you have to do," after which he had taken another hit from his oversize blunt.

Chuck dropped his head on his chest and looked away. He was obviously hurt. However, he didn't wallow in his misery much: after all, he was a U.S. marine! So he looked his former Portuguese mistress straight in the eye and said: "Affirmative, I understand. You like Randy more, you liked him before you even met me, I get it, fair enough. Actually, I'm relieved. I wanted to tell you before, but I kept avoidin' it: I'll probably be going away soon, in any case. I think they're about to transfer me. You see, besides the trouble in Yoman, which seems to be escalating, there's a crisis brewing in Yorack, too."

61. Interlude:
Another Place Another Time

A few hours later, in Greece, Finnegan became emotional and teary-eyed. Towards two in the morning, he crumbled and admitted his undying love for Amalia, who, to his relief, reined in her own cynicism and told him she loved him too. After which Finnegan said: "No, I'm serious, I really fucking love you," and so on and so forth.

At about 2:30 a.m. – after many hugs, caresses and kisses – Finnegan told Amalia that after their last "break", which had occurred around the time Amalia and Randy had finally left Kirkwall and gone for Amalia's walkabout, he had kept denying how he felt at first, even to himself. Then one day he realised he'd developed a habit of aimlessly walking around the town, but in reality he was revisiting all the places where he and Amalia had liked to hang out at. He'd go to their favourite bars, their cinema, their restaurants, he even checked if their secret hiding places in Vilewood forest were still secret – all that just to be able to feel close to her and sorry for himself in a remarkably elaborate way.

After Finnegan realised what he was doing, he decided he needed to get it all out, to exorcise it... To experience a catharsis by writing a truly nostalgic song... And he meant a *thoroughly* nostalgic piece, more nostalgic than anything he'd ever written before... So he wrote *Another Place Another Time*, which he now unveiled to her.

After Amalia read the lyrics and listened to the demo, they both became repulsively sentimental and diabetes-inducingly sweet. They sniffed and snivelled together and concluded there wasn't any reason they could think of that would cause them to ever have another one of those "breaks" of theirs. So Finnegan asked Amalia to marry him and she said yes.

Fortunately they didn't remember any of it in the morning. Well, save for the warm and fuzzy feeling that their new tune gave them.

After that track had been recorded a couple of months later, Amalia and Finnegan agreed that *Another Place Another Time* was one of their best works to date.

ANOTHER PLACE ANOTHER TIME
[https://soundcloud.com/cynicism-management/
another-place-another-time-augmented]

Incomplete
A fading vision
I still roam this darkened city
Altered and disguised
Stranger streets
With every season
As I sit there unperceived
And ponder our demise

Turned the tides
And wasted many months of
Slipping grips on what we thought
That some day might become
Something has gone
And hastened by while I
Returned time after time
To glimpse the things undone

Another place another time
Oh we used to be whole

All those long lost
Trains of thought end up
Derailed as I blend finally
With shadows you can't see

There I remain
A distant grain of memory
An epitaph a footnote
Signed yours respectfully

Of course, Finnegan had made it all up, fabricated a bit, embellished the truth. Well, frankly, he didn't really embellish the truth, he lied through his teeth. In reality he wrote the lyrics after a drunken schoolmate of his from the olden times, who habitually inhabited a certain bench in the park and preyed on the innocent passers-by, had pounced on him and pestered him with the "good ole days" for several hours. Finnegan later dedicated the lyrics to that sad bloke. However, he thought that such a tear-wrenching tale, if interpreted slightly differently, just might get him laid again and in a particularly sweet and succulent way, too… And he was right. He didn't feel bad about it, either – after all, that was why he wrote his 'poetry' in the first place.

62. Finnegan's Blog Entry No. 7

It's been a while since I've posted anything here. With good reason: some of you might have heard of the strange situation we found ourselves in last month... Bah, even if you haven't, it doesn't matter – due to reasons I don't want to go into I can't discuss it in detail even if I wanted to.

Suffice it to say that Amalia and I went on a little vacation. For a change we didn't take our computers with us, nor did we seek out and abuse any internet cafés. You wouldn't believe how good that felt for a change – we just focused on eating, drinking, sleeping, shagging, having a little swim in the warm crystal-clear sea if we really felt like it... And reading a couple good books. When was the last time you did that? Can't remember? Shame on you.

So what's new? Well aye, to answer the question you're most itching to ask: are we global rock stars yet? Nope, quite inconceivably not yet and I don't see how or why that unavoidable fate has eluded us for so long... Especially after everything we've been through.

It might be time to put my backup plan in action – that is, "to write and compose a literary musical". I know, right about now you're thinking I finally popped a gasket and went full-blown insane. But it's all quite rational, I assure you. You see, I'm working a cunning angle here, adapted to the evolving and booming e-book market. I figured – well sod it, if we can't sell our music on its own, we'll sell a book containing our music, like, with songs instead of illustrations that will work with those fancy iPads. Now if I can only make someone realise what an awesome concept that is...

Although, now that I think of it, it might be a better idea to scribble about a teenage vampire pop band and come up with a few teenage vampire tunes to go with that rather than writing treatises on a bunch of bitter old wankers who look awful and sound even worse. The thing is, however, that we're going for a cult art product here, of course. I'm sure you understand...

Cheers,

Finnegan Frotz

About the Author

Bori Praper, born in 1976 in Slovenia, graduated in English language and literature from the Faculty of Arts, University of Ljubljana, Slovenia, in 2000.

Worked as a translator of technical, literary and scientific texts – mostly in the field of EU legislation, contemporary history and audiovisual industry – for more than twenty years.

Also a musician (composer, producer, multi-instrumentalist and lyricist). Written and recorded music for numerous audiovisual projects and public events, including dozens of full-length theatre performances. Produced many works by other authors as well as recorded for them, most notably contributing drums as a session drummer. Work published on more than 40 digital releases, 15 audio CDs, and two video DVDs.

Finally, a writer who managed to finish his first novel in English at the tender age of 36, after a few failed literary experiments over the years.

Following a six-year stay in Izola on the Slovenian coast and then a five-year sojourn in Berlin, Germany, in 2017 Borut migrated to warmer climates yet again. He currently lives in the Canary Islands with his wife Monika and a flurry of free-range geckoes, focusing predominantly on translating, writing, horticulture, and tinkering with Cynicism Management, his progressive / alternative rock band (*https:// cynmanagement.bandcamp.com/*); Ray Kosmick, his psychedelic rock / indietronica / soundtracks alter ego (*https://raykosmick.bandcamp.com/*); and a few other side projects.

If you'd like to be the first to know about Bori's new books and music releases, head to his official site at *http:// boripraper.eu/* and sign up for his mailing list. Subscribers will not receive any spam – only updates on new developments and free music offers every two or three months, on average. Your email address will never be shared with anyone else and you can unsubscribe at any time. If you'd like to stay in touch, you can also write directly to *raykosmick@gmail.com*.

Music Links

For complete discography, head to author's music production site at *http://sur.si/*

For selected free downloads, head to author's blog / home page at *http://boripraper.eu/*.

Links

Author's blog:

http://boripraper.eu

Private page / free music for River Boat Books readers:

http://boripraper.eu/vault

(password: RiverBoat)

Author's music production site:

http://sur.si

Cynicism Management (the band) @ SoundCloud:

https://soundcloud.com/cynicism-management

Cynicism Management (the band) @ Bandcamp:

https://cynmanagement.bandcamp.com

Cynicism Management (the band) @ Facebook:

https://www.facebook.com/cynmanagement

Ray Kosmick @ Bandcamp

https://raykosmick.bandcamp.com

Ray Kosmick @ SoundCloud

https://soundcloud.com/ray-kosmick

Ray Kosmick @ Facebook

https://www.facebook.com/raykosmick

THE LIST OF SOUNDTRACK SONGS AND RELEVANT LINKS and where they intersect the text:

TOURING MY BACKYARD (p. 91)
https://soundcloud.com/cynicism-management/
touring-my-backyard-augmented

BAT LEFT THE BELFRY (p. 108)
https://soundcloud.com/ray-kosmick/bat-left-the-belfry

LIFE MALIGNANT (p. 161)
https://soundcloud.com/cynicism-management/
life-malignant-augmented

I FIND IT TWITCHING (p. 218)
https://soundcloud.com/ray-kosmick/i-find-it-twitching

INIQUITY (p. 239)
https://soundcloud.com/cynicism-management/
iniquity-augmented

GARDEN GNOMES (p. 270)
https://soundcloud.com/ray-kosmick/garden-gnomes

THE END OF THE VILEWOOD ROAD (p. 285)
https://soundcloud.com/cynicism-management/
the-end-of-the-vilewood-road-augmented

TIT (p. 321)
https://soundcloud.com/cynicism-management/
tit-augmented

WHENCE SHE CAME (p. 364)
https://soundcloud.com/cynicism-management/
whence-she-came-augmented

FOUR-CIRCLE PENILE SUBSTITUTE (p. 388)
https://soundcloud.com/cynicism-management/
four-circle-penile-substitute-augmented

RIGHT HUMPSTER (p. 419)
https://soundcloud.com/cynicism-management/
right-humpster-augmented

BAD BAD BOY (p. 443)
https://soundcloud.com/cynicism-management/
bad-bad-boy-augmented

TV TURNS ON YOU (p. 465)
https://soundcloud.com/cynicism-management/
tv-turns-on-you-augmented

NANITE RESET SIGNAL (p. 468)
https://soundcloud.com/cynicism-management/
nanite-reset-signal

HERBAL HAZE (p. 492)
https://soundcloud.com/cynicism-management/
herbal-haze-augmented

ANOTHER PLACE ANOTHER TIME (p. 520)
https://soundcloud.com/cynicism-management/
another-place-another-time-augmented